Cornbread Mafia

By

Sheree Le Mon

this book dedicated in honor of
Agnes Hallix
to Gallatin County Library

Cornbread Mafia
By Sheree Le Mon
Copyright © 2017

This book is a work of fiction. Names, characters, places, and incidents either are products of the author's imagination or are used fictitiously. Any resemblance to actual events or persons, living or dead, is entirely coincidental.

Printed in the United States of America

Publisher's Cataloging-in-Publication Data is available upon request.
Library of Congress Control Number: 2017934175

ISBN: 978-0-9972945-8-3

First Edition

With Indigo River Publishing, you can always expect great books, strong voices, and meaningful messages.
Most importantly, you'll always find... words worth reading.

To my children, my best work.

Summerville 2am

Ink-black striations streaked the gray night sky. There were no stars, no shadows, and no wind. A sliver of a new moon darted in and out of dense, dark clouds. It was a perfect night for a drop. Absolutely perfect.

Fifty-eight-year-old Barrett Lewter threw his cigarette to the ground after it burned his fingers. He covered the ember with his riding boot and ground it into the red dirt. His hand automatically sought another from his shirt pocket. He struck a match and looked down at the beagle sitting at his feet. The dog's eyes tracked the man's hand as he took a long, hard drag.

Barrett stood six foot two with hair dyed a ridiculous, gothic black revealing obvious white roots and telltale dark dye stains around his neck and brow.

Sweat dripped off the tip of his chin onto his black, silk shirt. He hated feeling nervous, but that sickening primal emotion crept up on him, making him feel vulnerable and weak. The three shots of Cuervo Gold he'd downed at Rustler's bar not thirty minutes before did nothing to calm him. Uneasiness came with the territory, and he knew very well that in this world of darkness, drugs, and guns, the hours of excruciating boredom would, within a matter of seconds, explode and climax in a heart pounding, thrilling moment.

Kinda like good sex.

The anticipation of a drop was enough to get him through a mundane week or even a month. He counted on it, needed it. Not for the money anymore, but the rush. There was something powerful about it, something wicked, something base. Why else did he need to fuck Candy afterwards?

The beagle's ears shot up.

Good little Booger.

Best hunting hound he'd ever had, not to mention the added bonus of having an infallible early detection device. The man held his breath and listened. He heard nothing, but trusted his dog.

"Let's roll," he whispered into the two-way radio, and, like magic, radiant halogen lights lit the dirt runway every sixty feet, revealing on each side white vans emblazoned with Candy's Catering on their side doors, as well as the man's black Bentley. Four anxious Mexicans on the right of the runway and six on the left stood silent with machine guns slung over their shoulders, awaiting the landing.

And there it was—the familiar soft purr, a good ten, fifteen miles out. All eyes focused south. The purring became a whirring, but still no sight of the Aero Commander 690. It wasn't unusual, because the pilot's standard operating procedure included turning off every interior and exterior light long before he had a visual on Summerville. There was never radio contact.

By the time Barrett's voice was heard over the two-way radio announcing "one o'clock," the darkened plane was on its final approach.

The 3,500 foot grass runway was set deep in the middle of four hundred acres of natural forest, barely visible even to those who knew it existed, but the sixty-eight-year-old pilot, on his ninth mission for the group knew the terrain and the routine like the back of his hand.

The darkened plane hit the runway hard, bouncing twice. The runway lights were immediately killed as the plane sailed down the runway before coming to a stop two hundred feet short of a row of tall pines. The props continued to turn as the Mexicans opened the plane's cargo doors and hurriedly removed vacuum-sealed ten-kilo packages of cocaine, transferring them to the vans. No words were spoken and no unnecessary movements were made. The plane was to remain on the ground for no more than ten minutes.

After each van was loaded to capacity, a Mexican jumped in the driver's seat, while another, clutching his trusty AK47, climbed in the back and sat on top of the loot. As soon as the doors closed, the driver slowly pulled away into the darkness without lights.

Within minutes the plane was empty and four Mexicans were pushing and turning the plane so it faced the open runway, taking extra caution around the deadly blades. Ever present was the memory of the two men who had been sliced to bits and forever forgotten in shallow graves, the victims of an unforgiving miscalculation.

Barrett clicked his two-way radio. "Ready."

The lights on the runway once again blazed, momentarily blinding Barrett. The pilot revved the engines, released the brakes, and the plane was off. Now empty, the aircraft quickly lifted, flying low over Barrett and his dog. A cold draft swept over them as the plane vanished into the night.

Le Mon

The runway lights were killed. Barrett looked up into the black sky, while listening to the dimming sound of the plane's engines. When the silence was whole, he looked down into his dog's yellow eyes and said with a sinister grin, "Come on, Booger, let's go see Miss Candy."

Madison 5:30pm

Thirty-six miles south of Summerville in the city of Madison, Alabama, Neely Glover left Dr. Roger Brown's office more depressed than when she had entered an hour earlier. She got into her car, put the key in the ignition, and slumped deep in the seat. A voice on the radio sounding a decibel short of a scream, announced the arrival of new models at the Chevrolet dealership. Neely looked up to see a young woman holding her little boy's hand emerge from her shrink's office. The little boy's face was red and his eyes were swollen. He looked like she felt. She turned the radio off. Her arms and legs were concrete and her mind, numb.

The thought of driving through rush hour traffic felt daunting. Her life was shit, and, even with the help of her sympathetic doctor and drugs, she couldn't see how it would ever get better.

It had been two years since Neely had discovered Eric's intimate relationship with a woman only a few years older than their daughter, Olivia.

After futile attempts at repairing the damage themselves, they reluctantly concluded they needed help.

Her husband came with her to the first obligatory appointment. At its conclusion, he made it crystal clear to both Neely and Dr. Brown that he was too old to change, and if their marriage was going to survive, she would have to make it happen. So, like an old mare that heads blindly back to the stable, Neely continued to go to therapy, not with purpose, but simply out of blind hope.

She was drowning in Prozac and Gestalt therapy, and couldn't find a way to escape the pain and anger that had become her new best friends.

It's almost dark...only an hour before everyone will be gone...if I just sit and be very still, I'll fall asleep...and with any luck, freeze to death.

Perhaps because the townspeople didn't want change, or maybe because the major roadways had bypassed it by a good forty miles, things never seemed to change in Summerville.

For almost a century, the town square, with its stately brick courthouse surrounded by huge oaks, a World War II memorial, and a couple of Civil War cannons appropriately facing north, remained the center of activity. Half a dozen wooden benches were strategically placed for the best viewing of the comings and goings of everyone, from orange-clad prisoners in leg irons, to well-dressed ladies browsing the square's many antique shops.

The population hadn't changed much either. In 2015 the local Better Business Bureau reported a fairly constant growth that had begun in the early 1990s, with the eventual county population hovering at about 10,000 residents. The old timers who settled on the wooden benches around the courthouse early each morning and who were affectionately known as the "dead pecker bench men," vigorously disagreed, labeling the Better Business Bureau and any of its allies as a bunch of damn liars, Yankees, or both. As they sat and whittled, the old codgers swore that if you counted every chicken, horse, and hog in all of Morris County, there'd never be more than 7,000—excluding "First Monday," of course. On the first Monday of every month the town square was transformed overnight from a somnolent gathering place into a bustling circus; a horse trader's empyrean.

The old men would be the first to boast of the population swell on First Mondays. Even the most conservative person conceded that an additional thousand converged on the town. And on First Mondays that fell on Memorial Day, one could count on two to three thousand additional visitors.

By sunup, every inch of the square would be claimed and quartered off by Mennonite women selling beautiful handmade quilts, crafts, and baked goods, along with shady individuals hawking knives of every size and guns of questionable origin. They barked out the merits of their wares from the back of tricked-out pickups parked amid antique junk dealers, horse traders, snow cone stands, NASCAR sports memorabilia peddlers, and the seasonal handshaking, baby-kissing politician.

The roads leading into the square were closed to traffic by 9 a.m., allowing the three municipal police officers to manage and direct vendors, as well as eager, early bird shoppers. The police force, made up of two male officers and one female officer, dreaded First Mondays. Their normal hour-and-a-half lunch at Bob's Place was out of the question, replaced, if they were lucky, with a dried out hot dog and a bag of chips from Sally's Doghouse kiosk at the corner of Main and Oak.

Sally Stophel was Summerville's hot dog queen and the daughter of Clyde Stophel, Summerville's twenty-three-year veteran sheriff. Sally was in her early thirties but looked years older, due mostly to her daily, amorous attachment to Jack Daniels.

Satch, a seventy-something-year-old black man with a three hundred pound, thirty-four-year-old girlfriend, was Sally's Man Monday. He was known for his happy nature and perpetual smile, illuminated by two gold front teeth. For as long as anyone could remember, he had worked the kiosk for Sally. She held the money and he took care of the hot dogs.

It was rumored she never applied for a city license nor paid the first red cent of tax on her cash take, but no one would challenge either issue out of respect and love for her father. The last thing anyone wanted to do was besmirch Sally's reputation and thereby offend the man who might one day save you from some crime or choose to look the other way if you were caught drinking and driving. But perhaps more accurately, over the years many of the townspeople had acquired a taste for Sally's dry dogs, which Satch so carefully nestled in the softest, lightest buns imaginable, topped with a secret sweet sauce that many believed was a mixture of nothing more than spicy barbecue sauce laden with chunks of canned pineapple, although a few thought the real secret to Sally's sauce was a little Jack Daniels. Regardless of the recipe, Satch made great dogs and Sally took good care of Satch. That was enough.

Cornbread Mafia

First Mondays were a traffic and crowd challenge for the local men and woman in blue, but rarely were they faced with anything more serious than settling a heated argument over whose space was whose or how early one was allowed to stake a claim in the courthouse parking lot. But in the back of their minds they secretly yearned for the excitement of the long ago First Monday of July 9, 1984, when, on the southwest corner of the square, a prominent local accountant was shot dead by a dairy farmer for sleeping with his wife. It took almost three hours to quiet the milling crowd, as each person seemed to be possessed by an uncontrollable, morbid curiosity to actually see the pool of blood left on the sidewalk in front of Lloyd Marshall's dry goods store. The fact that the farmer was sentenced to a mere eighteen months in the local jail and married his ex-wife's best friend a month after his release helped elevate the incident to Hollywood proportions.

Moments of drama and excitement were far and few between in Summerville. But when they occurred, the event was recited and chronicled with such furor and interest that, with each telling, it was honed and embellished to titillating perfection, worthy of generational endurance.

This sleepy, little southern town was to see drama in the next year as it had never seen before or since, and not even the five men who put this big, bad ball in motion could foresee the life-altering events that were to unfold as a direct consequence of their clandestine maneuvers.

David

"And how are we today?" a plump woman with a big smile asked, as she took a pad from her apron pocket and a pencil from behind her ear. Her white t-shirt, emblazoned with a big yellow smiley face, was tucked into her tight, waist high, pressed jeans.

"Bowl of cherries, Tilly! Bowl of cherries," David O'Donnell roared. An infectious grin swept his boyishly handsome face. At fifty-six, he was in better shape than most men in their thirties, with an energy level anyone over twenty would envy. He believed one should earn each day with a good dose of learning, laughing, and loving. His interests were as diverse as the people he surrounded himself with. He was a true renaissance man. In his current and past lives he held the title of attorney, Marine, baseball player, bricklayer, triathloner, local actor, voracious reader, political fundraiser, and wordsmith.

He was equally at home in the courtroom defending a low-life drunkard as reciting Yeats to his children. He stood six feet, with hazel eyes and graying temples. His body was rock hard. He dressed impeccably, in custom-made shirts and suits. Everything from his alligator loafers to his silver

Carrera Porsche epitomized his success.

His bigger-than-life persona left an indelible and mighty impression on everyone, whether they spent two minutes or two days with him. A positive "can do" attitude and relentless energy had brought him to a proud point in his career. He was blessed with more business than he could manage and wanted it no other way. He knew and appreciated he'd been lucky but he also knew he'd been smart enough to recognize when opportunity presented itself, regardless of how small it appeared.

"Is anyone joining you?" Tilly asked, placing utensils, wrapped in a paper napkin, in front of him with a big smile.

"Should be four of us. Just bring my tea, I'll order when everybody gets here."

He wanted the meeting to be a quick one. He hated when his schedule was disrupted. At eleven thirty, every day, rain, sleet or shine, he climbed on his custom-built, light-as-air Italian racing bike, and clicked away at least twenty-five miles. By twelve thirty he was back to the office for a quick shower, then lunch. By two he was back seeing clients or in the courtroom.

Tonight, I'll do an extra hour on the machines.

David opened his leather folder and pulled out a bound copy of A Life, a play by Hugh Leonard, and began reading.

A bellowing voice called out, "Afternoon, Counselor!"

Sally Stophel's dad entered the restaurant wearing his starched, tan sheriff's uniform. He sauntered up to the table and slapped David on the back. "You doing good?"

"Couldn't be better, Clyde." David placed the script on the table. "How's the world treating you, partner?"

"Making it. But I gotta lose some of this," Clyde laughed, patting his huge beer belly, which hung a good four to five inches over his low-slung holster. "It's killin' me."

David grinned. "I need to get you out on the road with me, Clyde. We could work that off in no time."

"There are easier ways to do me in," the lawman chuckled, imagining himself on one of David's skinny bikes. He gave another good pat to David's shoulder. "Speaking of grub, I gotta get some! Check you later."

Tobias Blount and Barrett Lewter entered the restaurant with Kate, an attractive strawberry-blonde woman in her early thirties. They spoke briefly to the sheriff before heading on to David's table.

Tobias, known to his friends as "T," was a short, heavyset, fifty-four-year-old man with bright red hair, wide set green eyes, and a round, fleshy face covered in freckles. Up until a year and a half ago, he ran five of the largest chicken processing plants in the South and had been happily married for twenty-six years. But life has a way of getting your attention when you're comfortable. So it was with T.

Seven years back, Nora, his wife and partner, was diagnosed with breast cancer. They made it through the surgery, chemo, and rehab, but as the magic five-year mark approached, lady luck vanished. Nora told T she had been experiencing an unrelenting pain in her hip for more than a month and had been afraid to tell him. An MRI revealed that the cancer had metastasized. She died six months later. His spirit was broken. He was a ship lost at sea with a broken rudder, floundering and barely upright.

A year, almost to the day of his wife's death, Tyson's Chicken approached him with a buy-out deal, assuring him complete financial freedom. His friends encouraged him to sell and enjoy the fruits of his labor. He took the deal.

Without his business or Nora he felt out of sorts, but was making a real effort to drag himself back into the world of the living. Kate was instrumental not only in bringing him back to life but giving him a life he'd never known before.

When T met Kate she was working for Barrett, breaking and training his polo ponies. Just thirty-two, she was uneducated but bright and she was pretty in a horsy sort of way, prettier, for sure, than anyone T had ever been with before.

Her life up to that point had been difficult and without the slightest bit of promise. It had been a little over four years since an Argentinian polo player had swept her off her feet. He was Barrett's featured celebrity player in the annual Make-a-Wish charity match. She fell deep under his spell. Their passionate affair lasted less than two weeks, a few days short of his entire stay. A month after his departure, Kate, to her horror, realized she was pregnant. She wrote a brief letter apprising the South American of her predicament. She never thought for an instant he would move to Summerville and marry her, but the response she did receive was one that left her sickened. A certified letter from the polo player's attorney arrived, curtly warning her that his client was happily married, knew without question that he was not the father of her child, and would appreciate her refraining from ever contacting him again. Enclosed was a certified check made out to cash in the sum of $100,000 and a release form that, when and if signed, would have probably allowed the polo player to murder her in the worship hall of the First Baptist Church, during church service without the slightest fear of reprisal.

In the midst of humiliating rage she wanted to tear the check into a million pieces, but her survival skills kicked in and, with stoic resolve, she wisely signed the documents and opened a trust account for her unborn child. She figuratively, as well as literally, pulled herself up by her bootstraps and went on with her life, never regretting once her decision to keep the child. She named the baby Tutt, for her father. The little boy was dark skinned with big, brown eyes, like his father. He was beautiful and, now at four, towered above his preschool mates.

T had a good notion why Kate was with him, but it didn't matter. She made his life bearable and she wanted so little in return. And as important as Kate was to him, her son had insidiously crept into his heart and captured it.

Barrett wore a shiny dark navy suit, which though expensive and custom-made, was wrinkled and in need of cleaning. A thin, off-white silk shirt was unbuttoned to the middle of his white hairy chest, revealing a heavy gold chain. His standard scuffed riding boots paired with his shiny suit projected a spot on manifestation of Hunter Thompson's lounge lizard.

Barrett's story was so obscure and convoluted, and under such continual debate, that one had trouble getting a handle on what was true. The most recited account of the sixty-year-olds beginnings, did little to explain how, an ex-cop once arrested for racketeering, could become an uber wealthy developer almost overnight. Barrett's own bravado would have one believe a mystifying "Cinderfella" story. He attributed the success of his multifaceted development business to his unorthodox business approach and simple hard work.

No matter the story, of which there were many, it took a leap of faith to fathom the sort of success needed to bankroll the three thousand plus acre farm, the Bugatti, the Maserati, the Bentley, several huge but tasteless homes, race horses, high-tech heated barns, a priceless collection of Louis XVI furniture, jets and prop planes, not to mention an important collection of Impressionist paintings any museum would covet.

Barrett came back to the table with a coke in hand and asked David, "What's happening?"

"Just trying to turn a buck," David said as Tilly set his tea in front of him.

"How are you, Kate?" David asked, after nodding at T with a smile.

"No complaints," She smiled.

"How's Tutt?" David asked.

Her face lit up. "He's growing like a weed!"

Tilly asked the group, "So what'll we have?"

"What'ya want, baby?" T asked Kate.

"Can I have a root beer float?"

"Don't you want something to eat?" T asked.

"I gotta pick up Tutt. Remember?"

T nodded, patting Kate's knee.

Tilly took everyone's order and headed for the kitchen.

Barrett waited for a moment, "So when did you talked to Escobar?"

"What the hell is wrong with you?" T demanded.

"What?" Barrett asked sarcastically.

"You know exactly what I mean."

"Like somebody is going to fucking know what we're talking about," Barrett sneered.

"And how do you know that?" T countered, his voice lowered to almost a whisper.

Barrett said, "Well let's see, we have the sheriff, Tilly, three old broads from the bank ..."

David interrupted, "I talked to him a couple of days ago. Everything is fine."

"Did you talk money?" Barrett pressed.

"No," David answered.

"Why not?"

"It wasn't the right time."

"When will it be the right time?" Barrett demanded frowning.

T jumped in, "When David says it's the right time."

Kate stood, picked up her root beer, and kissed T on the cheek.

"Let it go, baby," she whispered in his ear. She squeezed his arm and left.

"They think we're their little bitches and I for one am sick of it. I don't know why you won't say something," Barrett charged.

"Let David handle it," T interjected.

"Why don't you stay out of this? You don't have a fucking clue about any of this shit," Barrett charged.

"Oh right, I'm just a chicken farmer, aren't I Barrett? I hate to break the news but I get what's going on and I know if you go off half-cocked like you always do, you're going to fuck it up for all of us."

David looked at Barrett, "I told you I would talk to him and I will." He took a sip of his tea and went on, "I set the meeting in the islands. Do either of you want to go?"

"I'm in," Barrett said.

T shook his head No.

Barrett looked down and sniggered, "pussy" under his breath.

Atlanta 12 Noon

Wallace's white Jag turned off Peachtree towards Lenox. The weather was unseasonably warm for early March and the sky had a threatening yellow hue.

Neely and her two friends were making one of their frequent jaunts to Atlanta for two days of shopping, eating, and girly commiserating, away from husbands, children, and social obligations.

The minute they left Madison, Jan turned to Neely, who sat in the back seat next to a small ice cooler, and said, "Pour me a glass, Darlin'." By the time Chattanooga was in the rearview mirror, Neely and Jan had popped the second bottle of Veuve and were feeling no pain. Two hours later, Wallace pulled into the porte-cochere of the Buckhead Ritz Carlton with a dramatic threat to her friends: "Next time one of you is driving!"

"Welcome to the Ritz Carlton," a handsome young man greeted them, opening Wallace's door. She returned his salutation with a wide Texas grin and a "thanks honey." Born and raised on a Brahma cattle ranch outside Austin, her dad reared his only child like the son he never had, instilling in his five foot nine powder keg the self-assurance and tenacity of a pit bull. She was her father's daughter, fearless. And, like him, she appreciated power, a good roll in the hay, and Famous Grouse, in that very order. She exuded a sexual prowess that very few men, or women, for that matter, could miss.

Towering to almost six feet, blonde, and elegantly beautiful, Jan gracefully swung her long legs out the passenger door and held out a weathered Prada leather duffle. The young man who greeted them immediately took it.

"What about the cooler?" Wallace asked of no one in particular.

"Maybe this sweet boy could take care of that for us?" Jan cooed at the twenty-something man who held her duffle. Thoroughly charmed, he marched to retrieve the cooler. "Keep what's left, honey," Jan said with a big smile.

Cavalli sunglasses covered Jan's big blue eyes. She strolled casually through the doors held open by another valet and waited for her friends to join her. The palpable air of old money was nothing more than an ingenious mask created and perfected long ago to hide deep, ugly scars. Jan came from a place far from the couture clothing, fine champagne, and the privileged life she now enjoyed and seemed so comfortable with. Born in China, the third of five daughters to a career Army colonel and librarian mother, she came to instinctively anticipate the cyclical move to the next town or country, as well as her father's unprovoked and almost daily abuse. Making peace became her life's mantra, as well as her personal curse. She was gifted with brains, beauty, and the uncanny ability to size up those around her. But these attributes were diminished by an unhealthy and suffocating obsession to please, an anathema that would doom a string of personal relationships until the day she met Steven Howe, founder of Howe Aviation and a billionaire to boot. Despite a twenty-four-year age difference, they were blissfully happy. He was tolerant and gentle with his young bride, finding her pathology innocently childlike and endearing. When he looked at her, waves of happiness and gratitude swept over him. He wanted nothing more than to fulfill her every whim and keep her safe.

And she adored and loved him. He was everything she had ever imagined or wished for in a man, everything her father was not. Her husband was sexy, gentle, smart, and powerful. But most importantly, she knew with certainty that he loved her unconditionally.

Neely tipped the bellman and joined Jan and Wallace. They walked through the flower filled lobby to the reception desk. A slight man with red hair, redder cheeks, and brown eyes greeted them.

"Welcome back, Mrs. Glover. Did you have a nice trip?"

"We did, thanks," she replied, as she signed the standard check-in form.

He continued his pleasant greeting in a formal manner. "I believe your rooms are ready. Let me check."

Neely turned to her friends. "What do you wanna do for dinner? Should make reservations now?" She motioned across the lobby to the hotel's main restaurant, The Dining Room.

"Or do we just want to kick back, order room service, and watch porn?" Wallace blurted out, not caring in the slightest whether anyone around them heard her.

Jan drawled, "I don't care. Whatever y'all want is fine."

"I don't care either as long as we don't wait 'til' ten to

eat," Neely quipped.

"It wasn't ten," Wallace corrected.

"Nine forty-five? That's when we left the room," Neely persisted.

"God you're so strict! I say we come down, do the hors d'oeuvres and champagne thing, go back to the room, and order room service. I did the driving and I'm frikin' tired." Wallace leaned her elbow on the counter and closed her eyes, making sure everyone was aware she wanted to go to the suite. She'd had enough of the check-in routine and was ready to poke the desk clerk's eyes out with the hotel pen she was repeatedly clicking. The young man, sensing the crazy woman's seething impatience, held out three plastic keys neatly contained in paper holders.

"Ladies, your rooms are ready, and as you requested, you are on the concierge floor with rooms adjoining the Magnolia suite. Our staff will greet you upstairs. Have a wonderful stay."

Neely thanked him and took the keys. Wallace was already across the lobby on her way to the elevators when Jan turned and smiled at the young man, mouthing a sweet "Thanks."

Neely was not tall by the standards set by her friends. She was a little less than five foot seven in her bare feet, but her height was all in her legs. Growing up in a dysfunctional family of four children, she often joked to friends that she felt fortunate her mother hadn't eaten her shortly after being born. No one in their home was affectionate or emotionally demonstrative. Her mother believed if you did not acknowledge a problem it didn't exist or if you ignored it long enough, it would eventually go away. Avoiding unpleasant truths was the directive.

So, given her cloistered, puritanical and emotionally

stunted upbringing, along with being teased by her classmates with taunts like "giraffe legs" and "skinny Minnie" it was no wonder she was painfully shy and socially confused. Her mother, a devout Catholic, divorced her *irresponsible* father and remarried all before Neely's fourth birthday. Her mother never forgave the church for excommunicating her when it was her husband who was to blame for doing the *bad things*.

For years, the gawky giraffe look held. She slumped her way bashfully through her adolescent years, escaping into the magical world of literature. At eighteen and too late to have pleasant memories of high school, her transformation began. Her lanky, long legs, no hips, no definable waistline, and small breasts suddenly appeared to beautifully blend in the most seamless way. She had become a classic beauty with her willowy body, fine features, full mouth, big brown eyes, and thick chestnut hair. Sadly, regardless how others saw her, Neely would always see herself as the awkward giraffe.

Her husband, Eric, upon seeing her the day she first set foot on Dartmouth College Campus vowed he was going to marry "that girl". Four years later it was indeed, fact.

The twenty-first floor concierge lobby of the hotel was a second home to them. They'd spent many a late night and early morning in this private lobby with panoramic views of Atlanta, savoring their last nightcap or first espresso. The pale blue and yellow English prints covering the invitingly comfy sofas and chairs, along with the muted scrolled images on the Aubusson carpets, created an ideal environment in which to calm anxiety. A barely discernible Chopin prelude gently filtered through the air.

As they passed the unmanned concierge desk, Neely grabbed a copy of the *Atlanta Journal Constitution* from a perfectly flared newspaper display. A heavyset barefoot man in a hotel terrycloth bathrobe sat at a distant table nursing a cup of coffee. He looked up and nodded politely.

The women found their suite and proceeded to the first bedroom off the suite's living room. Neely plopped on one of the double beds and opened her newspaper as the bellman brought in their luggage. Jan stretched out on the opposite bed and closed her eyes, sunglasses still on.

"I love this place," Jan whispered, to no one in particular.

"We all do," Wallace replied impatiently, tipping the bellman. "What's the plan?"

"I plan on doing nothing unless it makes me happy," Neely smiled.

Jan laughed, "I need to pick up some fabric from Miami Circle but I can do that anytime."

A muffled cell phone ring was detected coming from Wallace's purse. She grabbed her bag and rifled through it until she found the phone. "Hello. Hold a second." Wallace walked from the bedroom to the living room. Her voice trailed off.

Jan lowered her sunglasses and looked at Neely inquisitively. Neely shrugged. It was several minutes before Wallace returned.

"I need to run an errand. I won't be more than an hour." Wallace's attempt to sound nonchalant appeared notably staged.

Neely asked, surprised, "What?"

"I'll be back in about an hour."

"Where are you going?"

"I have to meet that guy who's supposed to help me put the Montgomery fundraiser together. I told you about it."

"No, you didn't," Neely corrected. "Who is he?"

"What is this, the Spanish Inquisition?"

"I just think it's kinda odd that all of a sudden you've got to meet some politico in Atlanta, of all places. How did he know you were here?"

"What difference does it make? I'll be back in an hour, for god's sake."

Wallace and Neely stared at each other in a silent standoff.

Jan sat up in bed and removed her sunglasses. "Neely, we can go to Neiman's while she's gone."

Neely looked from Jan to Wallace, who was now heading for the door and before you could say Jack Sprat, she said, "I have my cell," and was gone.

Le Mon

6pm

The hour trip turned into two, then three. Periodically, Jan called back to the hotel to check on Wallace's whereabouts. No one answered their hotel room phone and all of Jan's calls to Wallace's cell went straight to voicemail and all texts went unanswered. Real concern began to set in when Jan's cell rang.

Wallace.

In her familiar Texas twang, Wallace almost shouted, "Are you two still at Needless Markups?"

"We're at Shaver's. Neely's trying to find some book on Poe nobody's ever heard of. Where are you? We've been worried."

Neely took a step closer to Jan, in a stance that demanded an explanation.

Jan held her hand over the cell and whispered, "She's in the room."

When they got back to the suite they found Wallace in the shower. Jan and Neely sat heavily in the down-filled loveseats that faced each other in the living room. Neely pulled off her shoes and rubbed her feet. She looked at Jan and grinned, "Must have been a rough meeting."

9pm

Rather than room service, they opted for dinner at American Cut. Neely tipped the girl at the podium with a crisp $100 bill, ensuring a choice table with unobstructed views of the very *hot* bar. Forty-five minutes and several rounds of drinks later, they were just getting right.

American Cut was Atlanta's new hot spot where young, beautiful, nouveau riche movers and shakers lined the bar two and three deep, talking the talk and walking the walk. In a sea of beautiful people, a couple of Atlanta Falcons, who appeared like bronze gods towering above the crowd, decked out in flashy platinum and diamond chains, grills and diamond encrusted custom-made watches stood in stark contrast to the young investment bankers who appeared anemic in their conservative starched, monogrammed, white tailored shirts, handmade suits, and English wingtips. Bartenders shook the latest exotic martinis as quickly as the deals, both business and personal, unfolded.

Neely leaned into the table, shouting above the crowd. "You never did tell us this person's name."

"Who?" Wallace asked innocently.

Neely ignored the stall and simply stared at Wallace, waiting.

Wallace pretended to get the attention of a passing waitress by snapping her fingers in the air. She answered Neely without missing a beat. "I don't think you know him."

"Try me," Neely prodded.

"You're such a nosy bitch," she sighed. "You don't know him."

"Maybe *I* know him," Jan chimed.

Neely and Jan both grinned at Wallace.

The waitress made her way to the table. "What can I get you, ladies?"

"Stay with the same or shall we do the bubbly?" Wallace asked.

"Bubbly," Jan immediately answered.

"Bubbly," Neely agreed.

"Bring a bottle of Veuve and make sure it's ice cold," Wallace instructed, emphasizing the *ice*.

The young woman turned to leave.

"Whoa, Honey!" Wallace called out, "Bring us some grilled shrimp, that artichoke thing with the feta, and some hot bread. Butter, too."

"I'll bring the champagne right out. Anything else?" the young woman asked.

"Y'all want anything else?" Wallace asked her friends.

Jan and Neely shook their heads no, in unison.

"Butter?" Neely mouthed to Jan.

Wallace dismissed the waitress. "That'll do it for now, honey."

The young woman disappeared into the milling crowd that now spilled from the bar into the restaurant.

Neely took a long sip of her Cosmopolitan. "Butter?"

Wallace ignored Neely's comment and asked, "How can you drink while you're taking all that shit?"

"What are taking?" Jan asked Neely.

"Nothing now. I quit taking everything two weeks ago. It put me in a fog. I figured if you're frikin miserable, there's probably a reason. I want to fix things not drug myself into oblivion. I'd rather drink my way there."

"Totally," Jan grinned.

"Enough about me. Who is he?" Neely asked.

"What?" Wallace asked trying her best to look clueless.

"You know what I'm talking about."

"Jesus Christ! What the fuck, are you my mother? You need a life Neely."

"Wallace, you know you're going to tell us sooner or later, so just tell," Jan said in her soft, little girl voice. Wallace stared at her friends and said flippantly, "Hop Farrington. You happy?" She leaned back and took a big gulp, finishing her whiskey. She set her glass down with a thump and waited for them to react.

Jan and Neely were stone cold flabbergasted.

"Hop, as in Wendy Farrington's husband?" Neely asked incredulously.

"One and the same." Wallace smiled smugly, conjuring up her tall, passionate blond lover with so many talents.

"Have you lost your mind?" Neely asked dumbfounded.

"Hop?" Jan muttered to herself as if recovering from a smack to the face.

The waitress returned with the champagne, ice bucket stand, and flutes. She set the glasses on the table, placed the ice bucket stand next to Jan, removed the bottle from the bucket, and opened it. She poured a little Champagne into Wallace's glass and waited for her to give a thumbs up but Neely commandeered the bottle saying bluntly, "It's fine."

Before the waitress could respond, Wallace took the bottle from Neely and poured the Champagne until her flute overflowed.

"What are you thinking?" Neely demanded. "You're co-chairing the ball with her *and* screwing her husband?"

"Well, yeah, I guess I am," Wallace responded casually, looking past both of her friends to the bar, as if distracted by something far more interesting.

Jan picked up the bottle of champagne and poured Neely and herself a glass. Jan asked, almost fearful, "What will you do if Wendy finds out?"

"Why would she find out?" Wallace responded, confident the idea was ridiculous.

"Well, we figured it out," Neely quipped.

"Somehow I don't think I'd offer it up to Wendy like I did to you two nitwits."

Jan wasn't sure, "What if Drew finds out?"

Wallace's mood instantly changed. She paused before answering, "He probably wouldn't give a shit."

"I wouldn't count on that, and you better be careful when it comes to that Wendy," Neely warned. "She's not somebody who's gonna lie down and play dead. She's a tough-ass broad behind that prim and proper performance of hers. You need to rethink this, Wallace. It could blow up in your face, big time."

"You're giving *me* advice?" Wallace asked with a nasty overtone.

Neely stared at Wallace blankly.

"I think it's kinda comical that somebody whose life is pretty much a disaster and can't get a grip on her own husband, should tell me how to handle my relationships" Wallace barreled.

The deafening silence was finally broken when Neely

asked, "Why are you being so mean? I'm genuinely worried you might get hurt."

"I'm not being mean, I'm being honest. Eric runs your little ass around, continually berates you, controls every move you make, and you pretend everything is just fabulous. Your *perfect* little life."

"My life's not perfect and I know that better than anyone," Neely said, as her voice undulated.

Jan touched Neely's hand, giving her a, *I'm sorry* look before turning to ask Wallace, "What's wrong with you?"

Silence returned as the waitress appeared with the appetizers. When she asked if they needed anything else and no one answered, she quickly left. Rather than look at Neely, Wallace's eyes followed the waitress until she lost her in the crowd.

After concluding no one was going to say anything, Wallace went back on the offensive. "You just come off like Susie-fucking-homemaker while making me out to be some crazy ass. Again, you're the victim and I'm the bad guy."

Neely stared at Wallace coldly, as she fought back the tears welling in her eyes. Wallace could see Neely's pain but it did not deter her from roaring on. "At least I *know* what I'm doing! You live in some fantasy world."

"You think you're so different from me?" Neely managed. "You're not happy, and yet you stay with Drew. You think he treats you any better than Eric treats me? He doesn't."

"You're absolutely right Neely, he doesn't. But I treat him like shit, too."

"And that makes it better?"

"No, just different, *very* different. I know why I'm staying. I made up my mind a long time ago. I'm in it for the money, the lifestyle, the glitz, all the shit. I know he doesn't love me. He's kept that whore in Birmingham for years. I know the deal. I don't want a divorce. I like being Mrs. Drew Macon Lee III. Unlike some people, I'm not pretending Drew and I are Ozzie and Harriet."

"You think I think Eric and I are Ozzie and Harriet?"

"I haven't a fucking clue what you think Neely. Why do you stay? The money? I don't think so. You have your own. The kids? Hell, they're not babies anymore. Why? You think Eric loves you?"

The cruel words excruciatingly tightened around Neely's heart and she found it difficult to breathe. Wallace had gone too far, she'd crossed that fine yet taboo line. But there the harsh words were, out there, like the reveal of a handicapped newborn at a baby shower. Everyone could clearly see the ache, but no one knew how to extricate themselves from the moment.

Wallace ravaged three shrimp in rapid succession, followed by a big gulp of champagne.

I'm being honest, goddamn it, she rationalized.

However, the truth was, she knew she'd screwed up and had to make nice. Immediately.

So she forged on in a matter of fact, business-like tone, ineptly trying to explain, as a shady CFO might, why there were no cookies, while her hand was still deep in the corporate cookie jar.

"I wish it was Eric I made cry," Wallace said, looking directly at Neely. She added softly, "He's the one who should feel like shit. Hell, I'm just drunk."

Neely was hurt and none of the words out of Wallace's mouth made a difference or lessened the pain. She wanted to go back to the hotel and climb under the covers and sleep forever. She sipped her champagne until it was gone, carefully avoiding Wallace's pleading expression.

"I think I'm gonna call it a night," Neely said, staring blankly at the empty flute in front of her.

Jan was so upset that she too was on the verge of tears. "I don't know why we do this. It's all about these asshole men. They hurt us, and we take it out on each other."

The clatter and voices in the room disappeared, leaving a silence that screamed.

Wallace looked at Neely and said with real sadness, for Neely, and for herself, "I'm sorry Neely. I really am."

April

David walked from the house through the perfectly manicured lawn to the teak chair under a big willow tree. He placed his books and yellow legal pad on the table next to the chair, sat deep in the comfy cushion and gazed out over his fifty-four sprawling acres. He felt proud he could provide his family with a magnificent home that touted a nine-hole golf course, tennis court, batting cage, and lap pool. He had everything he ever needed or wanted. He was happy; he was *comfortable*.

Blooming flowerbeds ebbed and flowed throughout the estate. Purple pansies, white geraniums, and yellow tulips were gloriously showy. A cool, gentle breeze rustled the sharp, long tentacles of the willow, singing a lulling, rustling sonata. A bluebird, perched high in the willow, chirped happily.

David looked up as the bird flew off toward the sun, low in the horizon. A good two hours remained before the light would be gone, giving him plenty of time to jot down his thoughts and finish *The Nightingale*. This was *his* time, no sleazy clients, no droning demands from Susie...nothing but peace, time to think about words, books, dreams, life...purpose.

He looked toward the house and garage after hearing a car door slam. He could see his wife, Susan Lee unloading groceries.

I should go help ... but

Although his wife was not particularly involved in community affairs, and in fact a little reclusive, she was credited with establishing the Summerville Historic Society, which in turn saved some of the most beautiful buildings on the square and most of the antebellum homes on Rosewood Avenue.

Her greatest achievement, however, at the ripe old age of thirty, was getting David, one of Tennessee's most powerful lawyers, to marry her. It was rumored her father called O'Donnell, demanding to know his intentions shortly before a proposal was forthcoming but perhaps it was O'Donnell who felt his days of bachelorhood had been sufficiently played out and he was finally ready to again take the plunge. But for those who knew him well, they recognized he needed a mother for the young daughter he was raising from a previous marriage and Susie was eager to fill that role. Whatever his reasoning, seventeen years later he seemed to have a marriage that worked. Susie was indeed a good mother to his daughter and the two children they had together. Her lackluster personality was noted by many in the community, who puzzled over why a man of such intellect, wit, and appeal would be happy with such a bland woman. But that *was* her appeal. She was invisible. *He* was the star.

Her size increased in direct proportion to the years of their union, and her ability to look the other way and, indeed, stay out of David's way, became an art. She was the perfect choice for this flamboyant man, who needed to shine as much as he needed to be entertained and distracted by the periphery of life, without competition or obligatory interaction.

Susie's brother, Franklin, ran the family banking business that supported, directly or indirectly, a large assortment of ne'er-do-well relatives. At thirty-five, he chose to relocate the banking headquarters from Summerville to Nashville, taking his wife Julien and their three children with him. Other than the obligatory Christmas trek, they wanted no part of their extended family or to live in what they considered, a small, two-horse town.

Susie's cousin, Michael Summers, who was in fact the only real intellectual in the group, returned to Summerville after graduating from Harvard undergraduate and Wharton Business to buy, with a longtime friend, a near bankrupt lumber business. Michael married his Cambridge college sweetheart and brought her back home as quickly as the ink on his business diploma dried. Their lives centered on their sixteen-year-old twin girls and the lumber business.

After a short two years, the business was in the black. Michael and his business partner were shrewd visionaries; having concluded one could make a fortune in specialty lumber. Gold wasn't in *them there hills*—it was in cherry, ebony, oak and mahogany. They cornered the market in specialty wood moldings, paneling, and floors by methodically buying up every little mom-and-pop lumber business within two hundred miles of Summerville, as well as acre upon acre of hardwood forests. They made Summer Lumber the number one source of specialty wood products in the South.

Michael's twenty-six-year-old brother, Scott, was another story. He turned out to be the black sheep of the family for many reasons, none of which was more publicized than the day he broke into what he thought was an unoccupied neighbor's house, only to scare the ninety-seven-year-old resident to death. Literally. The man had a heart attack and died.

The family beseeched David O'Donnell to represent Scott. He reluctantly accepted the duty. The case hinged upon the testimony of the old man's caretaker, a well-known and well-liked black woman by the name of Lula Mae Polk. At the trial she identified Scott as the intruder. She was Scott's mama's housekeeper when Scott was little. She had changed Scott's diapers, for goodness sake. She *knew* who broke in.

But as with most cases O'Donnell tried, by deliberation time the jurors were wondering who exactly *was* on trial. Doubts were planted. Was it possible Lula Mae had something to do with it? Why would Scott break into some old man's house where there wasn't anything worth stealing? Other than Lula Mae, who was well into her eighties, had cataracts in both eyes, and was known to take a nip or two, no one other than Lula Mae had actually seen Scott break in.

Hadn't Scott's family financially supported all of Summerville's charitable organizations? Weren't they the people who stepped up to the plate without hesitation when the church needed a new roof? Was Scott not just a good boy, perhaps a little off track, a harmless prankster with no sinister intent? Maybe he didn't show the promise of a typical Summer, but shouldn't he be treated like the next "Joe" and given a second chance?

When O'Donnell was performing, anything was

possible. He was known to work magic in the courtroom; he had a way of making you *believe.*

And this jury upheld the mythology...they *believed.* After less than an hour of deliberation, the foreman read a "not guilty" verdict on all counts. Scott turned to O'Donnell with tears in his eyes and dramatically vowed never to forget what he had done for him and promised to one day repay him.

It was a promise he would not keep.

Neely leaned back and closed her eyes. The sun was warm on her face. Nice. Her thoughts drifted as the soft hum of the highway lulled her.

Olivia's dress...Four months to look...Plenty of time...Book the Plaza Athenee... I'll wear Elie Saab... Right, like you could actually get in it... Four months... I have to lose this weight... I'm so weak... And he, never looked better... Obsessed... When was the last time we made love... Collin's party... Was that in April...oh

"Did you get the screw-up at the beach fixed?" his sounded combative. Neely opened her eyes but avoided looking at him, instead focusing on the road signs as they swept past in a blur. The last thing she wanted to do was to discuss the rental debacle of their beach house.

"Yes," she said closing her eyes.

Maybe he would let it lie.

"How?" he pressed.

She turned and looked at him, "I came with you today to get away...to get away from everything. Can't we talk about it later and just try to enjoy this afternoon?"

"I just want to know how much goddamn money I'm out. Is that too much to ask?"

"Is it *that* important?"

"What are you hiding?"

"I'm not hiding anything. I told you I took care of it."

"But in the end, I pay." He glared at her. "Right?"

She looked him, trying to make sense of his attack. The prematurely gray hair, falling tussled about his chiseled tan face, contrasted with the thick black lashes surrounding his water-blue eyes. He still looked like the man she had fallen in love with over twenty years ago, handsome and sexy but some insidious creature, some dark thief, had removed, one by one, bit by bit, any familiar mark or tender remembrance, leaving behind a man she no longer understood or liked.

"Right?" he demanded.

"I refunded their deposit."

"And that was?"

Neely lost it, shouting, "Three hundred fucking dollars, Eric!"

"Am I pissing you off? Forgive me, but I'm the sorry ass that has to go down to that little brown office every goddamned day and work like a nigger because of shit like this. And does anyone care? No. Give them three hundred. Give them three thousand! What the fuck difference does it make? Eric just has to work a little harder."

"Oh, god," she moaned, shaking her head.

"Don't want to hear it, do you?" he taunted.

"No, I don't. No one makes you work, you fucking racist. You do it because you want to. Quit! I don't give a shit."

"And who the hell would pay for all these fuck-ups?

You? Olivia? Sam? Yeah, right."

"I contribute," she said softly.

Damn it don't cry, don't.

"The way this family runs through money, we wouldn't have a pot to pee in if I weren't working like a nigger every goddamn day of my life. And just for the record, if it weren't for me, that company of yours would have gone down the dumper years ago."

She shivered as a cold chill rushed down her spine. She turned away from him and gazed out the window. The words she so deliberately chose caught in her throat. "That company is successful because of me, Eric, and me alone."

"Oh, now you're gonna cry?"

Without moving a muscle, she said sounding eerily calm. "No, I'm not."

Neither of them spoke until the "Welcome to Summerville" sign, standing tall and friendly, greeted them.

"You know, it's only taken us about thirty minutes," he said cheerfully, as if as nothing had happened. "Not bad, huh?"

There it was. He was done. He had extracted enough flesh to be purged. It was over. He'd put her in her place and robbed her of the little happiness she might have felt.

She looked out at the rolling green hills in the distance, capped by a pale blue sky, and wished she were someone else.

"There's a space," Eric said quickly parking his Land Rover. "I think that's it," Eric gestured toward the building on the northwest corner of the square. "He said it was gray. Does that look gray?"

Neely nodded. Eric grabbed his briefcase and got out of the car. She followed. They passed a barbershop that hadn't changed one bit since it opened in 1930. An ancient barber peered out at them as they passed. She smiled, doing her best to put away the angst of their altercation, as she had over the years learned to do. She was desperate to make peace for her family, even if the cost was her identity.

What an unbelievable town! It was as if they had been catapulted back in time. Next door to the barbershop was a ladies' dress shop. The large plate glass showcased two 1950's vintage mannequins, complete with their original antiquated wigs. Both had big boobs, tiny waists, and red lips, now faded to pale rust.

They passed Summerville Bank with banners touting "Cheap Fair Loans." They read the banners and looked at each other with perplexed expressions. They walked on to the building next door with a sign on the door reading, "Monroe Real Estate and Auction House."

Upon entering a young receptionist with cropped, brown hair and braces looked up from her computer and smiled as Neely and Eric entered. Before Eric could speak the young girl asked, "Are you Doctor Glover?"

"Yes."

"That's what I thought. Can I get you a cup of coffee or something? We have some Krispy Kremes. I think they're still hot."

"We're fine," Eric said.

The young girl hopped up from her desk. "I'll tell him your here."

Eric nodded, picking up a local real estate magazine from the girl's desk. He gestured for Neely to sit on the sofa next to him, across from the receptionist's desk. But before they could settle into the sixties-styled leather and chrome sofa, Charles Monroe entered, hand outstretched and smiling. He was a handsome man, tall and slender, wearing Wranglers, a starched, white shirt, and cowboy boots.

"Eric. How in the world are you?"

Eric stood, taking his hand. "Great, Charles. This is my wife Neely."

Charles greeted her with an enthusiastic handshake. "Nice to meet you Neely. We think the world of Eric. He's been a godsend to my family. You know he's taken care of my mama and my son, William. We really do think the world of him and we're so happy to hear he's thinking about putting an office here in Summerville. This little town could sure use the likes of him."

Neely smiled.

"Have you ever been to Summerville before?" Charles asked Neely.

"No, but I love it already. I feel like I've been taken back in time."

"I think it's a little piece of heaven, but then I'm partial. Y'all come on back and let me show you what I've come up with."

They followed Charles down a long narrow hall to his office at the back of the building. Two worn, brown leather chairs faced an antique mahogany desk. Pictures of Charles' family were crowded to one corner of the desk, behind neatly stacked manila folders. Behind the desk and taking up almost the entire wall hung a sepia photograph of the town square taken around the turn of the century. Neely examined the photograph and realized that if you replaced the horses and wagons with cars, you'd have a present-day photo of Summerville.

"Have a seat," Charles said, gesturing to the chairs across from the desk. "Can I get you something to drink?"

"We're fine, thanks," Eric replied.

Charles moved his coffee cup to the side and pulled a

file from the stack of folders.

"Here's what I have, Eric."

Before Charles could make his way around the desk, Eric stood and walked over to him. The two men immediately became immersed in the listings. Neely found she was out of the loop and looked around for something to read. The real estate magazine Eric had picked up in the lobby was abandoned in the chair next to her. She picked it up and flipped through it, stopping abruptly when coming to a photograph of a four story high, grand brick building, adorned with beautifully carved limestone pediments atop each window. Barely readable, a massive stone header centered above the main entrance spelled out *Faulkner Building 1897*. Neely continued to the text below the photo.

They were asking $175,000. It was a huge, probably over 20,000 square feet.

It had to be a misprint.

"Excuse me," she interrupted.

Both men looked up. She held up the magazine, the page turned toward them.

"Is this price right?"

"The Faulkner Building." Charles smiled.

Neely nodded.

"That's what they want...probably could get it for one fifty, maybe less."

"Where is it?" she asked.

Eric shot her a look that emphatically warned; *we are not here for that.*

Charles turned to the photo on the wall behind him.

"It's right across the street. The building marks the center of town. I personally think it's the most beautiful building on the square" he said pointing to the building in the photo. "Beautiful, huh? Just needs somebody that has the vision. Know what I mean?"

Neely nodded.

"You wanna take a look?" Charles asked with a big smile.

At the exact same moment, Eric said "No", she said "Yes."

Charles burst out laughing. Eric, not the least bit amused, forced a fake smile. Neely avoided looking at him and asked Charles if he could arrange for her to see it while they went to look for office space.

"Absolutely," he said. He picked up his phone and buzzed an agent down the hall. "Got a minute to show some property?"

A moment later a dishwater blonde woman in her forties with big brown eyes, a pug nose, and thin lips poked her head in the door.

"Come on in Lucille. This is Dr. and Mrs. Glover, Lucille...Lucille Holly. Dr. Glover and I are going to look at some property on the bypass. Mrs. Glover wants to see the Faulkner Building. Do you have time?"

"Well, I'd be proud." Her Tennessee drawl was heavy and her smile infectious. "Let me get the keys and we'll head on over there. You wanna come to my office, Mrs. Glover?"

Neely turned to her husband and asked, "Sound okay to you?"

He had no choice but to agree.

Awakening

The moment she entered the building she *knew...it* was extraordinary. She followed silently behind Lucille's dark outline. It was so quiet, the air moist and cool. She felt at peace, as though she were being gently encased in a silk cocoon. Safe.

The two large picture windows facing the courthouse, over fourteen feet in height from floor to ceiling, were haphazardly covered in brown butcher's paper. It took her eyes a few moments to adjust to the dark room. She found herself in the middle of a large open space that she estimated to be about 4,000 square feet. The architectural details created over a hundred years ago included massive plaster crown moldings and eight-foot cypress doors with hand-forged brass door locks. Neely's attention was interrupted by the clicking sounds of Lucille searching for a light switch that worked.

"Electricity's off," Lucille muttered.

Neely went back to admiring the yellowed chalk-like walls, partially hidden by layer upon layer of peeling wallpaper. The wall's magnificent pastel patina was veined in its entirety with faded cocoa discoloration, most likely the result of years of water damage. Broken linoleum floor tiles exposed beautiful wide-plank mahogany flooring. Carved support columns with Corinthian caps, evenly spaced every eight feet, stood like proud sentinels along the entire length of the right wall. They were magnificent despite being painted a putrid mauve color. About thirty large cardboard boxes in varying degrees of decay were stacked haphazardly against the back wall, overflowing with old clothes, real estate signs, and long florescent light bulbs. Alongside the boxes, piles of huge, brown leather ledgers numbering in the hundreds were covered in thick gray dust.

"Neely?"

Lucille's voice startled her.

"I'm sorry, Lucille. I don't know where I've been. I think I got lost in this fabulous place."

"I was saying the Grand Ole Opry use to come to Summerville in the 20s. They played in the ballroom on the top floor, about once a month for over ten years."

"There's a ballroom?"

"On the fourth floor. I haven't ever been up there, but I've heard it's something else."

"May we see it?"

"Why sure, honey! I've been dying to get up there and my time is yours."

It became dark as they headed toward the back of the building. Lucille felt her way by running her hand along the wall. Neely kept close behind her.

"The stairs are supposed to be back here someplace. I wish the lights worked so we could see where we're going but it's kinda exciting."

They came to the end of the room and a closed door. The air was noticeably cooler.

"This must be it," Lucille said, pulling on the glass doorknob. The door was stuck and wouldn't open.

"If you don't mind, honey, would you hold this?" She asked, handing Neely her heavy purse. Lucille put her foot on the door casing, grasped the doorknob with both hands and pulled hard. The door flung open without warning, throwing Lucille into Neely and the opposite wall.

"Lord have mercy! I don't know my own strength!" Both women laughed.

"Watch your step," Lucille said, taking her purse back. "It's pitch black back here."

Lucille rifled through her bag and removed a small black flashlight. She directed its beam to the steps in front of them. "Thank heavens I put this in my purse."

Lucille turned the light back to Neely, "Top two floors haven't been used in fifty years, so I want to warn you it's probably in bad shape, and dirtier than a yard baby, if you know what I mean."

"A little dirt never hurt anyone." Neely smiled, having no clue what she meant by "yard baby".

Lucille laughed, "I'm not sure about fifty years worth!"

Neely asked Lucille, "I know this is off topic but why do we see signs everywhere advertising *cheap fair loans*?"

Lucille turned back to Neely with a big grin, "It's a loan people get so they can go to the state fair. It's the big social event of the year…it lasts two weeks and everybody goes. Schools close. Lots of people round here can't afford to go, so the bank gives them a whole year to pay the loan. Just in time for the next fair!"

Neely smiled. What a town, what a building. Although she wasn't able to process in her mind how this place made her feel, or, for that matter, the logic, she felt connected, as if somehow she belonged. It seemed so wonderfully familiar. She laughed at herself. Was it possible that Eric pushed her to such a bad place that she now believed a building had a soul?

Not likely. She was pragmatic and levelheaded. She hadn't founded one of the most profitable clothing manufacturing companies in the country by putting her faith in puka beads or crystals. She was methodical, organized, analytical, and deliberate. Being carried away by the spirit of a building was as likely as finding her enrolled in a craft class at the local YMCA.

"Heavens to Betsy! I have no idea what this could be," Lucille winced, stepping over a fossilized dead rodent. "But it's nasty for sure."

Neely followed, skipping the step altogether. Sunlight broke through as they reached a landing and another set of twenty or so steps.

"You okay?" Lucille asked, looking back at Neely.

"Yes," she smiled. The smile wasn't for Lucille. It just was. She knew without a doubt she had to have this building.

Provo

Leeward Highway originated about a mile before Airport Road intersected it, and continued straight through the forty-two square mile island, ending conveniently at Gilley's Bar and Marina. Twenty-five years ago one would wave to every soul they passed on the one and only highway. Those were the days when the island's population was one tenth that of Bermuda's, although identical in size. Every car was identifiable and every person significant.

Providenciales (or "Provo," to those familiar with the once sleepy little British protectorate) was an easy hour and a half flight from Miami on American Airlines. In the "good ole days" there was one flight a day, an honor American Airlines held for many years until Delta, Air France, Air Jamaica, United, and many others, added daily flights. Now it's possible to fly daily, direct from most European cities, on several carriers.

For inter-island travel, TCI Airways provided a schedule of continual island hopping, with no flight over fifteen minutes in duration. Islanders long used TCI Airways much like a New Yorker might use the subway to get them to work. Living on one island and working on another was commonplace. When the pilot got caught up in a fiery political debate over breakfast or simply overslept, no one would get too worked up when they found themselves late for work. This was life in the islands and everyone accepted it.

As expats migrated to the island and found they had to rely on Turks Islanders (natives born on the island) in their development projects, the phrase *Island Time* became their thorny mantra. It described the particular lack of urgency and complete disregard many had when it came to time constraints or schedules. The local government worked feverishly, without success, to erase even the reference, going so far as to ban the playing of a local recording aptly named *Island Time*. The foreigners who came to the island to develop hotels and condominium projects had to either slow down and assent to the laissez-faire attitude, or go mad trying to change the local populace one at a time. Many businesses abandoned their island projects after a short stint simply because they could not adjust to the mentality of the local workforce.

Within just a few years, as a direct result of the explosive growth of tourism, the population of new residents more than tripled. Development of hotels and condominiums was soon at full throttle, with no slowdown in sight. The fragile infrastructure was stressed to its limits. Unfortunately, the laid back attitude remained steadfast. One might wait months for a phone or the next shipment of Klargeisters from England needed to complete their home's essential waste removal system.

Leeward Highway became a quagmire of antiquated, exhaust-spewing cars driven by illegal Haitians, Dominicans, and Islanders without drivers' licenses. Plans to widen the only main artery on the island were in the works, but like most projects not driven by expat money and supervision, they were slow to commence and even slower to complete.

But despite the miserable traffic, long waits for basic utilities, and lack of urgency regardless of the situation, the island grew. It wasn't just the white powder beaches or the blue crystal water, teeming with lobster and bonefish that brought them from the United States, Europe, and Asia. Provo had established herself as an offshore sanctuary for those looking to hide money. She wasn't a Liechtenstein or Cayman, but she was well on her way.

Ian Milson was a barrister, early ensconced on the island, who made his living hiding other people's money. He had been practicing law in Provo for more than twenty-five years and had made a personal fortune from the endeavor. Four of his partners were, like himself, white and British, while one, Pablo Lightmore, was black and an Islander. Many competitors, perhaps envious of the firm's success, accused Ian of bringing a token black into the firm for political and economic gain. Ian was not offended by the accusation, often replying to such affronts with a pat, "The proof is in the pudding." And there was lots of pudding. Ian's firm controlled more than eighty percent of the offshore investment accounts on the island. Financial management firms were growing faster than the island's development businesses or tourism.

Like many Brits in Provo, he seemed to be able to mentally and socially disassociate himself from the realty of island life. He built a house in Leeward on Millionaire's Row, where the pure white sand of Grace Bay met his perfectly manicured lawn. He and his equally fair British wife and children existed in a protected world that included frequent dinner parties at the luxury beach front homes of other foreigners, as well as long afternoons of golf and tennis at the lush Provo Country Club. All the towheaded children were shipped off to prestigious English boarding schools soon after the maximum seven-year stint at Longfellow School, conveniently located within the confines of the gated community of Leeward.

When they tired of the perpetual sun and eighty-degree weather and longed for gray rainy days, they merely hopped a plane to merry ole England for a week or two or three. One thing about the offshore business—you never had to be "on island" for the money to roll in. Offshore accounts demanded steep yearly maintenance fees that were *always* paid on time, as one would not want to bring attention to themselves or have their accounts dissolved, thus exposing them to vigilant, hostile eyes or worse yet, to have their money disappear.

Nestled among seven other islands in the Turks and Caicos chain in the British West Indies, Provo was an ideal place to hide funds from the IRS, business partners, and soon to be ex-wives and husbands. No one in these islands wanted to know the whys, wheres or hows of the money. Not the government, not the lawyers, and not the banks.

Over the years, an interesting and diverse assortment of individuals came to Provo to conceal money. Many of them unexpectedly fell in love with the island's spectacular beauty and slow, unpretentious lifestyle. The reefs of the Turks and Caicos Islands were ranked as the most protected in all the Caribbean, while *Dive* magazine rated its waters among the top five dive spots in the world, touting perfect reefs, and a massive hole. The spectacular water, pure white powder beaches, world renowned sail fishing, and year-round eighty-five degree temperatures were enough to entice many to invest more than their hot currency. They bought and built magnificent homes on Grace Bay's pristine beach, and they brought their friends.

David O'Donnell, his lifelong buddy Bill Corley, and Barrett Lewter made their first trip to Provo in 2004. They flew to the island from Miami on David and Bill's Citation, under the guise of entering Provo's annual world-class marlin tournament. They did more than tag a 500 pound blue marlin that week; they met with Milson.

They pulled into the parking lot at nine. They were early. Their appointment wasn't for another thirty minutes. The hotel staff at Grace Bay Club warned them the traffic on Leeward Highway could be slowed to a snail's pace during peak hours, so they left early and by some stroke of luck, found themselves with time to spare.

They sat in their rented white Suzuki Jeep surveying the two-story Barclays Bank building. Milson's office occupied over half the office space on the second floor above the bank, but the small bronze plaque to the left of the door reading, *Milson, Stewart & Lightmore* was only eight by sixteen inches. One would have to stand directly in front of the sign and have good eyesight to read it. They obviously didn't need to announce their existence.

"You want to see if we can get a cup of coffee?" David asked while surveying a small strip center across the street. Tasty Treats, a deli next to the American Airlines office appeared to be open.

"Maybe a bagel," Bill said offhandedly.

The men got out of the jeep and strolled over to the deli. David couldn't believe that the reported eighty-five degrees was right. The heat was stifling. He quickly concluded that the flaunted trade winds were— exaggerated.

David and Bill were almost identically dressed in faded

khakis, starched oxford shirts with sleeves rolled up to their elbows, and deck shoes. Barrett stood out like a sore thumb in shiny black slacks, a black dress shirt, and his riding boots.

After a six-year stint with the CIA in his early thirties, Bill burned out and opted for a completely different life. He bought a depressed strip mall for pennies on the dollar, remodeled it, found tenants, and sold it a year later, more than doubling his money. It was the beginning of a very successful commercial development business.

Bill, like David was in great physical shape. He was a confirmed bachelor, a good pilot, and an even better polo player. His one and only four-month marriage twenty-six years ago, now meant nothing more than it marked the birth of his only child, Beth. He never managed to maintain a romantic relationship lasting longer than two years, regardless of the woman's attributes. Finding the perfect mate became more improbable with each year, for as he grew older he required his women to be unrealistically younger, thinner, and more stimulating. He couldn't recall a woman he had honestly loved. There had been many worthy, but the curious truth was that the only person he ever really loved was David. They grew up together on the North Carolina coast. Summers were spent on Ocracoke Island, a quaint 16-mile-long island in the Outer Banks. Bill was a permanent fixture at the O'Donnell's hundred-year-old saltbox home, where views of the sea and sound were theirs. They ran the pristine beach chasing seagulls, or simply sat for hours on end under the great live oaks draped with lacy Spanish moss, talking of their dreams. It was on Ocracoke Island that both boys lost their virginity to innocent and sweet local girls, Bill at fifteen and David at seventeen.

Over the years things changed very little, only the topics and the size of the trophies. Bill made his home on a magnificent horse farm near Reston, Virginia and although the time the men now spent in each other's company was limited, there wasn't a week that passed in forty years that they hadn't spoken.

David removed his sunglasses and blue NC Tar heels baseball cap and wiped his brow as they entered the Tasty Treats deli. The cool air and the smell of freshly baked bread greeted them. A refrigerated display counter filled with all kinds of pastries separated them from the kitchen. On a counter to the right, three pots of coffee stood ready to be poured. Above the coffee, bins holding fresh bread and buns hung from the wall, next to a blackboard listing the upcoming day's lunch specials.

"Could use a shot of something," Barrett grumbled as he eyed the blackboard.

A young black girl in her teens, wearing a long white apron over her jeans and T-shirt, with short hair poking out in every direction, asked what they wanted without a hint of a smile.

After ordering a pastry each, they served themselves coffee and sat at a little ice cream parlor table near the front window.

None of the men said a word as they watched the activity in the parking lot. What they were about to do would leave a concrete trail, putting everything they possessed in peril. They were going through with it. It was part of the plan. Backing out was not an option.

"Good morning, gentlemen, I'm Ian Milson." Milson greeted them with his proper British accent, upon entering the dimly lit, paneled conference room where David, Bill, and Barrett sat at a long, shiny mahogany table, each with their cups of coffee and a plate of tea biscuits. They stood, shook hands and introduced themselves.

"I understand you have an interest in setting up an offshore corporation," Ian said, gesturing for them to be seated.

"We'd like you to give us an honest account of how the banks on the island handle audits and requests from agencies in the U.S.," David said, getting to the heart of the matter without the usual niceties.

"Government agencies?" Ian asked.

"Yes. As well as, say, other banks."

Ian's response was a pat one. "I was informed you are a barrister yourself, David and I'm quite sure you understand the legal ramifications we face as a firm in suggesting in the slightest manner, methods of avoiding laws our clients are bound to by citizenship. We can assist you in setting up an offshore corporation, but we make it very clear that our purpose in doing so is to assist in improving a tax situation, not to circumvent tax laws."

"I understand that," David responded, undaunted by the rote disclaimer. "I'm merely asking how your firm represents a client with regard to the banks here, when a request, say, is made by the United States IRS."

Ian pushed an intercom button. "Shirley, bring me a cup

of tea. Would you like a topper?" he asked his new clients. They declined.

"We had an interesting situation occur on island not more than three weeks ago. You might have read about it. Front page of *Washington Post? The Wall Street Journal* as well."

The men shook their heads, *no*.

Ian continued. "An American, whose funds were deposited in Provo's branch of Barclays Bank, was being investigated by the IRS. When Barclays refused to release subpoenaed documents to the U.S. government, a U.S. Federal Court ultimately fined New York's Barclays branch one million dollars a day for every day the Provo's branch failed to comply."

Bill looked like he had just been shot. His ruddy face lost all its color. He looked to David for reassurance. David didn't appear to be bothered but rather, deep in thought, which gave Bill some degree of calm. Barrett was extremely uncomfortable with the entire situation; more concerned that Milson was nothing but a pompous limey fag than with how the U.S. pressured banks in this goddamned hot box of a country.

A middle-aged black woman wearing a tailored navy suit with a white starched blouse entered the room carrying a small tray with a cup of tea, lemon, and a sugar bowl.

"Thank you, Shirley," Milson said.

"Can I get you gentlemen anything?" the woman asked in a very proper British accent. They, again, declined.

Ian put two full teaspoons of sugar and a squeeze of lemon in the cup and stirred before continuing, "After eighteen days Barclays gave them everything." He took a big sip, gently set the cup on the saucer and added in a matter of fact tone, "It was late on a Friday when Barclays reluctantly released the information to the U.S. government. The following Monday morning, according to conservative, unofficial estimates, approximately $3.4 billion in U.S. dollars was transferred before five p.m. from Provo's Barclays Bank to the Turks and Caicos Islands Bank."

"Because?" David asked, as if tracking prey.

Ian picked up the cup and finished his tea. "There's only one Turks and Caicos Island Bank, and it's in Grand Turk."

David spoke his thoughts out loud. "They can't be manipulated by an outside bank or government. No leverage."

Bill looked from David to Milson for confirmation. Barrett's arms were on his chest, crossed; his thoughts, god knows where.

"Precisely," the Englishman smiled. "I am not advising you to put your funds in TCI Bank to avoid U.S. tax laws. I am merely describing for you the local banking system. And specifically, the policies we follow when foreign governments request financial information of our clients. The situation I have cited regarding Barclays, however, did not involve our firm."

"Where's Grand Turk?" Bill asked, still looking a little unsettled.

"Fifteen minutes, as the crow flies," Ian chuckled, as if amused by his own analogy. "It's our capital, where our government offices are located."

Bill nodded.

"If you gentlemen would like to proceed, we can have a corporation for you within two weeks. I should mention that for a little more money you could buy an existing but dormant corporation."

"How much more?" David asked.

"Twenty thousand,"

"Probably a good idea," David said, turning to Bill.

"Why do we need an old one?" Bill asked.

"New corporations are always noted. Correct?" David asked Ian.

"You are correct, sir," Ian confirmed, smiling. He liked this O'Donnell...a smart chap.

David asked Bill and Barrett, "Okay?"

Bill agreed. Barrett nodded, looking strangely irritated. Ian buzzed Shirley, who appeared almost immediately.

"We need offshore documents. Select one that is, say at least five years old, if you would be so kind."

Shirley addressed the clients. "Would you like to open an account with a wire transfer, check, or cash?"

Barrett leaned to the side of his chair and pulled up two large navy canvas duffle bags with bold white letters spelling out Jimmy's Gym and Vitamin Shop. He plopped them heavily on the table, "Cash."

Shirley left the room.

"I think we would prefer our funds be deposited in the TCI Bank." David's words flowed as naturally as if ordering lunch.

"Shall we hold your summaries, or would you like them sent to your accountant?"

"Keep our summaries. We will make periodic trips to..." David paused. "...To fish."

"Of course," Ian nodded.

Shirley returned with a stack of legal documents and sat at the table next to Milson.

An hour later, the two men who shared every secret as little boys now shared the most enormous and chilling confidence of their lives.

Le Mon

Barrett, carrying the now empty duffle bag, snarled as they walked into the stifling heat, "I need a fucking drink."

Eric opened a bottle of a wine and poured them each a glass. He set hers on the kitchen table and went to the den, the evening paper tucked under his arm. The room was cozy and inviting. Neely had the talent of putting a house together, he'd give her that.

The bright yellow room's French doors opened to a brick walled English garden, which in the spring and summer was brilliant with the blooms of every variety of Austin rose and peonies. Neely joked with some hidden inquietude that her garden might have been a long forgotten Indian burial site, for everything she planted, from roses to fig trees, flourished beyond any horticulturist's hope.

Eric sat deep in his plaid chair, stretching his legs out on a matching ottoman. He placed his wine glass on the small table next to his chair and opened the paper.

Neely brought her wine into the den and sat on the blue and white print sofa. She pulled a black cashmere throw over her legs and watched Eric as he read, wondering how they had come to this terrible point. Was all lost? She took a sip of wine and closed her eyes.

"Can you get the wine?" he asked, holding his empty glass up above his head as he continued reading the paper.

She got up and returned with the bottle. "How was your day?" she asked, filling his glass. She scooted his legs to the side of the ottoman, placed the bottle on the end table and sat.

"Like every other," he said, still looking at the open pages of the paper.

"Were you busy?"

He laid the paper on his lap, looked at her frowning, and asked, "What do you want to know Neely?"

"It's called conversation." She stood, "Never mind."

"Sit down. We need to talk about the building."

She sat back down on the ottoman.

"I want you to explain how that building is going to help us, because I don't get it."

She overlooked his sarcasm. She wanted him to know it was a place that gave her a feeling of peace, a place without the painful reminders that haunted her, a place they might mend.

"We never seem to be able to get away from all that we've been through, and I hoped that maybe if we are physically away, in a new place, we'd have time to, you know, go back, to relax, forget, and maybe, just maybe, be nice to each other long enough to connect."

"You're the one who won't let it go Neely, and until you quit punishing me, a fucking building is not going to make any difference."

"I think it would help me do that. What do we have to lose?"

"A ton of goddamned money. Do you have any idea of what it's going to cost to just stop the leaks in that building? Let alone restore it? You don't have a clue and you don't care. What if the group decides we don't need to be in Summerville?"

"We'll sell it."

Eric laughed, almost choking. "This is so like you. Charles told me that piece of shit has been on the market for over five years. Until you, they've never even had an offer.   Everybody in that town is probably still laughing...the doctor's wife with more money than good sense. "

Neely looked at Eric. He was grinning as if having won something. She ached, so aware she was married to a man who smugly found perverse pleasure in her pain.

"You want me to ask Charles for the earnest money back, to cancel the deal?" She asked.

"No! The last thing I want is for those people to think I'm some fly by night. I'm trying to set up a business, for Christ's sake. But remember this Neely. This is *your* fucking mess. Don't pull my ass into it."

She said nothing, feeling such heartache for them both.

Two Months Later

Neely parked in front of her friend's house and hurriedly made her way to the porch to escape the rain that just started to fall. She knocked, opened the door without waiting, and called out, "Caroline!"

A voice shouted back, "In the kitchen!"

Neely walked through the living room down the long hall to the kitchen.

Caroline, who was barely five feet with naturally blonde shoulder-length hair, wide set green eyes, and a body that proudly declared a healthy and disciplined lifestyle was busy making lunch. She wiped her hands on a dishtowel and hugged Neely, "Making fish tacos."

"One of the many reasons I love you," Neely smiled as she sat at the round kitchen table.

Caroline had recently moved to Summerville with her ex-husband, Philip, with whom she had a child five years earlier and an on-again/off-again relationship of an equal amount of time. They were going to give their marriage another shot. But within days of sorting out the new living arrangements she had misgivings. She found him worryingly familiar. She knew in her heart he was the exact same man who, years earlier, left her for a barista employed at the local Starbucks, the same man who deposited her and their daughter, Dana, on the side of the road at night, in the rain, terminating a bitter fight.

She had been Neely's loyal friend for over fourteen years. They had been through a lot together, sharing both joys and sorrows.

"How's everything coming?" Caroline asked, setting a glass of ice tea in front of Neely.

Neely shook her head, "Eric's furious about all the money I'm spending and I don't blame him. It's awful. It's a horrible money pit and I can't see any end in sight."

"Well let me tell you something that might make you feel better. Yesterday I had about twenty minutes to burn before I had to pick up Dana from gymnastics so I went up to the loft to see the progress. I got there just as the sun was setting. It was beautiful. I'm talking beautiful. Do you know that when the sun sets it reflects off the tin ceiling tiles? The entire room looked like it been washed in a soft pink light."

Neely managed a little smile.

"I'm sorry. I wish I could do something to make you feel better," Caroline said.

"I don't understand why he can't see how it could be really wonderful for us. We could escape all the reminders and triggers. I try so hard to remember what it was like before…to recapture that feeling of…of love…to save…*us*.

But because he's so wrapped up with this latest girl, who I'm sure tells him he walks on water, the last thing he wants is to hear me nag about how shitty our relationship is and how he won't even try to fix it. He doesn't want to hear it. It's much easier and a lot more fun for him to continue seeing *her*. I'm the shrew that bitches and complains, the one who reminds him how fucked up he is, and I'm the one who won't sleep with him. He doesn't give a shit about keeping us whole, about our family and to be completely honest, I know I probably stopped trying a long time ago. Sometimes I honestly think we both would be better off if we just got a divorce."

Caroline squeezed Neely's shoulder and kissed the top of her head, She went back to preparing lunch.

Neely watched Caroline as her mind wandered.

Why and at what point do we relinquish the magic slippers that ferry us to our dreams? Why do we so easily give up so much of ourselves to stand on another's toes as they dance their *dance? Is it because we simply tire, finding it easier to surrender our desires and sometimes even our souls rather than battle the dragons? And when we yield, should we have only ourselves to blame?*

She raised her face to the warm water and closed her eyes. She didn't want to go to Jan's. She was emotionally drained.

She rinsed and stepped out of the shower.

"What time do we have to be there?" Eric asked, startling her.

He was standing behind her, naked. He pulled away her towel and pressed his body into her back.

"Eric," she moaned, protesting.

"What?"

"I just took a shower."

"So? We have time."

"We don't. We have less than an hour."

He turned her around, took her hand and placed it on his hard penis. "Plenty of time."

She pulled her hand away.

"I don't want to."

"Why not?"

"I just don't."

He stepped back and snarled, "You never want to! You're fucking somebody, aren't you?"

"How is it you expect me to feel close to you, to want to make love to you, when you talk to me like that?"

"What am I supposed to do?" he demanded "You never want to fuck! Ever."

"Fuck?" she asked with disgust.

"Fuck...Make love...We don't do it! I'm not a goddamn eunuch!"

Neely slowly picked the towel up from the floor and covered herself. She walked to the terry cloth bench in front of the draped window and sat. "I don't feel close to you, Eric. I feel like we're strangers."

He was furious, ready to blow.

"Do you really want to make love when I feel like this?" she asked.

"You're goddamn right I do," he shouted.

She looked at him with disgust. "And you wonder why we're in this mess?"

"If you wanted this to work, you'd fuck me. What am I supposed to do? Masturbate? You just punish my sorry ass until you force me to act like this, to look somewhere else," he seethed.

"You are so horrible. Take responsibility, for once. I didn't make you screw all those women. You chose to do that all by yourself."

"Go ahead Neely, beat me up. See where that gets you."

She stood and pulled the towel tight at her chest.

Eric cocked his head and asked mockingly, "Just so I'm straight on this shit, I'd like you to tell me exactly when think you *might* feel like ... making *love*?"

She glared at him before saying, "When I feel you love me. When you show a little tenderness, when we connect."

"Will it require I juggle three tennis balls, standing on one foot while I kiss your ass?"

She didn't answer, wanting instead to end the altercation by leaving the room. He grabbed her arm as she past him.

"I'm just so tired of trying to figure you out. Why don't we just go ahead and get a fucking divorce? Just get this shit over with, once and for all!" he growled.

Her eyes slowly moved from his eyes to his hand, which still held tight to her arm. He quickly let go.

An hour later they were at Jan's dinner party. And never once did anyone suspect they were anything but the perfectly happy couple.

Madness. Pure madness.

Jan stood next to Steven at the entrance of their country home, looking flawlessly stunning, as she greeted her sixteen dinner guests.

Eric and Neely motored up the long, walled private road where upon reaching the massive home, two valets simultaneously opened their car doors.

Neely looked spectacular in a black Gucci tuxedo with

an oversized white shirt opened to just short of her waist. Several strands of white pearls draped her chest. She wore deep red velvet stiletto Jimmy Choo slings.

Neely caught Eric out of the corner of her eye. He was shaking Steven's hand. She was unexpectedly struck with feelings of attraction and love for him; feelings that were once were so familiar. He was smiling, looking so happy, so handsome and so sexy. She suddenly recalled in detail, their passionate love making and how it felt. Emotions she thought were gone forever seemed so real, so authentic. Eric turned from Steve and his eyes met Neely's. She smiled. He furrowed his brow, suspicious of why she was staring at him and just like that, the moment was lost.

Jan, dressed in a short, vintage, water-blue, silk Chanel cocktail dress grabbed Neely's hands and kissed her on each cheek, bringing her back to the present. "I'm so glad you came," she said pulling her off away from everyone. "You can thank me now because you are sitting between two of the most interesting men."

Eric took Neely's hand from Jan's before she had time to react. Neely looked back and grinned at her friend as she moved along with Eric into the gallery.

A marvelous and rare early nineteenth century erotic art collection graced the walls of the long, austere room. Other than the beam from the LED tiny spotlights illuminating each piece, the room had a dramatic, dark flare.

Waiters dressed in black served champagne and Beluga caviar crepes from antique sterling trays. Laughter and conversation filled the room.

After forty-five minutes of libations and exchange Jan invited everyone into the dining room, which easily accommodated the massive five by eighteen-foot pine table. It was ladened with gold Limoges chargers, generations old, antique Odiot sterling, French linens, and a vast array of Lalique crystal.

Banks of eight-foot tall French doors, opening to a meditation garden, were framed with heavy, black velvet drapes that pooled luxuriously on the tumbled stone slab floor. A huge wooden candle-lit chandelier in weathered reds, rusts, and olives, rescued from an 1860 gypsy camp, hung, centered above the table, casting a flattering soft glow on everyone below.

All *oohed* and *aahed* as they milled about the table, looking for the placard displaying their names. Eric found his seat down and across the table from Neely, between a young blonde woman in her late twenties whose breasts were lifted and exposed like a wise farmer might showcase his most prized cantaloupes, and Dr. Diane Dubosky, a sixty-something professor of American History at the University of Alabama.

Eric went full throttle into his charm mode, leaning in close to the young woman with the spectacular breasts, who blushed and coyly swished her thick, shoulder length hair in rhythm with every word that spilled from her rosy pouting lips.

Neely found her place between the two empty chairs of her "very interesting" dinner partners. She read the card to her right: *Jack*. Before she could turn to read the card to her left, she felt someone touch her elbow.

"Allow me," a very attractive man with graying blonde hair and large brown eyes, said as he pulled out her chair.

Neely smiled and sat. Standing at least six two, he was lean and lanky with an easy way about him. He extended his hand. "Jack Bendix."

"Neely Glover."

"Joe Samples," came the introduction from her left.

They both turned, smiling politely, as introductions were completed.

Joe appeared to be in his late forties, early fifties. He was impeccably dressed and extremely handsome. In fact, gorgeous may have been more precise word to describe him.

Sweet Jan!

After a few pleasantries with Neely, Joe turned to an equally handsome man to his left, who, it turned out, was the *cantaloupe's* husband. The woman to Jack's right was now demanding his attention so she, found herself out of the loop. She felt decidedly boring. She eavesdropped on Jack's conversation with the woman to his right and found he was actually listening to her, which was quite remarkable since the woman's comments weren't very interesting. Neely looked around the table. She didn't see Wallace or Drew, but did note Eric was definitely enjoying his dinner experience. He now had his elbow propped on the back of the pretty young woman's chair. Their body language intimated a cozy familiarity.

"You okay?"

She turned to Jack and smiled. "Yes, why?"

"You look a little blue."

"Do I? Sorry, I'm really not," she lied, trying to appear cheerful.

"Well, in case you are, I'll do my best to brighten your evening."

She smiled, "What a nice thing to say."

Jack leaned in close to Neely, his shoulders touching hers, and whispered, tipping his head toward Joe in one quick motion. "I assume you know he's gay?"

"Joe?" she mouthed, her brow furrowed.

Jack nodded, "Just didn't want you to feel *we* don't

think you're beautiful or smart." She discreetly snuck another peek to her left.

"I've learned never to assume," Neely said smiling.

"That's one I haven't been able to master, although I try," Jack grinned.

"If the lesson is a particularly hard one, you learn," she laughed.

"You've peaked my curiosity. There must be a story here."

"You sure you want to hear it. I'm not sure I can do a *long story –short*."

"I'm all ears, give me the long of it!" His smile was broad and genuine.

"It's actually pretty funny or at least with the passage of time it has *become* funny. I was heading from New York to LA through Atlanta. I had a two-hour layover and went to Delta's clubroom. I had a couple of glasses of wine and grabbed, you know, two packs of those Biscoff cookies they have, on my way out. When I got on the plane to LA, I got settled, taking out my glasses, book, and the cookies. Once in the air, I have another glass of wine with lunch and I go to eat my cookies. I look down and the guy next to me has opened the cookies and has eaten one out of the first pack. I look at him but say nothing as I eat the second cookie. A little while longer into the flight he opens the second pack and eats another cookie. Now I'm trying to decide, do I burst out laughing or do verbally assault the guy. I opt for doing nothing except to freeze him out with the body language thing. Now remember we're talking cookies here, which were free.

When the flight attendant announces we have to turn off all electrical devices for landing, the guy takes the last cookie out of the pack and breaks it in half. He slides the broken cookie in the cellophane over to me with a smile. I give him a look of disgust and shove it back towards him. We land, I ignore the guy when he tells me "have a nice day", we deplane and I get my luggage and get into a cab. I open my purse and what do I see? My two packs of cookies. I was dumbstruck. We were eating *his* cookies! To this day I wish I knew who he was so I could apologize. Horrible. I'm still so embarrassed. Neely smiled, "So, there's my story of why I now try to, *never* assume."

Jack was belly laughing, "That is one of the funniest damn things I've ever heard."

"I'm glad you find my atrocious behavior humorous," she grinned. "Now that you know my darkest secret, tell me about yourself, Jack?"

He said with all seriousness, "I'm a wooly ole single, straight guy."

She laughed. "That is ridiculous but yet, strangely appealing."

"My charm," he quipped.

"What do you do, Jack, outside your comedic routine?"

"I'm in the security business."

"And that means you...?"

"Handle security for companies and individuals. Mostly in international settings."

"Is that how you know Steven and Jan?"

"Steven and I go way back. But yes, my company handles his company's security, as well as his and Jan's personal protection."

"Personal protection?" Neely was surprised.

"Most very high profile execs have security firms that look out for them when they travel. Every time he travels internationally, for instance, we get an advisory from the state department."

"For Steven?"

"No, not him specifically, but the general public isn't typically warned about a lot of the sensitive scenarios that exist."

"And the government tells you?" she smiled.

He smiled back, "I was with the NSA for a long time and I still have clearance."

"Oh," Neely nodded, not knowing the exact ins and outs of the NSA, but knew it was akin to the likes of the CIA or FBI, only more clandestine and, if her memory served her, they never had to report to anyone, not even congress.

"Depending on the client's profile and their relationship to the government, say, if they have serious military contracts, we're given classified information."

"Interesting," Neely mused.

"Not really."

"Where are you from?" she asked.

"Originally North Carolina and a little town in Tennessee. Now I mostly divide my time between Atlanta and D.C. Are you from Madison?"

Neely nodded. "I am, but speaking of Tennessee, I just bought a building in a little town just north of there."

"Where?"

"Summerville."

"Know it well." He grinned.

"Really?"

"It's my little town."

"You're kidding," Neely said.

"It's a small world, isn't it?"

"I'd say," Neely answered, truly surprised.

Joe interrupted, gesturing to his salad. "Did you taste this fabulous raspberry vinaigrette?"

Neely and Jack laughed.

"Did I say something funny?" Joe asked sounding a little hurt.

"No, no. Sorry, buddy. We've already had a little too much wine and we're acting pretty silly." Jack swished some spinach through the salad dressing and took a bite. "It's delicious," Jack said enthusiastically.

Neely quickly followed suit with a bite and an, "Mmmm."

Joe was pleased, nodding to them with a big smile.

Neely turned to Jack. They smiled at each other.

July

Eric's neurosurgery group's temporary office, located in the vacant wing of the decrepit Morris County Hospital, was cramped. The eight-man and two-woman group continued their search for a good piece of land near the newly proposed hospital but up until now hadn't been able to find something suitable. So until they did, they would make do.

Initially the clinic in Summerville was open once a week, but quickly expanded to twice a week, as the patient demand was considerable. All the doctors rotated their time through Summerville and so on the days Eric found himself in the Summerville, he tried to have lunch with Neely. They would meet in the hospital cafeteria, as it meant Eric would not, as he put it, "waste time driving around." They would break the long periods of silence with safe subjects that included children, business projects, and his practice. Everything else invariably ended in discord. She did anything and everything to avoid *the building* for it was sure to remind him of its monetary sucking sound.

He demanded control in his life and lately he had none. Neely's project had shot his comfort level to hell. He never knew where she was or who she was with and he didn't like it. It was time to pull in the reins.

After a quick mention of the group's offer on some land, and a call from Eric's uncle extending them an invitation to come to Palm Springs for a visit, they ran into the familiar and painful *brick wall*.

It was agonizingly evident that after all their years together they were strangers. They didn't share the same likes in people, books, films, or music. They had become that pitiful couple that others watch with vicarious sadistic smugness, or, in more compassionate souls, sad uneasiness. They were the couple that sat across from one another ordering the same meal; from a menu they knew by heart, while sitting at *their* table. They would say nothing as they ate and drank, avoiding each other's eyes; emotional foreigners bound by worn out, long forgotten marriage vows, money, and children. Tenderness, friendship, and intimacy had long abandoned them.

"When do you think you're going to wrap this up?" Eric asked, taking the last bite of his salad.

"As fast as I can," Neely answered, looking at the remains on her plate.

"Ballpark? A month? A year?" He persisted with an edge that warned her more was to come.

Her skin prickled. She suddenly had the urge to pick up her white plastic fork and stab him to death in front of the two teenage Candy Stripers at the next table, but decided to simply answer him civilly, to be the *good* wife.

"Probably about five more months."

"I want it wrapped up. Understand?" She knew that voice.

"I need to get back, Eric. I'm supposed to meet the heating and cooling people." She said, glancing at her watch. "In five minutes."

He stood, wiping his mouth with a paper napkin. They got up from their table, put their trays on the conveyor, and walked out of the cafeteria, down the hall to the hospital's main entrance. Neely turned to Eric to say goodbye.

"I'll walk you to the car. Come on," he said, taking her elbow and leading out of the building and out to the parking lot.

Not good.

When they got to her car she waited for him to say something. He seemed uncharacteristically slow to speak his mind.

"Well?" Neely asked.

"I told the bank to cut you off after another twenty-five thousand. That's it. No more."

Neely was startled, "I have to give Carl Wilson a check for seventeen thousand today, not to mention I owe the electrician his draw."

"It's not like I haven't warned you. Twenty-five thousand and that's it."

"No, Eric, that's not *it*. You can't cut me off. Our accounts are joint and some of that money is mine, money I earned."

Eric smirked. "Those accounts can be zeroed out with one phone call."

"You wouldn't do that."

"Watch me."

"You think I don't know why you're doing this?" she said, fighting back tears.

"I thought it was because I'm sick of you spending my money."

"You've never been able to stand it when I've done anything on my own, when I'm not right under your thumb."

"Oh, right. Like this building is *on your own.*"

"I'm not talking about the building. I'm talking about how you're worried I don't need you, that you won't be able to control me. You can't stand the thought of me being okay without you."

Eric burst out laughing, "You on your own? You know Neely, I would bet everything I have that if you were suddenly on your own, the money you didn't immediately blow, you would give away to the first big dick, who pretended he liked you."

"You are despicable."

"I know you better than you know yourself, Neely."

"You don't know me at all. That's the sad thing about all of this, you know absolutely nothing about me."

"Oh god, don't get dramatic. I don't have time. I have to get back to work to pay for that piece of shit building of yours. Twenty-five thousand…that's it."

"Screw you," she snapped.

He smiled, bathing in his perceived victory. She didn't care if he was the father of her children or what vows she took a million years ago. She hated him.

"I can make it without you. I've done it before and I can do it again," she declared.

"God, get a hold of yourself," he laughed.

"I've contributed to this family and you know it."

"Yes, Neely, you've contributed," he patronized. "Any idea of what I contribute? We'd need a lot more time than lunch to cover that." His smirked was gone, replaced with a threatening glare.

"All I'm trying to do is *be.* You rob me of every achievement, no matter how small. I feel I have to be self-promoting because if I didn't, I'd disappear. Nothing is ever enough for you," she murmured as the tears ran down her face.

A group of people walked past them, staring. Neely turned her head away and wiped her face with the back of her hand.

"You're making a scene," he scolded.

"I don't care! I don't care. I'll finish the building when it's finished, and *we* will pay *every* bill that comes in until it's done."

"I'm warning you, quit spending my fucking money! I mean it!"

"Don't threaten me, Eric, it won't work this time. If I have to, I'll use my own money!"

"Well fucking hallelujah! Finally, something we can agree on."

Neely pleaded, "I need to talk to you, Wallace. Please come. I know you don't want to but I really need to talk to you."

"It's *so* far Neely. Why are you making me do this? Why don't you come to Madison? We could have lunch at the club. Jan's gonna be there, she's playing golf with Sybil."

Neely waited. "I wouldn't ask if it weren't important."

"Shit. This better be pretty frikin' important. The idea of driving an hour to some *po dunk*, little-ass town is not my idea of a productive or fun afternoon."

"It's thirty minutes."

Silence.

"I can't believe I'm going to do this. Is there any place we can eat that doesn't specialize in sugar and grease, or should I bring something from here?" Wallace was not kidding.

"There are plenty of places to eat. You act like Summerville is in the middle of nowhere."

"It is in the middle of nowhere and you haven't answered me. What are my choices?"

"Wallace, we're talking food here."

"And?"

"There are two places you'd probably think are okay."

"Two?"

"Well, probably really only one, but I hear it has good salads and soups. You'll be fine. I promise."

"I'm sure," Wallace said sarcastically. "But know if I detect the slightest hint of banjo pickin', I'm outta there."

Wallace actually enjoyed the drive from Madison. The desire to bitch about the hardship and inconvenience of the journey waned as she drove through rolling hills of beautiful, pristine forests. She arrived in Summerville and pulled her Jag up next to Neely's silver Mercedes. Wallace looked at the clock on the dash. It indeed took just a little over thirty minutes. She got out of the car and gazed curiously at the building that had captured her friend's interest, not to mention her life, for the past six months.

Hell, it wasn't an interest it was an obsession.

What did Neely find so special about this building? At first glance it looked like any big old, brick building. Still sitting in her car, she took a harder look. Well, maybe it was a little interesting...in a hokey kind of way. Like finding a pair of outrageous Carmen Miranda shoes tucked away in your great grandmother's attic. Fabulous, but what in the world do you do with them?

She found her way around the corner of the building, past several plate glass windows towering from street level to over fourteen feet, on to a single glass-paned mahogany door that read Sammons & Sammons Insurance in chipped, faded lettering. Wallace opened the heavy door, removed her Chanel sunglasses, and cautiously started up the dark staircase.

"Neely!" she called out. "Jesus Christ," she grumbled to herself, after grabbing the soot covered stair railing.

Wallace peered up the dark staircase and shouted, "Neely!"

"Wallace!" a familiar voice called from somewhere far above her.

"Who in the hell else would it be?" she muttered under her breath, then shouted, "Yeah! It's me!" Wallace continued up the stairs, holding her dirty hand as far out in front of her as she could manage. You would have thought she had just touched road kill.

"Coming! Stay where you are." Neely called down.

Neely descended the stairs at a fast clip, grinning ear to ear. She wore faded jeans, a white t-shirt, and tennis shoes.

"I'm so glad you came," Neely said carefully hugging Wallace so as not to muss her. "I said casual, silly."

Wallace looked totally out of place in her Escada lime green slacks, hot pink silk blouse and Giuseppe Zanotti silver sling sandals. Her dark brown, shoulder length hair was pulled neatly back into a French braid fastened with a small rhinestone clip.

"This *is* casual. If you weren't spending your life in the boondocks, you might know that."

Neely frowned, squinting her eyes to slits. "It's a good thing I love you, otherwise I'd push you back down the stairs."

"Have you thought about getting a cleaning crew? This place is filthy," Wallace complained, turning up her dirty palm for Neely's inspection.

"Poor baby. Come on, you can wash that off upstairs."

Wallace followed Neely up a long flight of steep stairs to the second floor, and down a hallway lined on both sides with small offices. Each little office had a large snowflake glass window that took up most of the walls facing the hall. The sun entered the rooms through the outside windows before filtering through the snowflake glass to the hall. The brilliant light prisms cast tiny sparkles on the hall oak floor.

"Isn't it beautiful?" Neely asked. "Look." Her voice sounded childlike as she pointed to the light play on the floor in front of them.

"Uh-hum. But what in the hell are you going to do with this place? God, it's smack dab in the middle of nowhere and you have to walk up *all* these stairs?"

Neely smiled. "I'm putting in an elevator. But you'll see why, whether there's an elevator or not, you're going to love this place!" Wallace followed Neely to a closed door at the end of the hallway. Neely opened it, revealing another staircase.

"Where are we going?" Wallace whined.

Neely grinned dramatically waving her arm in a sweeping gesture. "After you, madam."

Wallace hesitated, looking up the next set of steps. "Why is it I feel Norman Bates is waiting for me up there? Maybe you should go first."

"Go on, you nut."

As Wallace hesitantly began the ascent a large dark shadow appeared at the top of the stairs. The figure began barreling toward them.

Neely reached out and gently grabbed the back of Wallace's arm.

"It's one of the carpenters," Neely whispered reassuringly to Wallace who was spooked.

"Afternoon, ma'am. Gotta get another blade."

The young man passing them wore tight, faded Levi's, work boots, and a sweatshirt with the sleeves cut away to his shoulders with the words, *Tennessee Titans* blazoned across it. His thick, curly, shoulder length hair was pulled back and tied loosely into a man bun. A red bandana was wrapped around his forehead. He was lean and muscular and his skin was tanned to a leathery brown.

Wallace stopped and turned to watch him disappear into the hallway at the bottom of the staircase. She looked at Neely wide-eyed and dramatically whispered, "Holy shit I think I'm in love!"

"Oh, Wallace, just go," Neely groaned, nudging her up the stairs.

Wallace continued to a landing at the top and found two closed doors on either side.

"To the right," Neely instructed.

Neely reached around Wallace and opened the door. Wallace turned and rolled her eyes with a sigh, walked two steps into the room, and stopped dead in her tracks. Her eyes grew to the size of saucers. She stood silently, taking in the enormous room.

"Voila," Neely whispered.

"Oh...my...god!" Wallace said softly, dramatically enunciating each syllable.

Le Mon

Her eyes scanned the sixteen-foot walls, the hammered tin ceiling, the magnificent carved mahogany panels bordering every wall to five feet, and the wide oak-plank flooring, all of which had been restored to their exquisite, original state. Centered in the middle of the room a gigantic turn-of-the-century Parisian crystal chandelier, replicating a hot air balloon, hung majestically. Massive fourteen-by-six-foot palladium windows encircling the entire room, warmly invited brilliant sunshine.

"If ever a room could be called eye candy, this would be it. This could be Paris." Wallace whispered, sounding almost wistful.

"I know," Neely beamed.

"I mean, it *really* could be Paris," Wallace insisted.

"I know," Neely repeated smiling proudly.

"Jan said it was spectacular but this is perfection," Wallace marveled.

A voice interrupted the moment. "Excuse me Miss Neely, but could I show you something?"

The carpenter was back, now holding a new saw blade and a paper bag full of nails.

"That was fast," Wallace drawled, while giving him her most seductive grin.

"It don't take me long. I've pretty much got those stairs under control," he flirted back. Swiftly, he returned to the business of the building and said to Neely, "Over here," pointing to the east, front window.

Neely and Wallace followed him past a man and a woman installing wall plates.

"How big is this room?" Wallace asked Neely, "It's huge."

"About forty-five by fifty, I think."

The carpenter interjected, "Actually, ma'am, it's forty-eight by sixty. And that's just this room, then you got the back."

"Blaine, please stop calling me ma'am."

"I'm sorry, it's just habit. My mama drilled it into me," he apologized, stepping up to the window facing the town square. He placed the new blade and paper sack on the floor and pulled out a screwdriver from his leather work belt, motioning for them to come closer. Neely came up next to him and placed her palms on the wide window ledge while Wallace moved in close behind the carpenter.

Wallace's eyes moved from the man's neck to the well-defined muscles in his back and arms. She was close enough to smell the sweat that soaked the small of his back. She wanted to reach out and grab his ass, but smartly refrained.

"I really hate to show you this, but..." With his last word trailing off, he stuck the screwdriver deep into the timeworn twelve-inch wide window sash. The screwdriver slid through the wood like a warm knife through butter.

"They're all like this...front ones are the worst."

"Oh god," Neely moaned.

"What does that mean?" Wallace asked offhandedly.

"All these windows gotta be replaced," he explained.

Neely shook her head sighing heavily.

"Bad?" Wallace asked, trying to feign interest, while still appearing as cute as possible to the carpenter.

Neely looked at her friend in disbelief, thinking, *how could this be anything but bad?*

"I don't know how much more of this I can take," Neely said. "Honestly, I really don't."

"Now you're talking! Screw it all and come home," Wallace smiled, slapping her hands together.

Neely was at a breaking point. She may have bought

the building for a mere $140,000, but five months and $700,000 later she understood why no other person ever made an offer on the building. She *was* the dumb ass doctor's wife.

"You want me to call a couple of people to get some estimates?" Blaine asked.

"Sure. What's another sixty, eighty or a hundred thousand? This will push Eric straight over the edge and I'm betting he'll take me with him."

"Fuck Eric," Wallace blurted. Blaine looked at Wallace, shocked and embarrassed.

"Oops." Wallace giggled, covering her mouth, smiling at Blaine, "I bet you think I'm just awful."

"No, no, ma'am," he said awkwardly. "I gotta get back to work."

"Thanks, Blaine" Neely said.

"You bet, Miss Neely. I sure hate this for you." He avoided eye contact with Wallace.

"He is just yummy" Wallace said dreamily as she watched him walk away.

"You scared him, Wallace. He probably thinks you're insane."

"Fuck him if he can't take a joke."

Neely shook her head, turned to look out over the almost deserted town square, feeling utterly exhausted and overwhelmed. Wallace put her arm around her friend and drew her in. Neely rested her head on Wallace's shoulder.

"Wanna sell? Come back to the real world with me? I'll drive," Wallace offered.

There was a long pause before Neely spoke. "No."

Wallace squeezed her friend's shoulder. "Well then, forget it, order the goddamned windows, and get on with it. It's only money."

Neely, still looking over the square, nodded. Wallace glanced back at the handsome carpenter, who was working on a cabinet across the room and whispered, "In the big picture, darling, we're talking pocket change here, and there are monumental perks lurking behind all those tool belts."

Neely looked at her friend while shaking her head and laughing, "Where do you come up with this shit?"

Wallace grinned like a Cheshire cat. "Comes naturally."

The two stood at the window silently looking at the little town's square below them.

"It is kinda nice here, isn't it?" Wallace said softly.

Neely nodded.

Wallace quickly added, "Key word is kinda."

It was almost one when they left the building and headed for Parker's Grill. Neither of them spoke as they stopped to peer in Sister's Antique store window. They scanned the displays on the other side of the plate glass window, which included glassware, linens, old movie posters, a small tapestry, a child's rocker, civil war memorabilia, and antique fishing lures.

After a few moments Wallace turned to Neely. "I know you didn't ask me up here to show me the building or to look at cheap antiques."

Neely kept her gaze on the items in the window, "Mind if we go in?"

Wallace followed Neely into the store knowing it had to be important because her friend was having such a hard time expressing herself. Wallace decided she would try to be patient, even if it killed her.

As Neely and Wallace entered the antique store, a heavyset woman looking well into hard lived seventy plus years greeted them. Her thin, yellowed gray hair was pulled up in a knot on the top of her head. She sat roosted on an antique barber chair behind a turn-of-the-century candy counter cluttered with hundreds of knickknacks and assorted pieces of pink Depression glass. She looked like a great, molting parrot high on her perch. She was jabbering on the phone and stopped talking just long enough to grin and instruct them to "look around."

The store was filled to the brim with everything from vintage clothing to old horse harnesses, all neatly divided into imaginary booths created by the items themselves. The whole store smelled of tobacco, although not one pipe or cigar was visible.

Wallace picked up a small, dark brown box with black hinges. She spit on her fingers and rubbed the box.

"Oh, my god! Neely, this is tortoise. Look," she whispered. "Eighteen dollars! The hinges are sterling. Look at the mark. It's English, probably early-to-mid-eighteen hundreds."

They meticulously examined the box.

"This is a goldmine! These fools have no idea what they have."

"I'm getting a divorce." The words spilled from Neely's mouth like jellybeans from a tipped jar.

"What?"

Neely turned away and picked up a small blue and white plate. She turned it over. "I saw Bruce Kennamer a couple of days ago. The papers will be ready by the middle of next week."

Wallace was shocked. "Oh, my god. What happened?"

Neely set the plate down and walked to the next booth. Wallace followed, clutching her new find tight in her hand.

"Twenty-three years."

"Shit. I mean why now? What happened?" Wallace couldn't imagine Neely going to see a lawyer without a cataclysmic event. It wasn't in the realm of possibilities, in the universe she understood.

"I found out he's having another affair. She goes to our church, is married, has three little children, and is a cokehead. Her husband called and told me. And here I am, going to therapy for the last affair he had and he's moved on to a new one."

"Goddammit why didn't you tell me before?" Wallace shouted.

"Can I help you ladies find anything?" The old woman startled them both.

"I'm going to get this," Wallace answered, holding up the box.

"You want me to take it to the counter whilst y'all look around?"

"No. I'll hold on to it," Wallace replied, not wanting to let the little box out of sight.

"Well, y'all just holler if I can help," the woman said, already shuffling her way back to the barber's chair.

Wallace looked at Neely, "What's her name?"

"Lisa McAllister. I don't know her. I'm sure I've seen her but I wouldn't know her if I ran over her."

"That's exactly what we should do. Run over the bitch!" Wallace blurted, almost shouting. "God."

"I told him the last time—if he did it again, it would be the last. I meant it."

"That fucking asshole!" Wallace's voice reverberated

through the store.

"Shhh. God, Wallace, this is a little town. People here don't talk like that," Neely pleaded.

"Like I give a shit what these hillbillies think!"

"I do. I'm going to live here," Neely said.

"Are you trying to give me a fucking heart attack?" Wallace shouted.

"You have the nastiest mouth of any woman I've ever known. Stop, please."

Wallace followed Neely who walked slowly down the aisle, "Let me check the back of your neck. The only logical explanation is you're a pod person. Not only are you actually going to divorce Eric, I realize you actually mean you want to *live* here. I have no words!"

"You have words, Wallace. You always have words."

"I have no words!" Wallace declared, in her best drama queen voice as she continued: "But I do want to say this, though. If you get a divorce, you need to be around your friends, not in the middle of Aintree. This place is not healthy, it's a redneck hell hole."

"I like it here. I feel like I belong, like..." She hesitated.

"Belong! Oh my god, ... you've lost your mind!" Wallace said, her face contorted.

Should I tell Wallace about the building? The magic? The peace? Would she understand, or would she just think I finally slipped away?

Neely decided that this would not be the most opportune time to go into that scenario, considering Wallace already suspected body snatching.

"I think it would be good for me to get away from all the social stuff, people looking at me pitifully and asking *'How are you?'* when all they want is some juicy crap they can pass on, you know, from the horse's mouth?"

Wallace knew exactly what she meant, unexpectedly feeling ill thinking about how few people they could call *real* friends, the kind that would support you no matter what.

As Wallace and Neely silently made the turn at the back of the store to the next aisle, they found themselves blocked by three women examining a small dresser. One of the women was on her knees peering up under the piece, while the other two stood unintentionally obstructing the narrow aisle. As soon as they saw Neely and Wallace, the two women quickly moved into the booth, smiling. Neely and Wallace walked around the other woman. Neely said "hi" as she passed.

"Well shut my mouth, you're Mrs. Glover, aren't you?"

Neely turned back to them, stopping. "Yes."

"I thought that was you. I see you go in and out of the Faulkner Building. My business is next door. Well, not exactly next door, but down the ways. You know, Candy's Catering?"

Neely nodded, although she had no inkling. "I'm Neely and this is my friend, Wallace Lee." Wallace stepped back without speaking, much like someone trying to avoid a toxic spill.

"I'm Candy Meade. My friends, Jessie Tidewell and Am Stilter."

The kneeling woman got up. Neely exchanged greetings and handshakes, while Wallace barely acknowledged them, keeping her hands, still clutching the tortoise box behind her back.

"Everyone is just so happy your husband has an office here. We think he's just wonderful and so handsome, my god!" Candy said, fake fanning herself. Immediately she began backtracking. "You don't mind me saying that do you? I don't mean no disrespect." The three women giggled.

Wallace looked at Neely; giving her the *can you believe this shit* look. Neely quickly looked away from Wallace, knowing her friend was primed to pounce on the woman like a starving mountain lion would on a whimpering rabbit dragging a bleeding, broken leg.

"None taken," Neely reassured the woman, who came as close to a real live Barbie as Neely had ever seen. She was fully equipped with big, teased, almost white platinum hair, big blue eyes enhanced with violet contacts, big white teeth, big fake boobs, and the teeniest, tiniest little waist. The Barbie woman never seemed to fully close her mouth, even when she spoke. "I'm so glad. You know a lot of women would get upset. You know, be jealous," she continued, still giggling.

Neely laughed, more as an emotional release than anything else. "I know he's really happy about being here," she said, doing her best to sound sincere.

"Do you work?" one of the women asked.

"Yes...I'm in the clothing business."

"You're kidding! I worked at Davidson's Pant Barn for ten years, after my kids got grown, in the boot department. Isn't it a small world, you and me in the same business?"

Every neuron in Neely's body fired. How long would it be before Wallace blatantly insulted these women or pulled out a Luger and shot them? She had to get Wallace out of there immediately. She looked at her watch.

"Oh Wallace, it's after one. I can't believe we're so late," Neely turned to the women. "It was so nice meeting you, but we have got to go. We're really late."

Without dawdling, they headed for the counter. Wallace's barbs began immediately. "This should be a lesson to you Neely Glover. I don't find this a bit funny anymore. How could you think of living here? Is this what you want? Friends like refrigerator hair Candy, or maybe your retail soul sister?"

Neely ignored her. "Pay for the dead turtle, and let's get out of here."

"You need to come home and I'm not kidding," Wallace commanded, walking up to the counter. She gave the old woman who was back perched up on the barber chair twenty two dollars and said in an offhanded way, "Keep the change."

"Wait, honey, you get ten percent off," the old woman grinned, exposing a missing front tooth.

Wallace looked at Neely and started laughing. She couldn't stop. Neely was at a loss for what to do or say, finally spewing apologetically, "She's from up north."

Neely's comment only fueled Wallace's wild laughter. The old woman frowned suspiciously as she placed the tortoise box in a used plastic Wal-Mart bag. She half expected them to rob her.

Wallace was completely out of control. Neely shook her head with an exasperated look of *I don't know what to do with her* and took the Wal-Mart bag from the frowning woman. Neely grabbed Wallace's arm, forcefully steering her to the front door and outside, where she demanded, "What is wrong with you? I can't believe how rude you were!"

Wallace was laughing so hard she had to stop and bend over, "Oh shit, I think I just peed."

An older couple walked past them deliberately ignoring the spectacle. Neely was mortified.

"I'm sorry, I'm sorry, I swear, give me a second," Wallace cried as she laughed. She braced herself against the side of the building with one hand, legs tightly crossed.

"Stop it, Wallace. I mean it."

"Okay. Okay. I've stopped," she said, taking a deep breath. She stood up straight while shaking her hands in the air. She took an exaggerated breath, smoothed her pants and pushed the wild strands of hair from her face. But as soon as she looked at Neely, she was laughing again. "You want me to go back and apologize?" Wallace managed to stammer, almost choking.

"I'm sure she'd call the police. You were so rude, Wallace. She's an old woman, for god's sake."

Wallace walked ten feet ahead of Neely and pretended to be window-shopping alone. It was the only way she could regain her composure.

They walked separately for the entire block before Wallace stopped her antics and waited for Neely to catch up. Wiping the tears from her eyes, she asked, "Are you really going to divorce him?"

Neely nodded, "Yes."

"Damn." Wallace looked at her friend; trying to place the part of her she'd obviously overlooked all these years. She would have bet everything that Neely would never leave Eric. She was obviously wrong.

"Confessing my husband's sins has made me ravenous. You hungry?" Neely smiled.

"I'm somewhat worried about the food deal here. Just tell me they don't eat squirrel."

"Don't worry, darling...tastes just like chicken."

"Well look at you!" Wallace drawled her best Texas twang at David O'Donnell, as he barreled out of Parker's Grill.

It took him a second to register who was doing the shouting.

"Wallace Lee! What in the world are you doing in Summerville?"

"Ask her!" Wallace said, pointing at Neely. "The question is, darlin', what are you doing here?"

"I live here," he grinned.

"I knew that, I was just pullin' your very fine leg," Wallace cooed. "This is my friend..."

But before she could complete the introduction, a gaggle of mostly obese women in a medley of medical uniforms packed in around them, maneuvering a pathway into the little restaurant.

"Allow me," David offered, holding the door open. Each woman smiled and thanked him as they passed. With the Florence Nightingales safely inside, David extended his hand to Neely. "David O'Donnell."

Neely shook his hand. "Neely Glover."

"I know," he smiled. She was immediately struck by how handsome and charming he was, and by how deliciously thrown she was. The attraction was immediate and fierce.

"Have we met?" she asked.

Two farmers in faded overalls, working toothpicks between their lips, made their way around them as they exited Parker's. They spoke to David, who addressed them by name.

"Are we gonna stand in the doorway all day or what?" Wallace bellowed. "I'm sure the hog grease is solidifying in there as we speak."

Le Mon

"Come in, ladies. Be my guest."

"Weren't you just leaving?" Neely asked.

"There's always room for a little tea," he smiled with a wink.

"Did you forget something?" Tilly asked David, as he directed Neely and Wallace to his table.

"Thought I needed a little tea."

The waitress frowned. "After that root beer float?"

He laughed. "Don't give me away, Tilly."

Neely avoided looking at him directly, fearing he might sense her uneasiness, or, worse yet, how attracted to him she was.

"Is there something here that won't raise my cholesterol fifty points?" Wallace asked, scrutinizing the menu. Tilly looked at Wallace and, right then and there, decided to poison her.

David said, "I like the soups...White chili is their specialty. Good Caesars." While stealing looks of Neely, he asked Wallace, "What kinds of things do you like?"

"Foie gras, Chilean sea bass, Cristal," Wallace's voice was aloof as she scanned the menu.

David and Neely laughed.

"I think the closest we can come to satisfying this uptown girl's palate is fried catfish with homemade tartar," he offered.

Tilly was not happy. The snotty woman's attitude was getting on her last nerve. The waitress impatiently tapped her pencil on her order book.

"What'll you have?" David asked Neely, gently trying to hurry things along.

"I'll have a cup of white chili and unsweet tea."

Tilly looked at Wallace coldly. Neely snuck a glance at David. He seemed so happy, so nice...and he wasn't wearing a wedding band.

Oblivious to Tilly's disdain, Wallace worked the poor woman over with inane questions about how each item was prepared and what was served with each dish.

David turned to Neely. "You know we've met before?"

Neely smiled nervously. "Have we? I'm sorry, I don't remember."

"At the Brooks Gallery, about three years ago? It was your friend's show, from Belgium?"

"Dieter Velter?" she asked, wondering where he was going with all this.

He nodded. "If I remember correctly, you were giving your husband a dressing down for describing a painting inaccurately."

Oh great.

"So you remember me as some kind of shrew then? Nice." She smiled; trying to pretend his comment was funny.

"It wasn't pretty," he continued, as his smile widened.

"Are you sure it was me?" she asked, hoping for a miracle.

"I'm sure," he said. "You called him an idiot. Funny, though, I don't remember you being this pretty."

Oh great. Now I don't look like a dog? What's wrong with this man?

"Gee, thanks," she stammered.

"Sorry, I didn't mean it the way that sounded. It's just that it's unusual to have such a different second impression. Do you know what I mean?"

Actually, no, she thought.

"I suppose," Neely answered, totally thrown.

"What are you two talking about?" Wallace asked after finally ordering.

David smiled at Neely. "We were discussing how we met, so many years ago."

"I didn't know you two knew each other," Wallace said, not sure if he was kidding.

"We don't. He only thinks he knows me," Neely looked directly into his eyes and felt breathless. "Actually, I think he has me confused with someone else, someone dreadful, *and* homely."

David laughed at their shared joke.

Tilly returned with David's tea and set it down hard in front of him. He smiled at the waitress, but she wasn't having it.

"Distracted by hog jowls five seconds and I'm out of the loop," Wallace complained. "This has truly been one hell of a day!"

David took a sip of tea and continued to watch Neely. His smile slowly faded, leaving an unsettled expression one might have when trying to master a difficult task without success. She could almost feel his eyes move across her skin.

What's wrong with me? Get a hold of yourself. I'm sure he's married. God, what are you thinking? You're married! Oh god. He's got to know you're crazy and he thought you were unattractive...Just look at him, not too long, be normal...He thought you were a dog. What are you doing? Say something.

"So, exactly what do you do in Summerville?" Neely asked, coming off like Inspector Clouseau.

Oh god, Neely. Why did you say, exactly? What are you doing? Calm down.

"I'm a lawyer. You know, nickel and dime kind of stuff."

Neely thought his self-effacing manner was so

attractive.

"Give me a shovel!" Wallace barked. "This man Neely, is the only attorney in the state to win several cases before the U.S. Supreme Court. Hell, he's a regular on Fox. Give me those nickels and dimes any day."

"Lucky is what I am," he said as if he was a simple country lawyer who fell off a cotton bale into good fortune.

"Luck doesn't have shit to do with it. If I ever decide to kill that son of a bitch I'm married to, this is the man I'd bank my fabulous widowed life on. Isn't that right, David?" Wallace asked seductively.

His smile transformed from a sweet, boyish demeanor into one of a cunning fox, and for an instant Neely thought she detected something very different, something very dark.

"Except that Drew has already given me a retainer in the event he kills you." David's familiar grin was back. "You know, planning ahead."

"That, my friend, is a total fabrication. Drew can't decide what tie goes with what suit without my help, let alone conceptualize and execute a murder."

Neely laughed.

David turned to her. "I've been watching your restoration progress. Nice job. What are your plans for the building?"

"Yeah, tell him your plans Neely," Wallace said, baiting her.

Neely looked at Wallace and shook her head slightly. She felt her face grow hot and knew it was probably turning red.

"Is it a secret?" David asked jokingly.

"Not for long," Wallace chimed in.

"I'm putting an apartment on the top floor, and I've

been talking with a good friend of mine about opening a restaurant on the main level. So far, that's about it."

"A restaurant?" Wallace ranted, "A restaurant? When did you come up with *this* harebrained idea?"

"Before Caroline was married, she worked as a chef at Palm Beach's E'Chaude. She thinks a restaurant would work and so do I."

"She's right on point, we could use a good restaurant," David said. "Right now, if we want something other than Rustlers, we have to drive to Madison or Nashville. You'll find you have a lot of support from the community."

"Don't encourage her, David, the thread is pretty thin."

"Are you going to rent the apartment?" he asked.

"No," Neely said simply. David looked at her curiously, as if expecting her to go on. When she didn't elaborate, he politely looked away and took another sip of tea.

"Tell him, Neely," Wallace said, egging her on.

"Wallace? Stop," Neely laughed uncomfortably, praying her friend would somehow magically morph into someone else, someone with discretion, someone who could *read* the situation.

"She's moving up there," Wallace barreled on, "if you can believe that deranged notion."

"Thank you," Neely said, not knowing if she should be angry, sad, or simply pretend she was in a fugue state.

"She's getting a divorce," Wallace rattled, like a tattling child.

Neely's mouth dropped. "Wallace. I'm sure David's not interested in my personal life."

David reached across the table and covered her hand with his. Her heart stopped and her stomach turned flips in the most wonderful fashion. "Why wouldn't I be interested? I'm sorry to hear that. Can't be a good time for you." His voice was so sensual, so familiar, she felt lightheaded, almost nauseated.

He took his hand off hers, long after what seemed to be appropriate. A warm sensation flooded her pelvis.

Run.

Las Vegas

Early Friday morning, Candy painstakingly chose the outfit she'd wear. She happily did the necessary tugging and pulling in order to fit into her hot pink lycra leggings and silver lame halter top. She teased her platinum hair a little tighter, adding an extra two inches to create the ultimate beehive, and adorned her bright blue eyelids with heavy, jet-black false eyelashes. Gigantic rhinestone loops hung from her ears. Before heading downstairs, she dusted her shoulders and arms with pink glitter, slipped into her purple, suede Jessica Simpson platform heels, grabbed her bejeweled Juicy Couture silver hobo bag and white rabbit fur jacket. She was ready.

The four-hour flight from Summerville to Vegas aboard Barrett's Hawker jet was uneventful; if you didn't count the blowjob Candy gave Barrett. By the time the limo pulled up to the plane, Candy had redone her hair and makeup and was ready for Vegas!

Barrett checked in at Caesar's high roller's private desk. With Candy at his side, they strutted like peacocks through the lobby and its hundreds of slot machines, each noisily identifying their existence. Barrett sported his standard Johnny Cash black outfit and scuffed riding boots. He wore two large gold chains around his neck; a gaudy diamond encrusted gold Rolex watch and a five-carat diamond pinkie ring.

The hotel bellman followed them with their cart of luggage. Barrett tossed the room key to the bellman and whipped out a hundred from a roll of cash and handed it to the man. "We're gonna get a drink."

"Yes, sir. Thank you so much. Good luck, sir," the young man said gratefully.

Barrett and Candy headed for the bar, strategically positioned in the center of the casino. After ordering, he peeled several hundred-dollar bills from the money roll and handed them to Candy. "Meet me in the room in an hour and a half. I gotta make a couple of calls."

Candy grabbed her drink from the counter, stood, and with the money wadded in one hand and her purse in the other, she leaned in to Barrett, stuck her tongue in his ear, and whispered, "I love you, baby." As she turned to go find a "lucky feeling" slot machine, Barrett slapped her on the ass. She grinned back at him before disappearing into the mass of people.

Barrett paid the bartender and, drink in hand, headed for the quieter sports bar across the casino. He took a seat in front of one of the many huge TV screens covering everything from soccer to basketball and gulped the last of his scotch. He ordered another drink from a Johnny-on-the-spot waitress. His phone rang.

"Okay. I'm in the sports bar."

The waitress sat his drink on a napkin in front of him with a smile. He pulled a fifty out of his roll and waved her off. She mouthed a thank you and was gone.

Barrett slipped his phone into his shirt pocket and

waited, passing the time focusing on a basketball game. He tried not to think about David and what he would do if he knew he was meeting with Escobar behind his back. He'd have a shit fit for sure, but what the fuck did he know anyway? It was time somebody took charge, instead of acting like a bunch of fuckin bitches, sucking these spics' dicks.

When he was done, they'd all be thanking him.

Escobar Montoya and his two *gorillas* approached Barrett, who was on his third scotch and feeling no pain.

"Barrett?"

Barrett turned quickly, caught off guard. He rose to his feet, hand extended. "Escobar, how are you?"

The dark eyed, dark skinned handsome Colombian man in his thirties did not appear to be happy. Escobar's two bodyguards immediately moved in and frisked Barrett.

"What the fuck!"

"Can't be too careful, my friend." Escobar gave a rapid nod to his thugs, who then moved to a corner table about twenty feet way. Their eyes remained laser focused on Barrett.

Escobar sat at Barrett's table.

"Do you know there are fucking cameras everywhere? "Barrett demanded.

Escobar looked at Barrett with unemotional steely eyes. He said nothing.

Barrett shook his head disgustedly. "I'd hate to see what'd you do to somebody you didn't like."

"Let me buy you a drink," Escobar tried to sound conciliatory as he snapped his fingers above his head.

"I've got a drink."

The waitress appeared. "Yes sir?"

"Bring my friend whatever he's drinking and I'll have a

club soda."

"And so, what can I do for you?" Escobar asked, curiously eyeing the glitter that clung to Barrett's face and hands.

Before answering, Barrett turned and glanced back to Escobar's thugs, who anywhere else but Vegas would have stood out like black men at a KKK rally. He was more nervous than he thought he would be. Sweat was pouring down the middle of his back to his butt crack. He shifted uncomfortably in his seat.

"I want to talk to you about the deal we have," he began, as he slid his glass around on the table. "We all feel we're taking the big risks, and yet getting the little piece of the, you know, *tamale*."

Escobar's chilly stare sent shivers through Barrett.

"We don't eat tamales in Colombia."

The two men stared at each other in an uncomfortable silence.

What in the fuck does that mean?

"So what do you think is fair, Barrett?" Escobar at last asked, in a disturbingly patronizing manner.

"I think...we deserve a bigger cut," Barrett stammered, feeling the sweat accumulate in his armpits.

"Is this the consensus of...*Everyone?*"

"Yeah, the consensus." His heart raced.

The waitress brought their drinks. Escobar took an obligatory sip of his club soda and sat the glass down softly. "How much more?"

"Another ten percent, on the front end? I think that's fair. We're handling more deals, doing a good job...You can't complain. Right?"

Escobar was expressionless. He stood slowly. "I'll get back to you."

Before Barrett could stand fully, Escobar's thugs were next to their boss. Barrett held out his hand to Escobar. "Sure, take your time."

Escobar was poker-faced as he glanced at Barrett's hand, and without taking it, turned and left. Barrett downed his drink.

Well, I think that went well.

July was one of the hottest months on record, so it was understandable that when the thermostat in the loft was turned on for the first time, the construction crew celebrated with "yeehaws" and thunderous clapping.

No one was happier than Neely, who had seriously considered abandoning the project until the heat dissipated. Now that she had air conditioning, she knew the renovation would soon be finished and the tension created by sharing a living space with Eric would soon be a distant memory.

After many arguments and standoffs, a list of what was hers, what she could take, was finally agreed upon. It wasn't all she wanted, far less than half, but she was ready to move on, reminding herself they were fighting over *things*.

Two weeks later, bright and early on a Thursday morning, the United Van Line truck arrived, packed with every possession she was begrudgingly allowed. Four very large and strong young men grunted their way up the stairs with anything that wouldn't fit in her little elevator, which essentially meant almost everything. The men worked nonstop and they were done by late afternoon.

The loft was suddenly and deliciously quiet. Neely sat heavily in a wooden chair in the middle of the room and surveyed the mess of boxes and furniture. Telling the movers to "put it anywhere" was a glaring miscalculation. All the things she had so thoughtfully chosen and fought for looked out of place and dwarfed in the huge, open space.

After several unproductive attempts to push furniture into some configuration that worked, she gave up and called Jan, who in her pre-Steven life worked as a fabulously successful designer, with frequent spreads featured in *Town & Country*, *Architectural Digest*, and *Vanity Fair*. With Neely promising dinner, a great bottle of wine and undying gratitude, Jan was more than happy to come. She was excited about seeing Neely and the loft she hadn't seen in well over a month.

Jan arrived a little over an hour later with a large bouquet of roses and peonies in hand. They hugged and kissed each other on each cheek. "You shouldn't have!" Neely said taking the flowers, "They're beautiful!"

Jan set her purse on the table and said with a big smile, "Wish I had but I didn't. The flowers were at the bottom of the stairs."

Neely set the flowers on the dining room table and found a small note card attached to the raffia that bound them. The note read, *Welcome to your new home. David.* Her heart raced.

"Who are they from?"

Neely looked at Jan, her face flushed and hot. "The Chamber."

"The Chamber sent you flowers? How odd." Jan said.

Neely shrugged her shoulders trying to look as confused as Jan seemed, "I guess they do that kind of thing in little towns."

Why did I lie to her?

Jan didn't give the flowers a second thought as Neely placed them in a glass vase before slipping the card in a drawer. "Help me move this over there," Jan called as she shoved the tan suede sofa to face the fireplace. It was clear the enormous room with sixteen-foot ceilings dwarfed most of Neely's things and it was going to take all of Jan's magic to make it work. So, for the next hour Neely simply followed her friend's direction, pushing furniture and placing accessories, as thoughts of David and the beautiful flowers he sent laced through her thoughts.

Fred, Neely's half Siamese, half unknown, eighteen pound rescue cat sauntered up to Jan.

"Well who do we have but my sweet Fred?" Jan cooed bending down to pick him up.

"It wouldn't be home without my big boy," Neely said while watching Jan scratch her pudgy cat's neck.

Jan gave Fred one last scratch and plopped him back on the floor. He looked up at Jan with a, *is that all,* look.

Neely smiled, "Ignore him. He's just like all the men we know. Never satisfied." They both laughed. The two women worked diligently for at least another half hour before Jan stopped, stepped back and surveyed the room. She asked, "What do you think?"

Neely smiled, "I think it's perfect. You've made it a home. Thank you, my sweet, dear, talented friend."

The sunlight was soft now, low in the sky, casting gentle shadows.

Jan smiled, curtsying. "Now, how about a nice glass of wine for this parched woman?"

"You got it," Neely said, heading for one of the two pantries abutting the back kitchen wall. "What's your pleasure?"

Jan grinned, "Alcohol."

Neely grabbed a bottle of red wine from the bottom shelf of a cabinet, emerging with a frown. "I have no idea where an opener is. I may have to open this with my teeth or maybe we can get Fred to scratch out the cork!"

"No worries," Jan said, lifting her purse from the floor. She pulled out a small plastic wine opener with the words *Meyer and Lee Jewelers* printed on it and held it high, like a prized trophy. "It's a Girl Scout thing. You know, always prepared," Jan grinned.

"For all the wine we Girl Scouts drink?" Neely laughed.

"Presactly!" Jan giggled, opening the bottle. "Glasses, my dear?"

Neely ran back to the kitchen in search of glasses. She stepped up on one of the room's stage platforms, which she knew was the past site of secret ceremonies and musical performances. She had visions of the ballroom filled with sweet music as merrymakers danced into the wee hours of the morning. She imagined the normally staid gentlemen of Summerville in their colorful silk ascots and black dress coats cavorting with the likes of the *fancy*—crinoline draped ladies imported from Nashville each Saturday night. Legend was the farmers, clerks, and shopkeepers traded in their normal attire, as well as their everyday lives, as they entered Queen's Hall atop the Faulkner Building seeking a little respite from their mundane lives. The steep and often painful financial compensation paid to the ladies of the night was hastily forgotten when dreamed up love alliances and titillating conversation became more than just fantasy.

The particular platform on which Neely stood was three steps up from the main floor, centered between a bedroom door and a foyer where the elevator was accessed. The platform accommodated two counters, complete with sink, dishwasher, and stove. The counter facing the living area was once a turn of the century, fifteen-foot, walnut church altar. It hid all the utilitarian items of the kitchen, perfectly.

Neely opened the cabinet under the sink and proudly lifted a bag of red plastic cups decorated with white snowmen. "Christmas in July!" She roared, ripping open the plastic, She pulled out two cups, returning triumphantly.

Jan poured the wine in the cups. "Here's to you, Jellybean. I wish you happiness, love, and most of all-- peace.

Neely sat next to Jan. She pulled her legs up under her. "To the first wine in my new home and to our friendship." They tapped the glasses together in a toast. "Peace, friend," Jan said.

"I wonder how many glasses have been enjoyed in this very place?"

"None as special as ours," Neely answered.

"I need to speak with Escobar. It's important. Tell him Barrett's calling."

"The woman spoke with a heavy Columbian accent, "He's not available."

"When will he *be* available?"

"I couldn't say. Would you like to leave a message?"

Barrett fumed. "And what the fuck good would that do? I've already left at least five goddamn messages. Does he ever call anybody back?"

"I will tell him you called."
"Yeah, you do that!" he yelled.

Le Mon

September

Olivia and Sam went back to school. Their departure gave Neely time to breathe and physically escape the obvious pain and disappointment she often saw in her children's faces, giving her a reprieve she so needed.

She loved being in Summerville. It was only thirty minutes from her closest friends, an hour to Nashville, and yet it was a different world. They spoke English (sort of), drove on the right, and the stores offered all the familiar staples, but, interestingly, she didn't have to interact. She was an outsider, allowing her the previously unknown luxury of communal detachment—complete anonymity. If she chose to say hello it was her choice alone, without the social pressure to behave in any particular way. It was a wonderful, unfamiliar freedom.

She and Caroline laughed at the farfetched rumors that abounded surrounding her relocation to Summerville. The funniest scuttlebutt alleged she was opening a Chinese restaurant. The most ironic twist, however, was that most people in the little town had no idea she and Eric were divorcing, while a few miles away in Madison, with a population of over four hundred thousand, it seemed everyone from the crossing guard at Camdon School to the nail girl at The Spa knew every detail of her derailed marriage and impending divorce.

Her mind drifted to David and tried to imagine the exchange they would have when she could finally thank him for the flowers. As it turned out, it was over a week before she saw him again. He was sprinting from his office just off the square to the courthouse when he saw Neely coming out of the drugstore. He came up from behind and tapped her on the shoulder. He was grinning as he explained he was running late for a court case. She barely time had to acknowledge him let alone say anything. All the words she had so carefully chosen were lost in the moment, leaving her to simply say, "Thank you for the flowers." He smiled, saluted her and was gone. She felt ridiculous having made such a big deal out of him sending flowers. He was just being nice.

However, her defeated mood didn't last long. That evening she found a hand written note in her mailbox.

We must stop meeting like this. There has to be a better place than the courthouse.   O'Donnell

The morning sun radiated through the prisms of the massive chandelier that hung high above her bed, reflecting an incredible light spectacle on the far wall. Each morning she delayed getting out of bed so she could take a moment to plan the day as well as marvel at the dazzling light display.

As the weeks passed, Neely found her children were doing better, too. She spoke with them almost every day, discussing their class schedules, professors, sorority and fraternity socials, and their lives in general. The uncomfortable family dynamics that overshadowed everything all summer were slowly diminishing, and just as Neely found relief in her new town, her children found theirs in their college campuses. And because they were physically removed, they were no longer confronted with the awful and unfair emotional dilemma as to which parent they should side. At school they were on their own, with friends and challenges of their own.

Everyone seemed to be doing better, except Eric. He was drinking too much and running through women like a junkyard dog on Viagra. His approach to finding himself was not working. Neely felt for him, despite all their issues. She couldn't seem to completely bury the love she felt for him, for so many years.

But in time she slowly separated herself from her old life and found a solid resolve to never go back. She felt a contented stillness for the first time in years.

Parker's Grill became Neely's almost daily destination for lunch when she found it was also David's. He'd always insist she join him, and she'd almost always say, she had just a minute, that she had to get back to meet someone or was expecting a delivery or whatever popped into her head that sounded believable. She couldn't admit to him or herself she was there to meet him. But in reality, they both knew and understood the pretense of the dance. She now appreciated the fact he was married and knew better than to continue the *relationship*, but rationalized that nothing had happened. She told herself they shared nothing more than a friendship.

They spent hours learning about each other, discussing topics encompassing everything from children, to their dreams, and to the books they were reading. He made her feel strangely unseated, emotionally precarious, and yet she was drawn to him.

Like the moth to the flame?

Within a month she was so totally consumed with thoughts of him, she worried about her judgment, worried that after years of feeling so emotionally isolated she was distorting the significance and purpose of their relationship.

She wanted to believe it wasn't all in her head, something she conjured up, because he was nothing like any man she'd ever known.

He was better.

Her once immaculate, hundred thousand dollar plus Mercedes had become something of a trashed-out pickup truck. She hauled everything, from bags of mortar to lumber and today was no different...today the car was full of cans of polyurethane.

"Let me get those, Miss Neely," Blaine called as he emerged from the building. She was parked in a handicapped space and was hurriedly unloading the cans.

"Thanks, Blaine," Neely said, handing him two cans.

She pushed the strands of hair that fell haphazardly, out of her face. She searched for the hair tie she thought she had in her jeans pocket but found nothing. So she ignored her messy hair and continued with Blaine, unloading the cans from the trunk.

A car horn honked loudly. Neely jumped and turned to hear a vaguely familiar voice call, "Need some help?"

She didn't recognize the gray BMW. Squinting, she shielded her eyes from the sun.

"It's Jack. Jack Bendix," a voice called.

"Jack! How are you?" she smiled.

"Great. And you?" he called.

She made a sweeping gesture toward the building. "Other than this big bad monster, I'm great" she laughed.

"It looks like you're almost done."

She grinned. "Almost."

"Excuse me," Blaine interrupted, "I'm gonna start taking these up."

"Thanks, Blaine. I'll be up in a minute."

Neely walked up to Jack's window with a big smile. Jack said, "Don't let me hold you up, I just wanted to say hi."

"There's no schedule around here. Believe me."

"Are you and Eric moving up here permanently?" he asked.

"I am. Eric and I are getting a divorce."

"I didn't know. I'm so sorry."

"Thanks."

"So what are you going to do up here?"

"I have no idea. Hide out?"

He laughed.

"Why are you here?" Neely asked.

"Business."

"Oh, that's right. I forgot. Sorry."

"I imagine you have a lot on your mind."

She laughed. "I could tell you that, but I'm pretty much this way all the time."

It suddenly became awkward, neither of them knowing what to say next. He finally asked, "Do you have time for lunch?"

"I wish I did, but I have so much going on. The floor guy is finishing the office spaces and..."

Before she could finish, he interrupted, "Totally understand."

His invitation made her feel uncomfortable. She wasn't used to talking with a man in an *unmarried context*. It seemed strange.

"Next time I come through I'll give you a call, you know, to see how things are coming along," he said in the most unthreatening, pleasant way.

"That would be nice, Jack. I'll take a rain check if that works for you."

He smiled, "I'll hold you to it!" he said before pulling away.

David and Bill sat at David's personal table in Rustlers' dining room. It was a few minutes past five. The restaurant was empty, as David had hoped.

"What do you suggest we do?" Bill asked. All the reservations he had going into the deal were bubbling to the surface. David didn't immediately answer. He looked troubled and unsure. Bill went on, "We need to get rid of him, diffuse him. He's a loose cannon. I told you that months ago."

David nodded. The waiter came to the table with a bottle of wine and two wine glasses. "Have you had a chance to look over the menu?"

"I'll let you know when we're ready to order," David said without looking up. Once the waiter was out of range, David said, "Getting rid of Barrett right now isn't an option. We have to contain him without making him feel trapped or out of the deal. The last thing we want is for him to go rouge. He …"

Bill interrupted. "But he already has! He's going blow us all out of the goddamned water, David, and I'm telling you right now I'm not gonna let him take *me* down. I haven't worked my whole fucking life to have it pissed away because some dumb shit is trying to make up for having a little dick!"

David shook his head and sighed. "We have to figure out a way to contain him."

"Does he know Escobar talked to you?" Bill asked.

David shook his head, no.

"So what now?"

"I'll talk to him," David managed trying to sound confident.

"You need to fix it, David or I will," Bill replied.

October

It was a little before eight when the magnificent South American white roses with a hint of pale pink frilled petals were delivered in sixty big, white plastic water buckets to the Madison Civic Center. Neely and Wallace arrived as the roses were being wheeled into the ballroom on carts.

"They're flawless!" Neely said softly as she reached into a mass of stems, pulling one rose free. She brought it to her nose and inhaled, "Oh, they smell so good."

"They used this rose at the Swan Ball last year," Wallace bragged, bunching some of the stems with a few Calla Lilies and Jackson vine, "What do you think?"

"Beautiful. Really, absolutely beautiful," Neely smiled.

Within minutes, the West Hall was teeming with over fifty Symphony Guild members, each with a mission that would ultimately transform the cavernous, sterile room into a fairyland, where later in the evening thirty-two young women, in splendid white ball gowns, would make their social debut.

Jan called to Wallace and Neely from clear across the room, "Morning! Looking fabulous girls!" She carried two large bags full of snack foods and was trailed by three women carrying similar sacks. Jan placed the bags on one of the many six-foot, folding worktables lining the east wall and made a beeline for her friends.

"How are you, sweetie?" Jan asked Neely while giving hugs and kisses all around.

"Good," Neely smiled.

"Really?" Jan persisted.

"Yeah, really, I'm doing pretty good."

"Pretty good, my ass," Wallace interjected, "Now that Eric's figured out she's actually going to divorce him and take some of the money, *his* money, she's the enemy. Amazing isn't it? He screwed around all these years, treated her like crap, and now he's pissed and doesn't understand why she wants a divorce. Typical."

"Where are you on the property settlement?" Jan asked, trying to direct the conversation back to a more practical course.

"Basically nowhere. I'm so sick of fighting over every little thing."

"Son of a bitch!" Wallace ranted. "None of these guys who get caught with their pants down want a divorce, because they don't want to have to give up anything, let alone half. There's no downside to wearing your ass down because it goddamn works."

Jan interrupted. "It does. Look what happened to Margaret Rolland."

Neely nodded weakly. Jan continued: "She just couldn't fight anymore. Gary had finally broken her. Remember how she kept telling us he would be fair in the end? Remember? Hell, he got everything Neely. Everything. And after twenty some years of being a good wife and mother, she ends up selling mascara at Merle Norman. She's poor, Neely, poor. And what does Gary do? He buys his redneck girlfriend a tacky red Corvette and parades her through the country club like a 10-point buck. What do you bet he brings her tonight?"

"He wouldn't!" Neely grimaced, finding the grotesque idea totally out of the realm of possibilities. She couldn't imagine that even a schmuck like Gary, who apparently had lost all sense of decency would be so insensitive as to bring his twenty-three-year-old, ex-roller skating rink worker to the social event of the year to mingle with his ex-wife's friends.

"You think not? He's such a sleaze; I wouldn't put it past him. And you know the saddest part? Every man we know would secretly be envying him, wishing they were with some twelve-year-old whorelet on roller skates." Wallace's tone lacked the bravado of moments earlier. Somehow the truth was so caustic, theatrics were unnecessary.

"You need to hang tough and I mean tough." Jan's tone was uncharacteristically stern. Neely again nodded, like an attentive, good pupil.

"Love is fleeting, poverty is forever. Remember that Neely," Wallace said with a kind of strange sadness.

"OH, MY GOD! Neely Glover!" Before anyone could turn, Wendy Farrington had grabbed Neely's arm and was squeezing it. Her gestures became hyper animated. "Hop and I were so upset when we heard about you and Eric. We were shocked! Really. We were s-h-o-c-k-e-d! We thought y'all were just the happiest couple. You just never know, do you?"

No one said a word.

"I'm sorry, I didn't mean to interrupt," Wendy said covering her over-plumped, filler enhanced lips with her blood red, perfectly manicured long nails.

"You're fine," Neely offered half-heartedly.

"I haven't heard any juicy gossip in days and I'm in complete withdrawal," Wendy babbled on. "So tell me everything!"

A devilish grin swept Wallace's lips and even Jan, who was a master of control, found she was dangerously close to breaking into laughter. Neely found nothing Wendy uttered to be of importance or in the slightest bit funny.

"Are you okay?" Wendy asked dramatically, stroking Neely's arm.

Neely knew to choose her words carefully, as they would be repeated within minutes to anyone who would give Wendy an ear.

"I'm doing great, Wendy. Thanks for asking."

"Are you going to keep Glover?" Wendy pressed.

"What do you mean?"

"Your last name, honey."

"I haven't really thought about it," Neely said, puzzled at where Wendy was going with the inane question.

"You should. It's important. It gives you credibility," Wendy sighed, throwing back her blonde, shoulder length hair, while shaking it like a wet dog. "Just a thought." She scrunched up her over-arranged pug nose and leaned in close to Neely, feigning a whisper. "I heard her husband is leaving her and taking the kids. Exactly what she deserves, if you ask me. What a stupid bitch."

Neely drew back. "Who are you talking about?"

Wendy looked crestfallen. "You know. That woman. Eric's…whatever."

"I don't know anything about her," Neely said dismissively.

"Well, I don't know, that's just what I've heard." Wendy was becoming irritated with Neely's refusal to engage.

Jan jumped into the fray, "Wendy, Neely has better things to do than worry about what that woman is doing. Why would she even care?"

"You're right, why would she?" Wendy's hand fell from Neely's arm, only to reach out and grasped Neely's limp hands, shaking them dramatically. "I'm on *your* side, and you know if you need anything, anything at all, all you have to do is call me. I mean...*anything*."

"Thanks," Neely said, slipping her hands out of Wendy's, acutely aware that the woman in front of her would just as soon knife her, as she would Eric's... *whatever*.

Wendy brusquely turned her attention to Wallace, switching her demeanor as if flipping a light switch. "We need to make sure someone instructs the orchestra about where they're supposed to set up and really gives them a good talking to about how long they have to play. You know, we don't want a snafu...play thirty minutes...break forty-five..."

Wallace found it increasingly difficult to mask her contempt. "Belinda already met with them and gave them instructions. It's all good."

Wendy grinned. "Isn't Wallace just amazing? She's so organized. I swear I don't know what I would do without her. Even Hop thinks you're wonderful."

Neely's eyes widened as the irony of it all unfolded. This poor, ridiculous woman, who subjected herself to every plastics procedure imaginable in a desperate attempt to hold back time, was left with a facial expression reminding one of Batman's Joker. She had absolutely no clue about Hop and Wallace's liaison.

Wallace grinned wickedly. "You know, Wendy, I can't

imagine what I'd do without you, either."

By mid-afternoon the room had been draped, lit, and fluffed. The hundred some odd tables, with raw silk taupe cloths overlaying the white to-the-floor table cloths, held tall, square crystal vases two feet tall, filled with Wallace's Winchester Cathedral white roses, calla lilies, and Jackson Vine. The entire arrangement towered to almost four feet and was surrounded by several terracotta trays each containing black votives, nestled in green moss. White dinner plates were placed on elegant black chargers. An assortment of crystal flutes and wine glasses were positioned according to the sequence of the dinner courses. The everyday grotesque overhead lighting was off, replaced with dim spots strategically placed to softly wash every wall. Thousands of tiny, white twinkle lights wrapped columns, trees, archways, and anything else that didn't move, creating a shimmering wonderland.

The orchestra arrived on time and, just as Wallace predicted, they had been adequately instructed. They set up their equipment amidst a sea of lush, feathered ferns and magnolia trees potted in giant distressed stone containers.

By five o'clock there were only a handful of people left in the hall. Most were there to give last minute instructions to the lighting and sound crew.

Wallace, Neely, and Jan walked silently through the room, checking every table for the proper silver, glasses, napkins, and table numbers. Wendy and her program committee concluded their meeting with the local news personality who would be introducing the speakers. She waved to Wallace with a "see you later," as she left the hall.

"That does it," Wallace said to herself, making the last tick next to a long column of table numbers that were listed in a notebook. She followed Neely and Jan to the stage where they sat.

"I hope everybody appreciates this because it's the last time I'm doing this shit. Last time." Wallace was emphatic.

"You say that every year," Neely laughed.

"Sometimes, darlin', we mean it."

Neely smiled at Wallace. "Sometimes we do. Don't we?"

"Stay. Come tonight," Jan said to Neely. "I know it will be boring, but you'll have fun with us. Steven would love to be your date!"

"Driving back to Summerville to change is more than I can handle right now."

"Spend the night," Wallace chimed in, "you can wear something of mine! Hell, I might still have that dress I borrowed from you. Do I? The black one?"

"You returned it. I just want to go home, put my feet up, have a glass of wine, and watch a *Seinfeld* rerun. I'm beat."

"God, that sounds so good," Wallace said wistfully.

"You wanna grab something to eat before you head back?" Jan asked. "I don't think I can wait 'til ten to eat."

"No, you go ahead. I'm going to call Caroline and see if she'll fix something for me. If I call now, it'll be ready by the time I get there."

"Jesus, and here we were worried about her little ass," Wallace laughed, looking to Jan. "We'll be eating grilled chicken at Burger King and fake eggs at midnight, while she'll be chowing down on something fabulous."

Neely kissed both her friends. "A great job, Wallace...as usual. Don't forget to take pictures!"

Wallace grabbed her arm and whispered, "I hate to ask you this, but can I borrow your apartment next Wednesday between three and five?"

"For what?"

"You know for what."

Neely frowned. "Why not a hotel?"

"That's so gross." Wallace looked genuinely hurt.

"You know I can't stand Wendy, but..." Neely said meekly.

"Oh, god! You're going to lecture me? My husband's had a fucking mistress for as long as I've been married to him, and I have to be the faithful wife?"

Neely looked at her friend, not knowing what to say.

"You're making me feel like a whore Neely."

"I can't help thinking how Wendy would feel if she found out. I've been there, I know what it feels like."

"Forget it! I don't need a fucking lecture on morality."

Neely felt awful but worse than that, a hypocrite.

How could I act so righteous when I'm consumed with continual depraved, sexual thoughts about David? Would I act on those thoughts given the opportunity? Probably...

"I'm sorry, Wallace. Of course you can use the loft."

"How will you live with yourself?" Wallace asked sarcastically.

"Okay, I deserve that. I'm sorry, really, take the key. I want you to have it."

Wallace's anger quickly disappeared, as she couldn't contain the smile that swept her face. "Thanks, Jellybean."

Neely opened her purse, took out her wallet, removed a key from the change compartment, and handed it to

Wallace. "Don't lose it, don't give it to anybody, and don't get caught. The security code is 4444."

"Wait, will I see you before we leave?" Jan asked Neely.

"Where are you going?"

Jan shook her head, smiling. "Uh, France?"

"Oh god, I completely forgot. When do you leave?"

"Five days and I can't wait."

"Let's all do lunch before you go. Okay?"

Jan hugged Neely. "Sounds good."

Wallace smiled and gave Neely a big, wet, noisy kiss on the cheek. "I love you more than she does."

Jan frowned at Wallace and said to Neely, "We all know she's a liar."

The Faulkner Building's new restaurant, The Mustard Seed, looked extraordinary from the street. It dazzled. Summerville had never seen the likes of it. Rustlers, the town's oldest and only real dining experience, could be best described as a Western Sizzler with good food. Its lack of style defined its peculiar ambiance; sort of Cowboy Bob meets Dale Earnhardt.

Neely, on the other hand, selected her restaurant furnishings as if she planned on living smack dab in the middle of the dining room. She admitted halfway through the project that she may have lost perspective, creating an atmosphere New Yorkers on the Upper East Side would have found elegantly familiar. It was at once apparent that Summerville might not "get" the sanded and sealed original walls, when the painters asked Neely what color she planned on painting them after they finished sealing them. It never occurred to anyone working on the building that the layers of faded butter-yellow, lime green, and aqua chipped plaster created an exquisite patina only age could create. It was truly "Tres recherché."

Large, rust carriage lanterns hung from the walls every six feet, directly above the white clothed tables, casting soft light on all below. Padded khaki squares with giant tabs piped in black suede hung on the back wall threaded through heavy copper rods. Black suede seat cushions matched the squares. Centered on each table was a large off-white candle placed on a round sand stone. Three massive antique chandeliers hung from the sixteen-foot ceilings, nine feet off the floor. Each chandelier held thirty-eight lights, all dimmed to a faintness that reduced every woman's age by a good ten years. A fireplace with a towering limestone mantle faced the front of the restaurant. Oversized, deep red, full hide leather club chairs were snugly nestled to face the warmth of the fire.

From the start, Eric had warned her that every penny she put in "the rat hole," as he so venomously named her building, would be deducted from any monies she would eventually receive. He made it clear that the building and everything in it was an asset he did not want to divide. She could have it...lock, stock, and barrel.

She approached the door and saw the place was packed. A large group of people were enjoying their drinks by the fireplace as they waited for a table. She debated whether to go in, considering the way she was dressed, but knew her dinner had to be ready. She also knew Caroline could not afford to lose a waiter, not even for the few minutes it would take to deliver her food upstairs. She looked down at her jeans and loafers, quickly ran her fingers through her hair and pulled her coat closed. She entered the restaurant and made a beeline for the kitchen with her head down. She made it unnoticed about halfway to the back, before a voice called out above the loud chatter and soft jazz.

"Neely!"

She turned. David O'Donnell stood waving from across the room, motioning for her to come to his table. He was wearing gray slacks and a black cashmere sweater, under a gray tweed jacket. He looked yummy.

Suddenly her fur coat might as well have been a nightgown. Except for what was left of the little blush she'd applied before entering the civic center eight hours earlier she had on no make up. She felt grungy and knew she looked a mess. She shook her head no, smiling, waving him off as she opened her coat just enough to expose her t-shirt and jeans, as if to explain her predicament. But before she could be on her way, he was up and approaching fast.

"You look beautiful. Join us. I insist," he whispered in her ear, as he pulled her close. "Mmmm, you smell good." He clasped her hand firmly and guided her through the tables.

She mumbled something to the effect that she'd already ordered and didn't want to disrupt his dinner. He either didn't hear her or chose to ignore her mumblings. His hand felt so big around hers. It wasn't until he began introducing his wife that he let go of it.

"Neely, this is my wife, Susie. Susie, Neely."

They were seated at a table for four. Susie was sitting directly opposite her husband. David pulled out the chair to his right and helped Neely with her coat, placing it on the vacant chair to his left.

"I apologize for the way I look. I'm just coming back

from working all day at the civic center. I came in to get my dinner, to take it upstairs. I don't want to intrude."

"You look pretty and you are definitely not intruding," David's wife said sweetly. "I have to say, it's nice finally meeting you. David has told me so much about you."

Neely looked at David.

What could he have said about me? Was she just making polite conversation? Why do I feel betrayed?

"I told her how you paint, write, and have a successful business. I knew Susie would be interested in your building because she's very involved with the Historical Society."

Can he read my thoughts?

"The Hysterical Society," Susie laughed.

Can she not see?

Neely looked at him and their eyes locked, with a knowing that was so sensual, so deep, she froze for an instant. She turned away from him and looked at Susie.

The woman saw nothing.

"You said you were going to eat upstairs? Have you moved in?" Susie asked.

"I've been in for about two weeks but more things are in boxes than not. But I love the apartment, it feels like home," Neely said trying to sound as natural as possible, continuing the stream of conversation, all the while afraid the intimate, sexual sensations she felt deep in her pelvis were as glaring as the flashing neon sign one would find at a cheap motel.

"I've heard through the grapevine it is beyond words." Susie sounded oddly giddy.

"It's very special," Neely said, as a waiter placed silverware and a water glass in front of her.

"Will you tell Caroline I'm having dinner with the O'Donnell's?" She asked the waiter.

"When you get settled, I'd love to see it," Susie smiled. His wife seemed genuinely nice. Neely immediately questioned why she felt surprised. Why did she expect her to be an ogre?

"Sure. Absolutely. Anytime," Neely said, nervously placing her napkin on her lap.

"Does the invitation include me?" David asked, grinning from ear to ear.

She could not have felt more sexual tension had his hand been under the table, between her legs.

"Of course," Neely answered casually, before turning to his wife. "Just call me and let me know when you want to come. We'll have a glass of wine and I'll give you both the grand tour."

Neely straightened the silverware in front of her. She could feel his eyes on her. Out of the corner of her eye she saw him unconsciously rub his thumb and index finger together, ever so slowly.

The waiter picked up David and Susie's salad plates and placed their entrees in front of them.

"Please, go ahead. Don't wait for me," Neely said, speaking to the woman David chose to marry. It was hard to believe she was fifteen years younger than David. She was frumpy, heavy set, and matronly. Her chin-length hair was black and coarse. She was fair skinned, with brown eyes. She was the kind of woman you could not recall with clarity after an hour of her departure. But Susie seemed completely content, and Neely deduced there had to be more than met the eye.

Caroline brought out a beautifully prepared Ahi tuna and placed it in front of Neely. Caroline gave Neely a peck on the cheek and a gentle squeeze to her arm. "Enjoy."

"Looks so good," Neely smiled at Caroline, who was

radiant in her red toile chef's coat, baggy black and white checked pants, and red clogs. She was in her happy place.

The seared tuna was presented on a bed of sautéed seaweed and drizzled with a wasabi glaze. A mountain of crispy, sweet potato shoestring fries was heaped next to the tuna. Caroline took a set of chopsticks and a tiny bowl of soy sauce from the waiter standing beside her and sat them carefully next to Neely's plate.

"Is there anything else I can get you?" she asked.

David smiled. "Not a thing. I think we're set."

Caroline bowed with a grin before leaving them.

"We are so happy she's here. Everything we've ever had here has been wonderful," Susie said as she began eating. David picked up the bottle of Cain Five and poured Neely a glass, before topping off Susie's and his. He raised his glass. "To Neely's new life."

"Hear, hear," Susie chimed.

Their superficial dinner conversation was interrupted when a couple stopped by the table to apparently thank David for something *incredible* he had done. Neely nodded politely when introduced. Susie turned to Neely as David continued his conversation with the couple.

"He can be exhausting," she whispered dramatically.

Neely's expression begged for an explanation.

"David sometimes just wears me out. He's *always* on."

Neely smiled, thinking of Eric's morose demeanor, and said, "It's got to be better than being with someone boring or, worse, unhappy."

Susie laughed loudly. "It's never boring. That's for sure. The last big excitement he created was when he bought some radio stations without telling me. You have no idea how hard I had to work to get us out of that mess."

Neely smiled politely, but wondered why Susie felt the

need to emasculate her husband, to portray him as someone without any business sense, someone she had to manage and why she would reveal this to someone she just met.

This match was indeed odd.

The couple's departure brought David back into their space.

"He's the new school superintendent. I gave a piece of property to the city for a new ballpark and he wanted to thank me, again." David seemed genuinely embarrassed by the attention. "Doesn't take much around here to be idolized."

His smile was infectious.

"I heard Caroline's going to start opening for breakfast," David said. "I thought I'd bring some of my ragtag crew by. Do you know how early she'll open?"

"I think she said six thirty, but you better ask her."

David and Neely looked at each other, knowingly, intimately, as Susie enjoyed her rib eye. The tuna was delicious and she was about to share that fact with them, when out of the corner of her eye she observed Susie smile furtively at David.

It suddenly struck her, Susie knew exactly what was going on and this scene had been played out before.

A wave of nausea swept over her.

David followed Barrett from the grand foyer to the massive veranda where they sat in wicker chairs facing each other.

David looked out over the rolling pasture. The cool

breeze reminded him winter would soon be upon them.

"You've got a nice place here, Barrett."

"Thanks," Barrett said, lighting a cigarette.

A quiet awkwardness prevailed.

"I know you didn't come here to tell me you like the farm," Barrett said finally.

David looked directly at Barrett, "I know you've been talking to Escobar."

Barrett immediately stood, taking a defensive, combative posture, "That's bullshit. I haven't said shit. If somebody's talking shit, believe me, I'll take care of 'em!"

"Sit down, Barrett."

Barrett didn't move for what seemed to be an eternity before begrudgingly settling back in his chair.

"Whether you have or haven't is irrelevant. We're talking prison here if we get careless. Do you understand, Barrett? Prison. For a long, long time."

"Don't bitch at me like I'm a fucking child."

David stood. "You don't fuck with *me*, Barrett. Not me. I know you met with Escobar. Next time it won't be me coming to talk to you, I'll let *them* do it."

Barrett bit his lip and shook his head. "I was trying to help, goddammit. We're getting screwed and you know it. I'm sick of those spics getting the big bucks and we're picking up what's left! Doesn't it fucking bother you? It should."

David glared at Barrett as he struggled to check himself. "Don't open your fucking mouth. *I* call the shots here," he paused, "understand?"

Like a whooped dog, Barrett, his chin hanging down to his chest, bobbed his head.

Neely was crouched over, picking up nasty discarded cigarette butts from the sidewalk in front of her building, when a voice interrupted, "I think we should kill them." Neely looked up to see a statuesque redhead with her hands on her hips, grinning.

Neely asked, smiling, "Who might *they* be?"

"Those suicidal fools who throw these horrible things on the ground for people like us to pick up," she continued, as she gathered up several butts and pitched them into Neely's trash sack.

"Good thing you're not the queen," Neely laughed.

"Actually, I am, but darn it if I can get anyone to acknowledge it." She held her hand out. "Lanie Jackson."

"My hands are filthy," Neely said, standing as she wiped her hands on her rear.

"Mine too."

Neely took her hand. "Neely Glover."

Lanie's handshake was firm and strong. "I'm...I suppose..." She hesitated, in the mists of trying to explain, "An artist in a desperate quest to find a place I can *express myself...*"

Lanie was a pretty woman who looked to be about forty, with flaming, shoulder-length red hair and crystal blue eyes. One would have expected her to fling brilliant neon paint across a massive canvas with complete abandonment, while dancing stark naked to aboriginal fertility ritual drum rhythms, but Neely was to find out her new friend's creative juices were expressed in the most delicate, intricate and detailed pencil strokes.

Lanie went on, "...away from kids, husband, dogs, cats, and an iguana."

"That's some tall order," Neely chuckled.

"As Virginia Woolf once said, *'a room of one's own is essential.'* My husband says I just want a place to hide."

"Sounds like you might actually need one," Neely laughed.

Lanie grinned. "I was hoping you might have an office or room I could rent. I've always loved this building. And since you've renovated it, I was hoping."

"You know, there are several rooms on the second floor that I thought I'd rent out as office space, but you know what? They'd make perfect studios. And having artists in the building instead of accountants or lawyers would seem...natural and, I'm positive, much more fun. Would you like to see?"

The rest was history. Within a month, four of the second floor rooms, the ones with the beautiful snowflake glass windowpanes, were home to engaging and creative artists. These artists were some of the most fabulous women Summerville had to offer. It was as if these gifted women were inexplicably drawn to the magnificent old structure just as Neely had been.

The women of the second floor bonded, sharing friendship, an interest in art and life experiences. Neely sensed she was given a little window, a tiny glimpse, into the camaraderie Gertrude Stein's salon at 27 Rue de Fleurus on the left bank, provided the painters, writers, and poets that were her friends.

David brought, just as he said he would, his office staff to The Mustard Seed for morning coffee and pastry. And as the days passed he added clients and friends to the list of people he brought to the restaurant, single-handedly trying to promote what he called Summerville's only "coffee shop." Neely seized every opportunity to be in the restaurant whenever she thought he might be there. Within two weeks, David had his own special table where he and Neely would sit and talk.

She could count on him walking through the front door, alone, every morning at about seven. He'd enter smiling, his leather notebook tucked under his arm, ready for his standard fare of hazelnut coffee or green tea and a blueberry muffin. Perhaps because others read the intimacy of their relationship, or because Neely and David blatantly ignored anyone who had the audacity to seat themselves at "their" table, it wasn't surprising that after a short while no one but a fool would disturb them. And occasionally one would turn up, like a bad penny, trying to engage them in conversation, only to be shut out by a united, frigid front.

They bathed in their wonderfully selfish daily exchange without the slightest thought of consequence. As days and weeks passed, she came to need and count on the time they spent with each other. It was the focus of her day. She had survived years of emotional and intellectual deprivation and now would not question the whys or the rationale of being with this man who fed her emptiness with fascinating thoughts, self-effacing humor, and who amazingly, had awakened her sexual desire.

He was the only man who had been able to touch her heart and her head and she knew, when looking into his eyes, he, too, needed her. But to her dismay not knowing where he was or when she would see him again proved more painful than the hurt she felt at the hands of Eric.

This could not be healthy.

November

"We need to meet," the familiar voice said without a hello. It was Eric.

"About what?"

"I've worked out the last of the property settlement. I want to go over it with you."

"When?"

"In the morning? I'll be in Summerville for clinic. I can meet you at the restaurant. Does she serve any protein?"

"What are talking about?"

"Can I get anything other than shit like donuts?"

Neely grimaced. It had been just a little over two months since they had lived in the same house yet it felt like an eternity. She found it interesting she could forget all of his rules, demands, and idiosyncrasies as if they never existed. His long-standing refusal to eat anything white, like rice, sugar, potatoes, and bread, was now no longer her concern.

"Caroline's a master chef" she said indignantly, defending her friend. But as fast as she so righteously protected Caroline, not wanting her to be forever labeled the *carbohydrate queen*, she regretted the protest and quickly suggested, "Why don't we meet at Baby's Diner where I know you can get eggs and bacon?"

"No, I'll meet you at the restaurant around seven. Just tell Caroline to have something I can eat. You know what I like."

Why did I agree to meet him there? God.

Eric addressed a litany of issues, almost all skewed in his favor. He presented the papers; bound neat and tidy in a traditional legal blue cover. He wanted her to *go ahead* and sign them, insisting they were not binding in the final analysis but only a preliminary agreement. She looked at him, so thoroughly at home in the bullying mode, and was reminded of why she left.

"I need to have someone look at these before I sign them."

"Why?" he demanded.

"I would just feel more comfortable if I did, that's all."

"You are going to fuck this up. We're going to have to pay some goddamned lawyer just so you feel more *comfortable*?"

"Would you tell Olivia to just sign something without a lawyer if she were getting a divorce?

"Don't start."

"Would you?"

"If you get lawyers involved, they're going to tell you you're getting screwed. The bigger the mess, the more money for them. Just sign it."

"I told you I am going to have someone look at it first."

"Who?"

"I don't know."

"Somebody you're fucking, no doubt."

"Oh god, not again. That's something you'd do, Eric, not me."

She looked down at her watch. Five after seven. By the grace of god, maybe he wasn't coming.

"You expecting someone?" he asked suspiciously.

Shit, maybe he does know me?

She ignored his question. "Is there anything else?"

Caroline's normally soft, discreet voice bellowed, in an attempt to warn Neely. "Well, good morning to you, Mr. O'Donnell. How are you this morning?"

Neely's heart plummeted. David was heading straight for them with his hand outstretched. "Bowl of cherries, Caroline! Morning, Eric! Morning, Neely! Mind if I join you?"

The two men shook hands. David nodded to Neely with a wide grin.

Oh no.

"Join us for breakfast?" Eric beamed as if everything was just peachy keen.

"You working here today?" David asked Eric.

"Somebody's gotta bring it in. Know what I mean?" Eric laughed like it was a man's joke no woman could possibly get.

"Sure do," David said, smiling at Caroline as she placed a cup of green tea and a blueberry muffin in front of him.

"I see you're a regular," Eric said distrustfully, his smile frozen like a Miss America contestant's might look after realizing she just lost. Neely shuddered as a foreboding chill ran down her spine.

"Caroline's got me hooked on these muffins. Have you

had one?"

"I don't eat bread." Eric's tone was noticeably cool and forced.

"I couldn't live without it," he said softly. "You know…a bottle of wine, a loaf of bread, and…"

Oh god, please don't look at me.

But he did, he looked directly at Neely and said, "…and thee." Neely looked away with an awkward jerk while offering a weird, almost bizarre smile.

"Bread is my downfall, isn't it?" Neely asked Eric trying to recover. Eric said nothing but Neely saw the fury he was suppressing and she knew, he knew.

"Speaking of bread, I forgot to give Caroline a message from one of our vendors. Excuse me for a second." Neely got up and made her way to the kitchen. She grabbed Caroline and dragged her to behind the walk-in cooler.

"He knows," Neely said, crumbling.

"Knows what?"

"About David."

"He doesn't know anything. There's nothing *to* know. Don't get crazy."

Neely put her hands over her face. "Oh, god."

"Is there something to know?" Caroline questioned.

"No. No."

Neely stayed hidden in the kitchen trying to muster enough courage to go back, when she heard David's voice call out, "Thanks for the muffin. Wonderful as usual." He took a ten out of his wallet and set it on the table. He patted Eric on the back. "Good seeing you."

"See you," Caroline called to him from the kitchen. Neely watched him walk to the door. As he opened it he turned, looked at Neely, and did a quick Marine salute complete with a cocky wink.

What the hell is he doing?

Neely gathered her composure and walked to the table with a pot of coffee. Her hands were shaking.

"Do you want a refill?"

"You're fucking him, aren't you?"

The handle of the pot slipped down her fingers before she caught it. Tiny drops of coffee splattered the floor.

"I'm not the one who's cheated in this relationship, Eric. I never have and you know it."

Eric's voice was low and unfamiliar, "Not until now maybe, but I know what I saw. You've been with him."

"I haven't."

"I don't believe you" His voice was raw.

Neely sank into the chair next to him. She steadied her hand and slowly poured coffee into her own cup, long cold.

"I have never been with him, ever. On our children's lives, I am telling you, I haven't."

He continued his deathly stare. She was afraid to look at him.

He said with a strange, despondent resignation, "In all the years we've been together, you have never once looked at me the way you look at him. Not once. A blind man could see it."

He stood and slowly slid the folder to her. "Have your boyfriend look at them."

He threw a twenty on the table and left.

IN THE CIRCUIT COURT OF DAVIS COUNTY, ALABAMA

Le Mon

```
CASE NO: STG05-358-JTS
Laura Neely Glover, Plaintiff
vs.
Eric Campbell Glover, Jr., Defendant

FINAL DECREE OF DIVORCE
This cause coming on to be heard was
submitted upon Complaint for Divorce, Answer
and Waiver, Agreement of the parties and
testimony on behalf of the Plaintiff; and upon
consideration thereof, the Court is of the
opinion that the parties are entitled to the
relief requested in said Complaint.  It is,
therefore, ORDERED, ADJUDGED and DECREED by the
Court that the bonds of matrimony heretofore
existing between said Laura Neely Glover and
Eric Campbell Glover, Jr. are forever divorced
for and on account of incompatibility of
temperament.  It is further,
    ORDERED, ADJUDGED and DECREED by the Court
that the Agreement heretofore entered into
between the parties, a true and correct copy of
which is…
```

She quit reading the document and placed it on the stack of mail. She pulled out a chair at the old farm table and sat heavily, placing her hands in her lap. She stared at the pile. This is what it all came down to—a piece of paper no more significant to anyone who touched it than the phone bill it lay upon. Her identity for over twenty years was simply dissolved by the pen of an unknown circuit court judge. She imagined the judge's clerk lining up her divorce decree alongside all the others, early on the morning of November 12th, so all he had to do was pen the documents without flipping, turning, or even reading them. Why would he? He had no interest, no claim, and no stake. All he had to do was sign.

Her emotions vacillated between waves of grief, resignation, regret, and exhausted relief. She sat silently, numb. She was divorced.

Neely's only safe constant amidst the upheaval of her life was David. Yet in the recesses of her resolve remained a nagging uncertainty about her break with Eric. They had been together so long, she had loved him with that young love you feel only once. He was the father of her children, who were her best work, the people she loved more in this world than anyone or anything. But Eric created a hole that burned through her. With the knowledge that he shared his body and part of his mind and soul with many people, including friends, not once but many times, impaled her with searing unrelenting sorrow.

She needed so much, too much. All the years of feeling rejected and intellectually lonely left her with a constant need, like a heroin addict needs a fix. She wanted someone to love her, someone to validate her significance, someone to cherish her.

Whether Eric couldn't or wouldn't try and meet her needs, David filled them effortlessly. He made her feel beautiful and smart and he made her feel desired. He valued her thoughts and knew her worth.

For David, Neely was an unimagined gift that opened a world to him he'd never envisioned. She was the succor in his life. Years and years of David telling himself he had it all, while trying to bury the insidious flashes of ghost-like longings that crept into his heart, were exposed as the deceits they were, when he fell in love with Neely. With her smack dab in front of him, the ghost became a living, haunting and demanding entity.

They had come together in the most innocent way, never conceiving the fanaticism or lust that would mushroom without restraint or contemplation. They were oblivious to the dangerous consequences their liaison had set into motion. They had fallen deeply in love.

Neither spoke of how they felt. They knew it down deep, where a person hides their recondite thoughts, elegiac ghosts, cloaked dreams, and decadent fantasies. They merely had to look into each other's eyes to know.

The restaurant was empty, the doors locked. They sat drinking green tea. Caroline wouldn't be back for at least an hour.

"It's nice, isn't it?" she asked.

He looked at her as if studying a lovely painting. Everything was still, peaceful. He wanted to reach across the table and touch her face, to cover her with his body, to consume her, to breathe her in. He physically suffered the throbbing void in his gut and groin. He softly rubbed his index finger and thumb together before making a fist.

Neely reached over and touched his hand. "Why do you do that?"

He questioned her with his eyes.

"You rub your fingers together when you're deep in thought."

"I don't know why I do it."

"What were you thinking?" she asked.

A slight curve formed at the corners of his mouth. "I'm

astonished I've lived all these years and have never known...*this*."

They looked at each other for a long time without speaking.

"Where do we go from here?" she asked hesitantly.

He looked directly into her eyes and slowly shook his head. Grief covered her. She knew in her core this road would lead nowhere, but desperately tried to believe otherwise.

He was too close and she loved him too much. She took a deep breath, set her cup on the table, and as her eyes fell away from his, said in an almost whisper, "I can't bear more pain in my life, David. I'm trying to heal, trying to find myself, to be better. If this is bad for me, please tell me now."

He reached across the table and covered her hand with his. "I know I never want a day to pass that you are not in my life. That, Neely, is the truth."

She looked at his beautiful face and knew his words were not enough. She knew that one day, she would have to have more.

After two splendid weeks at their St. Paul de Vence hundred-year-old stone cottage in the south of France, Jan's and Steven's lives were turned upside down. Steven suffered a stroke.

Their Learjet 85 left Nice for Teterboro and then on to Rochester, Minnesota, where an ambulance waited for them on the tarmac. The ambulance team's instructions were clear. They were to take Steven Howe and his wife to the Mayo Clinic, where a cardiac staff awaited their arrival.

Jan called Neely and Wallace from the jet just before landing in Rochester, telling them of Steven's emergency.

It wasn't until the following morning that Neely heard from her again.

"Neely? It's Jan."

"How's Steven?"

"He's good, finally resting. They just brought him back to the room."

"What do the doctors say?"

Jan climbed out of the big leather lazy boy in the darkened room and walked past Steven, who was sleeping. She opened the door to the hallway and the bright florescent lights. She hadn't slept in over twenty-six hours and was exhausted and frantic at the same time.

"They think he'll make a full recovery," Jan said.

"Thank god."

"He's having trouble speaking Neely. He's confused and cries for no reason." Jan broke down in sobs. "He doesn't know who I am. I'm so afraid for him."

"Oh Jan, don't cry. It's normal, it's just going to take time, it happens when people have strokes."

"I don't know what I'd do without him," Jan cried "I don't."

"Let me come. You shouldn't be alone."

"No, no. I'm just tired. There's nothing you could do here. It's just crazy. His kids are on their way. They should be here in a couple of hours."

"You sound exhausted. Have you had any sleep?"

"No. People come in and out of the room. You know?"

"Yes."

Jan started to cry again and Neely let her.

Jan managed, as she gathered herself, "You know, when we first got here, no one really knew if Steven was going to make it and I was so humbled. I realized it doesn't matter who you are, or who you think you are, or how much money you have, or who you know. There's only God, and you pray he'll forgive all the bad things you've done in your life, and just this once...just this once...He'll hear you," Jan's cries became sobs.

Tears streamed down Neely's face, "You've never done a bad thing in your life, Jan. Not one thing."

Jan brought Steven home after two weeks at the clinic. His speech was improving daily, and with it, Jan's optimism. The doctors' opinion was that Steven didn't need in-home nursing care; that he was in fact on the upside of the recovery curve. But Jan wanting to err on the side of safety hired three fulltime RNs and a physical therapist to insure her husband continued his road to recovery. Elizabeth Terry, their dear friend and well-respected cardiologist, made daily visits to the house first thing in the morning and again late in the day. Jan rarely left Steven's side.

When Wallace and Neely came by to see Steven, they were relieved to find him sitting up in bed, having a cup of tea while going over Howe Aviation's quarterly reports. He looked great and his color was back. And although his speech was noticeably different, slower and more annunciated somehow, he seemed happy and spoke freely. Jan looked good too, finally sleeping, comforted in the knowledge that her husband was slowly improving and that they were home, surrounded by familiar things and the people who loved them.

For everyone privy to Wallace's and Hop's entanglement, no one was more astonished than Wallace herself when she discovered her feelings were real, that what she shared with Hop was an honest-to-goodness love affair. Usually a cynic, never buying into the *true love* myth, Wallace found, to her own delight, that she embraced love and all its trappings. Her typical repertoire of barbs and condescension was falling to the wayside, replaced with silliness, laughter, and almost ridiculous blind optimism.

Wallace's use of Neely's loft became a regularly scheduled Monday and Thursday afternoon intrigue. Often the two lovebirds would show up unexpectedly with pleading, desperate miens. Neely, sympathetic to their longing, was reminded each time they came of the ache she could not escape on the days she didn't see David.

What lengths would I go to, if I already knew the touch of his lips on mine or his breath on my body?

And so, Neely would retreat to The Mustard Seed to read or talk with Caroline or go for a long walk until she received a "coast is clear" text from Wallace.

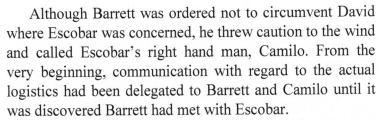

Although Barrett was ordered not to circumvent David where Escobar was concerned, he threw caution to the wind and called Escobar's right hand man, Camilo. From the very beginning, communication with regard to the actual logistics had been delegated to Barrett and Camilo until it was discovered Barrett had met with Escobar.

"Listen, buddy, if you can help me out and get Escobar to give me a call, I promise won't forget it. He won't take my calls or call me back. He thinks I'm trying to screw him when I'm not. You see that don't you, Camilo?"

"You should talk to Escobar."

"He won't talk to me. I just told you."

"I don't know what I can do. I schedule, nothing else." Camilo sounded nervous. He knew talking with Barrett was not a good idea.

"You know he's not the only game in town if you know what I mean. We can take our business else where."

Camilo said nothing.

"Look, we all have a good thing going. Right? Just talk to him. You can *guide* him."

"You are mistaken. I can't" Camilo said.

"Just talk to him. He trusts you. I know you two are tight."

"I'll try. But if he says no, don't ask me again. It could be bad for both of us."

"Buddy, all I'm asking is for you to give it a shot."

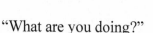

"What are you doing?"

Her heart fluttered. He had never called her; they always managed to just *run into* each other.

"I'm cleaning my brushes."

"Brushes, like in painting a wall?"

"Like in a landscape."

He chuckled. "Meet me for lunch. Parkers. I'm waiting."

"I've got paint all..."

He interrupted. "No excuses. See you in ten minutes. Bye bye." He hung up.

Barely able to contain her excitement she ran to the bathroom and stripped off her sweatshirt and jeans with one hand, while trying to twist her hair up on top of her head with the other. She turned the water on in the shower, and then ran back to her bedroom to grab her hair clip off the nightstand. She stepped into the shower with her hair secured with the clip but found the water was still cold. "Shit!" She hurriedly lathered her entire body, and by the time the water started to feel warm she was rinsed and out.

She walked down the east side of the square past Miss Linda's Antiques, a.k.a. Wallace's crime scene, focusing on the courthouse, trying to avoid catching the old woman's evil eye.

What am I doing?

Cold, she pulled her black wax coat tight at the collar and looked up at the dark sky. It looked like snow.

With Christmas a little more than a month away, the

town square was gloriously festive. Fresh white pine garlands, huge red bows, and white twinkle lights trimmed every light post. Every storefront displayed a vast array of Christmas trees and Santa scenarios. A life-size nativity scene was set up on the courthouse lawn next to the cannons. Summerville *never* understood the separation of church and state and never would.

Neely couldn't have been happier. She loved Christmas, and her life felt so full.

She opened the restaurant's door and found David sitting at a table, alone, reading. He looked up as she approached and stood, pulling out a chair next to his. His usual million dollar luminous smile radiated. He looked very much in the season in a dark gray suit, white shirt, V-neck, light gray cashmere vest and bright red tie.

"How did you know I'd come?" Neely asked him, smiling.

"I hoped." He grinned.

"Looks like you're planning on doing some serious reading," she commented, eyeing the large stack of books to his left.

He pulled a book from the stack and handed it to her. "I brought this one for you."

Neely smiled at him. For a book lover to share a book with another is a very personal gesture...offering one's impressions, ideas, and likes to another, inviting a shared memory, a common experience. Neely held the book with both hands before pressing it to her chest. She was flattered. It meant something sweet, intimate.

"I think you'll like it. Lola Montez was a very interesting, strong woman." He said as if implying, "Like you."

The magic of the moment was broken with the arrival

of David's friends.

"You must be Neely. I'm Will Bibb and this is Daphne Polansky," said the young man, shaking Neely's hand enthusiastically. David often spoke of Will. He was in David's law firm. He was in his late-thirties, married with two little girls, and the one man, other than David's lifelong friend, Bill, in whom David confided.

William, or Will as his friends called him, was young, handsome, and clean shaven, with short, sandy blond hair, and gray eyes. Neely couldn't imagine him ever doing manual labor: he seemed, soft. With him stood a woman in her forties, who reminded Neely of one of those stereotypical, mannish "libbers" of the 1960s bra-burning era. She was a good five inches taller than Will, with strawberry blonde hair, small, close set brown eyes, thin lips, big hips, and a sharp, narrow nose. She wore no makeup and her fine hair draped limply about her face. Around her neck hung a braided leather strap necklace with a polished pink stone looped in the center. Her mid-calf, olive green skirt and pale blue shirt with navy piped ruffles around the sleeves did nothing to improve her dated look. Neely watched as she ambled to the chair on the other side of David and envisioned her as a molting ferret, perhaps the "*child*" of the *parrot* antique dealer. Daphne greeted David with a wide smile.

David told Neely. "Daphne is our Chamber president and a fellow thespian."

"Nice to meet you," Neely offered genuinely, extending her hand.

"Same here," Daphne responded curtly with a half-baked handshake. The woman immediately turned back to David. "Are you going to rehearsal Saturday?

David nodded.

"Can you give me a ride? My car is still in the shop."

She spoke with a nasal twang. It was clear she wasn't from the South. Definitely from somewhere up north. Not a trace of southern charm anywhere.

"Pick you up about 11:30?" David asked.

Daphne smiled. "That'll work."

She was masculine with a no-nonsense air to her, and it was obvious to anyone within striking distance she was not a woman to waste time fluffing. She considered it frivolous to dribble away one's time on superficial issues like personal grooming. She made fun of women who were, as she put it, "nothing but show," and she surely did not have time for the dumb ass flavor of the week that David presented this lunch hour.

"Neely bought the Faulkner Building," David said, as if explaining her existence.

"The whole town's been watching the progress," Will said with a smile, " I know it's been a tough undertaking. I bought a little rental house a couple of years ago, and I thought redoing the bathroom was going to kill me. I can't imagine what it's been like tackling that building."

"I'd be lying if I said it hasn't been a huge challenge. I think if I knew back then, when I bought it, what I know now, I would have probably passed," Neely smiled, "but since I didn't, at the end of the day, I'm glad I bought it."

Will chuckled, "How close are you to being done?"

Neely laughed, "Do you really ever finish a building that old?"

"How about when the money runs out?" Daphne cracked rudely. She was bored with Neely. She turned her attention back to David. "What's new on the reading list?"

Daphne didn't think Neely warranted her time and didn't particularly care whether her slight was obvious. In fact, Neely quickly concluded, Daphne wanted it clear she did not consider her deserving of her or David's attention, and that Neely was infringing on what she considered hers. And that *hers* was David.

Daphne asked David some convoluted question about a book they both were reading. Within moments they were engrossed in an intellectual debate over a character's lineage, an issue that appeared to Neely as nothing more than mental masturbation, but she admitted it was in the realm of possibilities that she might be wrong. She studied this woman, who was busy pontificating about this and that, and decided Daphne was nothing more than a sciolist.

She watched the *ferret* bob her head up and down as she wrinkled her brow in synch with each word leaving her tight little mouth.

Liking her was going to be a monumental feat, but Neely was going to do her best. David seemed to really like her, so Neely concluded her best course would be not to alienate the woman with the rodent face.

What was it with the women in his life? None of them fit. Do I look like one of them to the outside world?

As Will asked Neely several questions about the renovation, she couldn't help eavesdropping on Daphne and David's conversation. The nasal, snippy tongue had been replaced with a soft, almost feminine warble. This woman, who was now and forever imprinted in her mind as the *ferret*, was laughing happily, all the while acquiescing to all of David's intellectual impressions.

Meanwhile Will, also aware of Daphne's slight, did his best to entertain Neely. "What's your book about?"

She picked up the book from the table and turned it over to look at the back cover. "It's a biography. David said he thought I'd like it."

As if on cue, Daphne turned from David. She glared at Neely with a hardened frigidness. She transformed instantly from the happy chatterbox into a calculating predator. Daphne looked from the book to David, smiling smugly. "Isn't that the book you gave me two, or was that three, years ago?"

Neely looked at the woman and felt sorry for her. Daphne was so plainly insecure and so terribly unattractive, inside and out.

"I gotta see you." T's words spewed out fearfully.

"Can't. I have an office full of people and my daughter's on her way. What if I meet you after my ride, say about 12:30?"

"The feds picked up Barrett." The words spilled from T's mouth.

David tried not to panic, to grasp and evaluate the magnitude of what may have happened. "I'll be there as soon as I can. Don't do anything until I get there."

The dial tone sounded in T's ear. David placed the phone in the cradle and sat back heavily.

A rage overcame him. He took a deep breath before buzzing his secretary.

"Yes?" her voice called over the intercom.

"Get me Clyde."

"Sheriff Clyde?"

"Yes. And clear my schedule, something's come up...and when Sandy gets here, tell her to go to the house. Tell her I'll see her when I get home."

"Clear everything?"

"Everything."

David's meeting with T lasted less than ten minutes. Things were falling apart.

Clyde's patrol car was just where he said it would be...at the end of Capshaw Road, near old man Deever's catfish pond. David pulled his Porsche up next to the sheriff's car and got out. He walked around to the passenger side of the patrol car and got in. The gray haired sheriff with the big belly looked fearful.

"What's up, partner?" the sheriff asked, not really wanting to know.

"The feds picked up Barrett. Have you heard anything?"

"Shit! Haven't heard a word...you know I woulda called you right off...shit...son of a bitch! What do you want me to do? Just tell me and I'll be all over it."

David's voice was deliberate, slow and calm. "Find out what the charges are and where he is. Do not mention my name. Do you understand, Clyde?"

The lawman's head bobbed up and down as sweat rolled down the sides of his face in tiny streams. "I, I understand. I'll find out and I'll call you."

"When you call me, don't use your cell phone, the car phone, or your office phone."

"What phone should I use?" Clyde sounded short of breath.

"A payphone, Clyde."

Before Clyde could acknowledge the instructions, David was out of the car and gone.

The Highland Pike Airport was as quiet as a bankrupt morgue. Three full-time employees managed the nondescript, 4,000 square foot, cinderblock main building, constructed in the early 1980s as a skating rink and converted in the early 1990s when the one runway was built. It more than filled the needs of Summerville's reluctant travelers, with one scheduled Delta flight a day to Atlanta and back.

Other than the occasional corporate jet filled with Branum Furniture Company executives arriving to check on their Summerville plant, the little airport went unused. Most people in Summerville suspected they needed Atlanta about as much as a visit to a Zimbabwe witch doctor.

Today, however, the airport would have an unscheduled arrival. David's pilot Tim radioed ahead, notifying Summerville Airport of his approach and planned immediate departure just as soon as David could board.

After Tim landed the Citation and taxied up to within twenty feet of the building and parking lot, he could see David had not yet arrived, for the parking lot was empty except for a Harley motorcycle and a Volkswagen bug. Tim cut the engines and made an entry in his logbook, before going into the building.

Two Naugahyde plum sofas with frayed, broken piping sat under two windows on the wall facing the parking lot. Two spindly end tables piled high with old flying and pilot publications were at each end of the sofas. There was no sign of the local controller, although Tim knew he had to be somewhere close, as he had just spoken with him.

David entered with his eldest daughter, Sandy, as the controller emerged from the men's room at the other side of the room.

"Evening, Mr. O'Donnell," the controller greeted David as he walked to the counter. David nodded.

"Anytime you're ready, Mr. O'Donnell," Tim said, flight plan in hand.

David turned to Sandy, his "first baby girl," as he endearingly called her. She was in her early thirties, but looked not a day over twenty. She was an attorney like her father, but not practicing, an agreement she made with her husband. They decided it would be best if she put her career on hold until their two small children were in school. She had come to see her dad for advice. She was having difficulty coming to terms with being "just a mommy," coping with the apparent loss of her intellectual identity and drowning in a seemingly unappreciated world of wifely tasks. Things were bad. She was seeing an old flame on the side, but didn't have the gumption to get a divorce. She needed her dad to help her sort things out. But her problems could wait. She wasn't sure why her father was leaving, but knew when he abandoned an office full of people, paired with his strange behavior, something was very, very wrong.

"Papa, if there's anything I can do, I want you to tell me."

"Sure, sugar." He smiled lovingly.

"You promise?"

"Promise."

He pulled her to him and gave her a hug so big it hurt.

"You okay, Papa?"

"Bowl of cherries."

She smiled at him. Sandy was the spitting image of her mother, the beautiful woman David had loved and let down so many years ago. The two were married shortly before he left for Vietnam and divorced shortly after his return. Yet they remained close friends, a testament to David's devotion to all those he ever loved.

"If you did need me, you would call me, wouldn't you, Papa?" Her smile was gone. She wanted the truth.

"No, sugar."

"Papa!" she pleaded.

He managed a small smiled, took her small hand in his, and pounded it against his chest. "Feel this. Nothing's gonna happen to this Marine."

She wasn't reassured.

"Don't worry."

"I love you, Papa."

He kissed her forehead and squeezed her hand before picking up his duffle and exiting the building. Once on the tarmac, he sprinted to the jet. His daughter watched and waited at the window, until the jet carrying the most important man in her life raced down the runway and disappeared into the night.

David reclined the seat back as far as it would go and closed his eyes. He wanted to clear his thoughts before making the call.

A tone sounded and the illuminated seatbelt light went dark.

David released his seat belt, unlatched the panel door of a small cabinet directly in front of him, and retrieved a bottle of scotch and a glass. His pour was generous. He gulped the scotch in one motion and took his phone from his coat pocket and dialed.

"Hello?" a small child's voice answered.

"Mary Catherine?"

"No sir, this is Reilly. Who is this?"

"This is Uncle David. What are you doing up this late, sweetie?"

"I'm not tired."

"Is your dad around?"

"Uh huh."

"Can you get him for me?"

"Uh huh."

David waited, hearing the little girl call her dad.

A minute later, Franklin picked up the phone in the den. "I've got it, baby." The phone rattled as the child maneuvered it back on the cradle.

"David?"

"We...may have a small problem...with the accounts I opened recently."

Silence.

"Franklin?"

"I'm here." Franklin's fear came through loud and clear. "What do you want me to do?"

David chose his words carefully. "I need to have a look at the... Accounts. If you can't get them from home you may need to go down and get them. I'm heading for Washington but will be back, I hope, tomorrow. Maybe we can meet then."

"Sure."

"And Franklin?"

"Yes?"

"Transfer what's in the corporate account...today...to the *other* account."

"Done."

David ended the call and immediately dialed again.

"Hello."

"Can you talk?" David asked.

"Yes."

"There's been a fuck-up, Jack. The feds picked up Barrett."

"Don't contact him until I get back with you" Jack instructed.

"But I'm on my way to Washington to see you. Where are you?"

"The Pentagon."

"This late?"

"Just wait until you hear from me. Hang loose until I get back with you."

"Jack, what do you think happened?" David asked.

"Shit if I know. I can't believe this is coming apart when we're this close."

"If my cell doesn't work for some reason, I'll be at The Madison, near the White House," David said.

"Just don't do anything until I call you."

The line went dead.

David turned his phone off, poured another drink, and sat back in the seat, spent.

Medellín, Colombia

The calls of exotic birds and friar monkey's cries echoed through the dense jungle, where thirty-five foot trees canopied the moist floor. The stifling heat and suffocating humidity were unbearable.

A lone man sat in a wooden chair, bound, gagged and hooded. He slowly repositioned himself in the chair and softly moaned as if every motion caused him pain. His exposed flesh showed signs of a beating as well as exposure to the elements.

The man managed to move his hands, which were bound behind his back, upward. As he tried to raise them above the back of the chair, the chair tipped over. When he landed on the ground the hood over his head, fell to the side, partially revealing his bloody face. It was Camilo.

He blinked his blood caked eyes and slowly scanned the jungle around him, trying to determine just how precariousness his situation was.

The sound of rustling was heard. As he slowly turned toward the sound, the hood fell back over his eyes. A coral snake slithered toward him.

After five days, anxiety gave way to depression. Her imagination had gotten the better of her, envisioning him in a hospital somewhere, unconscious. Or worse yet, he'd simply tired of her.

Neely entertained any outlandish scenario that happened to pop into her head including his odd relationship with Daphne, concluding David's relationship with her had lasted at least four years, and she was fairly confident David's attraction to the woman was nothing more than an shared intellectual curiosity. So, if that peculiar woman could hold his attention for years, surely she had enough interesting qualities to keep him entertained for a few more lunches.

So why did he quit coming to the restaurant without so much as a goodbye?

She reassured herself that she would have heard something if he was sick or hurt. It was, after all, a small town, where secrets weren't kept.

The phone rang, waking her.

"Can you come down?" Caroline sounded excited.

"What's wrong?"

"Just come!"

"Is he there?"

"No. Just come."

Neely looked at the clock on the table next to her bed. 8:03 am. She'd overslept. She jumped out of bed and put on the jeans that she'd dropped on the floor the night before and scanned the room for her sweater. She found it on the back of the brown velvet club chair next to her bed. She pulled it over her head and slipped into her loafers. Not bothering to brush her hair or teeth, she ran down the back stairs to the front of the building and over to the restaurant. She rubbed the sleep from her eyes and ran her fingers through her hair before entering. Several people she didn't recognize were eating breakfast.

Caroline emerged from the walk-in cooler. As soon as she saw Neely, her eyes lit up.

"What?" Neely asked, half fearing what might have happened.

Caroline continued to beam as she took a piece of paper from her apron pocket and handed it to Neely. "Will left this a few minutes ago. I read it. I'm so sorry...but I couldn't help it...I'm so sorry...forgive me?"

Neely grinned at Caroline, not a bit upset about her indiscretion. She unfolded the paper. It was written in his hand.

I will pick you up tonight...6:30...out front. No excuses. Have missed you. O'Donnell

Neely held the paper to her lips and closed her eyes. She smiled from ear to ear!

Janet knocked before opening David's office door. "I was asked to give this to you as soon as possible."

"One second," he said to his client as he opened the note. It read: Barrett/good. Call me. It was signed, Jack.

Janet asked, "Do you need me to do anything?"

"No" he said with a sigh of relief.

Neely was ready at six. Her hair and makeup were perfect. She had no idea where she was going or what to wear, but finally settled on black leather pants, a tailored white shirt and a cashmere jacket. She sprayed the air with her favorite perfume, Must by Cartier, and moved through it, thinking of the many times David commented about how he loved it.

As she sat waiting for the time to pass, she wondered where he had been for the past week.

She looked at the clock on the wall. 6:12. Time wasn't standing still; it was frozen. At 6:25 she could wait no longer and slowly meandered down the stairs. As soon as she opened the door to the street, he called to her.

He stood outside a dark blue Yukon. The door to the back seat was open.

"Hello, David," Neely mumbled, completely thrown by the bizarre situation. His entire family was in the SUV, smiling at her. In the back seat sat two of his children. She climbed in with them.

"Hey, Neely. How have you been?" Susie greeted her warmly from the front passenger seat.

Neely was shaken, confused, and sick.

I'm going to dinner with his wife and children?

Neely miraculously formed the words in her mouth. "I've been great. How have you been?"

"Pretty good...busy with Brooke's dance recitals. She has a big performance next week, and with David being gone it's been hectic. You know, double duty..."

No accident. No sickness. He'd been gone.

"Coop and Sylvia Manning are joining us at Rustlers. Do you know them?" Susie asked. "They're from Madison. He's an account exec with Baldwin Engineering?"

"I don't think so," Neely said, actually fighting the urge to vomit. Her stomach was upside down. She felt lightheaded.

"Great couple," Susie went on.

Neely nodded, turned to the two children sitting with her, gathered her senses, and addressed them. "Hi. I'm Neely."

"My goodness, you've never met the kids! This is Brooke and Bud. Ms. Neely," Susie laughed. Brooke looked to be about twelve, favoring her dad, while Bud appeared to be fifteen or sixteen. He looked just like his mother.

"I don't know why I thought you knew them, but I did," David said, smiling, while turning back to look at her.

Are you insane? Are you a frikin lunatic?

When they arrived at the restaurant they found the Mannings already seated at a large table, several drinks to their credit. Jimmy, the proprietor, walked them to the table, making polite conversation. David sat Neely next to him, to his right, and Susie to his left. Sylvia and Coop sat across the table. The kids sat at either end of the table.

Despite its Fellini-like beginnings, the evening softened and seemed almost normal after a while. Neely liked

David's children and his friends, discovering that Coop and Sylvia's children also attended Camdon and they shared many friends in common.

The nausea was finally subsiding.

David smiled at Neely and asked if she would choose a wine. She was flattered and, for once, was thankful to Eric for his libation wisdom. She had learned a lot about wine over the years, particularly reds, from Eric. She scanned the pages and was surprised to find such an extensive and sophisticated offering. She chose a 2010 Francois LeClerc French Burgundy.

Before the waiter could return with the wine, David's children began begging their father to relent and let them go to an eight o'clock movie. He was steadfastly opposed to their early departure, but, by his second glass of wine, acquiesced. No sooner was the salad placed on the table than the children wolfed it down and left to meet up with friends.

With the children gone alcohol flowed freely, as did the topics and laughter. Everyone was happy, including Neely. Not used to having more than a glass or two with dinner, she was well on her way to her fourth and no longer even thought about how clumsy and bizarre the situation was.

The owner of the restaurant, Jimmy, did know good food, serving some of the best steaks you ever put in your mouth, and he didn't do such a bad job on the sea fare despite being in the middle of nowhere.

Coop was enticed to join some business associates at a table nearby for a quick drink and conversation just as Susie excused herself to go to the ladies room. David smiled across the table at Sylvia who held her empty wine glass in the air. He walked around the table and refilled her glass.

"This is the most amazing wine," Sylvia said, smiling broadly before taking another sip. "I love it."

"Thank Neely," David said, turning to her as he walked back to the other side of the table. He topped off Neely's glass.

"It deserves more than just a thank you!" Sylvia laughed, feeling no pain.

"What does it deserve, Sylvia?" he asked, placing the bottle back on the table.

"It deserves a kiss!" she announced, holding her glass out to Neely grinning. "Give Neely a big kiss for me. I don't think I can walk!"

David looked down at Neely, she at him, and without a word, he leaned down and softly placed his lips against hers. She closed her eyes and their lips melted. When Neely finally opened her eyes his lips were still pressed to hers. Sylvia's enthusiastic clapping was a distant eidolon.

She felt as though she were drifting through a drug-induced trance. The rest of the evening flowed like a living, breathing Monet. It was surreal—an imaginary walk through soft lights and muted sounds.

No one mentioned the kiss when all returned to the table. David and Neely were unusually quiet. They both were reliving the moment, while barely maintaining a presence.

The evening finally concluded around eleven. Everyone said his and her goodbyes in the parking lot. Neely climbed in the back seat of Yukon.

Susie spoke, breaking the soothing silence. "We're so glad you could join us tonight. I'm still gonna take you up on seeing the apartment."

"Yes, of course, anytime you want," Neely answered.

David pulled the Yukon into the handicapped space

directly in front of the now closed restaurant and put the car in park.

"Be right back," he said to Susie, hopping out of the car. He opened the back door.

"Thank you again, Susie. I had such a good time," Neely said.

"See you soon," Susie smiled.

"I'll walk you inside," he offered.

"The elevator's this way," she said, unlocking the restaurant door. She did not turn on the lights. "When you leave, just pull the door to. The door will lock automatically."

They said nothing as they walked through the dark. The light from the full moon reflected off the white draped tables. The walls were luminescent with the shimmering tiny reflections of the bright moon.

She stopped at the elevator and put her hand on the door to opened it when he stepped to her and stood so close she could hear his soft breathing and imagined if she moved, his mouth might brush the back of her neck.

Can he hear my heart?

He placed his hands on her shoulders and turned her to face him. The world stilled when they found each other's eyes. She reached up to gently hold his face in her hands. He kissed her lips softly. She slid her arms around his neck and pressed her body hard, to his. They kissed passionately, lost in each other. As his lips left hers, she bit his lower lip.

He was taken aback. She smiled wickedly. He grinned, and kissed her again, hard. Neely opened the elevator door. He touched her face before turning and walking back through the restaurant to the entrance. He turned back and for a moment, saw her in silhouette before the elevator door closed and all went dark. He smiled.

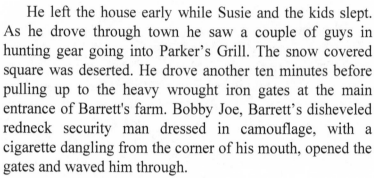

He left the house early while Susie and the kids slept. As he drove through town he saw a couple of guys in hunting gear going into Parker's Grill. The snow covered square was deserted. He drove another ten minutes before pulling up to the heavy wrought iron gates at the main entrance of Barrett's farm. Bobby Joe, Barrett's disheveled redneck security man dressed in camouflage, with a cigarette dangling from the corner of his mouth, opened the gates and waved him through.

David made his way down the snow covered, mile long, winding paved road, past the huge, disproportionate, and poorly reproduced replica of Scarlet O'Hara's Tara. A quarter of a mile past the house he veered off the paved road, down a one-lane gravel road, and continued on for another three quarters of a mile. A small white building, no larger than 800 square feet and surrounded by landscaping paraphernalia, sat in the center of a clearing, where variations of gravel paths and roads radiated out in a starburst pattern. Two John Deere tractors were parked side by side at the far end of the clearing.

The snow was falling heavily as David pulled up to the nondescript structure; next to Barrett's snow covered black Mercedes. Parked a few feet away was T's vintage '55 blue Ford pickup. David got out of his car and walked around the building to its only door and opened it to a single room. Barrett and T were seated in mismatched lawn chairs, facing each other. Snow from their boots had melted into puddles around their feet. It felt colder inside the block building than outside.

"Is this really necessary?" David asked. No hint of the familiar grin or life being a *bowl of cherries*.

"I'm about to crap in my pants. I haven't slept in days. Everything is fallin' apart," T said anxiously before turning to glare at Barrett. "*You* said this would be a cakewalk...I wouldn't be involved...you just needed the money. Well, I gave you the money and look what's happened!" He turned back to David. "I admit it, I'm afraid. Call me a pussy, a fuckin' chicken farmer, a redneck...I don't care, I want out."

Barrett smiled smugly. David glared at Barrett, finding his unabashed disdain for T repugnant.

David pulled a lawn chair from a stack by the door and placed it between Barrett and T. He sat heavily, lowered his head, and stared at his wet; hand stitched alligator loafers and shook his head.

T continued. "I have a life now...Tutt and Kate are important...they are everything to me...I don't want this shit. I want my life back. I'm not a fucking criminal. I'm a chicken farmer, for Christ's sake."

Barrett's laugh was mocking. "Calm down, T, we all know you're a chicken farmer. You've told me twice in the last minute. Trust me, we're not confused about who you are. And why are you so bent out of shape anyway? I'm the son of a bitch they picked up, not you. You need to fucking calm your ass down."

"Fuck you! I'm not gonna calm down! You think because they let you go, we're all okay? We're not! The Feds are going to nail you! Watch and see. His eyes shot to David. "I'm sorry, but you didn't fix this, David. Do you know they're watching Kate?" T turned back to Barrett and exploded. "They're watching all of us, you fucking son of a bitch! They've got my bank records, phone records and god know what else! All because you can't keep your big mouth shut – have to try to be the big dick and pretend you're some fucking mafia drug lord, making deals behind our backs!"

As Barrett lunged for T's throat he screamed, "I *am* a drug lord you dumb ass!" But before his boots found the ground David had Barrett's right arm wrenched up between his shoulder blades. Barrett groaned as his knees buckled.

T smiled, "You're a joke, Barrett, nothing more than cornbread mafia … not a thing more."

David's mouth was at Barrett's ear as he whispered, "Enough." He slowly lowered Barrett's arm as T picked up David's overturned lawn chair.

The men settled back in the chairs. A terrible silence followed. Barrett's pride hurt far worse than any real injury, but he rubbed his shoulder dramatically all the same. "They don't know shit. They were just fishing. I was out in three hours. I'm good. They don't know shit."

T had to physically restrain himself, screaming. "Fishing! Are you as stupid as you look? The feds don't just fish! They're on to us."

David asked T, "You want out?"

"Yes, I want out."

"Then you're out," David said flatly.

Barrett's eyes shot to David. "What in the shit are you talking about? Things get a little dicey and we let him walk away 'cause his *life is good* and he's *afraid*? Why should we take the heat and let this little Alice ass walk?"

"You think we should force him to stay?" David demanded.

"Fucking A!" Barrett yelled.

T's face was bright red, his eyes bulging. "Y'all keep

the money, except for what I put up in the beginning. I don't want anything else. Nothing. I just want out."

"And what stops you from talking or turning on us if it all goes to shit?" Barrett shot back.

"You're the son of a bitch that's been running your mouth!" T shouted. "Not me!"

"Fuck you!"

"Fuck you and the horse you rode in on!" T fired back.

David shook his head.

Keep it together, O'Donnell. Keep it together.

"T's not going to talk. You wanted his cash, you got it, it worked for us, and now he doesn't want a cut. I see this as a windfall. Instead of a five-way spilt, it's four. Right?"

Greed seized and held Barrett's attention, but he couldn't let T walk without a little more ridicule.

"It makes me nervous with him just out there, with nothing to lose," Barrett babbled on, while eyeing T suspiciously.

"How long have you two been friends?" David asked.

"What the fuck difference does that make? "Barrett growled.

David stubbornly waited.

"Thirty fucking years. So what?"

"Has he ever once screwed you?"

Barrett stared at David defiantly, but reluctantly admitted, "I've never given him the opportunity."

David continued to stare at Barrett. He waited.

Resentfully, Barrett finally muttered, "No, he hasn't screwed me."

"Then he's out."

Barrett looked squarely at T. "You fuck me, and you'll not live to regret it."

"Don't you threaten me, you asshole."

"Are you both finished?" David sighed deeply as he looked from Barrett to T and then at his watch. "I had an eight o'clock appointment, which I've obviously missed."

David backed his Porsche into his reserved space in front of his office at 8:46. Upon entering the building, Janet, his heavyset and normally cheery receptionist, greeted him with a scowl and a stack of legal manila folders. Every telephone line was ringing and the office waiting area was overflowing with an assortment of guilty criminals, all professing innocence of varying degrees and in desperate need of O'Donnell's legal expertise.

"I know. I know. Is he in there?" David's expression acknowledged he grasped the consequences of his late arrival, while his body language made it very clear that he did not need or want to be admonished. He grabbed the files from Janet's hand without looking at her.

"Since 7:45," Janet said, managing to get in a barb.

"Green tea. See what he wants."

"He's on his *fourth* cup of coffee."

David was a blur as he wrestled with his overcoat while juggling the files. His face reddened as the files and overcoat spilled to the floor. He cursed and left them on the floor where they fell, and headed for his office. Janet yelled after him, "Susie's on her way, said she had to talk to you *before* you get started."

"Shit" he said, exasperated.

"I'll go over these with you whenever," she added, waving a thick stack of pink message slips in the air.

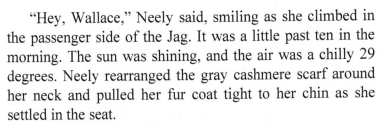

"Hey, Wallace," Neely said, smiling as she climbed in the passenger side of the Jag. It was a little past ten in the morning. The sun was shining, and the air was a chilly 29 degrees. Neely rearranged the gray cashmere scarf around her neck and pulled her fur coat tight to her chin as she settled in the seat.

"It's freezing."

"I sure have missed you, Jellybean," Wallace grinned. "You look great."

Wallace was decked out in a red turtleneck, herringbone wool slacks, her most outrageously gaudy black and gold Gucci loafers and vintage Jean Paul Gaultier sunglasses. Her full-length fur lay draped across the back seat.

"Thanks," Neely smiled.

"I mean it, you look great."

"You hitting on me, honey?" Neely asked flirtatiously, opening her coat to reveal a white t-shirt, black cardigan, and gray wool slacks. Prepared for a day of walking, she chose her old, tried and true, black suede Chanel loafers.

Wallace giggled. "Would it get me another day in the loft?"

"No."

Wallace suddenly eyed three women a block up from Neely's building, loitering outside a beauty salon on the corner of the east side of the square. "Oh my god, look at what we have here!" Wallace cackled.

As they approached the corner, the light turned red.

Wallace's car slowed to a stop directly in front of the salon. The three women in white, mid-calf smocks covering black pantsuits huddled together, shivering. They clutched tightly at their thin, white salon coats, futilely staving off the frigid temperature. Their hair color was identical—fried platinum. They propped themselves around the front door like crazy ass imitations of Cirque Du Soleil performers. Spying Neely in the passenger seat less than five feet away, they waved their cigarette clutching frozen fingers.

"Oh, my god. Who would ever believe this shit?" Wallace laughed.

"Just drive," Neely said, waving to the women as the light turned green. The beauticians continued their wave as the car passed them.

Wallace, still laughing, turned off Main Avenue onto Highway 68 and headed for I65 and Birmingham.

"Where to first?" Neely asked. She felt everything was right with the world. It was a beautiful, bright sunny day, she was with her dear friend and they were laughing. For the first time in a long time, she knew in her bones things were getting better.

"I had some luggage made for Hop. After we pick that up, we can do whatever you want."

Neely opened her red Prada bag and pulled out a small note card. "My Christmas list."

"What am I getting?" Wallace grinned like a child bursting with Christmas anticipation.

"Let me see" Neely whispered, placing her fingers on her lips while scanning the list. "Hmmm...Strange...I don't see your name. Could it be you've been bad?"

"I've been terrible," Wallace laughed, as she pulled onto the main highway.

"Well, at least you and Santa agree on something,"

Neely grinned.

"I told Drew."

Neely's happy face vanished. "Told him what?"

"I told Drew about Hop."

"Why?" Neely sounded concerned.

"I don't know. I was drunk and pissed. It seemed like the thing to do at the time."

"What did he say?"

"He called me a cunt."

"God. I hate that word," Neely said.

Wallace didn't offer more, so Neely sat back in her seat and stared at the Office Depot delivery truck directly in front of them, wondering what terrible things would come of Wallace's honesty.

"Hop and I are going to try and make this work."

Neely did not know what to say.

"I want to be with him," Wallace added.

"You're going to leave Drew?"

"Yes."

Neely chose her words carefully. "I'm surprised..." She hesitated. "I never thought you and Drew would...not be together."

"I'm in love with Hop. Can you believe it, Jellybean? Me, in love?"

Neely smiled at her friend. "Yes, I can believe it."

They drove in silence for about twenty minutes before they got on the interstate. Within moments the speedometer read 93 miles per hour.

Neely turned and looked at her friend who always made fun of Neely's easily manipulated heart and wondered:

Could love really change one's life, temper loss, accept potential poverty, and give one the strength to endure whatever was necessary to possess it? It appeared so.

"We've decided to wait until after Christmas to tell Wendy. His kids will be coming home for Thanksgiving, and Christmas comes right after that, so we thought it would be best to wait."

A stabbing pain cut through Neely's gut.

We?

Surely Hop intended to tell Wendy and he wasn't just dangling Wallace out there.

"I know what you're thinking but you're wrong. He wants me as much as I want him. I have to pinch myself sometimes because it's hard for me to believe he really loves me. But he does."

"And why wouldn't he love you, Wallace?"

Wallace looked pained. "Do you ever worry when things go a little too right that something bad is about to happen?"

Neely hesitated before admitting, "All the time."

"Me too."

"When I was little and demanded the light be left on at bedtime, my sweet, dear grandmother used to tell me that there were no scary boogie men hiding under my bed...just dust bunnies," Neely offered.

"What does that mean?" Wallace asked.

"I think a lot of the things we fear aren't real, they're just imaginary."

"Is this the same grandmother who told you when she was a little girl she had the measles so bad they had to scrape them off of her? The same one who froze every piece of food she ever brought into her house?"

Neely burst out laughing. "Yup!"

"Dust bunnies my ass! There are frikin monsters under the bed, and they're just waiting for us. And I mean us, specifically!"

Nelly and Wallace roared with laughter.

After the moment played out, they continued on quietly, as only people who feel comfortable in each other's company can do.

Wallace asked softly, "What do you do every day in that ridiculous place?"

"Talk with my office, paint, read. I've met some wonderful women."

Wallace grimaced. "What do these women do?"

"Mostly, artists. Talented, funny, and interesting."

"And what in god's name are they doing in Summerville?"

"They live there," Neely continued. "Not everyone wants to live in a city. Some people actually like small town life. Like me."

"We'll see how long that lasts. You know, I have a wager with Jan—one year and you're outta that place."

"I hope you didn't bet the farm."

"A week at The Golden Door."

"You poor, poor baby."

"You wanna make it double or nothing, smart ass?" Wallace taunted.

Neely enjoyed the banter. "Hell yeah."

"You move out of Hee Haw within a year and I get a week from each of you, or, you stay and I pay for you buffoons."

"The idea of making you pay for my massages is so alluring."

"So?"

"Deal."

Wallace smiled haughtily as she turned on the CD. Etta James belted out *Love's Been Rough on Me.* Neely closed her eyes and relaxed deep in the seat. Her thoughts drifted to her friends and in particular how infrequently she'd seen them since Steven's stroke, Wallace's "love affair," and her ensconcing herself high in the Summerville loft.

"Do you know Robin Warner?" Wallace asked.

Neely opened her eyes and shook her head, no.

"He's recently widowed, owns some high tech company that does a lot of government contract stuff, and is *very* nice looking."

Neely shot a look at Wallace. "Are you trying to fix me up?"

"I worry about you in that little town, worry you're gonna turn into some weird old woman who owns ten cats and becomes a hoarder, who's afraid to leave her home."

"I have only Fred, I don't hoard and I go out, thank you."

"On dates?" Wallace's look at Neely curiously. "Or what if..." her voice turned menacing, "What if you start thinking brothers Darrell and Darrell down at the local stockyard look good. I can just see you going to rodeos, church bingo, NASCAR races and local *'wrasslin'* meets."

"You are so dramatic and, totally mad."

"Seriously, why don't you at least let me introduce you? I know the kind of men you like. You'd like him. He's nothing like Eric."

"Funny."

"What do you have to lose? It's not like the farmer's in your new home town are beating your door down."

Neely looked out the window and debated whether or not to confide in Wallace about David.

"What?"

"I didn't say anything," Neely said.

"I know, but I can always tell when you're thinking. What are you thinking?"

"I'm trying to decide whether I should tell you."

"Of course you should tell me!"

Neely knew she was about to jump off a big cliff without a chute, but went ahead with the death plunge. "I think I'm in love."

Wallace's head jerked to Neely, the car veering into the right lane. Thank god there wasn't a car in the other lane. Wallace quickly recovered control of the car, moving back into the left lane.

"Good God, Wallace, watch where you're going!"

"Well what do you expect when you drop a bomb like that?"

"I don't know if it really even matters...it's an impossible situation...I don't even know if he feels the same way. Oh shit...What the hell...He's married."

"Jesus! Who is it?"

Neely looked catatonic.

"If you don't tell me right this second, I'm pulling over."

"David O'Donnell. Your friend."

Wallace's reaction was surprising. She said absolutely nothing. Her face became expressionless, her playful tone, gone. She looked somber as she stared into the traffic ahead.

Neely was unsettled by her reaction. "Wallace?"

Wallace turned to Neely, her nose scrunched, her brow furrowed, and asked incredulously, "David O'Donnell?"

Neely, nervously bobbed her head.

"When did this happen? I don't understand. Didn't *I* introduce you, or did you really know him?"

"No, I met him with you at lunch. I mean I had met him before, but I didn't *know* him. I don't know how this all happened. It wasn't planned. It just sort of grew and, before

I knew it, it was too late."

"Too late for what?"

"I don't know. It's complicated. It's like I woke up one morning and I just knew."

"What the shit are you talking about?"

"God, I don't even know what I'm saying. He doesn't even know."

"How you feel?"

Neely nodded, before correcting herself. "Well, actually, that's not true, he probably knows now. I think I made it pretty clear Friday night."

"What did you do?"

Neely squirmed. "I kissed him."

"Where?"

"On the mouth."

Wallace looked at Neely disbelievingly. "Oh my god, I mean...*where were you*? Like home, a movie, you idiot."

Neely laughed as she felt her face flush. "It was in a restaurant and again when he brought me home."

"You were on a date?"

"I went to dinner with him..." Neely said laughing uncontrollably. "...And his family."

"You were with his family when you kissed him?" Wallace's eyes were the size of saucers.

Neely laughed inappropriately, mimicking a hebephrenic. "I know it sounds crazy..."

"Fuck a mighty, no shit it sounds crazy!"

"We were alone when we kissed."

"Well, thank god for small favors!"

Neely grew serious. "I've never felt this way, never even...you know...thought this kind of love existed...for anyone."

"Have y'all, you know..." Wallace hesitated, bobbing

her head around. "Slept together?"

"No. Friday was the first time anything like that has ever happened." Neely hesitated and then added, "But I know if I had the opportunity, I probably would. The sad part is, I don't know if *he* would."

"My head hurts," Wallace said frowning.

"What do you think?" Neely asked reluctantly.

"You want me to be honest?"

"No, lie. Of course I want you to be honest."

"He has a reputation..." Wallace quickly looked at Neely before going on. "...With women."

"What do you mean?" Neely was suddenly thankful she wasn't standing.

"Affairs. Who knows if the rumors are true? There's so much bullshit we hear and rarely is any of it true, but I don't want you to get into something that's bad, something that will hurt you."

"Who's he supposed to have had an affair with?"

"None of it may be true," Wallace backtracked.

"Would you just tell me!"

Wallace turned the music down.

"An office manager who did way more than manage his front office got caught embezzling. Initially shit hit the fan, but nothing came of it. When David, in the end, refused to prosecute, she made a quiet, quick exit, unscathed and miraculously with enough money to open a little florist shop right on the square. And from what people say, the two of them are good buddies, thick as thieves, even today." Wallace paused. "Interestingly though, people say he wasn't worried about the affair but everything else."

Neely's own head was now pounding. "Is she the only one you know of?"

"I think there have been several, but who'd blame him,

being married to that woman?"

"Maybe it's all rumors. People can be just awful. You know that Wallace. I'm sure he's made a lot of enemies being in the kind of business he's in and I imagine there are people out there who are jealous of his success."

"It's the other stuff, Neely." Wallace took a deep breath. "Rumors that have made the rounds for years, rumors about drug running."

Neely's mouth gaped.

"Well, think about it. How does a small town lawyer make enough money to have all the shit he has? A sprawling estate, a jet, race horses?"

"You're the one that went on about how successful and smart he is! Was that just bullshit?"

Wallace stared straight ahead.

"I'm not saying he's not successful and smart. He is. I'm saying there's probably a whole lot more to him than we know."

"I know everything I need to know. He's a good man and I love him."

Wallace sighed deeply, not sure what else to say. The quiet was broken when Neely said defensively, "Some lawyers make that kind of money, even small town ones."

"I guess," Wallace said with resignation, realizing they were now stumbling through inescapable emotional wreckage, without logic. "What I'm saying Neely, is he wasn't worried about the affair. He was worried about her talking about the drug stuff. She supposedly helped him out once when one of the deals went bad. Something about her husband taking the fall. He's still in prison."

Neely couldn't believe they were talking about the same person. All these disparaging rumors had to be wrong, fabricated by jealous, bitter, small minded people with nothing better to do than attack a successful, powerful man...a good man with a good heart. A tear trickled down her cheek to the corner of her mouth. She licked the salty tear and then wiped it away with the back of her hand.

"I'm sorry Neely. I know you think you love him. He's bigger than life and is *so* charming. But remember, he's an actor, a lawyer. Rumors don't persist over years without *some* truth. At least not usually." Wallace glanced at her friend, who looked so sad, so dispirited, and asked sympathetically, "What are you going to do?"

"There's nothing to do. He's married and *appears* to be happily married despite the *alleged* affairs. I think the drug stuff is crazy, though, off the wall."

"Are you okay?"

"No! If I'm wrong...It means I haven't learned a fucking thing." Neely's expression vacillated between anger and despair. "The only thing I know is I'm consumed with thoughts of him. I'm in love with him, and the really scary part is I don't think I'd feel differently, short of finding out he's a pedophile."

They drove another twenty minutes before Wallace revisited her earlier suggestion and said, "Do me a favor and go out with Robin. I swear, Neely, you being in that goddamn hellhole is screwing up your head and all this just confirms it!"

"Maybe you're right," Neely admitted sadly.

"You're goddamn right I'm right."

The traffic ahead slowed to a standstill.

"Oh great, it looks like an accident," Wallace muttered, craning her head to see around the cars ahead.

They sat in silence a good five minutes before the traffic began inching forward.

"What are you doing for your birthday?" Wallace

asked, trying to ignore their predicament.

Neely faked a smile. "You remembered."

"Of course, darling." Wallace grinned proudly.

"The fact that I share your dad's birthday doesn't have anything to do with it, does it?"

"Well maybe a little. But I did remember."

"Yes, you did."

"Big Daddy's coming into town. It will be his seventy-fourth so I'm going to have a huge, kick ass party. We'll celebrate both your birthdays! What do you say, Jellybean?"

"Sounds like fun." Neely said, trying to put the hauntingly disturbing information about David out of her head. She continued, still trying to manage the overwhelming anxiety she couldn't shake. "How's your dad doing? I haven't seen him in ages."

"Remember me telling you about that little Mexican girl, Lupa? She's moved in with him. He tells everyone she's his housekeeper. Can you frikin believe that shit?"

"Maybe she is."

"Ever heard of a housekeeper sleeping with her employer?"

"Yeah...I think the Vanderbilts, Hearsts, and Dukes started that tradition a long time ago."

"Very funny. He bought her the biggest, gaudiest, Pepto-Bismol colored Cadillac you've ever seen. She put these...I don't know what you call them ...they go on your tires... rims! They are so horrible you have no idea. Suffice it to say she has a pimped out Cadillac!"

Neely laughed. "Oh my god, he's such a stud muffin. He's just trying to keep his little love baby happy"

"I think she's like twenty. It's beyond disgusting."

Neely teased her friend. "I think it's funny. Is he

190

bringing her?"

"I'd have to kill her," Wallace said.

Neely grinned from ear to ear, laughing. "Can you imagine if he did?"

"No."

The cars and trucks ahead began to slowly inch forward as a police car in the far left median, blue lights flashing, zoomed past. Wallace shook her head.

"Can I help you with the party?" Neely asked.

"Heavens, no. Deenie's doing it all."

"Keep it low key, Wallace. I know Big Daddy, and he wouldn't want a big to-do without you inviting his little Mexican love bug."

"You just love tormenting me, don't you?"

"Actually, I do, but I know your dad and he really would want it low key."

"Isn't that my style, darling? Simple and low key?"

"Yeah, that's exactly how you roll!"

Neely woke at 4:30, and after thirty minutes of tossing and turning, gave up trying to get back to sleep and got up. She walked through the dark loft lit by the half moon and went to the front corner window overlooking the square. It was still very dark with so little moonlight there were no shadows. The old courthouse and bell tower appeared to be a miniature movie set. Snow fell, blanketing the deserted streets. She watched as big white snowflakes landed on the outside limestone window ledge. They melted almost immediately. It was beautiful and so quiet. Her thoughts drifted to him.

Was he asleep, his eyes closed, his breathing shallow and soft? Were his lips gently parted? Was "she" next to him?

Neely left the window and the slumbering square to feed Fred and make coffee. She did not turn any lights. Her cat waited patiently as the coffee grinder whirred. She opened a can of cat food as he snaked through her legs, rubbing and purring loudly.

She went to the sofa and sat, coffee in hand. With the click of a button the flames in the fireplace instantly roared, and the heat washed over her. She turned on a nearby reading light and picked up the latest book David had given her, *The Choiring of the Trees*, and began reading. After a few minutes, Fred joined her by climbing on her lap and book.

The book was one of many books by southern authors David had given her over the past few months. She loved every one of them and reciprocated by giving David many of her favorite books, which included her thoughts notated discreetly in the margins, a habit she began in college and never abandoned. He told her how much he delighted in her notes, finding them intimate and revealing.

She looked at Fred, who had moved to a sturdier resting place in the corner of the sofa. She petted him gently and stretched her legs straight out to rest on the coffee table and curled her toes. The clock across the room was visible as daylight arrived. It was 6:58.

Thirty pages later she placed her book on the table and got up, ready to face the day. After a quick shower, she slipped into her jeans and a red Patagonia. Fred was at her feet, wanting attention.

"Be back in a minute, sweet man," she cooed, bending

down to pet him.

"Morning," she called, entering the restaurant kitchen.

"Well, good morning to you. Is your Mr. O'Donnell coming this morning?" Caroline asked with a bright smile.

"Don't know. I got up early, did a little reading, and thought I'd come to see you. Do you have time?"

"Let me put these in," Caroline said, sliding a large tray of homemade biscuits into the oven. "I'd love a big cup of coffee."

Neely went to the coffee station and poured Caroline and herself each a cup and headed to her and David's regular table. She sat and waited for Caroline to join her.

Caroline came to the table with a plate of sliced banana bread. Neely smiled at her friend and asked, "How've you been?"

"Pretty good." Caroline said, pulling out a chair. "I'm almost afraid to say it, but I swear Philip has been wonderful. I think he's really changed. Is that possible?" Caroline asked.

"I don't know," Neely answered, smiling.

"I really think he has."

"Maybe you've changed?"

Caroline looked puzzled.

"Think about what was going on in your life a year ago. You depended on him for everything. Financially and emotionally."

Caroline nodded.

"If he was happy with you, you were happy; if he

wasn't, you were miserable. When he questioned you about something you knew was a sensitive issue, you might lie rather than tell the truth. You've grown, Caroline. You've made a success of this restaurant, you bought a great house, and all by yourself. Your life is the way *you've* made it."

Caroline listened as she dissected the idea that is was she that had control over her life and not her husband.

"Philip's smart. I think he sees how you've grown and respects you for it, even if he isn't totally comfortable with it."

"Do you have a low fat bran muffin?" a nasally voice whined.

The ferret.

Daphne walked up to their table, her unwashed hair plastered to her scalp. She removed a wrinkled brown wool coat, revealing a pink cable knit sweater covered in little matted balls and tight, powder blue, polyester slacks that were inches too short. A guest Press Pass dangled from her neck.

"Let me check," Caroline said, getting up to go look.

"How have you been?" Neely asked.

"Busy," the ferret answered brusquely.

"You want it warmed, Daphne?" Caroline called from the kitchen.

"Sure." Her tone suggested she really didn't care. "Mind if I sit here?" she asked without waiting for a reply as she deposited a stack of folders, newspapers, and a book on the table next to Neely. She was off to the coffee bar and was well out of hearing range when Neely said sarcastically under her breath, "Don't mind at all."

Caroline came back, placed the plate with Daphne's warmed muffin on the table, picked up her coffee mug, and leaned over Neely's shoulder. She whispered, "Count to ten."

As Neely smiled, Caroline squeezed her shoulder. "He's here."

David rushed into the restaurant in his Groucho Marx posture, perfectly suggesting his life's constant state of motion.

"Morning!" His radiant greeting was directed at Neely.

"And to you, Sir," she countered, with an equally enthusiastic grin.

Daphne returned to the table as David sat.

"Hello, David."

"Morning, Daphne," he greeted her. "You said you had big news?"

"Perfect Mattress is closing its doors Tuesday. Don't you just love it when a company screws its employees just before the holidays without the least bit of warning?" She had a look of revulsion as she took small repetitive sips of tea, making a slurping sound each time her lips touched the rim.

"How many people do they employ?" Neely asked.

Daphne ignored her and called to Caroline, "Can I get some jam?"

"What are there...four hundred or so?" David asked, trying to cover the slight.

"Between four hundred and five hundred, depending on production."

Neely could feel her blood boil.

Who did this ugly ass, beak nose think she was?

"No chance of it just being a layoff?" David asked.

Daphne shook her head, her mouth full.

"Has this company been around for a while?" Neely asked David directly, dismissing Daphne altogether.

"Thirty years. Susie's youngest brother Scott works

there."

"Did," Daphne corrected, washing down the last bite of her muffin.

"Did," he repeated.

Caroline came to the table with David's green tea, a blueberry muffin, and Daphne's jam.

He smiled. "Thanks, Caroline. How are you?"

"Great."

"A little late for that," Daphne pouted, eyeing the jam.

"Oh, I'm sorry," Caroline said apologetically.

Daphne, with a crumb caught in the corner of her mouth, looked directly at Neely as she stood. "Can't dillydally. I work."

Neely decided she was not going to let the remark slide. She'd had enough. This wasn't the first time Daphne had implied she was not productive or relevant.

"Actually, I work too Daphne, but I'm lucky enough to have a successful business that doesn't require me to be there 24/7. I have employees that take care of the daily operations. I just have to oversee things occasionally. I'm lucky."

Both Daphne and David looked surprised at Neely's declaration. But within seconds a grin swept David's face, while Daphne's angry expression declared war.

Daphne's beeper buzzed, halting a possible altercation. She turned it to mute and began rummaging through her purse as though she were looking for something.

"I've got it," David said, offering to pick up her tab, as he *always* did.

She slid her check to him, gathered up her belongings, and smiled.

"Tuesday, 11:30?"

"Best Western?"

She nodded. "I'll call to remind you. Okay?"

"Good idea." David nodded.

She left without even looking in Neely's direction.

"She doesn't like me," Neely said after Daphne left the restaurant.

David looked at Neely as if he were clueless as to what she was referring to.

"Haven't you noticed?"

"I think she's just a little gruff."

"A little?" Neely said.

His thick salt and pepper eyebrows furrowed.

"She's jealous," Neely blurted.

He smiled.

"You think that's funny?" Neely asked, not the least bit amused.

"Yes, because she's probably the most asexual woman I know," He answered.

"I know what I see. She has a thing for you *and* does not appreciate the fact I've come into the picture."

He grinned. "Since you've come into the *picture*?"

Neely's face turned red. "You know what exactly I mean. Since you've been coming here, having..." she stammered, "coffee...lunch with me. She sees me as a threat."

"Hmmm."

"You're enjoying this, aren't you?" she asked, now a little embarrassed as well as being a little irritated.

He said nothing, choosing to simply smile innocently.

"And you're not going to answer, are you?" she asked.

He shook his head no, still grinning.

How long would this charm be enough?

She noted a difference in his demeanor, something very slight. She studied his face. Although he was quick to smile and all the familiar charm was there, she saw a sort of melancholic undertone in his manner.

"Is everything okay?"

He looked at her with a surprised look and answered with a weak "Bowl of Cherries."

She frowned, waiting for further explanation. He rubbed his thumb and index finger together and sort of shook his head slightly. It was obvious something *was* bothering him.

"What?"

He still didn't answered. He was struggling.

"Is it me?"

He looked at her and shook his head no with a smile, "You're the only thing that's right in my life." He reached over and covered her hand, "It's work...More crazies than usual."

"You sure?"

"I'm sure." he smiled. "What are your plans for today?"

"Are you trying to change the subject?"

He bobbed his head, grinning.

"I'm down to the last of the boxes. It'll be good to be completely moved in."

For a moment they sat in silence.

"Would you like to see what I've done up there?" she asked, avoiding his eyes.

"I would" he smiled.

Her heart pounded.

What do I say now?

But before she had time to agonize over the tact to take, he asked, "How would Wednesday be? I can be there around six."

"Wednesday would be perfect. Will you have time for a glass of wine?"

"Absolutely."

Should I tell him to leave the family at home?

"Will Susie be coming?" she managed.

He smiled. "Just me."

As soon as he left, Neely ran to tell Caroline. Neely's excitement was dashed as Caroline reminded her, "Isn't that the night of Wallace's party?"

"Oh shit," Neely moaned.

"He'll understand," Caroline offered.

Neely laughed. "I'll just tell Wallace I'll be a little late. *She'll* understand."

Waiting for him was excruciating. She stared at the clock. Only another twelve and a half hours! After the normal rituals of coffee making, unloading the dishwasher, feeding Fred, a shower and dressing, she looked at the clock. Great, now I only have eleven hours to go.

With coffee cup in hand and Fred trailing, she walked to the front window and looked out over the square. It was snowing again. For the first time in years it would be a white Thanksgiving. As the morning sun rose, the streetlights on the square went dark, leaving only the faint glow of some shop lights. She felt, as her grandmother would say, nervous as a long tailed cat in a room full of rockers. She turned and surveyed the loft she'd spent the past day preparing.

Candles throughout the room would be lit and lights dimmed. The romantic mix she'd put together was ready to be played. She decided on her faded jeans and a navy sweater. She wanted the mood easy and casual. And as soon as he left, she would change for the party and be off.

The phone rang.

"Hello."

"Are you up?" Caroline asked sounding cheery.

"I have coffee. The alarm is off."

"See you in a second," Caroline said.

Neely made her bed and poured Caroline a cup of coffee.

Caroline unlocked the door with her key and called out from the back staircase, "Hey!"

"Hey you," Neely called back. Her friend entered the living room carrying a small serving tray. She kissed Neely on the cheek. "Happy Birthday, Neely."

Neely looked at the tray and with a grin asked, "What did you bring?"

Caroline set the tray on the counter and pulled back the foil. "Just a little salmon mousse, your favorite stuffed eggplant and everyone's favorite, Ahi tuna."

"How sweet!" Neely smiled. "This is so thoughtful."

"I figured you and your Mr. O'Donnell might want a little something to nibble."

"It's perfect. Thank you. Come sit." Neely said handing Caroline a cup of coffee. They sat on the sofa in front of the fire.

Caroline pulled a small gift-wrapped box from her apron pocket and gave it to Neely.

Neely smiled at the friend she loved so much.

"Open it."

Neely untied the bow and lifted the lid. She pulled a small, ornate, antique sterling frame from the white tissue paper. "It's the one we saw at The Nest!" Neely exclaimed.

"It was the easiest gift I've ever gotten you."

"I love it," Neely whispered, turning the frame over. The engraving read: *To the best year ever! Love, Caroline.*

Neely hugged Caroline tightly.

"I have to get back downstairs before everything goes

to hell in a hand basket. I have a new girl and I'm afraid to leave her alone." Caroline got up, put her coffee cup on the kitchen counter and said, "Have a happy, happy birthday! Call me if you need anything and enjoy your evening with David! I can't wait to hear all about it!"

Susie barreled into the office, loaded for game, demanding, "Is anybody in there with him?"

Janet nodded, the phone cradled on her shoulder.

"Tell him I'll be in the library."

Janet nodded again.

Thirty minutes later David sprinted up the stairs to the library. Susie was on the phone. David pointed to his watch. She quickly concluded her call.

"No sooner did Bud leave for school," she seethed, "than I got a call from the headmaster's office informing me he has not been to his afternoon classes for the last three days. They're not going to pass him and for all I know they might throw him out. Camdon doesn't put up with this kind of crap! I want you to be home when he gets there this afternoon and I want you to straighten him out."

"Fine."

"You need to be there when he gets home, not when you feel like it!" she yelled.

David suddenly felt lightheaded, his chest tightening.

"What's wrong with you?" she demanded.

He touched his hand to his forehead. "Nothing."

"You don't look right."

He took a deep breath and straightened his spine,

determined to shake it off. "I said there's nothing wrong with me."

"You need to be there when he gets home, David."

"I said I would. So stop! I'm working. I don't need to hear this bullshit. You could have talked to me about this tonight."

"This isn't bullshit and you never want to talk about anything when you get home! Your damn son is about to screw up any hope of a scholarship not to mention he could get thrown out. Have you forgotten how much shit we had to go through to get him in, in the first place? He's barely been able to keep up when he does go to class! He's out of control and, to top it all off I think he's screwing that fourteen-year-old girl who seems to have moved into our house.

David closed his eyes and took a deep breath.

"I know you don't worry about shit like that but I can tell you, it won't be funny when he gets her pregnant!"

David opened his eyes and stared blankly at his raving wife.

"You're not even listening to me!" she screamed.

"I'm not that talented", David said sarcastically. Susie opened her mouth to start the assault when David said forcefully, "If you'd put your foot down once in a while, we wouldn't be talking about this crap in the first place. You baby him, he fucks up and you don't do shit. And when things get really out of hand, you make me come in and be the heavy!"

"You make it where I *have* to protect him" she fired back.

"From what? Me! You can't have it both ways. One minute I'm too hard on him, the next, you're demanding I get him in line?

A knock at the door interrupted the heated free-for-all. Will cautiously poked his head in the library. "You're ten minutes late for your deposition. The clerk just called... judge isn't happy."

"Fuck!" David shouted.

"How you doing, Susie?" Will asked uneasily.

She glared at Will, looking like she wanted to kill him. He quickly shut the door.

David turned to Susie. "Don't worry about Bud, I'm gonna set his sorry little ass straight tonight, and when I do, I don't want to hear one fucking word from you!"

Neely's day, despite every effort to speed it along, dragged in excruciatingly slow measure. Several people called to wish her a happy birthday, including her mother and children. She called Wallace to let her know she might be late for the party, but it made no difference to her friend. She had problems of her own. Hop had spilled the beans to Wendy, which Wallace said he did because of guilt, exacerbated by his children's return for the holiday. Wendy understandably went crazy, threatening to take Hop "*to the cleaners*" and told him in no uncertain terms to "*get rid of the bitch or else.*" And to top it all off, Hop warned Wallace that Wendy was demanding he take her to Big Daddy's birthday party, "*to show Wallace and everyone else that he wasn't going anywhere.*"

"Just hold your head high," Neely instructed.

"Do you think she'll really come?"

"No."

"I need a Seconal, Wallace moaned."

"God, no, Wallace. That's the last thing you need."

"Why did he have to tell her now?" Wallace cried.

"I don't know. I'm sure he feels guilty."

"Do you think he loves me?"

"Yes," Neely said trying to sound convincing.

"Oh shit! Deenie and his people are here."

"Deep breath, have a stiff drink and remember to stay above the fray. If she comes, try to remember Hop *is* her husband. She has every right to do what she thinks she has to, to protect her marriage. Remain a lady. Remember, it's your dad's birthday and I know you don't want to spoil it for him."

Wallace didn't say anything.

"Does Jan know what's going on?" Neely asked hopefully.

Wallace nodded her head, tears in her eyes. "Yes, she's coming early."

"Thank god. Call me if you need me. Okay?"

"Okay."

Neely hung up and felt her stomach turn. Why did so many men pretend to be so big and strong, and then fold like pussies when faced with real life problems, ones that demanded a little character and conviction? The thought of David coming, now somehow seemed tainted, distasteful and seedy.

What in the hell am I doing?

Neely looked at the clock and tried to rid her head of foul thoughts. One forty. Four and a half hours. She went into the bathroom and started to fill the tub. She lit the three scented candles clustered in the corner of the tub and turned off the overhead light.

She undressed, and just as she stepped into the tub she

205

caught her reflection in the floor mirror at the end of the room.

What would he think? What am I thinking? He's coming for a glass of wine!

My breasts are too small, she thought, placing her hands over them. Then she smiled, remembering her free thinking grandmother emphatically reassuring her, all through her long, awkward adolescent years, that anything more than a handful was an absolute waste. She slid into the warm water and closed her eyes.

Please, God, let this be a good thing.

Wallace stood in the living room drinking her Famous Grouse, personally greeting guests as they arrived. She was decked in her *Texas getup* in honor of her daddy—wranglers, rodeo belt buckle, ostrich Luchese shitkickers, her custom made cowboy hat, and a totally, politically incorrect, floor length lynx. Her alcohol level was constantly checked and maintained by Deenie's well-trained staff and, miraculously, by her third drink, Wendy's threats were nothing but a fading nag. Wallace grinned as she looked over the rowdy party makers.

The bitch wasn't coming. Hah!

Big Daddy was definitely in his element, loving every minute of his party, with spirited guests and all attention focused on him. The food was spicy and plentiful and the tequila…flowing. His little baby was at the top of her game, being the perfect little hostess. He was damn proud of her.

Wallace made a quick sweep and evaluation of the food tables and bottles of champagne, before heading for the kitchen to prepare her daddy's birthday cake.

"Come on! Quick! I don't want these little suckers to burn out before we get this son of a bitch out there." Wallace hurried the staff as they finished lighting the seventy-four candles.

With the candles blazing, Wallace escorted the four-tiered chocolate cake, carried by two young girls, from the kitchen to the living room, where over sixty guests spontaneously broke into a raggedy rendition of "Happy Birthday." The cake was placed on a library table in front of Wallace's grinning dad. The candles weren't as bright as the smile on his face as he looked at his daughter.

"Make a wish, Daddy! Make a wish!" Wallace shouted, clapping her hands like a little child.

"Come here, honey," he called to her.

"Make a wish, Daddy, before the candles melt!" she pleaded, coming to his open arms.

"They'll be fine, baby," he whispered, pulling her close.

"Howdy folks! Let me have your attention. This ole cowpoke wants to share some words with y'all." Big Daddy smiled, gently patting Wallace's shoulder.

The crowd gathered close around them.

"First, thanks for coming. I know y'all have other things you could be doing tonight. Not half as much fun, that I'm sure of, but I appreciate y'all coming to celebrate my birthday. I'm one crusty ole son of a bitch and don't take to this kind of hoopla, but I'm kinda liking this 'cause, the truth is, I don't know how many more of these I might have."

"Couldn't kill you with a stake to the heart!" a man's voice was heard shouting from the back of the room.

"Only the good die young!" another man yelled.

"You see, I'm surrounded by people who love me," he laughed while hugging Wallace tight, "but no one is more important to me than this little filly and I want to take a minute to tell her how much, and to thank her for taking the time to do all this for her ole man."

"Daddy, don't."

"Hush, honey."

"Daddy," Wallace pleaded.

He held up his empty glass high into the air. "To my baby...my only child. Most of you who've known us a good spell know her mama was taken from us when Wallace was nothing but a little tumbleweed. And as much as I tried to be what she needed, I failed in lots of ways. I wasn't always there when she needed me."

Wallace shook her head, saddened by his words. "Daddy..."

He went on with a smile looking down at his daughter, "But you've always been so strong, baby, finding your own way, being your own person, even when you were just a tiny little thing. You've never been afraid—spunky, like your mama. She knew how to keep my sorry ass in line. You're not so good at that, are you honey?"

She smiled at her father.

"I know I drank a little too much over the years, carried on with *this* or *that*..." He was briefly interrupted by laughter and cat calls. "...And I didn't always set the best example but in spite of me, you've grown into a fine young woman, a good woman. Here's to my baby!"

He took a deep breath and blew out the few little stubs still burning.

The crowd broke into thunderous applause as outrageous, off color toasts commenced.

Revelers recanting wild stories of past birthday celebrations in Juarez, sent the more refined women scattering.

Wallace looked at her dad smiling so happily, his nose big and red from years of hard drinking, and wished she had invited his little Mexican love bug. What the hell difference would it have made? She giggled at the thought as she looked at the many happy faces in the room, finally stopping with her husband. He was laughing, talking with their friends, drunk.

Maybe this was as bad as it was going to get.

It was six twenty eight and no word from him. Her heart sank as her head filled with abysmal thoughts. She was a fool...again.

She got up from the sofa and paced, finally stopping in front of the fireplace where she stood staring at the flames. She felt so foolish acting like a young girl with a silly crush.

Some night. Poor Wallace. Poor me.

Neely turned away from the fireplace and walked to the kitchen where she opened a bottle of Chateauneuf-du-Pape. She poured herself a big glass fightening back tears. The beautiful tray of tuna and eggplant now mocked her, a reminder of how outrageously naive she apparently was. With the bottle in one hand and the glass in the other, she went back to the sofa and sat.

I need to put the food up...maybe I should take it to the party.

The phone rang. The caller ID read: David O'Donnell.

"Hello," she answered, trying to sound cheerful, yet fully prepared for disappointment.

"I'm on my way if I'm not too late," he said apologetically.

"No, you're fine."

"How do I get up there?" He said, sounding hurried.

"Come up the staircase through the artist studios. There's a door at the end of the hall. Do you know where I mean?"

"I think. I have my cell if I get lost," he laughed, breaking the tension.

"The door's unlocked."

"Leaving now."

She stood completely still, and then breathed a sigh of relief. But in the next instant, she was overcome with an unexpected feeling of anxiety, jumbled with waves of dread. She was seized with the urge to turn on every light, blow out the candles, turn off the music, pour the wine down the drain, and lock the door. But of course, she just waited.

The phone rang again. It was Wallace.

"Are you alright?" Neely asked hurriedly.

"Is David there?" Wallace voice sounded frantic.

"He's on his way. He just called. What's wrong?"

"Wendy and Hop are here."

Neely winced. "Oh god."

"What am I gonna do? I can't go back in there. I can't!"

"You have to. You don't have a choice. It's your party, your home."

Wallace started to cry. "When they walked into the living room, I honestly thought Drew was going to attack Hop. And Wendy...she looks like a fucking peacock,

210

prancing around with her nose in the air, like she's so happy. Shit!"

"What did you expect, Wallace? All you can do at this point is be gracious. Where's Jan?"

"Gracious? Are you crazy?"

"Yes, gracious. You can do it, Wallace. Rise above it. I mean it. Rise above it. Where's Jan?"

"The last time I saw her she was at the bar," Wallace answered. Precious seconds ticked by.

Oh god, Wallace, hurry. He'll be here any second.

Wallace ranted on, "You're right, I'll be so fucking gracious it'll make her puke."

Neely sighed. "That's not what I meant. Go find Jan."

"This *is* my fucking home and I won't be intimidated by some psycho bitch, not on *my* Big Daddy's birthday." Wallace was sounding more and more like herself …crazy!

David's voice called from the foyer. "Neely?"

Neely whispered into the phone, "He's here, I gotta go. You okay?"

"I will be!"

Neely ended the call and headed for the foyer. She met David as he entered the living room.

He stopped abruptly, amazed by the room's beauty. He shook his head, carefully examining every detail before turning to Neely.

"You like?" she asked, taking his overcoat.

"Unbelievable."

She hung his coat in the foyer closet and turned back to him. He looked extraordinary. His perfectly tailored pale gray suit, white dress shirt, and stunning blue tie made for a dazzling display. After a full day's work he still looked crisp and smart. She could have eaten him with a spoon.

"Can I get you a glass of wine?"

"I'd love one. What a day!"

"Red or white?"

"Red, if it's open."

She grabbed a wine glass from the counter. They walked to the sofa where she poured him a glass. He was so handsome, so charming. She was so smitten, so completely taken with him.

He continued taking in the room. "It's beautiful Neely. It's hard to believe I'm in Summerville. You did a amazing job."

"Come sit down," she offered. He sat next to her on the sofa. She hoped he could not see how nervous she was.

"How was your day?" she asked.

"Best forgotten" he said. He looked at her and smiled, "now, things couldn't be better."

She loved the fact he was always seemed so positive, never once being able to recall him complaining.

The phone rang. "Sorry," Neely said apologetically as she went to get it.

God, Wallace. No.

"Hello."

"Happy birthday, darling."

"Who is this?" she asked, not recognizing the voice.

Neely smiled at David, who had gotten up from the sofa and wandered across the room to a large, draped table, home to black and white photographs of family and friends in beautiful sterling frames.

"It's Mimi, darling."

"Oh, Mimi, I'm so sorry. You sounded like a little girl. How are you?"

"Fine. Dodaddy and I are both fine, honey. Your Aunt Beth left this morning after a week. You know, she just needed a little sunshine after her knee surgery. How are you spending your birthday, dear?"

David turned and smiled at Neely, who gestured apologetically. He smiled, unconcerned.

"A friend is here visiting and Wallace is giving a party tonight."

"For you?" her grandmother asked excitedly.

"For me and her dad. You remember we have the same birthday?"

"Oh, that's right."

The conversation lasted less than two minutes, but felt like an eternity. She adored her grandmother, but couldn't wait to get off the phone. After hanging up she thought of muting the phone but imagined it might look a little too designing.

"My grandmother," she offered, smiling.

"Am I keeping you from a party?" David asked.

"Wallace is having a little get together. It's really for her dad. I just happen to share his birthday."

"Today's your birthday?" he asked with surprise.

"All day," she said, as they both returned to the sofa.

He raised his glass to hers. "Happy birthday. I would have gotten you something had I known."

She laughed nervously. "Really?"

"Yes. What would you have liked?"

"I'm happy you're here, sharing a little wine with me."

"Surely there's something you'd want," he coaxed with a big grin.

She felt an overwhelming urge to reach out and touch him, to tell him what she really wanted but "I'd like you to dance with me" flew out of her mouth as if she were a ventriloquist's doll.

Dance with me? OMG, I am crazy.

Neely's lungs suddenly seemed to have a mind of their

own, totally ignoring the need for oxygen. She struggled to reverse the real possibility of self-induced asphyxiation while attempting to appear normal. He took her wine glass and placed it on the table next to his. He found her hand and led her to the open area of the room and pulled her close.

She really *was* having difficulty breathing. Her terrible state brought back dreadful memories of her ninth grade science project presentation, where panic and nausea battled furiously, before mutating horrifically into a profuse sweating incident.

He slid his arm around her waist, cradling her right hand in his left.

I'm seconds away from imploding. How will
he explain my death?

At last she drew a deep breath when he pulled her tight, surely saving her from fainting straight away. His movements were smooth and strong as they danced to the sexy, soothing voice of Michael Buble'. She felt a wonderful release. All the muscles that were faultlessly impersonating taunt rubber bands now eased and her breathing was even. He looked down at her, his mouth so close she could feel his breath. She looked up at him before resting her cheek against his chest. She could feel and hear his heart beating. He pressed the palm of his hand firmly in the small of her back, pulling her body flat against his.

The song ended yet they remained in each other's arms, perfectly still. Seconds passed in quietness before Rod Stewart's sweet words, "I'll be seeing you in all the familiar places..." began to filter through the room.

They looked into each other's eyes. She slipped her hand from his and placed it gently on the side of his face. He covered her hand with his, turning her palm to his lips.

She closed her eyes. As he slowly parted his lips from her hand, she opened them. He pressed his mouths softly to hers. Hunger consumed them as the tender kiss became untamed and frenzied.

She moved her hand down his back to his ass and pulled him in. Suddenly, without warning, he drew back, slowly withdrawing his lips from hers as he lifted his face upward. His exaggerated breath was forced as he exhaled in a regretful sigh. He looked down at her beautiful face, and said, "I can't do this."

She was stunned and embarrassed and didn't understand.

"Come here," he said, taking her hand and leading her back to the sofa where they sat facing each other.

He put his fingertips under her chin, lifting her face. "I want you. You know that."

She fought the tears forming in her eyes. "Then why did you stop?"

"I can't do this. I'm married."

"You've never done this before?" she demanded accusingly.

"No, I haven't."

She jerked her face from his hand. "I find that difficult to believe."

"It's the truth."

"Your reputation would indicate otherwise."

He appeared dismayed as he shook his head. "I've had a lot of women... friends. Susie is a remarkable woman. She's always allowed me the freedom to have friendships with women that most wives would find unconventional, if not completely unacceptable."

"How convenient for you," Neely sneered sarcastically.

"I think you know how I feel about you but I have

never been unfaithful to Susie regardless of what you've heard, and I never will be."

"Fine. You've made your position perfectly clear."

David took Neely's hand and brought it to his lips. He looked at Neely. "I don't want our relationship to end. You have no idea how important you are to me."

Her stare was ice cold. "Let me get this straight. You want to continue this *love affair* just short of the actual screwing? How perfect for you and the little woman who is so remarkably understanding. No muss, no fuss. Right?"

"No," he said softly, "That's not what I want or mean."

He looked so sincerely vulnerable and wounded.

He was good.

"Let me tell you, David, I am not Daphne or one of your old secretaries or whomever you have *used* to fill some empty void in your life because you chose to marry a boring, unattractive woman with whom you have nothing in common. You may not have had actual sex with any of these women, but you might as well have, and if you want the intimate, intellectual, and the emotional *sex* we've been having for months and months to continue, you are going to have to have a sexual, physical relationship with me or it's over. You will not use me. I don't want you to think of me while you screw your wife."

"I don't think you understand. I love Susie. She's a decent woman."

Neely looked at him incredulously and laughed out loud. "Decent! If the man I loved described me as a decent woman, I'd hang myself—after I strung his ass from the nearest tree."

He sighed, turning his head. "I'm sorry. I'm not trying to hurt you."

"Please, don't apologize. I'm a big girl, David. Believe

me, I'll survive."

He looked crushed. But she knew his heart could not be any more broken than hers.

"I need to change, I'm supposed to be at Wallace's party." Her words flowed hard, detached and unemotional.

He looked pale and drawn as he stared at her before turning. His shoulders were markedly slumped as his made his way toward the foyer. She followed him to the closet and handed him his coat. He tenderly kissed her cheek. She gave nothing.

"Happy birthday, Neely."

She remained frozen at the staircase door until the sound of his footsteps faded to silence. She quietly closed the door and emotionally shut down.

She plodded back to the living room, where the romantic music now cruelly scorned her. Blanketed by numbness, she wandered through the room, blowing out candles. Tears ran down her face in streams. The sense of loss and humiliation was all consuming. She went to her bedroom and opened her closet. She put her hands to her face, and sobbed uncontrollably.

Fred came to her and made two rubbing sweeps at her legs. Disturbed by her crying, and being ignored, he bit her ankle.

"Fred!"

The cat scampered.

She wiped the tears with the top of her sweater and looked at the clothes in her closet. She continued crying as she pulled a short, red velvet cocktail dress off the rod. She threw the dress on the bed and pulled the navy sweater up and over her head.

A distant sound startled her. She stopped.

What was that? Someone walking? She listened, not

moving. The sound of footsteps became louder. She grabbed the sweater from the bed and clutched it to her chin.

Her eyes darted to her bedside table for the phone. It was not in the cradle! She'd left it in the living room. Someone was in the apartment. Frozen she stared at the bedroom door.

David stepped into sight. Their eyes met and instantly they shared a singular knowing.

They moved to each other, stopping as their bodies were within a breath of touching. The course was set. She let her sweater fall to the floor.

She stood barefoot in nothing more than her jeans and a small French cut black bra. The corners of his mouth formed the smile she loved so much. He gently placed his hands on her shoulders, moving them slowly, softly down her arms. She felt her whole body quake.

The countless times she imagined this moment suddenly paled. Never had she wanted a man so much or felt such recalcitrant urges rage inside her body.

She slid her arms around him, gliding her hands slowly over his strong back. He moved his mouth gently over her neck, over the side of her face, to her ear, nose, and lips, kissing her passionately. Her body trembled.

"Slow," his hot breath whispered softly.

She was blown away. He was passionate, sensitive, and in control. He would take his time. He wanted nothing more than to savor every inch of her.

Never taking his eyes from hers, he removed his jacket. He reached around and unfastened her bra while she unbuttoned his shirt. Her bra fell to the floor. His shirt was open. He was exquisite, his body beautiful. He placed both palms flat on her collarbone and ever so softly moved them down her chest, as his lips slid down her neck to her nipples. His tongue moved over them slowly.

She reached down between his legs. He was hard and big. She felt lightheaded...fabulously delirious. He smiled seductively as he unzipped her jeans. His hand moved down the front of her jeans. She wasn't wearing underwear. He grinned wickedly.

He pulled her jeans down, over her hips, letting them fall to her ankles. She stepped out of them. He looked at her, studying her exquisite body. He wanted her in every way imaginable.

A savage unfamiliar passion had been awoken in him. His mind and body were engulfed in torturous desire. It was the first time in his life he felt such magnificent ecstasy. He marveled at this woman. She was not only his intellectual match, but made his dick so hard he could have used it to pole vault out of the loft to the street below. She was everything he had ever wanted...and more.

He was alive.

The house phone rang, waking her.

Shit. Where in the hell is the phone?

She jumped out of bed and followed the ringing to the living room coffee table. She picked up as the answering machine clicked on.

"Can't take your call. Please leave a message and I'll get..."

"Hello."

"...back to you as soon as I can."

"What happened to you last night? " a voice asked.

"Wallace?"

"Uh huh."

"What's wrong? You sound horrible," Neely asked.

"I am horrible! Everyone knows. Everyone! I'm in such trouble," Wallace sniffled, her voice hoarse.

"What happened?" Neely asked, searching for her robe. The apartment was freezing.

"Wendy called me a whore in front of everyone. She threatened to kill me if I ever saw Hop again. In front of my daddy, Neely…Oh god, all in front of my daddy."

"Just a second. Let me turn the answering machine off." She stopped the recording and put on her robe. "Wallace, where is Drew?"

Wallace continued crying. "He left."

"Where did he go?"

"Birmingham. He went to *her*, to his whore. He told me it's over."

"Oh, Wallace."

"And your dad?"

Wallace sobbed like a child.

"Is he still there, Wallace?"

"Yes, he's here but Hop left with Wendy. Hop wouldn't stay with me," Wallace wailed.

"He had to go," Neely said softly.

"That's not true. He could have stayed."

"Not last night. You know that." Neely wasn't sure she should ask, but did anyway. "Have you talked to him today?"

"No." She cried. "I am so fucked."

"You want me to come over?"

"Yes," she sobbed, "please come."

More than a week passed before Wallace heard from Hop. When she picked up the phone and heard his sweet voice say, "I'm sorry, Wallace," all the emotional damage and concerns evaporated. The words she was waiting to say, or waited to hear him say, were lost somewhere between joy and dread.

The prescribed Prozac in addition to Valium she used to self medicate beginning the day after the incident, numbed the awful pain, but left her unable to clearly grasp the events around her.

"Wallace?" Hop sounded beaten down.

"Yes?"

"How are you?"

"I'm here," she said in a whisper.

"Are you okay?"

"No."

"I'm sorry I haven't called. It's been really bad. I wasn't even sure it would help if I did. My kids are with Wendy at her brother's. One minute she's threatening to divorce me and take everything, and the next, she's telling me she'll never give me a divorce. What about Drew?"

"He's gone...moved out."

"Shit."

Complete silence held.

"Hop?"

"Yes."

"Do you love me?" she asked.

He didn't answer right away.

221

She sobbed.

"Oh god, Wallace...Don't...You know I do."

"I need you, Hop," she cried. "I'm so afraid. Christmas is in three days. Please come...I have nothing. I'm all by myself. I need you."

"I can't, Wallace."

"If you loved me, you'd come."

"Don't say that. Please, I can't right now. It's Christmas, I have to be with my kids, especially now, after all this."

"Why don't you feel like I do? Why don't you want me like I want you?" Her words were slurred. She was so sedated and crying so hard, it was difficult to understand her.

"I'll come as soon as I can...I promise."

"When?"

"Soon. It won't be long."

"Promise me," Wallace begged.

"I promise."

"I love you, Hop."

The warm and fuzzy feelings Neely had come to enjoy and expect, promptly vanished when David told her could not see her for at least eight days. Between his children's Christmas vacation, and his mother, oldest daughter and grand children visiting, he saw no way to break away. Neely was broken-hearted as she realized that the romance she thought they had was probably nothing more than a cheap, sordid affair.

Neely spent Christmas Eve with her children in the loft. They had a late lunch, opened gifts, and talked of upcoming trips, friends, and life at school. They left early so that they could have dinner with their dad in Madison.

It was all so different from the festive holidays they once enjoyed as an intact family. Everyone could feel the emptiness but no one spoke of it. Like the phantom pain of a missing limb, they all would have to learn how to cope with a loss that would forever remain.

Christmas Day, her favorite of the year, was unbearable. By choice she was completely alone, declining invitations from Jan, her mother, her grandmother, and Wallace. She spent the morning reading and paying bills. She could not rid herself of the thoughts of David with his family, opening gifts, laughing, and enjoying dinner around a festive Christmas table. She felt sick, angry and repulsed, and mostly, at herself.

Another dumb ass, self-destructive path.

About four in the afternoon she finally opened *his* gifts. A platinum Irish charm, the symbol of eternity, set with a single diamond, on a long chain was nestled in a cotton filled, red velvet box. Tears welled as she fastened the chain at the back of her neck. She sat holding the eternity symbol in her fingers, considering it.

Eternity? How about just fucking Christmas?

She opened David's other two gifts. One was a CD and the other, lovingly inscribed, was the book, *The Fifty Greatest Love Letters of All Time*. She read the words he wrote, over and over.

I love you Neely. You are my heart, my last and forever love. David

She put the CD and book on the table and went to bed. She couldn't suffer another minute.

Le Mon

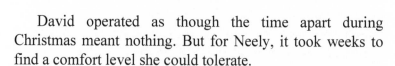

David operated as though the time apart during Christmas meant nothing. But for Neely, it took weeks to find a comfort level she could tolerate.

It would never again be the same. She loathed being the *other* woman. But more than that she was disappointed and angry with herself because she had allowed it to happen.

After making love, David rolled on his side to face her. "Do you like the necklace?" he asked, brushing a wisp of hair from her face.

"It's beautiful," she said, holding it with her fingertips.

"What's wrong?"

She let the necklace fall back to her chest. "I missed you. I was alone. I would rather have had you with me than gifts. And it seems being apart didn't bother you like it did me. You had your family, the intact Christmas, and, you have...*me*. I had hours of being alone, of imagining you with your family: dinner, opening presents, laughing." Neely shook her head, "I don't know what I'm doing anymore. What are we doing?"

He rolled to lie on his back and stared at the ceiling. "You told me you'd be fine."

"What was I supposed to say? That I feel cheap? That I can't believe you would do this to me? That I'm apparently more fucked up than ever?"

He turned back to her and placed his hand on her arm. "Was I supposed to tell my children, *excuse me while I go see Neely?*"

She closed her eyes tightly fighting back the ache, the

tears.

Who was this man...so cold, so matter of fact?

"Neely, I love you. It killed me to think of you up here alone. It killed me. I thought of you a thousand times Christmas day. I wanted to be here with you. There is no place I would have rather been. You have to know how hard it is for me, too." He kissed the small of her neck and pulled her close.

Not too hard to have stayed away.

Neely felt guilty every time she spoke with or saw Wallace, for her own life was pretty much back to the old routine: seeing David several times a week while Wallace was at her saddest. Neely wanted to call Hop and scream at him, to demand he take better care of her friend, to make him love her and protect her. Instead, she consoled Wallace as best she could, with outlandish promises and conjured images of love and commitment that she insisted would come. But the truth was she had no idea what Hop would eventually do and prayed she wasn't just postponing the hurt and sorrow Wallace would know if it all fell to pieces.

She had to mask the truth. Wallace was so fragile. Neely and Jan were both certain she could not face the real possibility that it was over with Hop. It was troubling to them that he might not possess the strength or love for Wallace, that it would take to make it right.

But miraculously, after two excruciatingly painful weeks, Hop finally called again. Although still living with Wendy, he decided he would go through with the divorce regardless of the consequences. He told his children, his broker, his attorney, and his mother and father. There was no need to tell friends—Wendy had enlisted a group of her girlfriends early on to spread daily, one-sided updates of Hop and Wallace's affair. Wendy relished the opportunity to provide the sorted details of their divorce madness to anyone who'd listen.

He sat at his desk, flipping through a stack of mail. A letter addressed to him in her hand caught his attention. Before opening the letter, he brought it to his face and inhaled deeply. It was her fragrance...one that would forever haunt him.

He opened the envelope and removed a single sheet of paper.

A breath...a smile...a touch.
Your presence quickens me
Awakening a soul long numbed by dreams
unimagined...unrealized.
Cavernous voids we conceal deep within
are at once filled ...
A perfect union.
Pray this shimmering light is not
but a final glimpse of simply, what might have been.
For without will or purpose,
my heart is yours.

Neely

He reread the words she'd written, while replaying in his head their lovemaking. Again, he brought the paper close, to smell her fragrance. His thoughts were moved with the essence of her and with the sadness he brought her. He wanted to pick up the phone and call her, to hear her voice, to tell her he was in love with her, but Susie was in the next office going over the accounts. It was all too surreal and grim.

"Got a minute?" Will asked with his shoulder propped against David's office door. He held a manila folder in one hand and a cup of coffee in the other.

"How long have you been there?"

Will looked confused. "Just a second. Something wrong?"

David grinned. "No. Everything's fine."

T settled back into his old life, trying his best to forget ever having been involved with Barrett and the whole drug thing, while Barrett spent time convincing himself his actions had always been in the best interest of the group. Rather than worry about the feds investigating them, he concluded David and Bill should be worrying whether T might throw them all under the bus.

The drops had stopped, the money was moved, and documents and hard drives were destroyed—yet a constant uneasiness shrouded everyone's lives.

Nothing was what it seemed.

"Franklin's on line three," Janet's voiced was heard over the intercom.

David picked up the phone. "Morning."

"Can you talk?"

"What's up?"

"Are you coming up anytime soon?"

"Do I need to?"

There was a protracted pause.

"I've heard you may be getting yourself into trouble."

David felt a sudden angst. "I thought everything was...good."

"I'm talking about you and your *friend*."

David was unseated by the comment.

"Rumor is you're seeing someone."

David said nothing.

"It's none of my business, but with all that is going on I question your judgment if it's true." Franklin waited for a response that didn't come. "Susie's been a good wife to you, David, and a good mother to your children. She deserves better and, as her brother, I just felt I had to say something."

"Nothing's going on."

"Good. I'm glad to hear that."

An awkward silence followed.

"Anything else?"

"No."

After they said their strained goodbyes David stared at the papers in front of him and felt a sickness in his belly. It was the first time he'd ever lied to Franklin.

Neely and Jan tried to spend as much time with Wallace as they could, worried she might be pushed over the edge by Drew, who now demanded she move out of their home with basically nothing. She had already been put on notice by her husband's high profile, high-powered attorney, who gloated that he was naming Hop as the correspondent in the proceedings and that he intended on assigning most of the assets to Drew's coffer.

Things were going to be ugly and very messy and Wallace was going to need every faculty she possessed, firing on all pistons, to avoid losing everything. In order to protect herself, she would have to reveal Drew's expose his longtime mistress, who was married with a ten-year-old son.

Whether Wallace was up to the challenge was extremely doubtful.

David's normal routine was to call Neely twice a day, usually once before eight in the morning and once before leaving the office at the end of the day. If he could, he would have seen Neely every day but that was impossible, and if they managed to see each other twice a week, they were happy.

After his bike ride, he'd come over for lunch in the loft. They'd sit at the old pine farm table, her big chair facing his, her bare feet in his lap, and discuss books, Wallace's predicament, politics, their children, each other, and anything else that was relevant to their lives—except where their relationship was going. The wine was never sweeter, no thoughts wiser, or feelings more passionate. They were happy, full to the brim with each other. As he so aptly described it, he was all *swoll up.*

After lunch they'd walk hand in hand to the bedroom and undress each other. They'd grin like children getting ready to ride the biggest, baddest roller coaster before climbing into bed. Under the sheets, they'd slip into each other's arms, and remain still, as if taking time to breathe, to savor the moment.

"You feel so small in my arms."

"Is that good?"

"Yes."

She snuggled as close to him as she could, wishing their bodies would melt into one.

"I love you, Neely," he said, before kissing her.

"I'm so glad you do."

He felt so big, so strong. He should have made her feel safe, but he didn't because the reality of it all was he wasn't *really* hers, it was only real, here, in the loft, in her bed, for that moment.

Sensing her disconnect, he pulled her so tight she could barely breathe. "I will always love you…it will never be over. No matter what happens. No matter what I might say or do. *We,* my love, will never be over."

More than anything, she wanted to believe him but wondered why his words didn't console her.

"What are you doing tonight?" Lanie asked before Neely could say hello.

"Lanie?"

"My friend, Simone, is here from Paris and I'm getting a group together for GNO. You know, *girl's night out*," Lanie rattled on. "You'll love Simone, she's so French. Sandy Hannigan, she's Dana's new partner, and Will Bibb's wife, Kathy, will probably come. We never know for sure who will show up. There are about ten of us who try to do this, like every two weeks. It depends on kids, dinner, and homework—you know, the usual stuff. I'd love for you to join us. Do you think you can make it?"

"I think so. Sounds like fun. What time?"

"6:30 in the bar at Rustlers. Invite Caroline if you think she'd like to come."

"Thanks, I will."

"Great. See you about 6:30."

Neither of them ever found the bar scene a comfortable or preferred place to socialize. But here they were walking into the dark, smoky bar at Rustlers. Who would have thought?

"Neely! Over here!" Lanie yelled from the far side of the room. She half stood at a big round table, waving. Caroline and Neely walked past the bar of mostly men, dressed in various ensembles that included trucker hats, overalls, and phony cowboy get-ups. Caroline and Neely looked at each other and laughed out loud—at absurdity of it all.

They met several women they probably would have never come in contact with, if not for this particular evening. Kathy Bibb, wife of David's partner, was there; Simone, an art professor from the Beaux Arts in Paris; Sandy Hannigan, an OBGYN new to Summerville; Danielle Brown, a real estate agent; and Cynthia Walker, an elementary school music teacher.

For the first hour and a half the women got to know each other, sharing a little about themselves while polishing off a few bottles of wine, two baskets of cheese sticks, a basket of wings, a plate of stuffed jalapeno poppers, and two orders of nachos.

A couple of pseudo cowboys at the bar sent over a cheap bottle of Chardonnay, while dramatically tipping their spanking new Wal-Mart cowboy hats to the ladies.

"The tall one's cute," Cynthia giggled, making it clear the three and a half glasses she'd already had were three too many.

The conversation gravitated toward the topic of men and, specifically, what dick heads most were. Simone had been married for nineteen years when her husband came home one night and classically stated that he didn't love her anymore and wanted *more*...basically he wanted a divorce and *more* of his young mistress. He married his paramour the week his divorce was final. Simone gave up men entirely after surviving a year of what felt like emotional death and decided to give women a shot. She found happiness with her now girlfriend of five years and decided without reservation, she would never go back to the other side.

Danielle, a local real estate agent, couldn't conceal her shock of finding out she was in the presence of a lesbian, let alone a French lesbian. Her total exposure to the world outside Summerville was limited to a spring break trip to Panama City, Florida many years ago. She found the encounter with Simone very titillating and scandalous.

Sandy seemed the only one truly happy with her man, but then again, she'd only been married eight months. Perhaps even more telling was the fact she'd only known him two months before they married. The pheromones were no doubt still feverishly plentiful, raging and intoxicating.

Kathy congratulated Lanie on her daughter getting the lead in the school's production of *Annie*. "Is she excited?"

"Oh she's excited but I'm about to wring her little soprano voice box! I'm serious...she's driving me to distraction. I hear those damn songs in my sleep."

"She does have a beautiful voice, but I have to agree with Lanie." Simone laughed.

"You teach music at Summerville Elementary, don't you?" Caroline asked Cynthia.

"Yes, and reading."

"Cynthia is a great teacher, but her real gift is acting. That's her real talent. You would have died if you'd seen her in *Desire Under the Elms*. She was unbelievable!"

"Oh stop." Cynthia beamed, pouring herself another glass of wine.

"Are you working on anything now?" Neely asked.

"Uh huh," she said, carefully directing her very full wine glass to her lips, "*The Importance of Being Ernest.*"

Neely smiled. "Funny play."

"Who else is in it?" Danielle asked.

"Carla Baker, Jake Westheimer, Blake McCain... me...uh...Daphne Polansky...and Terrance Layne."

"I know Daphne," Neely said.

"I heard," Cynthia said with a knowing undertone, implying she knew *much* more.

"What do you mean?" Neely asked.

"Nothing."

"What are you talking about, Cynthia? You can't insinuate something more and then say *nothing*," Lanie insisted firmly.

"I don't think I should say."

"Yes, you should," Kathy pressed.

"Well," she began tentatively, turning to Neely, "you know I don't even know you, so don't take this personally." She gulped more wine. "Remember, I'm just the messenger."

"Okay, we get it. Just say it," Kathy instructed.

"Well...I overheard Daphne telling some people at rehearsal that Neely was stalking somebody."

Neely looked gob smacked.

"That's what she said," Cynthia said defensively.

"Who am I supposed to be stalking?" Neely asked.

Cynthia squirmed. "Oh gosh."

"Who?" Lanie demanded. "For god's sakes, just say!"

"David O'Donnell."

No one said anything as each person processed the claim.

Neely, looked to Caroline, who thankfully was very quick to take the reins.

Caroline laughed out loud. "I can't even imagine how anyone, let alone someone who doesn't even know Neely, could say such a stupid thing with a straight face. I have known Neely forever and she would be the last person to stalk anyone! And David O'Donnell? Preposterous."

"I know, I thought it was, well, not believable when I heard it, but hell, I didn't know you then." Cynthia grinned at Neely, tilting her head, almost touching her shoulder. The woman was way past, three sheets to the wind.

"This is how rumors get started in this town," Lanie said, looking at Neely. "If I were you I would call her and demand to know why she's saying this crap." Lanie was fired up.

Neely shrugged. "It's probably better I just let it go, it's so bizarre. I don't want to give something like that credence."

"Hell, I don't think you should drop it, I think we should call her right now!" Cynthia shouted. She almost fell to the floor as she bent over and rummaged through her purse, looking for her cell phone.

"Wow, hold on!" Lanie laughed. "No more for her. Is she driving?"

"Not anymore," Kathy said.

"I can drive. Shit, I'm a great driver!" Cynthia boasted, pounding the table.

"Here, eat these," Kathy said, shoving the plate of soggy nachos in front of her. Cynthia dove in.

The women continued drinking, talking, and laughing, totally abandoning the stalking accusation. But Neely and Caroline could not let it go and found they were no longer mentally in the moment but were simply waiting for an opportune time to leave. They looked at each other often, knowing full well they were going to have to get the *ferret*.

A mix of freezing rain and snow pelted them as they walked across the parking lot a little before midnight. After helping Kathy pour Cynthia into the passenger seat of her car, they all made their way to their own cars. Safely inside Neely's, Caroline looked at her friend, wiping the wetness from her face and shouted, "I cannot believe that bitch! What are you going to do?"

"The idea that I'm stalking *him*? God!"

"She is just bad," Caroline seethed.

The GNO women were tucked warmly in their beds and sound asleep when the snow and ice mixture turned to pure sleet. Within an hour the roads were covered in a thin, frozen, bluish layer of ice.

He drove slowly, carefully, grateful the weather was terrible. His pale metallic blue Mustang would be veiled and, as he'd imagined, the roads were deserted.

He passed several farms, lit only by a few halogens high on tall light posts, marking their entrances.

As he approached T's farm he started to sweat. Within seconds the moisture that formed on his brow and the back of his neck cooled in the freezing air, making him shiver. A hundred yards from the turn he switched off the headlights and slowed the car to a snail's pace. The boundaries of the one-lane road were obscured by packed snow. He pulled his car off the road into the deep bank of snow a few hundred feet from T's house, grabbed his bowling bag from the back seat, and got out of the car. He pushed the door closed carefully, trying not to make a sound. The snow gathered on his head and shoulders as he walked from the road, past the house to the barn where T kept his John Deere tractor, his Ford truck, a Saab, and Kate's truck. He entered the barn and moved between the Saab and Kate's truck, careful to not touch either.

He heard a dog bark. The yapping was coming from T's house. He froze. He waited, crouching low, between the automobiles until the dog barking stopped. He stood and walked around to the front of Kate's truck and knelt down, placing the bowling bag on the ground close to the bumper. He took off his gloves, shoving them into his coat pocket and opened the bag. He removed a pair of pliers and wire cutters and slid easily under the front of the truck. He discovered moving his frozen fingers were another issue. His hands were so cold he had difficulty moving his fingers. He opened and closed his hands, squeezing them into tight fists. Feelings quickly returned to his fingers. He worked hurriedly, completing his mission in just minutes. He inched himself out from under the truck, put the tools back in the bag, and soundlessly walked out of the barn, grinning.

After hearing of Kate's accident, David canceled his appointments and immediately left his office for the hospital. As he drove through town, the sleet quickly began coating his car. The windshield wipers slowed until they stopped, freezing to the glass.

I have to get to T before they talk to him.

David pulled into the hospital's main parking area and

found no empty spaces. He continued on to the restricted physicians' parking area, waving at the security guard as he passed. He parked in front of a sign reading, *Emergency Room Physician Only.*

"Shit," he grumbled, stepping into a deep puddle of frozen slush as he got out of his car.

A security guard appeared out of nowhere.

"You Doctor Phillips?" He called out in an authoritative tone.

David unbuttoned his coat and reached into his back pocket. He pulled a hundred dollar bill out of his wallet and handed it to the guard.

"My daughter's in the emergency room...just had an accident. Can you give me a break?"

"Try not to be too long.... I could get in trouble."

"Thanks."

David buttoned up his black cashmere coat, pulled the collar up, and dashed to the doctor's entrance.

David walked down the green and white speckled linoleum hall, past a bank of patient rooms, and on to the nurses' station. He unbuttoned his coat, brushed the icy droplets from his shoulders and sleeves, and waited for someone to return to the station.

After a couple of minutes of listening to bells and phones ring without any sign of a person to answer them, he decided to look for the ICU on his own. He walked past a couple of more rooms and found himself standing in front of an elevator marked EMPLOYEES ONLY. As he turned to head back, the doors opened and two hospital workers pushed an empty gurney out past him.

David asked, "Could you tell me how to get to the ICU?"

One pointed, saying, "Go back down this hall. At the

nurses' station take a left and keep going until you see a sign that says Nuclear Medicine and ICU. It will be on your right."

David was already halfway down the hall when the second worker called out, "Visitation's not 'til two!"

David nodded with a wave, not missing a step. The smell of alcohol and odd human odors mingled unpleasantly. The hall lights were too bright and the temperature too cold.

How in the hell was somebody supposed to get better in this shit?

An arrow to the left directed him to Nuclear Medicine and the ICU. David turned the corner and half way down the hall to the right, found T sitting in a one of two pale green, plastic chairs placed just outside the hospital room guarded by two sheriff' deputies. T was slumped over, his face in his hands. A Styrofoam cup and a coke-can were at his feet. The deputies, nodded to David as he sat next to T.

T looked up. His red eyes welled with tears. David put his hand firmly on T's shoulder.

"They tried to killed her, David."

David stared at T's pained face and bit his lip. T looked down and wept.

"They tried to kill her."

The caller ID on David's phone illuminated the name *Bill*.

"Hey," David said, answering his cell.

"Jack and I should be touching down in about twenty

minutes."

"I'm leaving now."

"How's Kate?" Bill asked.

"The doctors say she'll recover. She's in surgery now."

"And T?"

"Devastated." David answered.

"Barrett?"

"In Vegas."

"Have you heard from him?" Bill asked.

"Not a fucking word." David was furious.

"Son of a bitch," Bill added. "You need to get to him as soon as you can."

"What do you think I've been doing? He won't answer his phone."

"I need to match this trim, or at least find something close," Neely explained to the young man helping her. She turned the piece of door trim, as if a different angle might help him understand what she wanted.

"Uh huh," he said, taking the wood from her. "Let me go see what we got in the back."

Neely waited as the man disappeared behind doors displaying a big sign in red lettering reading, WAREHOUSE. She checked her cell phone. No missed calls.

Why hasn't he called? This is becoming the story of my life.

After a couple of minutes of waiting, she concluded it might take him awhile, so she meandered down the old wood plank floors that creaked with every step, moving from aisle to aisle. She stopped to study and marvel at the shelves of hundreds of wooden boxes that contained every imaginable screw, nail, widget, seal, and nut known to man. She wondered if someone really knew the purpose of all these things.

"May I help you?"

Neely turned around to find Jack Bendix standing before her, smiling.

"Jack! What in the world are you doing here?"

"I work here," he smiled.

"Really?" she asked, looking confused.

"This is my business. Michael Summers and I own this old place."

"I love it. It's like a museum," she laughed.

The young salesman reappeared holding Neely's piece of molding, "We don't stock this, ma'am, but we can get it milled for you. It would take about two weeks. How much do ya need?"

"I'm not sure. I have three or four doors, maybe more. I guess I need to get the measurements before I get back with you."

"Sure thing," the young man said, handing her the piece of trim. "I wrote the number of the molding on the back, so you know what to ask for. Can I help you with anything else?" She shook her head no. "Thanks for your help."

She turned back to Jack with a smile. He reached out and took the piece of wood from her. "How about lunch? Looks like the perfect day to claim that rain check."

"It's a little early for lunch," she smiled

"Then how 'bout breakfast?" he asked.

She hesitated for a moment then said with a smile, "Sounds perfect."

Le Mon

"You want to meet me at your restaurant?"

She hesitated. The Mustard Seed was the last place she wanted to meet him. There was always an outside chance David might show up.

Oh great! Now I'm worrying about my married boyfriend thinking I'm cheating on him. OMG.

"What about Baby's Diner? I hear it's pretty good," Neely offered.

"I'll meet you there." He smiled, handing her back the trim. "Twenty minutes?"

"Perfect," she smiled back.

Most of the regular patrons of Baby's Diner were gone by the time Neely arrived. They included the laborers of Summerville—the painters, carpenters, roofers, bricklayers, and farmers. Most were in and out well before 8 a.m.

The women behind the counter with teased and sprayed beehive hairdos eyed her suspiciously as she passed them, on her way to claim a seat in one of the booths that lined the opposite wall. She'd only been in the restaurant/pool hall once before, almost a year ago, and vowed she'd never come back after finding, next to her table, a used Q-tip. She didn't mind funky; she did mind nasty. But Baby's Diner was the perfect place to meet Jack because she knew, without a doubt it was a place David would never go.

One of the women came from behind the counter, holding a plastic, amber glass of water, utensils wrapped in a paper napkin, and a menu. A lit cigarette hung precariously from her bottom lip. She put the glass and napkin on the table and handed the menu to Neely. She said nothing and was decidedly surly.

"I'd like a cup of coffee, please, black with one sweetener. I'm expecting someone. He should be here any minute."

The woman turned and left. For the first time since coming to Summerville, Neely had never been made to feel unwelcome, until now.

Jack entered the front door with a broad smile and waved. He came to the booth and sat across from her. "I had trouble getting outta there. Sorry. Have you been waiting long?"

"No, just got here. I didn't order you coffee because I wasn't sure what you wanted."

"Well, I'll be a tater's ass! Where in the hell have you been, stranger?" Hollered the same woman who had just waited on Neely. She quickly wiped her hands on a towel; grabbed Neely's coffee and almost racing came toward Jack. She put Neely's coffee mug and a packet of Sweet and Low on the table, and held out her arms to Jack.

"Patsy Boyd! My god, how long has it been?" He stood, giving the rough-as-a-cob looking woman a bear hug.

"Too long...too long, my friend." She smiled, uninhibitedly displaying two missing bottom teeth.

"I want you to meet my friend, Neely Glover. Neely, this is one of my very, very good friends, Patsy Boyd."

"It's nice to meet you," Neely said, shaking her hand.

"Patsy worked with me when Michael and I were just getting the lumber business going. She did everything—ordering, selling, keeping us in line, tracking inventory, and bringing us the best pecan pies you've ever put in your mouth. Patsy did it all."

The woman squeezed his shoulders hard. "This is my

man. We been through it, ain't we?"

"That we have, Patsy."

"Well, enough of this slobbering. You came in here 'cause you're hungry. What can I get ya, honey?"

Jack looked at Neely. "Do you know what you want?"

"I think I'll have scrambled eggs and wheat toast."

"All's we have is white, honey," Patsy grinned.

Now I'm "honey?"

"That's fine."

"Now what about you, Jack?"

"Let me have the Big Boy Feast." He smiled, winking at Neely.

She couldn't help laughing. Everything seemed so comical—the diner, Patsy, the Big Boy Feast.

"How'd ya want them eggs, darlin'?" she asked, hankering for things to be just right for her man.

"Over medium, crisp on the bacon, and bring me some Louisiana Hot if you have it. And some coffee."

"Comin' right up!"

"Thanks, Patsy."

The woman left to cook up the Feast herself. Jack smiled at Neely. "I love this place."

"It's growing on me," she smiled.

He looked down to his right, lifted a paper sack from the bench, and opened it. He took out a beautiful box. It was wrapped in a dark rust velvet fabric tied with a heavy black satin ribbon. A tiny, gold metal tag tied to the ribbon read, "Valencia". He handed the box to Neely.

"What's this?" she asked.

"A late Christmas present."

She was so surprised.

"Christmas is my favorite time of the year, and I love sharing it with the people I care about" he said.

244

Neely smiled. "It's my favorite too," she said, suddenly reminded how sad this past one had been.

"Really?" he asked, detecting her sadness.

She smiled, forcing the blue thoughts away and joked, "Do you keep gifts in your car for all your friends?"

"No. You can open it later if you want."

She realized she might have hurt his feelings. "It's too beautiful to open later," she said as she pulled at the ribbon. She looked up at him as the lush velvet fabric fell away from the clear box, revealing a most exquisite crystal globe. Suspended within the globe was a delicate, hand-painted angel. A thick ecru card lay on the top of the box. She opened it.

Merry Christmas, Neely
Jack

The gift is for me!

"It's beautiful, Jack. I don't know what to say."

"Say you like it."

"I love it, it's lovely. Thank you," she whispered, holding the box up for a better look. She looked at Jack. "What a sweet thing."

"Here you go, honey!" Patsy placed the Big Boy Feast and Neely's plate of eggs and white toast on the table with a thud. No finesse in this joint. She pulled a bottle of Louisiana Hot from deep in her apron pocket and placed it next to his plate. "Thought you might wanna see this," she said, handing Jack a copy of the local biweekly paper that moments before had been folded and held tightly in her armpit.

"That girl that breaks Lewter's ponies was just bout kilt' the day before yesterday. Run off the road. Looks like her little boy was in the car, too. Front page."

Jack unfolded the paper as Patsy ran on.

"Think it says her young'n is okay. I didn't get a chance to read the whole thing yet. Sure is a shame, though. Nice girl, hard worker, always friendly. She's a regular in here. Just sad, huh?"

Jack's whole demeanor changed as he nodded to Patsy. His whole body became rigid as a frown settled on his face.

"Do you know her?" Neely asked.

"Yes."

"I'll be right back with a refill, honey. Need anything else?"

Jack looked up from the paper. "I don't think so." He asked Neely, "Anything for you?"

She shook her head. He went back to reading the paper.

"Do they say how the accident happened?" Neely asked.

"It wasn't an accident," Jack said, still reading.

"What do you mean?"

He put the paper down and said, "Someone tried to kill her."

"Can I see you?" The strain in David's voice was clear.

"Well, I think I might be able to arrange that," she teased.

"When?"

"What about now?" he asked.

"Do you have your key?"

"I don't know what the hell I did with it."

"I'll leave the door open."

"Okay."

"David?"

"Yes?"

"I love you."

"Ditto."

Ditto? Gee, that's romantic.

He took off his khaki trench coat and Burberry hat, and threw them on the chair across from the sofa where she sat smiling, her legs tucked up under her. The things he came to say would wait. He wanted her.

"Hey you," she greeted; as he leaned down to kiss her. His hair was wet.

"Is it raining? She asked.

"Just started."

"Wanna sit in front of the fire?"

"Come," he said, leading her to the bedroom.

"I thought you wanted to talk."

"Later."

She unbuttoned her blouse as she watched him.

Something's wrong.

After undressing he came to her and whispered, "I love you." His mouth moved down the side of her neck. "I'm addicted to you. Do you know that?"

She laughed, grabbing his hand and pulling him into bed.

They made passionate love and afterwards lay in each other's arms, basking silently in their bliss.

She looked up at him and asked, "You happy, baby?"

He grinned like a Cheshire cat. "Bobo's happy as a clam!"

"What is it with you men, having to name your...your penis?"

He laughed, "Maybe because most men's lives are ruled by it. They're owed a little respect."

"No wonder half of the world is mad!" They both laughed, "I made my world famous crawfish bisque and sweet cornbread. Are you ready to eat?"

"As long as I'm back by ten 'til two."

"Plenty of time." She kissed him and got out of bed. She put on her robe and turned to him, taking in his body. "You're beautiful, you know that?"

They sat at the farm table like so many times before and smiled sweetly at each other. He poured the wine.

"Incredible," he said after finishing lunch.

"Glad you liked it."

"Loved it. Seriously, though, you're really a good cook."

"And I make my own shoes," she laughed, making a silly face.

"I'm sure you could if you set your mind to it," he mused.

"Oh, by the way, I met somebody through Jan who said he's known you for years."

"Who?" David asked about to take the last bite of his cornbread.

"Jack Bendix?"

David suddenly seemed uncomfortable.

"What's wrong?" Neely asked.

"Nothing."

"You look like I said something wrong."

"No," he insisted.

"He told me he was in partnership with your brother-in-law."

"He is. He doesn't live here, so I don't run into him that often."

Neely understood at once David was not interested in discussing Jack, so she let it drop.

"What did you want to talk to me about?" Neely asked, changing the subject.

He hesitated, and from the look on his face she knew it was something she didn't want to hear.

"I think Susie knows about us."

Neely knew her happiness was about to end. "Did she say something?"

"She said she heard some rumors, rumors I was seeing someone. I told her I wasn't. Her brother called me, sort of a warning kind of thing. He'd heard it, too."

Neely waited for her world to come crashing down.

"I was awake most of last night, trying figure out a way to make this work. I don't want to hurt Susie. She was crying and Brooke was asking what was wrong. I can't do this to them."

"What are you saying?"

"I don't want to hurt you. You know that. But you're strong Neely. Susie's not. If the kids were grown and gone, it would be a no brainer, I'd be here with you. But they aren't. And when Susie cries, asking me what she's done to deserve this, what do I tell her?"

"You tell her you don't love her anymore. That you're in love with me."

"But I do love Susie. Not the way I love you, not anything like it, but I think about taking away the life she's known and leaving her with nothing, and I don't know if I can do that. I don't want her to feel like she's a loser."

"Are you saying you don't want to see me anymore?"

"You know better than that. I will never say that to you. Never."

"Then what?"

"I don't know. I just wonder if I could live with myself if I left her. Could *we* be happy at her expense? I have a terrible feeling if you knew the real me, Neely, you wouldn't want me, you wouldn't love me."

"You want me to tell you I won't see you anymore, to make it easy for you? Or maybe you just want me to go away?"

"I don't know what to do. I'm just hurting her and I hate it. I don't want to hurt my children. And...I don't want to hurt you. Maybe we should lay low for a while. Just for a while. I just can't deal with any more blowups right now. There's too much going on."

"You waited to tell me this until *after* we made love?"

He hung his head, ashamed.

For the first time, she found him truly despicable.

David drove through the empty parking lot to the back of the building and parked next to the loading dock. He was the last to enter Summer Lumber. The security light above the door was burned out.

He fumbled in the dark before finding the doorknob. He opened the door where two small ceiling globes full of skeletonized insect carcasses faintly lit the hall. He walked past the entrance to the warehouse and a couple of closed doors, to the end of the hall where the business offices were located. He made out a muffled conversation coming from Michael's office.

He found Jack sitting in Michael's leather chair behind a large, black metal desk. Bill sat opposite the desk in a schoolroom-style wooden chair. A small radiant heater's fan made an irritating grinding sound. Everything in the room looked grimy, and the combination of the heater's bright red coils and the hooded florescent desk light create an eerie, harsh effect in the room and on the men's faces.

"Sorry I'm late."

"The Company says it's over," Jack said. "If they can't get the others now, they'll go ahead and take Barrett, if they can find him. It's obvious he's gone rogue...ignoring everyone and everything. Last we heard he was leaving Vegas but since a flight plan wasn't filed, we're not sure where he's heading."

"What about T?" David asked. "We can't let him get screwed."

"I've done all I can do," Jack answered pointedly. "The Company will ultimately make that call."

David looked down. "This is bad, Jack. T's already had enough shit in his life. He doesn't deserve this. He had no idea what he was getting into. Barrett bullied him into this. T was just trying to fit in, to be a friend."

Jack offered nothing.

David wouldn't let it rest. He turned to Bill. "Who do you know that could help? Surely there's somebody from the old days..."

Bill thought hard before answering. "There is one person who has that kind of clout, but I haven't talked to him in years."

"Call him."

"We went through some real crap together. Should count for something," Bill said.

"Thanks" David nodded to Bill.

Bill asked Jack. "When's it going down?"

"Within days."

"What do you want us to do?" Bill asked.

"Nothing, stay low, stay out of the way. If I can, I'll give you a heads up when the operation gets underway."

David felt the tightness in his chest grow.

"He's such an asshole," Neely said with conviction, but to her friends it appeared she was merely trying to convince herself.

Neely had invited Jan and Wallace over to catch up. They'd finished a wonderful dinner at The Mustard Seed and came up to the loft to where they could talk in private. Neely opened a bottle of wine and poured each a generous glass. They stood at the counter.

"He's a shit," Jan said flatly.

"But I know he loves you," Wallace said offhandedly.

"The point is, Wallace, if David can't or won't do what he should do, it doesn't matter, does it?" Jan asked.

"I'm not sure if that's true," Wallace resisted.

"That's bullshit, Wallace! You're giving Neely bad

advice," Jan barked.

"I've known him almost as long as I've known you," Wallace said, looking at Neely. "And I know without any doubt that the two of you belong together. You both are a little different..."

"What does that mean?" Neely asked.

"You know, all that artsy fartsy shit, reading all the time, painting. Hell, you're different and so is he. I've known Susie as long as I've known him and, believe me, I've never been able to figure that deal. At best it's just odd. He's exciting, smart, and cute. She's like one of those old women who, without a shit load of maintenance, would sprout a unibrow and need a full-time management team to control the hair running down the inside of her thighs!"

"Oh, god, Wallace, that is so disgusting!" Jan moaned.

Neely couldn't help laughing.

"It's true and we all know it. She reminds me of those village women in that Borat movie." Wallace headed for the club chair across from the sofa. The girls followed, settling comfortably in the seating around the fireplace.

Wallace kicked off her shoes, "and there's always been that rumor floating around that she's gay."

"Really?" Neely asked.

"I've heard it too," Jan, said. "A friend who's gay told me she was."

Neely looked shocked, "Why would he stay with a woman who's gay? Maybe she's bi."

"He's definitely a man's man. Why he stays with her is a mystery, whether she's gay or not. Could be she needs a cover and likes her lifestyle, but I wouldn't be surprised if she has something on him. That makes more sense," Jan surmised.

Neely's mind was racing, trying to process the new

information.

"Jellybean, you need to stick it out. You and that schmuck are perfect for each other."

"Gee, thanks, Wallace," Neely said sarcastically.

"I don't know why anyone would listen to you, Wallace," Jan fired back. "You're an idiot. David either doesn't have balls, or he's one of those dickheads who thinks he can have it all. He wants his cake and eat it too. He's an egomaniac *and* a pathologic liar. You deserve better, Neely. A lot better."

"He does love me, Jan."

"So what? He won't leave her, no matter how gross she is. He's using you. When someone truly loves, there is nothing in the world that would keep him or her from that person. *And*, if he loved you he wouldn't put you through all this pain. He just wouldn't."

You are so right, my sweet Jan.

Jan turned to Wallace. "And you're no help at all. You're encouraging her to go down a path to hell. So just stop."

"Well, thank god somebody is encouraging her!" Wallace declared, raising her glass in a toast. "To love, and having it your own frikin' way!"

"I think you need to call Jack and give him a chance. He's a great guy," Jan said, ignoring Wallace. "Get out of this *doo doo*. It's not your style. It's so sordid Neely. David is not going leave Susie, and you couldn't pry her out of that marriage with a crowbar. She has *zero* options. She'd never, ever get a man or woman again, let alone one like David. The tiny bud she had long, long ago is but a distant memory. Why do you think she keeps that ridiculous life-size portrait of herself in their foyer? Have you seen it? First and foremost, the artist, and I use the word lightly, has absolutely no talent and second, the thing looks *nothing* like her. Dorian Gray would be embarrassed."

Wallace laughed, "I've seen it. It's really bad on so many levels."

"I want to say one more thing and then I'm done," Jan said. "He's not *all that,* Neely. Really. I think you just want to be in love so much you've blinded yourself to his flaws. He knew you were vulnerable and he took advantage. He's very selfish and self-centered. There, I've said it."

"I'm trying to stop the image of that big ass woman climbing in the bed with David. She's almost twice his size and," Wallace grimaced," looks so soft, like mushy dough."

Jan rolled her eyes, "God, just stop, Wallace."

"Is Jack that gorgeous metrosexual you introduced me to at the club?" Wallace asked.

"That's Joe Samples," Jan said.

"He's not metrosexual, he's homosexual," Neely clarified, getting up to get the bottle of wine.

"How do you know he's gay?" Wallace asked, not convinced.

"Actually, it was Jack who figured it out."

"Tell me about this Jack!" Wallace demanded.

"Jack Bendix is an old friend," Jan said. "Handsome, smart, sweet. Neely sat next to him at my party. And he's really nice, and did I say handsome?"

"He *is* nice," Neely agreed.

"And did I say *single*?" Jan added sharply.

"I had breakfast with him the other day," Neely said.

"Really? Breakfast?" Wallace asked seductively.

"It was just breakfast, although he did bring me a beautiful ornament from Venice."

"*Really*? A gift?" Wallace repeated dramatically.

"Yes, Wallace. *Really*. Stop being so dramatic, you

sound like a fool."

"Well excuse me!" Wallace said pretending her feelings were hurt.

"Are you going to go out with him again?" Jan asked hopefully.

"It really wasn't a date. I don't know if he's interested in that way."

"Jan smiled, "I bet he is."

"You know it was weird though, when I mentioned him to David… about having met him. It's like David freaked out. Not like jealousy, but just that the fact I'd met him. I don't know why, but I feel like there's some strange deal going on there."

"Between David and Jack?" Jan asked.

"You mean like, gay?" Wallace jumped in.

"No, not gay," Neely answered. "But I can't figure it out, it's like David is hiding something."

"Well, what's new? Everything about David involves some form of hiding!" Jan said sarcastically. "But Jack's in business with Susie's brother, so they would know each other."

"It's probably nothing, but I couldn't help feeling he didn't like the idea I'd met him."

"He's probably jealous," Wallace chimed in.

"No, I already said that's not it."

Wallace, bored by it all said, "Well, then, stop worrying about it!"

"Fine, let's change the subject. What happened at your hearing?" Neely asked Wallace.

"They call it 'marriage arbitration.' Can you imagine? One good thing did come out of it. Drew agreed that if I didn't drag his whore into the deal, he won't ask for the house."

"Well that's something. Where's he living?" Neely asked.

"He rented a townhouse near his office."

"Why the change of heart?" Jan wondered. "I've never seen Drew as the gallant type, you know, putting protecting a fallen woman's reputation before his well being."

"You're right, he's not. I think it has more to do with the big guns Big Daddy hired."

"Now that makes sense," Neely said.

"Regardless of why, I'm glad you don't have to worry about the house. How's Hop?" Jan asked.

"He's wonderful. You know, he worries about me. No one's ever done that before."

"We worry about you, Wallace," Neely corrected.

"No one I've ever slept with."

Neely laughed. "Well, that eliminates us."

"He does love me, though." Wallace stopped, her voice choking up.

Jan reached over and squeezed her hand. "Oh, sweetie, don't."

"He wants to see me next week. It will be the first time since the party. It feels like it's been forever. I've been so sad without him."

"Do you think you should risk seeing him in the middle of all this?" Jan asked.

"I don't think it matters. Wendy couldn't be any meaner than she is right now. She's basically taking everything, badmouthing him to anyone who will listen, including his kids. Did I tell you she shredded all his clothes and threw them in the pool?"

Neely winced. "Jesus that is pissed."

"We don't care. Hop and I made a pact, that we'll get through this, together."

Jan and Neely smiled at Wallace, proud of their friend.

"I've never felt so unselfish about anything or anyone before and you *know* how selfish I am."

Neely and Jan burst into laughter as they nodded in agreement.

"I've never loved anyone like this, ever," Wallace said.

"We know, sweetie," Neely smiled.

Wallace brusquely rubbed her teary eyes and giggled. "Actually, there is this little matter of reclaiming our time in the loft..."

The weeks passed so slowly. She did everything possible to keep thoughts of him at bay. She painted, rode her bike, ran, saw friends, visited several of her retail stores and got away with Jan for an antique shopping trip to Charleston. And she did okay during the day, but when she climbed into bed each night it was a different story. She missed him so much. And if he loved her as he had so fervently professed, she didn't understand how he could simply choose not to call, not to see her. How could he think she was so strong? She, in fact, was so fragile. It was Susie who was a hard and frigid soul. If she truly loved David she wouldn't have been able to stay with him knowing he loved Neely. Susie's only concern was to preserve the status quo at all cost because without David, she was and had nothing.

Just another Hillary.

It was as if someone turned off a light, leaving Neely to walk alone in the dark. Her life seem to stop while those around her continued on. Olivia was going to Aspen for spring break with two girlfriends and asked her mother to join them. It was hard enough to maintain a semblance of sanity, alone, without trying to hide her pathology and pain from three young women full of happiness and life. She declined the invitation. Sam and his dad were going to Europe. She could mourn alone, in complete and utter self-indulgent misery.

Hop and Wallace fell deliciously back into their sweet affair, spending every Monday and Thursday afternoon in Neely's loft. With their divorces in the works, they no longer worried who knew.

David set his book down and sank back into the sofa. The house was quiet. He looked at the clock on the bookcase, 11:08 p.m.

He got up, walked down the hall from his study, and went to the bathroom before noiselessly entering the bedroom. He unbuttoned his shirt and, as quietly as possible, unzipped his pants. The last thing he wanted was to wake his wife.

The bedroom was dark and cool. He hung his pants over the back of the chair next to the bed, dropped his boxers on floor and climbed in, slowly pulling the sheets up to his chest. He felt every muscle in his body ease as he silently exhaled. He was spent.

Susie turned over and whispered softly, "David?"

Shit.

"Yeah?"

"What time is it?"

"It's late."

"What were you doing?"

"Reading."

Her hand found his arm.

He didn't want her. Her touch repulsed him. He didn't move, wishing she would leave him alone.

She moved her fingertips slowly up and down his arm. He turned on his side, away from her, but she moved close to him, pressing her thick body against his back. Her hand slid to his groin. She was determined, moving her hand lustfully over him. He closed his eyes, tight. He was flooded with self-loathing as he became hard.

He struggled to visualize Neely, furiously desperate to shut out the reality of the physical lust he could not control. He *saw* Neely and could almost feel her soft, full mouth, as if she were there, that moment. He tried to imagine every part of her, the pieces of her that gave him so much pleasure. He envisioned touching her face with his hands. He *saw* her eyes searching his, her mouth open. He could *feel* her breath on his neck; *hear* the sounds she made when her body quaked, as their ecstasy swelled to a crescendo.

"David?" Susie murmured seductively, instantly fracturing the precious illusion.

He rolled over and faced his wife. She smiled triumphantly. He hated her. He closed his eyes and hopelessly fought to recapture the vision of his sweet baby, to mask out and rid himself of the endomorphic woman hunching herself against him.

If only I could smell her perfume...breathe her in.

Susie moved her fingers to his ass.

He reached out and roughly pulled his wife, this *thing*, to him. The exquisite thoughts of his love could not be saved as he forced his hand over his wife's fleshy, protruding belly. He shut his eyes tight before putting his hand between her thighs.

He spread her short legs with his and fucked her, making a loud, guttural grunt as he came. The grotesque debacle lasted less than three minutes.

Neely sat at the table drinking a glass of wine while finishing off a bag of chips. She picked up the latest edition of the local paper and flipped through the ten pages of mostly advertisements, when a small header reading, Local Horse trainer goes Home from Hospital caught her attention. Neely read with interest, trying to find, perhaps, a clue as to what connection Jack had to David. The short paragraph revealed nothing. It appeared the young woman was to make a complete recovery despite numerous serious injuries and major surgery. The last line however, gave her pause.

"The crash has been determined to have been a deliberate act of sabotage although the police have not identified any leads or suspects."

How did Jack know with such certainty someone had tried to kill her only days after it happened?

Le Mon

Neely flipped through the stack of mail. She removed a letter addressed to her. It was a letter from David. Her heart stopped. She set the rest of the mail on the table and opened the envelope.

A winter's sleet of nerves frayed raw
A voice from within the soul screams out
A voice not heard but felt.

The remembrance of youth
The thoughts of age
I cannot recall without some memory fault
blown together in an imperturbable blur.
Obe and cello, an elegante melody

Footsteps in the sand
Snow melting into the earth

But with clarity I loved you close
No dim thoughts have I

And you remain, my love,
The closest thing to a permanent possession
I will ever have.

Cornbread Mafia

David

She sat at the table, put her head down, and cried.

February

Endless rainy and cold days mirrored her emotional state. His letter crippled her. He was in pain, too. So much so, he was compelled to write this beautiful, heart-wrenching poem. In some sick way it gave her hope but sadly, not enough to keep her from sleeping fourteen hours a day. Her bed, her sleep, were her only respites' from the physical ache of breathing without him.

It was after Neely cancelled Wallace and Hop's use of the apartment for a third consecutive time, feigning the flu that her friends realized Neely was suffering from love sickness, a much more threatening illness than a virus. They decided to come to Summerville and rescue her from herself.

Wallace unlocked the door with her key. She looked to the alarm pad. It was off. Jan called out from the bottom of the stairs, "Neely! Don't freak…it's us. Neely!"

Neely woke as they entered her bedroom. Fred was curled up next to her. Two petrified, half empty cereal bowls were stacked next to an assortment of dirty glasses on the nightstand. Clothes were scattered all over the floor.

Jan and Wallace sat on the bed next to her.

"What are you doing here?" Neely asked, straightening the t-shirt she'd had on for three days.

"Do you know what time it is?" Wallace asked.

Neely shook her head.

"It's one o'clock…in the afternoon."

Neely said nothing. She looked haggard despite her sleep marathon. Her hair was wild and tangled.

"Come on," Jan said softly, "hop up and go get in the shower. We brought some lunch. Come on."

Neely shuffled to the bathroom.

The sound of running water gave cover to Jan's words. "Good god, she looks horrible. This is bad. We need to get her out of here."

"No shit," Wallace agreed, as she gathered up dirty clothes from the floor.

"Then that's what we're going to do, right?"

Wallace nodded.

While Neely finished showering, Jan and Wallace changed the sheets, cleaned the kitchen, and set the table for lunch.

Jan revealed their plan minutes after they all sat down to eat.

"Wallace and I are going to Atlanta and we are taking you with us. The Ritz is calling us…*all* of us," Jan laughed.

"We'll leave by ten next Thursday and return sometime Sunday. We won't take no for an answer," Wallace said resolutely.

Neely looked at them sadly. "I know what you're doing, but going to Atlanta is not going to help. I'm going to get a hold of this, I promise. I'm fine."

Jan stood firm. "Don't even start. You are going."

It had been four days since her friends came to Summerville. She sat in front of the muted TV, drinking coffee, with Fred curled up in her lap. After Wallace and Jan's visit, she slowly reduced her daily sleeping time and made a real effort to get up in the morning and push her way through the rituals of life.

Thursday

Her bag was packed and on the elevator. Just a couple of hours before she'd be on her way to the Ritz, just like old times.

The phone rang. She looked at the clock on the wall. Six forty-two.

Oh God, let it be David.

She looked at the phone. The caller I.D. read David O'Donnell.

Breathe.

"Hello."

"Come to the front window. Hurry."

She jumped up, throwing Fred in a half-sleep state to the floor.

She looked out of the big window, down to the street below.

"I see you," he said.

He was at the stoplight. He flashed the Porsche's lights.

"Did you get the poem?"

"Yes."

She watched as his car passed her building and out of sight.

An uncomfortable silence prevailed.

He finally said, "Can I see you?"

She did not answer.

"Please. There are things I want to say."

"When?"

"Tomorrow?

No, Neely...No!

"What time?"

"The usual?"

Say no, Neely!

But "okay" flowed out of her mouth, as if her tongue and brain belonged to the enemy.

"I've missed you, baby girl," he whispered, before hanging up.

What have I done?

"Jan?" Neely said into the phone.

"Neely?"

"I can't go."

"What?

"I can't go."

"Why?"

"I'm just not feeling good."

"You'll feel better if you go. I promise. It'll be fun. You need to get out of there, change the scenery. Listen to me, I know."

"I just can't. I'm sorry, Jan."

"He called you, didn't he?" There was rage in Jan's voice.

Neely said nothing.

"Don't do this. He's bad for you. I'm telling you this because I love you."

Neely remained silent.

"What the hell did he tell you? That he loves you, wants to see you? What words did he use to make you think he'll leave her? I can tell you, nothing's changed!   Nothing! He's married, he's selfish, and he's a fucking liar! He's not thinking about you!"

Neely held tight to her silence.

"You know, it's rude to do this to me, to Wallace. You put Eric first and now you're doing it with David! I'm sick of it, Neely. Fed up. You're not acting like my friend or anybody else's."

"I know it's wrong, but I have to see him. I'm so sorry. I am."

"What's wrong with you? I don't know who you are anymore."

"Please be my friend. Don't abandon me. I may be wrong but I need you."

"No, Neely, you don't," Jan's voice was flat, void of emotion. "You know, I'm beginning to see that *this* is not good for *me*. I can't stand around with my hands tied behind my back and watch this train wreck one minute more. Call me when you wake up."

"Jan don't—please."

"I'm going to tell you something I hope will open your eyes."

Neely waited for the next blow as tears welled.

"Wallace said she heard people at the Guild meeting talking about how you've gone off the deep end and were stalking some guy."

How much more can I endure?

269

"I've heard," she said wiping away tears.

Jan was stunned.

"A woman in town started it. She has a thing for David and I guess she's angry."

"Oh my god Neely, can't you see that if he loved you, he wouldn't let this happen to you? He'd protect you, defend you, not have you exposed to all this sleazy shit. Steven would never let this happen to me. Can you see the difference Neely? Jan pleaded, "God, please come with us."

"I have to talk to him. Maybe I can finally put it to rest if I talk to him."

Painful moments passed before Jan said sadly, "I'm finished. I'm done. You're blind and on a path to pure shit and I won't be a part of it, I don't want to see it and I won't enable you, because I love you, unlike David."

Jan hung up.

She heard him running up the stairs at a fast clip. He came around the corner with a single red rose between his teeth. He stopped for just a moment, took the rose out of his mouth and came to her. He encased her in his arms and lifted her off the ground. He began passionately kissing her, on her neck, on her face, and chest.

She didn't care why. He was here. He was with her.

Neither of them spoke as they undressed each other, almost tearing their clothes off in passionate delirium. They discarded clothes haphazardly on the floor, sofa, and chair. They kissed as they crab walked, naked, toward the bedroom. Just as they moved around the kitchen church altar, he stopped, and lifted her up on its counter top. He moved in close and spread her legs. She lay back and closed her eyes. He slowly ran his hand from her knee to her pelvis, while his mouth, as soft as a velvet glove, slid up the inside of her thigh.

A half hour later he lowered himself off her and helped her down from the counter. They looked at each other and burst out laughing.

She walked to the bedroom to get her robe and called back, still laughing, "Mr. O'Donnell, I think I have some of that yellow crime scene tape in the pantry and I suggest you cordon off the kitchen before someone really gets hurt."

From that moment on, it was like old times.

T nursed Kate back to health. The surgeries to repair her ruptured spleen and broken leg were successful and her recovery was progressing well. T kept fresh flowers throughout the house to cheer her in the dark hours of winter and Tutt, her sweet little boy was happy to cuddle with his mother every afternoon upon returning home from day school.

T's efforts to make Kate feel safe were working, but for T, he feared the worst was yet to come. He was afraid to his core.

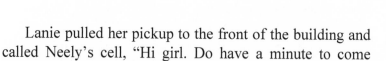

Lanie pulled her pickup to the front of the building and called Neely's cell, "Hi girl. Do have a minute to come down and help me get a little sofa up to my studio?"

Neely tucked her cell phone into her jean's pocket, put on a down jacket and slipped into her loafers. She headed down the stairs.

"You're a doll! Isn't this the most outrageous thing you've ever seen?" Lanie asked, walking to the back of the truck. Lanie let the tailgate down revealing a hot pink sofa.

"Outrageous and fabulous!" Neely grinned. And it was. A very dainty Victorian love seat's frame was painted a shiny bubblegum pink and upholstered in black and white cowhide.

As they slid the sofa to the end of the truck bed, a nasally voice offered, "You need some help?"

They turned to find Daphne standing next to them.

"Hi, Lanie," Daphne greeted, totally ignoring Neely.

"Hi, Daphne. We sure could use an extra hand," Lanie said, giving Neely a look, as if to say, *what can I do*?

The three of them brought the love seat up the stairs and set it in Lanie's studio.

"Looks pretty cool if I say so myself," Lanie said proudly. "Thanks ladies!"

Daphne was already at the door. "See you later, Lanie."

"Daphne?" Neely called to Daphne.

"What?" she turned back to Neely, looking irritated.

"Do you have a minute?"

"Why?" Daphne asked.

"I want to talk to you. It won't take but a minute."

"I have a *minute*," Daphne said firmly.

"We can talk up in the loft."

Lanie busily placed and fluffed the cushions on the sofa, trying to physically extricate herself from the exchange. Neely give Lanie a little wave and a stolen, exaggerated grimace before leaving.

Daphne kept a scowl on her face as she followed Neely down the hall, up the stairs, and into the living room.

"Have a seat," Neely offered.

"I'd rather stand."

"Suit yourself," she said, looking directly at Daphne. "I've heard you've been telling people I'm stalking David and I want to know why."

"I don't know what you're talking about."

"Daphne, I've heard it from several people and they all say they heard it from you."

"What you do is none of my business. I could care less. I'm not interested in discussing you or your problems," Daphne quipped.

"You're absolutely right. It isn't any of your business, but when you go around saying things about me that aren't true it becomes *my* business and *your* problem. Why are you talking about me? You don't even know me."

"I'm simply defending a friend."

"David?"

"Yes, David. I'm protecting him."

"David doesn't need protecting."

"I think he does. You're lying about him and it's wrong and I'm not going to sit back and let you get away with it."

"What you are talking about? I don't talk about David to anyone in this town."

"You're telling people you're having an affair with him

and he's too much of a gentleman to call you a liar."

"We *are* having an affair," Neely heard herself saying, as clear as day.

Shit!

Daphne smiled smugly. "You're such a liar, no wonder people don't like you."

People don't like me?

Neely was mystified by Daphne's apparent self-directed need to protect David's reputation. She was still trying to sort out the ferret's odd motivation as she continued in a matter of fact tone, "The truth is, Daphne, we *are* having an affair. But what I don't understand is what business is it of yours? Aren't you married?"

Daphne's face turned a frightening shade of magenta that flushed down her neck to her chest in big streaks. Her thin nostrils flared wide and she snorted before shrieking, "You're a bitch! For the record, if he were going to have an affair with anybody, it would be with me! David O'Donnell happens to be in love with me."

Holy shit!

Neely's body flinched. She didn't see that coming. She quickly composed herself and walked over to the phone base on the end table next to the sofa and pushed the *play* button of her message center. As one after another of David's messages played, expressing intimate messages of love, the purple blood vessels in Daphne's face appeared to grow and throb. Neely could see Daphne's body become hard as her long fingers started to twitch.

Neely spoke calmly, "From now on, don't speak my name or say anything about my relationship with David. *We* are not your business."

Daphne's icy stare unexpectedly transformed as the corners of her mouth curled. Her wild eyes and bizarre smile were completely abnormal and frightening. Neely shuttered.

The ferret freakishly cackled, turned, and walked out, slamming the door behind her.

Neely had a wonderful conversation with David over her first cup of coffee. He was on his way to Leeton for a jury trial and called her from his car. He laughed about how his daughter Brooke came to him the night before, requesting he pull her loose tooth, and the crazy antics leading up to him pulling it. He then surprised her by telling her was planning a trip to South Carolina to see his mother, and he wanted her to go with him. His mother knew about Neely and was happy her son was finally happy. She had never been a fan of Susie's.

Neely was over the moon. The idea of being able to be *normal* with him, to go to dinner, meet his mother and not worry who might see them, to fall asleep and wake up in his arms, sounded like pure heaven.

What great way to start the day!

She took a shower, made her bed, and began working on a large canvas. She was excited about the piece. She'd never done anything quite so big or ever worked with a palette knife. As she squirted large globs of oil in every color onto the cover of a Neiman's catalog, the phone rang. The caller ID read "private."

"Hello."

"This is Susie O'Donnell."

Neely was stunned. "Hello, Susie."

"We need to talk," she said. "We can meet at your apartment, at David's office, or in a field for all I care."

A field? Was she suggesting a dual?

"I don't think that's a good idea."

"You've been through this yourself," Susie said. "I know you understand how I feel."

"I'm sorry, but you need to talk to David."

"I want for all of us to sit down and talk."

"Please, call David."

"I've asked him and he denies everything. I know he's seeing you."

"You think if we meet, he'll tell you the truth?" Neely asked.

"Yes, if he has to face us both."

"He would lie."

"Not if we both confront him," Susie insisted.

"I don't want to confront him," Neely said. "I'm sorry, but I don't have anything to say."

"You're not sorry. You're some crazy bitch who needs to get a life and leave my husband alone. You're a fucking whore."

"I'm going to hang up."

"You think you know him? Trust me, you don't know him."

Neely didn't answer. She didn't want to argue with her. "I am sorry. I am, I mean that."

"Yeah, you're sorry all right. I do want to thank you, though. Our sex life has never been better. You brought him back to me."

Susie's words cut to Neely's heart. She tried to sound confidant saying, "If everything is so wonderful, Susie, why are you calling me?"

Susie exploded. "Are you just out to destroy my life?"

"No."

"Then why are you doing this to me?"

Neely said nothing.

"Answer me! Why are you destroying my family?"

"We fell in love…it just happened…it wasn't planned. I do know how you feel and I'm sorry but we love each other."

Susie burst out laughing. "He doesn't love you. You're deranged, you need help."

"I'm going to hang up now," Neely said.

"I want you to know one thing—I'm not going anywhere!"

"Neither am I," Neely said quietly and hung up.

Later that Afternoon

She heard the courthouse clock tower strike six and, like magic, the phone rang.

"Hey, baby." His voice was cheery.

"You're still alive?" Neely asked, truly amazed by his upbeat mood.

"What do you mean?"

"Have you talked to Susie?"

"No."

"She called me right after I talked to you this morning. She knows everything and told me she wanted all of us to meet...*in your office, in my apartment, or a field.*"

"A field?"

"Yes, that's what she said, a field."

He laughed.

"Why are you laughing?"

"What did you tell her?" David asked.

"Nothing at first and then, well, that I wasn't going to meet with her and that we couldn't help how we feel. She kept saying she wanted all of us to meet, so you'd tell the truth. I told her you'd lie."

He roared.

"I swear, David, I can't believe you're not upset, that you find this funny."

"Well, I'm not happy, but there's nothing I can do at this point." He laughed again. "I can't believe you told her I'd lie."

"Why is that amusing to you?"

"It just is."

"There are only two things I'm sure of, David. One, you love me, and two, you're a liar."

"I only lie to her."

"Right."

"If she calls back, don't say anything."

"What do you mean?"

"Just don't engage."

"I'm not going to lie, David."

"Are you angry?" he asked teasingly. "Does this mean having a glass of wine is off the table?"

"Are you kidding?"

"No, I was planning on coming over for a minute if that's still okay. Is it?"

Bewildered and unsettled, she agreed.

"I'll see you in about fifteen. Leave the door unlocked."

"Have you not found your keys?"

"They're around here somewhere."

"I don't want her to get ahold of them, David."

"You worry too much, baby."

"I can just see her barging in, shooting us both."

He laughed. "She'd never do that."

"I wouldn't bet my life on it."

After they made love, he held her tight.

Don't ask him.

"What's going to happen to us?" she asked, unable to stop herself.

"I don't know."

"What do you want to happen?"

He frowned. "I'm here, aren't I?"

"What does that mean?"

"It means I love you and I choose to be with you."

"But...she knows."

"I told her I wouldn't see you again."

"But you're here."

He pulled her close. "I know I love you and will until the day I die. You are...my last and only love."

He kissed her and said, "The other day as I was on my bike ride, I started having chest pains..."

She reached out and touched his arm.

He took her hand and squeezed it. "I'm fine. It lasted just a couple of seconds but the only thing I could think of was *you*...not my children...not Susie...just you...worrying if something happened to me, you'd never know until it was too late. He went on, "When I got back to the office, I told Will that if anything happens to me, I want him to call you, first."

The sun had long set and the mix of rain and sleet pelted the big windows in the loft. The pure, innocent love she felt for him only a short time ago was tainted, bittersweet, because she understood with a terrible certainty, each time they made love, he would leave, perhaps forever. Every time he left, pangs of regret and loneliness reigned. She knew somehow in the deepest part of her heart it could not last.

A heart that raced to dance with mine
now slows gentle in rhythm
while the sweet chorus of love's spent labored breath
rises and falls to silence
My legs curl and wrap your hips,
my breasts against your back,
my pelvis snug in the small of your spine
We cling...wet...bodies now cool...spent.
Time ticking...running out...running out...running...running
Out.
The voice I love whispers, "stay".
Our lips melt but hunger keeps.
More
Time...running out...running
Out.
Disappearing soft steps rob me...

Le Mon

no air...no light...no joy.
And with the click of a lock
the cavernous black void of gnawing want
slips in to lie beside me·)
I am cold.

She never gave the poem to him but the words she wrote were a presage of the terrible things to come.

On Monday morning, he called at a little past seven thirty, as he always did.

"Hey, you," she answered smiling. "How are you this morning?"

"I'm here."

"No bowl of cherries?"

The silence set in like a hard freeze.

"What's wrong?"

"Susie has had a private investigator follow me for the past week. She somehow has gotten copies of your phone bills and basically knows every time we've talked or been together. Leslie, Susie's gay friend from Madison, who isn't capable of keeping his nose out of other people's business, and is a snake, hired a private eye for her. I'd like to break the little prick's legs but his feet are so fucked up naturally, I will let them torment him for me" David said furiously. "I had Clyde pick up the PI. They questioned and roughed him up enough to send a clear message to stay out of Summerville. I got the copies of your phone bills back, but Susie rummaged through my office and found your letters and poems and won't give them back."

Neely remained silent, knowing it was the end.

"She threatened to pull Brooke and Bud out of bed last night and take them, god knows where."

Tears rolled down Neely's face.

"She's using the kids to keep me from you."

"What kind of mother uses her own children to control her husband?"

"I can't hurt my children Neely. I know she's wrong but I won't hurt my children."

Silence.

"What will you do without me?" she asked. "What will we do without each other?"

He said with a broken heart, "Slowly die."

She fell to the floor sobbing and awoke, hours later. The room was dark. Her eyes were swollen almost shut and her body ached.

She stumbled in the dark to the bathroom. She turned the on water in the shower, took off her clothes, and stepped into the warm water. She leaned her full weight against the stone and wept.

Le Mon

The torrential sleet pounded the roof of his Porsche until the car was well into the garage. There was a relief in the silence. He turned the car off and sat as the garage door rumbled closed. He stared at the wall in front of him, cluttered with tools, sporting equipment, and bicycles and thought of Neely, how she must be hurting. He leaned forward, resting his forehead on the top of the steering wheel and closed his eyes. He felt complete and total loss.

The door to the garage opened. Susie sneered at him before closing it. He gathered up his papers and got out of the car. He didn't want to talk to her. He wanted Neely.

The kitchen was dark. He put his keys and papers on the counter and headed for the den.

"David," Susie's voice called from the darkened corner of the room. He turned, squinting. He could barely make out her silhouette. She sat at the kitchen table.

"Why are you sitting in the dark?"

She didn't respond.

"Fine. Don't answer," he said.

"Sit down, David."

"It's been a long day."

"Sit down."

He flipped on the light, revealing Susie's bloodshot eyes. He sat in the wooden chair next to the computer desk and waited for the other shoe to drop.

"I've always let you do what...what you needed to do, to have your... *freedom*."

He said nothing.

"You've always had the good sense to be discreet. We both have. I knew they meant nothing, and no one ever really knew but me. But now, everyone knows... about...her and you've made me the laughingstock of Summerville. The fucking kids know, David."

"Because you told them!" he yelled,

"I had to. How else could I make you stop?"

He shook his head in despair, realizing how sick the whole mess had become, "I told you, it's over."

"How am I supposed to believe you when I heard you were at..."

"You heard what?" he screamed.

"Do you love her?" She asked, sounding pitiful, broken.

His eyes were steely, his voice harsh. "No, I don't."

"I want you to promise you won't see her again."

"Goddamn it! Didn't I just fucking tell you it's over?" he shouted, knocking the chair into the wall as he abruptly stood. "I don't want to hear about this again!"

"David...I just need you to..." she continued, pleading.

"It's done." He walked out of the kitchen.

Two days later Neely wrote Susie. She decided she would not lie down nor simply fade away into the woodwork, unheard. She knew he loved her and she knew it was not over.

Susie,

You may have won the battle, but the war is not yours to win or lose. David and I share a love that will remain intact until the day we die. It is not a choice either of us has. I don't expect you to understand.

He is trying to remain fair to you because he feels a sense of commitment and responsibility. He loves his children and doesn't want to hurt them. His personal fear of the unknown and his honest desire to limit the hurt and humiliation he has caused you torments him.

He cares for you and loves you but don't confuse the love he has for you with the kind of love that compels a man to breathe the essence of a woman into his soul, the kind that completes him, the kind that makes him feel immortal, the kind he has with me.

I know deep in my heart with absolute certainty, that at the end of each and every day for the rest of his life, when he lies down and closes his eyes, his thoughts will drift to me. The singular magic of us, created by our laughter, our intellectual symmetry and the exquisite passion we feel for each other, has woven a complex union that cannot be broken. Haunting thoughts of "what might have been," will creep like an evocative demon if you keep him from me. These treasured thoughts of "us" will, in time, become my insidious warriors.

When he chooses to come back into my life, he need only come. The door will never be closed to him. I write these words not to hurt you, but to be honest, finally, as you have professed to want.

Neely

At 8:15 a.m. Jack walked past Janet at the front desk, straight back to David's office, ignoring all the dregs of society who had congregated in the waiting room hoping to be saved. He opened the door without knocking. David was on the phone. Jack closed the door and took a seat across

from David, who quickly ended his phone call.

"They raided Medellin four hours ago. It was a good hit," Jack said.

"And T?" David said looking anxious and worn.

"You got lucky. The Delta boys stick together. You owe Bill, big time."

David's head dropped like a discarded puppet with broken strings and took a deep breath. He looked up at Jack and asked fearfully, "And me?"

"You *are* one lucky son of a bitch. Why? I have no idea, but you are."

David put his hand to his mouth and squeezed his lips. Tears filled his eyes.

"But, David, the Company can only do so much. We didn't get them all. There will be suspicion...you didn't go down...and they'll wonder. I've done everything I can do to keep your cover, but there's no guarantee."

"I know."

"Well I guess that does it," Jack said, rising.

"Jack." David's voice sounded uncharacteristically shrinking. "And Sandy?"

"I told you a long time ago, David, you do everything you should as a father, and I'll keep quiet. She'll never know, unless you tell her. My word is my bond."

David nodded gratefully.

Jack walked to the door. Before opening it, he turned to David and said dispassionately, "With any luck, I'll never see you again."

David sat deathlike long after Jack was gone.

Three Days Later

He left the office early. He was having unrelenting, sharp chest pain. His mind whirled with visions of Barrett being arrested, if they could find him, the raid in South America, T, his family's safety, Sandy and...Neely. He pulled into his garage, noting several cars and trucks belonging to Bud's friends in the parking area adjacent to the garage.

Fuck!

Susie was in the pantry looking for something. She poked her head into the kitchen as he entered from the garage. She had been crying, again.

How much more can I take?

Susie stormed into the room to her purse on the counter. She tore through it, ripping out a letter. She shoved the paper into his chest, pushing him back.

"You son of a bitch."

He opened the letter and began reading.

Susie,
  You may have won the battle, but the war is not

288

yours to win or lose. David and I
    share a once in a lifetime love that will remain until
the day we die...

He stopped reading and looked at his wife.

"You better understand something, you son of a bitch. You fucking leave me, and I'll tell Sandy everything. Everything! And your sorry ass, I promise, will be in the goddamn slammer when I'm done."

"Don't threaten me about Sandy."

"I'll threaten you about any goddamn thing I want!"

"If you tell her, you are fucking yourself."

"I'm already fucked!"

He put the crumpled paper on the kitchen counter and walked past Susie. She grabbed the letter.

"Don't you walk away from me while I'm talking to you!" she screamed.

He continued walking.

"I want you to get on the goddamn phone and call that bitch right now. You tell her it's over! You hear me? I want to hear you tell her it's over!"

David continued to his study where he collapsed in his reading chair. He closed his eyes, fumbling with the buttons of his overcoat. Susie wildly waved the letter inches from his face.

"You will not ignore me, David O'Donnell!" She shrieked. "You call that bitch now!"

Brooke appeared behind her mother. "Why are you yelling, Mom? What's wrong, Daddy? Everybody can hear you."

"Go downstairs, Brooke," David said firmly.

Brooke looked fearfully from her dad to her mother.

"Baby girl, go downstairs, now," David repeated

strongly without looking at his daughter.

Brooke didn't move.

"Now." Her father shouted.

Brooke caught her mother's eyes before she retreated back downstairs to the rec room. Susie was crazed, out of control.

"David, look at me!" Susie screamed.

He turned the TV on and scanned the available shows with the satellite programmer.

"You son of a bitch," she panted, trying to catch her breath.

He stared at the TV. She no longer existed.

Her arms dropped limply to her sides, letting the letter fall to the floor. With a red face and tears streaming, she turned away from him and left, slamming the door so hard the walls shook.

He found a North Carolina basketball game on ESPN and intently focused on it, struggling to put everything out of his mind, including the pain in his chest that now cut like a knife all the way to the middle of his back.

Five minutes into the game, the pain in his chest slowly began to subside. He stood slowly and took off his coat, throwing it to the floor in a pile. He sat back heavily in his chair and took the first deep breath he'd had in hours.

He watched the TV screen as head coach Roy Williams pulled Brice Johnson off the court during a timeout. Suddenly the TV screen flicked and the game was gone, replaced by The Voice. David jumped up with such ferocity he knocked his leather recliner on its side. He swung the door open and headed for the down the stairs rec room. He yelled, "Bud!"

As he hit the landing, he tripped and fell into the wall at the bottom of the stairs. Bud, four of his friends, and

Brooke who were sitting on the floor in front of a gigantic flat screen TV, froze, as their David struggled to get up. Once on his feet he headed for Bud, whose hands went up in a defensive posture.

"No, Daddy!" Brooke screamed.

"I told you're never to change the goddamn satellite when I'm watching upstairs!" He shouted, jerking Bud by his t-shirt up off the floor. He began pounding his son's chest with his fists, all the while Bud tried to protect himself. But David being twice his son's size, Bud was no match. It wasn't until David realized Brooke was hanging on his arm, screaming, that he stopped. Bud fell to the floor, broken, holding his chest. Brooke continued screaming hysterically. Bud's petrified friends were motionless and horrified. Susie stood in the doorway of the room, her hands covering her gaping mouth.

David's eyes were wild. Gasping for breath, he pushed Susie out of the way and staggered up the stairs.

"Mom? I'm sick," Neely's son, Sam moaned. His sounded wretched.

"What's wrong, sweetie?"

"I think I have the flu and I'm really sick."

"Did you go to the clinic?"

"I'm too sick."

"You want me to come?"

"Yes. Can you?"

"I'll leave as soon as I can. I'll call you when I get on the road."

"Thanks, Mom. I'm so sick."

She hadn't been out of the house in days, holed up with her grief. Now she had to be a real person, a mother, and leave the loft to take care of her son.

She rang Caroline. "I've got to go to Auburn. Sam's sick. It sounds like he has the flu."

"Oh, no, poor thing."

"I think he'll be fine, he just needs a little TLC. Would you check on Fred? I probably won't be gone for more than a couple of days."

"Have you heard from the asshole or the *big woman*?"

"No, and I won't."

"Oh, you will."

"Don't, Caroline. I can't think about it."

"Sorry, just try to forget about everything here and enjoy your visit with Sam."

"I'm going to try. Oh yeah, I almost forgot, Wallace and Hop are still coming up on Mondays and Thursdays. If I'm not coming back by Thursday, I'll call you."

"Text me when you get to Auburn, so I don't worry. I'll check on Fred and bring in the mail. Give Sam a big hug for me."

"Thanks, Caroline. I love you."

"Love you, too."

"Where in the hell are you?" Wallace asked.

"Auburn. Sam's sick. He needs his mama."

"Why don't you let somebody know when you up and leave?"

"I did. I told Caroline. She's going to check on Fred."

"Well, thanks a lot. I could check on Fred."

"Wallace, you know you wouldn't come to Summerville every day to check on Fred."

"I'm there twice a week. I could have checked on him then."

"You still can, darling. I told Caroline when you'd be there and for her to stay away."

"Thank you."

"How are you?"

"Great. Drew and I have sort of worked things out. I think he's about as sick of me as I am of him."

Neely laughed. "I guess that's good?"

"Very. And by the way, Hop thinks he found a place for us, so darling, in very short time your wonderful loft will again be yours and yours alone!"

"Well good for you. Have you seen Jan? I haven't talked to her in over a week. She's still mad at me you know," Neely said.

"She's doing good, busy, raising money for the museum. And yeah, she's really upset with you."

"I know."

"She'll get over it. She's just too damn strict" Wallace laughed.

"I think she is too, but I hate it anyway. I miss her, miss talking to her." Neely sounded sad.

"Guess what? I met your friend the other night at Christopher's and Libby's party," Wallace teased.

"Who?"

"Jack Bendix. He's a cutie Neely."

"He is, isn't he?"

"When I told him I was your best girlfriend in the whole wide world, he told me he thought you were pretty

293

fabulous. The man is charming…he told me I was cute, too."

"No wonder you think he's charming."

"And I suspect, he has balls. That should count for something."

Neely raised her eyebrows. "What's this? You, down on David?"

"All I said was I think Jack has balls."

"Are you insinuating David doesn't?"

"Hell no, I'm telling you flat out. He fucking has no balls."

"What? You, his biggest fan? What happened?" Neely asked sarcastically.

"I *have* been his biggest fan but you know, as time goes on and he does nothing, I have to figure I was wrong. Chalk it up to my previously drug-induced state."

Neely said nothing as the floodgates of pain opened.

"Too much?" Wallace regretted bringing him up.

"Uh huh."

"Not my intent. You know?"

"I know. No one can help he's a dick," Neely said.

"Still, I didn't mean…"

"It's fine. You're just speaking the truth and it's hard."

"I get it, Jellybean. It's shitty. He's shitty."

"But you know, Wallace, I have always believed things happen for a reason and I want to believe something good will come out of this."

"Me too. I know that when all is said and done you'll be better than ever."

"Thanks, Wallace."

"When are you coming home?"

"Thursday, I think. I might stay a couple more days and visit if Sam doesn't run me off. I'll let you know."

"Hop and I will be there Thursday until about three, unless that's not good for you."

"No worries. I wasn't planning on coming back until six or so. Your afternoon is safe." Neely grinned.

"Tell Sam his *aunt* Wallace misses him."

The sound of frozen grass crunching broke the early morning quiet as FBI agents crept toward the darkened trailer. They slipped by the silver Mustang and a mixed-breed hunting dog chained to a dirty, broken down doghouse. The hound, curled up deep in the doghouse lifted its head in half-hearted interest as the five men continued to the front door. It was too cold for the dog to investigate the activity.

The sun broke over the distant pines as two agents moved in to stand on either side of the front door. Another agent ran toward the door, hopping the two concrete block steps, and flung himself, full force, into the hollow door. It fell off its hinges and into the trailer with a crash. The agents quickly charged through the small living room and kitchen, toward the back of the trailer.

They rushed down the narrow hall to the bedroom where they found their target trying to climb out the window. A scraggly young girl, barely in her teens, sat up in bed screaming.

"Please don't hurt me!" she squealed, pulling the thin, faded, floral sheet to her chin.

The man, attempting escape, wearing only his underwear, was pulled from the window and thrown face down across the bed on top of the girl's legs. The agents cuffed him.

"Scott Summerville, you are charged with the attempted murder of Kate LeBron and her minor son, Tutt LeBron. You have the right to remain silent and refuse to answer questions. Anything you say may be used against you in a court of law. You have the right to consult an attorney before speaking to the police and to have an attorney present during..."

"Fuck you!" Scott yelled, as they pulled him by his arms from the bed.

"...Questioning now or in the present. If you decide to answer questions now without an attorney present..."

"I know my fuckin' rights! I want my goddamn lawyer. I have nothing to say to you fuckers!"

The agents pushed him down the hall.

"Get me some fuckin' pants!" Scott yelled.

They continued moving him through the trailer. One agent went back to the bedroom to get a pair of pants and question the girl.

"Watch your head," were the last words Scott heard before they slammed the back door of the black, unmarked Ford.

Fifteen miles across town, three unmarked black SUVs raced through the open gates of Barrett's compound. The cars continued down the long drive to the main house, screeching to a halt at the front door. Eight men in black SWAT gear jumped out of the cars with their guns drawn.

They climbed the steps to the verandah and waited in total silence as one agent tried the front door. It was unlocked. He motioned for them to enter, as he stayed at the door. The team divided up and soundlessly moved through the massive foyer as one force. They advanced through anterooms, searching.

"Here!" an agent yelled from the library, just off the foyer. Three of the agents quickly found the room. An antique cherry desk was in the middle of the room. Two large, brown leather armchairs faced the desk.

A man in the chair behind the desk was slumped over. His head was twisted, resting awkwardly on his chest. A tamale jammed down his throat, protruded grotesquely from his open mouth. His chest and feet were bare; his black slacks unzipped.

Two agents moved toward him as they continued to scan the room. One agent stood guard at the door. The rest continued silently through the house, guns drawn.

The dead man's hands had been tied behind his back with a phone cord. He was still wearing his five-carat diamond pinkie and gold Rolex. The agent noted three bullet holes to the back of his head.

An agent returned to the library from somewhere in the house and reported, "Three deceased males in the kitchen. Professional hit. Joe, call in the lab. Have you ID'd this one?"

"Barrett Lewter."

Hours Later

Neely pulled up to the building. The sun was setting. She grabbed her overnight bag from the back seat and got out. Before heading up the stairs, she checked her mail. Her mailbox was empty. She smiled. Someone was doing her job. She walked up the two flights of stairs and inserted her key. She opened the door, turned to the alarm panel, and saw it was not armed.

Damn, Wallace...you left the system off again.

She walked into the living room and threw her keys on the kitchen counter.

"Wallace!" Neely called out.

No answer.

She walked to the farm table where her mail was neatly stacked. Fred appeared at her feet.

"Hello, big boy," she said, reaching down to scratch his neck. She went to the front window and placed both hands on the windowsill. She leaned deep into the window. Almost all the cars were gone by five thirty and today was no different. She spotted Wallace's Jag. Other than a couple of cars here and there, the parking lot was empty. There was no sign of Hop's Mercedes.

Where are they?

Neely bent down and stroked Fred. He purred loudly.

"Did you miss me, my sweet man? I missed you."

She walked back to pour herself a glass of wine. The cat followed her. She turned on a small lamp by the sofa and continued to the kitchen where she grabbed a wine glass from under the counter and a bottle of Malbec from the cabinet next to the sink. She opened the wine and poured herself a glass. She took a sip and, with glass in hand, kicked off her shoes and wiggled her toes. It was good to be home.

She stopped, suddenly noticing dark marks on the wood floor in front of her. They looked like Fred's paw prints. She knelt, placing her wine glass on the floor. Fred meandered over to help investigate the situation. She touched her fingertip to her tongue and rubbed the spot. She held her finger to face the fait light coming from the living room.

What is this?

She grabbed Fred as he brushed against her back and caught his paw to take a look at what might have caused the stains.

"Did you hurt yourself, big boy?"

His right front paw was caked with something dark and sticky. She grabbed his other front paw and it too was matted. She swept her hand across one of his back feet. It was sticky, too. She looked at her fingertips again.

Blood.

She instantly released Fred who then scampered off. Still on her knees, she stared out over the silent loft. Her heart pounded. She grabbed the side of the kitchen counter and slowly pulled herself up. The sunlight had all but vanished and she found herself encircled by distorted gray shadows. She stepped from the kitchen, past the partially opened pantry door, to the bedroom. She shuddered as her silhouette's reflection flickered in the window at the end of the room. She stopped suddenly and looked down at her feet. She stood in sticky, still wet, blood soaked shoeprints.

Oh, my god.

She took one step closer to the bedroom. She could hear the deafening sound of her own heart in her head. She knew if she had to run, she couldn't. Her legs were dead, heavy, incapable anything more than a slow stagger. She stood motionless, without breathing just outside the doorway, her head down, terrified of what might be.

Fred reappeared, rubbed on her leg, and meowed loudly. Her eyes opened wide as terror gripped her.

In front of her...legs...ankles...stained a red so dark they appeared black.

Oh, god, oh, god, oh, god.

She stumbled back against the door facing, not wanting to awaken the carnage, as if she might be able to somehow change what had happened, if she were just quiet enough, if she left silently, if she disturbed nothing...it might all disappear.

Mercifully, the darkness initially shrouded the gruesome details as her eyes slowly adjusted and focused. Her bed, only a few feet in front of her, revealed a still body.

Wallace.

Her friend was on the bed, naked, arms and legs flayed, eyes wide, mouth open. Her pale blue blouse, which only hours earlier had been so crisp and fresh, lay on the floor next to the bed soaked in blood.

The ghastly hush was marked only by Neely's tortured breathing and the horrific sound of droplets dripping from

Wallace's fingertips, as they dangled lifeless off the side of the bed, into the pool of blood on the floor.

Wallace's face and arms were smeared with blood, her chest open and gaping, mutilated by massive, frenzied stab wounds. The splatters across the back wall spoke for her, telling of her desperate struggle. Wallace had battled ferociously for every last moment of her life.

Neely looked at her friend's face, into her doll-like eyes that peered expressionless at the ceiling. There was no trace left of the horror someone had so viciously inflicted upon her.

Neely's struggled for breath as silent tears poured down her face. The odor of blood and noxious smells permeated the room, seeping into her nostrils. She closed her eyes tightly, screaming silently for it to go away. But there was no escape. She cried uncontrollably as her chest heaved. Her friend was dead.

Neely fought sickening nausea as she gathered her friend's limp, battered and bloody body, cradling her in her arms, rocking and sobbing, "No...No...Oh god...No, Wallace...No."

"Thanks for coming." Steven greeted Jack as a valet took Jack's coat.

"How is she?"

"Better. We're all just in shock," Steven said solemnly as the two men walked through the foyer, past the living room and dining room, to the kitchen. "They're in the breakfast room."

Steven stopped, reaching for Jack's arm. "I don't want her worked over by those goddamn morons in Summerville. Jack, they wanted her to come down to the station first thing in this morning. I don't want those Barney Fifes within ten feet of her. I want her interviewed by the feds, and I want it done here."

"I'll see what I can do."

Jan and Neely sat at a round table, in the center of a large bay window alcove. The morning sun was bright. Beautiful red tulips were on the table but not even they could improve the dark pallor that overshadowed everything.

Both women were in their robes. Neely's face was freshly scrubbed, her vacant eyes were red and swollen, and her cheeks, hollow. Her hair was pulled back in a ponytail. She was barefoot.

The men entered. "Hello, Jack," Jan smiled, as he placed his hands on her shoulders and kissed her cheek.

"Good to see you, Jan."

He walked over to Neely and sat in the chair next to her, placing his hand on hers.

"How are you?"

She shook her head as tears formed in her eyes.

"How about some coffee, Jack?" Jan offered.

"Love some."

Jan turned and called to a large black woman preparing breakfast in the kitchen. "Betty, will you please get Mr. Jack some coffee?"

The woman smiled. "Yes ma'am."

Jack kept his hand on Neely's. "This is going to be difficult. There's no way around it. I'll do what I can. Okay?"

Neely nodded. She felt nothing but inconsolable,

throbbing grief.

"Do you remember who you spoke with when the police arrived?"

She shook her head, no.

"By the time we got there, she was in the middle of giving a statement. Shortly after that, the coroner arrived," Steven said. "I remember an officer by the name of Jason...Josh? Something like that."

Betty brought Jack a cup of coffee and refilled everyone else's.

"Thanks, Betty." Jan smiled at her housekeeper.

"She's supposed to be at the police station at ten. That's the best I could do," Steven continued.

Jack set his cup down. "Let me make a couple of calls. We'll see if they can come here." He turned his attention to Neely. "Do you have an attorney you want me to call?"

Neely looked at Jack, confused.

Jan looked worried. "Why does she need an attorney?"

"I don't think she *needs* one, it just might be prudent."

"Do you want me to call David?" Jan asked Neely.

Before Neely could respond, Jack quickly said, "No."

Everyone looked at Jack, startled by his forceful stance. He realized he had created alarm and promptly attempted to soften the impression. "There's some other stuff going on in Summerville right now, and I don't think it's a good idea we use David."

Neely searched Jack's face for a hint of what other terrible thing might be looming. Surely, nothing could be worse than what had already happened.

Steven offered, "I'll call Peter Harriman's firm in Nashville."

Jack nodded as he looked at Neely, wondering if her friend's death was somehow tied to their sting. He hoped not.

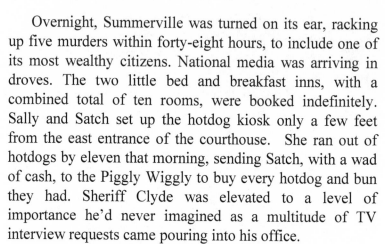

Overnight, Summerville was turned on its ear, racking up five murders within forty-eight hours, to include one of its most wealthy citizens. National media was arriving in droves. The two little bed and breakfast inns, with a combined total of ten rooms, were booked indefinitely. Sally and Satch set up the hotdog kiosk only a few feet from the east entrance of the courthouse. She ran out of hotdogs by eleven that morning, sending Satch, with a wad of cash, to the Piggly Wiggly to buy every hotdog and bun they had. Sheriff Clyde was elevated to a level of importance he'd never imagined as a multitude of TV interview requests came pouring into his office.

It was more than most citizens of Summerville could process. By seven that morning, after discovering Barrett and the others had been murdered, the town was seized with fear, excitement, and morbid curiosity. The courthouse square teemed with people. It had predictably become the site where one might discover the latest leaked information from loose-lipped sheriff's deputies and local attorneys. Many were more than happy to dole out juicy tidbits as they milled in and out of the courthouse, eager to snatch their fifteen minutes of fame.

Early on the town's people had concocted a list of suspects that included drug lords, ex-wives, boyfriends, girlfriends, mistresses, business associates, and loan sharks.

Curiously, Wallace was mentioned only as a peculiar afterthought, as if her death was such a wild card it couldn't be of any bother to them, let alone be linked to *their* people. *Or could it?*

David made his way through TV remote set-ups, townspeople, and reporters. Several voices, some familiar, some not, called out to him by name. He kept his head down, ignoring all, and entered the jail entrance, now guarded by familiar county deputy sheriffs. He spoke to no one.

He walked down the hall to the sign in desk as his wingtips tapped the gray painted, concrete floor. He grabbed the ledger, signed his name, the time, and the name Scott Summers.

The jailer greeted David. "Can you believe all this?"

David did not speak. His dark mood was noted by the jailer who, hastily removed a massive key ring attached to his belt and proceeded to unlocked the heavy iron door and said, swinging it open, "Just holler when you're done."

David nodded and entered the most secure block of the jail. He quickly walked down the hall where another guard sat outside a cell, reading a magazine. The jailer, a black man well into his seventies, looked up and, upon seeing David, immediately began to unlock the cell directly behind him. David could see Scott seated on his bunk, his head in hands.

"Evening, Mr. O'Donnell," the jailer greeted.

"Evening, Japhus. Can you give me a few minutes alone with Scott?"

"Sure. I'll be down the hall if you *needs* anything."

David, stone faced, entered the cell. Scott stood. David pulled the only chair from the opposite wall to the center of the room. Scott reached for David's hand as David sat down. He found his lawyer's hand limp and unresponsive. Scott sat back down on the bunk across from David.

"Thank god you're here. This is just fucking crazy. They think I had something to do with some wreck…said I tried to kill Kate! Can you believe that?"

David unbuttoned his suit jacket and stared at Scott as he let him continue to babble nervously. "I don't know shit about any of this. I swear. You gotta get me out of here, David. I'm going fucking crazy. I mean it, I'm going crazy."

David remained remote as he leaned back. "I know you did it, Scott."

Scott jumped up and began pacing around the tiny room. He had to maneuver around David with each turn. "That's bullshit! Why would I? I like Kate. This is a setup David and you know it. They're trying to fuck with me, trying to pin this shit on me."

"Barrett's dead, Scott. Shot three times in the back of his head. It was a professional hit. You fucked up real good this time. I wouldn't be the least surprised if they're looking for you."

Scott felt faint. He sat down on his bunk with a dull thud, his legs suddenly unsteady. Scott put his hands in his face, and started to cry like a baby, begging, "I am *so* fucked. You have to help me David. You have to. I'm family, David."

"You did it, didn't you, Scott?" David's bizarre soothing voice had an unexpected calming affect.

Moments passed before Scott bobbed his head up and down. "I'm sorry, David. Barrett made me." He peeked at

David, trying to gauge the precariousness of his predicament. "I was afraid. You can see that, can't you? You know how Barrett can be. Shit, I had to do it. He made me! I had no choice. He said T had screwed him."

David's tired and worn eyes fixed on Scott, his wife's sorry ass redneck nephew, and, with utter and complete disgust, said very slowly and very menacingly, "I'm going to help them fry your ass, you little fuck."

Scott's face appeared to have been wiped clean by a ghost sucker punch. He was catatonic with shock.

David got up and called out, "Japhus!"

The old black man appeared at the cell and unlocked the door. David walked out without looking back. He was well down the hall before he heard Scott scream at the top of his lungs, "You can't leave me here! I know too much, David! I know too much!"

David walked out to his car. A couple of reporters clamored around him. One pushed to the front with a cameraman as they filmed. "NBC affiliate, WZKN, Nashville. Bob Hudson. David O'Donnell...please ...are you planning on representing Scott Summers? What's your strategy?"

David said nothing as he slammed the camera into the cameraman's chest before getting into his car. The reporter placed his hand on the car's door handle, "Can you give us a statement." David yanked the door shut, fastened his seat belt, and drove away.

Two Days Later

Drew sat heavily in a faded plastic peach colored chair at a sterile looking Formica table. He set his steaming cup of coffee on the table and traced the rim with his fingers. He looked haggard, his mouth drawn. The hunter green pullover he wore was wrinkled, as were his khakis. His hair was unkempt. He had deep dark circles under his eyes and hadn't shaved in days.

"Drew," a familiar voice called softly, as a firm hand came to rest on the back of his shoulder. He turned. It was Big Daddy, his face and eyes red. He reeked of alcohol.

"Big Daddy."

"How are you doing, son?" the old man asked as he sat next to Drew.

Drew shook his head as tears filled his eyes. "All the things they're asking me...crazy...we had our troubles...sure...but...you know I loved her, don't you?"

"I do, partner."

They sat in silence for a few minutes.

"You want something? Some coffee?" Drew asked, wiping his eyes with a paper napkin.

"Naw, I'm good."

Tears continued to pool in Drew's eyes. He looked at Wallace's dad, who had aged a millon years since his child's death. He wanted to say so many things to the old man, to apologize for not protecting his daughter, for running around on her, for being a worthless husband, for every goddamn thing he had or had not done that ended up hurting Wallace. But the words wouldn't come out of his mouth. His tongue was paralyzed. He squeezed his lips together hard with his fingers, as if punishing them for not functioning. His voice breaking, he finally managed, "I couldn't let her go through this alone...you know, for her to go through this all alone...in this place."

Big Daddy, with tears streaming down his face, placed his hand back on Drew's shoulder. "I know, son, I know."

They sat in silence, both crying as they waited for the coroner.

So far, the coroner's findings were unremarkable. He had identified and noted thirty-four stab wounds over five millimeters in depth and twenty-nine additional stab wounds, mostly defensive in nature, along with several contusions, mostly around her hands and wrists. The cause of her death, which had not been painless or quick, was a loss of blood.

His experience told him the murder weapon was probably a serrated kitchen knife. He estimated the weapon to be eight to ten millimeters in length, four to five millimeters in width, and one half millimeter thick.

He stared at the woman on the table, studying her

carefully. He wanted to find evidence to aid law enforcement officials in finding out who did this to her, but so far... he found nothing that was conclusive.

He began closing her up when he noticed a small off-white piece of something lodged in the superficial fascia of her abdominal wall. He grabbed a camera and moved in close to photograph the object before disturbing it. He took several pictures, placed the camera back on the counter and selected a pair of sterile tweezers off a towel-draped tray on the stand next to the examining table. The coroner peered at the small, milky piece, analyzing it before picking it from the clear sheath with the tweezers. He held up the fragment to the bright operating room light, while angling it in different directions.

Well, what do ya know...a nail.

He took the plastic bags off Wallace's hands and examined them. Two nails on her left hand and three on her right were broken off, but her nails were painted a blood red. This nail was unpolished, much shorter and wider.

He placed the nail on a piece of sterile paper and walked across the room to an area housing lab equipment, including several very sophisticated microscopes. He positioned the nail under the lens and adjusted the focus. The nail appeared broken off at the quick. A small amount of tissue clung to the base, and around it was a tiny bit of dried blood. He noted a small speck of white material in the tip area. With the tweezers he removed the tissue and placed it in one specimen tube and the nail in another to be sent off for DNA testing.

"I'm not gonna say another fuckin' word 'til I talk to my lawyer. I know my rights! David O'Donnell's my lawyer. Did you know that?"

"We're trying to help you, Scott. You need to come clean. If you don't let us help you, you could end up taking the rap for Barrett as well as the other murders," the federal agent pleaded, as if trying to help a close buddy.

Scott didn't buy the man's pitch. He was terrified and suspicious of the agents.

What other murders?

"I'm not saying shit!" he said.

"We hear David O'Donnell's not helping you, and in fact, Scott, he's left you high and dry. Why is that? A lot of people in town are talking, saying you had something to do with Lewter's murder, and that's why he's told you to take a hike."

"That's a fuckin' lie. I never killed nobody and he knows it! Did David tell you I killed Barrett? If he did, he's lying!"

"I thought David was your lawyer, Scott."

Scott was panicking.

"Bad talks going around. Scott. And why in the world would David O'Donnell wanna set you up?"

Scott stared at the agent, steadfast in his refusal to talk.

"Let me help you, son. You don't want to take the rap for a murder you didn't commit."

"Shit," Scott muttered under his breath as he scratched his crotch.

"What do you know about all this, Scott?"

Scott looked at the agent, at the locked cell door, and back at the agent. "What kind a deal can I get? I didn't fuckin' kill nobody. I didn't, and that's the truth, I swear to god."

"Let me turn this tape recorder on, Scott. Do you mind? Can I?"

Scott stared at the agent before saying reluctantly, "I guess."

"I wanna know what I get for talkin'."

"We won't charge you with attempted murder of Kate LeBron."

"Will I get charged with something else?"

"Nothing serious...some misdemeanor, Scott."

"What's that mean?"

"Worst case? Six months...a year tops."

Scott thought about it for less than ten seconds. "Okay then."

The agent had Scott state his name and address.

Scott then asked, "Where do you want me to start?"

"Wherever you want. Tell us what you know, Scott."

"I know lots...about O'Donnell...Barrett...drug stuff... O'Donnell's girlfriend. You know, that's where that woman was murdered...that's David's girlfriend's place...did you know that? Yeah, I know a lot of shit."

Despite their best efforts not to, the agents smiled.

The Funeral

Over six hundred people came to pay their respects. The receiving line snaked through the mortuary and into the parking lot, like a line at Disney. Despite the light rain and cool air, no one went home without penning the guest book. It seemed everyone who loved, hated, or knew her in the slightest way wanted to be part of the circus.

The press interviewed those under black umbrellas in the parking lot, who were foolish enough to speak to them. The press pried, hoping to discover some unknown, juicy detail about Wallace. All hoped they would specifically uncover some sorted unknown fact about her marriage and affair.

Jan became Drew and Big Daddy's savior. She took charge of every detail of the service. She ensured Wallace looked as beautiful lying in her coffin as she did at any event she'd ever attended. She fixed her hair, applied her makeup, and chose her cherry red Chanel boucle cocktail suit. She knew Wallace had to be smiling. Somehow it was so *her*.

Olivia and Sam brought Neely to the chapel an hour before the scheduled visitation. Jan and Sam held her hand

313

as they walked into the quiet, dimly lit chapel where Wallace's open casket lay in a blanket of white Calla lilies. Neely stepped to the casket and looked down at her friend. She turned to Jan as tears welled in her eyes and whispered, "She looks beautiful."

Neely leaned in and kissed Wallace on her cheek while gently placing her hand on her face. Tears streamed as she whispered, "I miss you so, so much. I'm so sorry, Wallace. I love you." She turned back to Jan. They held each other and cried.

Wallace would have liked the service. Many of her friends spoke of her spirit, her zest for life, and simply how much fun she was, but nothing would have made Wallace more proud than seeing Drew's poignant gesture of standing in the line to greet the mourners between Hop and Big Daddy. He had never been as big a man as he was today.

Wallace had to be smiling down at the men she loved.

A day after Wallace's funeral, federal agents came to Jan's and Steven's to interview Neely. It was the best Jack could do in delaying the inevitable. The authorities had pushed to get her statement the day after the crime, but Jack convinced them she was too fragile, which was, in fact true. She cried continually and ate almost nothing. Her sleep was constantly interrupted by nightmares, reliving the gruesome details.

It was a quarter till' ten. She sat in a chaise in the glassed-in sunroom. Peter Harriman, her newly hired attorney, was with Jan somewhere in the house. Neely waited for the agents in silence, with Fred, curled up in her lap. She gently stroked him as she gazed out across the rolling lawn to the lake where two graceful Canadian geese swam effortlessly.

A blurred image of a bloody arm dangling flashed.

She trembled, powerless to stop the violent images that often seized her without warning.

Jan came in the doorway to the kitchen. "Neely?" She turned. Fred woke and stretched, almost falling off her lap. "They're here. As soon as Caroline gives her statement, which is scheduled in the morning, Jack says you can leave."

Neely nodded.

"Did you know Steven and I used to go to Blowing Rock every fall? His sister's husband's family has a place there. I'm so glad you and Caroline are going away. I think it's the best thing you could do."

Neely couldn't think past the interview she was facing, "Where's my attorney?".

"He's in the library, laying the ground rules for the interview. Steven said they'd be in directly."

Neely nodded.

"I'll be right in the kitchen, if you need me."

"Jan?"

"Uh huh?"

"Has anyone called?"

Jan looked crestfallen. "No."

Neely nodded, as she felt the ground beneath her slip away.

"You want me to call him?"

Neely shook her head no.

How empty could empty be?

Neely looked down at Fred and stroked him softly. "We'll be okay, little man...I promise...it will be over soon and we'll be okay."

Jan came to Neely and wrapped her arms around her, hugging her tightly. Fred jumped to the floor, as the sound of footsteps approaching grew louder. Neely stood and pushed her hair behind her ears. She was ready.

Peter Harriman and two men in gray suits entered the sunroom. Peter made the introductions. "Neely, this is Ben Oldman and Cory Chambers. This is Neely Glover." Neely shook their hands and they all sat.

The interview began with the standard fare of recording personal information, including birth date, prior addresses, Social Security number, relationship to victim, and on and on. After ten minutes the questions began in earnest, when they asked her to describe in detail her discovery of the crime, beginning when she entered the building.

After several excruciatingly painful minutes of describing the specifics of finding Wallace, Neely placed her hands on her lap, hung her head, and wept. The men waited a respectful two to three minutes before continuing with their questions.

"Did you notice anything unusual or out of place in your apartment?" Oldman asked. "Was anything disturbed or missing?"

"No."

"When Wallace Lee used your apartment to meet Hop Farrington, do you know if it was her habit to lock the door while they were there?"

"I don't know, but probably not."

"Why do you say that?" Oldman's partner asked.

"She wasn't afraid."

Oldman opened a manila folder, flipped through some

sheets of paper, and asked Neely, "Do you know anyone who would want to kill Mrs. Lee?"

Neely looked at Peter, who nodded, suggesting she try to continue. She focused, thinking about the question, wanting to be as honest as possible. She wanted them to find the person who did this terrible thing to Wallace. "I don't know anyone who would do this to her."

"What about Mr. Farrington's wife, Wendy?" Oldman pressed.

"No."

"We retrieved from your answering machine a conversation you had with Wallace the morning after her father's birthday party. She's recorded telling you that Wendy threatened to kill her if she didn't leave her husband alone. Do you recall that conversation?"

"Yes. But Wendy didn't kill her."

"How do you know she didn't?"

"I just do. Wendy didn't kill Wallace."

Oldman studied Neely and decided to let that line of questioning rest for the moment.

"Did she have any enemies you were aware of, who you feel might be capable of harming her?"

Neely, for the first time since the murder, smiled. Her reaction seemed odd to the agents.

"Wallace...always spoke her mind...she wasn't afraid... she..."

Neely stopped, overcome with uncontrollable grief, as the vision of her friend's battered and bloody body wiped out previous thoughts of her beautiful and vibrant life.

She sobbed.

The agents said nothing as Peter extended a handkerchief to her.

"I'm sorry Peter," she said, trying to gather her

composure. She took the handkerchief, wiping her eyes and nose and went on slowly, tears still running down her cheeks.

"She was brave...really brave...not afraid to be who she was...she didn't give a damn about what people thought. She offended people sometimes...actually, a lot of the times, but no one I know would want to kill her. She was a good person, a wonderful person."

"What do you know about Susie O'Donnell?" Oldman's partner asked after an appropriate moment.

Neely looked to Peter, then back to the agents. "I don't know what you mean."

"What kind of relationship do you have with her?"

Neely looked again to Peter.

"They need some insight into your relationship with David's wife, Neely."

"Has she ever threatened you?" Oldman asked.

Neely looked bewildered and confused.

"I don't understand. Do you think Susie killed Wallace? Why would she want to kill Wallace?"

None of the men spoke for almost a minute. Slowly, the implication of their silence sunk in.

"You think the murderer thought it was me?"

David, despite the upheaval of the past week, went to his office. He had to maintain the illusion of normalcy. He would not react with any more or less shock than the Church of Christ's minister down the road. He would not bring any attention to himself by not following his routine.

He would follow it to the letter.

And so he sat at his desk, making notes on his yellow legal pad while seated across from his client, who watched him scribble away. He had long ago perfected the art of pretending to listen to a client while working on another case. It was one of the many techniques he used to, as he put it, "to turn a buck." It also helped when he didn't want to hear Susie drone on about her day, the kids, or any other boring topic she found pressing.

A woman in her early fifties sat across from him. After handing over the five hundred dollars in cash to start her divorce proceedings, she was hell bent on getting her money's worth. In her mind, the hard earned money she'd given to this dandy, her "spensive law'r," as she described him to friends, meant she should be able to thrash out every detail of every event leading up to the violent altercation with her husband, which began when she walked in on him banging their sixteen-year-old niece. David looked up from his notes and nodded every few minutes, with just enough of a furrowed brow to feign reflection and interest as he jotted away. He was diligently listing every point he wanted to make, later in the day, when he would be before Judge Evers defending a thirty-two-year-old father of two who was charged with driving without a license and resisting arrest.

His intercom buzzed.

"Yes?"

"Susie is on line three."

"Janet, I'm with a client."

"David, pick up," his receptionist instructed firmly.

Maddened, David pushed the blinking light on line three. "I'm with a client."

"I just got off the phone with the police chief. I have to

meet some investigators in the morning, you son of a bitch."

"I'll go with you."

"They told me I could bring an attorney as long as it wasn't you. Isn't that just perfect, David? Look what you've done to me ...to our family."

"What did they say to you?"

"What are you asking me?"

"I'm asking what they said to you? What did they ask you?" he demanded.

"I'd say they're gonna want to know about Barrett, drugs or maybe they want to know about your girlfriend! Or maybe it has something to do with that woman who was murdered... in your fucking *slut's* apartment."

"I'll talk to you later. If they call back tell them nothing."

"I'm not going to lie for you, David."

"I didn't ask you to lie."

"Well, I'm not going to."

He leaned back in his chair and envisioned his world imploding.

"I'll get Will to go with you."

"Fine," she said sharply before hanging up.

He put the phone back on the cradle and looked at the woman sitting across from him.   She looked worried. Maybe she saw the terror that caught him and reckoned she made a big mistake.

Oldman sat at the bar in Rustlers. He was waiting for

Cory, his partner to arrive. He was tired and wished he hadn't agreed to dinner. He wished he'd gone back to the bed and breakfast, taken a shower, and hit the sack.

It was Thursday night and the bar was crowded. Oldman had just ordered a third beer when a black man in his forties, dressed all in white, hair slicked with Gerri Curl, sat down on the barstool next to him. A white woman in her early twenties, with light brown hair and green eyes, hung on his arm like he was the only life preserver left on the *Titanic*. She sported tight faded blue jeans, a purple silk blouse, and white stiletto open-toed pumps. Her hair was teased, her make-up overdone, and her demeanor telling. She placed her hand firmly on her man's thigh after she sat.

Upon eyeing them enter, Jimmy, Rustlers' proprietor, sauntered behind the bar and stood before the black man. Sensing the potential clash, Cherry, the bartender, smartly moved to the other end of the bar.

"What will you have?" Jimmy asked the black man.

"My lady will have a strawberry daiquiri and I'll have a Jack straight up."

Jimmy turned to the wall lined with every imaginable bottle of spirits, grabbed a bottle of Jack Daniel's from the bottom shelf and poured a generous shot in a short tumbler. He set the drink on a napkin in front of the black man and turned to Oldman. "You good?"

"Excuse me," the black man interrupted.

Jimmy turned back to him, expressionless.

"My ladies drink?"

Jimmy placed his hands on the bar, leaned in, and with a nasty swagger said caustically, "By law, I may have to serve your nigger ass, but I don't have to serve your whore."

Oldman almost fell off his stool. Coming from D.C. and

the federal arm of the Justice Department, hearing the racist assault was inconceivable.

How could this son of a bitch get away with this? What century are we in? Should I arrest this fucking racist? Do I have the authority? What do I charge him with? Jesus Fucking Christ!

As his brain raced, trying to figure out what he could and should do, the black man and his companion left without incident. Oldman's partner, Cory Chambers passed the couple leaving as he entered the bar. He walked up and took a seat on the vacated stool next to Oldman.

"Hey, buddy. Sorry I'm late. I had to make a call to Margaret...had to hear about Meagan's recital" Cory offered apologetically

"You just missed it, buddy."

"What?"

"You wouldn't believe me if I told you."

"Try me."

"I just wanna get out of this frikin place, alive. This place is beyond crazy! I swear to god it's scarier than when we worked West Englewood."

Cory laughed. "Did you mess around with one of the local lasses and get yourself in trouble? Some big ole farm boy after your ass?"

Oldman shook his head. He simply wanted to pack up his shit and take the most direct route out of Summerville. The fact that all these people were murdered in this little town suddenly didn't seem so improbable.

"Any news from the coroner? Oldman asked.

"The report came in as I was talking with Margaret. Real interesting."

Oldman took a swig of his beer as Cory ordered one for himself. Cherry popped the top and placed the beer in front of Cory with a flirty smile. Jimmy was at a table of inebriated men, laughing, as he exaggeratedly flayed his arms about, probably recanting the "N" story.

Cory continued, "The coroner found a fingernail in the victim's abdomen. Appears to be a woman's by the size and length. It's been sent it off for testing. Interesting, huh?"

Oldman winced. "A woman's? No shit, in her abdomen? Wow."

"Yeah, pretty gross."

"Do you remember Neely's nails?"

"I can't remember any of them being broken, but I think we need to go back and check. Not that I see any reason she'd want to kill her friend."

"Stranger things have happened."

Cory nodded. "What time's the O'Donnell interview?"

"Nine."

"And Farrington?"

"Eight. It shouldn't take long, they both have air tight alibis and have lawyered up."

Oldman asked, "Anybody else?"

"The housekeeper and a friend, Caroline somebody. I can't remember her name off the top of my head...one of Neely's good friends...she's coming at eleven, lives here in town, had a key...and, oh yeah, that boy, Scott Summerville. He's singing like a canary. It's ironic he probably knows more than he even realizes." Cory then asked, "When do we bring in O'Donnell?"

"I want to let him stew for a few days. But you know I still can't figure out why we're having so much trouble getting any info on him. Something's not right; I know it in my bones. I have one of the guys I worked with at the CIA running a check on him under the table. He's not just some country lawyer. He's cool as a cucumber—way too cool—and all the threads lead back to him. I want to wait until I hear back before we sit him down."

"Maybe his wife will spill the beans." Cory laughed. "You know she can't be too happy about any of this."

Oldman laughed with a nod and took another swig.

Caroline sat outside the tax assessor's office that, immediately after the murders, had been commandeered by the federal agents to serve as their center of operations. She arrived way too early. She was so nervous.

Why do they want to talk to me? I don't know anything.

The sound of footsteps caught her attention. She turned toward the main entrance of the courthouse and saw federal agent Cory Chambers enter. He walked down the long hall toward her. His gate was sure and fast. He was holding a Styrofoam coffee cup in one hand and a fried pie, probably from Baby's Diner, in the other. Just steps from her, he hesitated slightly and nodded without smiling. His expression did not help ease the growing anxiety she felt. She wondered what they'd do to her if she just left. Weighing the unpleasant possibilities, she decided to wait.

The agent fumbled with the doorknob, juggling the pie and coffee before opening it. The door closed and the hall was once again silent. She wished she had brought something to read or better yet a drink. Nobody would have noticed a little orange juice and vodka. She looked at her watch. Ten twenty-eight.

The double doors at the opposite end of the hall opened with a burst. She could make out two silhouettes against the backdrop of the bright morning sun. The figures made their way down the hall, toward her. She couldn't hear what they were saying, but their exchange was heated. She looked away politely, trying to appear disinterested.

A man's voice addressed her. "Morning, Caroline."

Standing in front of her was Will Bibb and Susie O'Donnell. Susie's black hair was coifed and sprayed into a helmet type do. She was wearing an unflattering, matronly cut black mink that hit her at the knees and was buttoned tightly around her thick neck. She wore light, sheer hose and navy pumps. She looked like a big black bear.

Caroline looked down at her red clogs, jeans, sweater, and red fleece jacket and decided it was probably not the best choice. Sitting next to the big bear, she couldn't decide if she looked like little red riding hood or a leprechaun.

"Hi, Will, Susie." Caroline greeted, but was immediately shut down but Susie's obvious and directed hostility.

"Cold out there this morning," Will said, offering distracting small talk, all the while sounding as if he were defending Susie's fur choice. "I think it's the coldest day we've had so far."

Caroline nodded, thinking how ridiculous his comment sounded. It had to be at least fifty degrees. She avoided looking at Susie wrapped up tight is her fur, still stewing.

Will finally knocked on the door. Cory Chambers opened it.

"Will." Cory greeted him formally as they shook hands. Will waved his arm, allowing Susie to enter before him. Caroline heard Will introduce Susie to the agent as the door closed.

Le Mon

Caroline felt sorry for Will...and the agent.

Jack and David sat in David's Porsche behind the goal posts at the end of the high school football field. It was after six in the evening.

"What am I supposed to do with the money in the account in the Turks & Caicos?" David asked. "I don't want it to catch up with me down the road."

"I don't care what you do with it," Jack said without a hint of emotion,

"And I don't ever want to know."

"Well, I don't want it. Do you think it could hurt T if I gave it to him?"

"What is it with you? Are you fucking deaf? I told you, I don't want to know about it and if you remember, the last time I saw you I told you I never wanted to see you again. That's still how I feel. I have no idea why you insisted we meet. Don't you get it? I want to put this behind me, once and for all. It's over, David. Fucking over."

"You don't think I want it to be over?"

"I don't know what you want. I think you're as crazy as Barrett was."

"I want this over just as much as you do, Jack but there are loose ends."

"I don't like you, and the only reason I've helped you all these years was to protect Sandy. What you did, David, to fuck up your life, is of no concern to me. I don't care and for the last time, it's over!"

David nodded. Jack reached his hand toward David's

passenger side door, when David asked, "Have you seen Neely?"

Jack turned and glared at him feeling absolute contempt. "You're a piece of work, you know that? You're a lowlife, a prick."

"I know you see her," David said cowardly.

"You son of a bitch."

"You don't understand, I love her…I'm worried about her," David continued, attempting to defend himself.

"Love? Worried? Fuck! You don't know the meaning!" Jack shouted.

"*She* knows I love her."

Jack opened the car door and got out. He hesitated for a second, resting his arm on the roof of the car. He then leaned down to look directly at David.

"What you ought to be worrying about is, does Susie believe you love Neely? For your sake, you better hope she doesn't."

"Where were you Thursday, March eighth, between the hours of two and six?"

Susie answered disdainfully, "I have no idea."

Agent Oldman looked at Will, exasperated. The interview had been arduous from the get go. Susie made them work for every tiny tidbit she divulged.

"Susie, that's the afternoon Wallace Lee was murdered," Will coaxed.

"What difference does it make what *I* was doing?" she fired, attacking her own attorney.

Oldman's voice was stern. "We are trying to establish the whereabouts of all persons who had a connection with Mrs. Lee."

"For god's sake, what connection am I supposed to have had with that woman? I knew her casually. Period."

Ben Oldman had enough of her belligerent, combative attitude.

"Mrs. O'Donnell, we are investigating a murder, a very brutal murder, and because your husband was having an affair with the owner of the loft where the murder was committed, we require you to answer our questions."

"I don't think I like your attitude."

Oldman was seconds away from losing it.

"Could you give us a minute?" Will asked the agents.

Before Oldman and Chambers left the room, Oldman told Will sternly, "Five minutes."

With the agents out of the room Will demanded, "What are you trying to do?"

"The question is, why aren't *you* defending me? What the hell are you here for anyway? All you do is stand around like some moron, with your finger up your ass not saying a damn word while they attack me!"

"You're going to have to answer their questions, whether it's now or later. They can take you in. There's no way around it. Why make it harder on yourself?"

"I didn't have a thing to do with this and you know it! Why should I have to listen to that little prick tell me David was screwing that bitch? This is so outrageous."

Frustrated, Will pulled at his face with his hands. "That's the whole point. You didn't have anything to do with it. Let's establish your alibi and get the hell out of here."

"You better damn defend me, Will. That's what you're

here for. Don't forget it. You're not supposed to just stand around looking like a fool."

Will left and returned with the agents. Oldman sat down on the edge of the desk across from Susie.

"Again, where were you the afternoon of March eighth between the hours of two and six?"

Susie took a dramatic, exaggerated breath and stated, "I picked up Brooke, my daughter, from school..."

Will interjected, "Camdon School on Revere, in Madison."

"As I was saying, I picked her up from school around 3:15 and dropped her at a friend's house where she was to spend the night. I went to Marshall's and I think Publix."

"What is the name of her friend whose home she spent the night?"

"Henry and Paula Blalock."

"What purchases did you make that day?"

"I don't remember buying anything."

"You went to the grocery store and bought nothing", the agent followed up sounding skeptical.

"I went there for a specific item, which they did not have."

"Where did you go after Marshall's and Publix?"

"I went home."

"You didn't go anywhere else before going home?"

"No."

"Was anyone at your home when you arrived—a maid, gardener, a friend, your husband?"

Susie thought. "No."

"Is it a common practice for you to allow your daughter to spend the night with friends on a school night? It was a school night, wasn't it?"

"Yes, it was a school night," Susie answered

sarcastically. "It's something I do if I have an appointment in Summerville the next morning."

"And did you have an appointment that Friday?"

"Yes."

"And what appointment would that have been?"

"An appointment with Dr. Garber, my gynecologist. I had a pap smear. Would you like me to send you the results?"

"That won't be necessary." Oldman looked at Will and said, "but I would like his number."

Susie sneered. "*Her* number."

"Her number," Oldman corrected himself. This woman was pissing him off royally. He went on, "How did you feel about your husband being in love with another woman?"

If looks could kill, Oldman would have been in a box six feet under.

"My husband does not love that woman."

"I have evidence to the contrary."

"Do you think you can intimidate me by resorting to such obvious, cheap tactics? Do you expect me to break down and confess some deep, dark secret? You've been watching too much TV, Mr. Oldman."

"The only thing I expect you to do is answer my questions."

"Will?" She looked to him for help.

Oldman pulled a stack of papers from a manila folder on the desk and handed them to Susie. She read a couple of lines before placing the entire stack back on the desk.

"Those are but a few examples of the poems and letters your husband wrote to Neely Glover professing his love. There are many more. How do you feel about your husband loving another woman?" Oldman asked again.

"He did not and does not love her, and if you'd done

your homework, you'd know she is not the first woman my husband has had a dalliance with."

"We did our homework, Mrs. O'Donnell, and are very acquainted with your husband's past relationships, as well as yours." For the first time Susie looked unseated. Oldman continued, "We have interviewed those women and, interestingly, he never once wrote or told any of those women he loved them. In fact, they all stated that he made it very clear, from the beginning, that he was married and had no intention of disrupting his family situation. And they all said their relationship never included sex."

Oldman watched Susie seethe. He *had* her. He went on, "But this time was different. He fell in love with Ms. Glover…deeply in love, and I think you knew it. I also think, for the first time in your marriage, you knew you were in trouble…that he might actually leave you."

"How dare you talk to me that way? You don't know shit. David would never leave me."

"But he told Ms. Glover, and I think he told you, Will that in fact he was planning on leaving his wife."

Will was shocked and could not have been more aghast if Oldman had pulled a gun and shot him in the leg. Susie's eyes were wild as she jerked around and stared at Will in absolute disbelief. She turned back to Oldman exploding, unleashing her rage, screaming, "He would *never* leave me! Ever."

"Mrs. O'Donnell, I think you have deluded yourself into believing you could control your husband, that he valued you and your children more than Ms. Glover, but to anyone objective it's quiet apparent it was simply a matter of time before he left you to be with her."

"You pompous, pencil-pushing, little shit! You don't know who you're dealing with!"

Oldman's antagonistic attack was relentless. "Everyone in this room and probably in this town thought he was going to leave you, and you knew there was nothing you could do to stop him."

Will was freaking out over how Oldman was badgering Susie and decided to physically step in between them, to stop the onslaught. Cory knew his partner was simply provoking Susie to gain more information and it was working. Susie shoved Will to the side and screamed, "I'd fry him! I'd put him away!"

Everyone stared at Susie as the air felt like it was instantly sucked out of the room.

"What do you mean you'd *fry* him...put him away?" Oldman asked with a smirk.

She didn't move.

"What did you mean, Mrs. O'Donnell?" Cory repeated.

"I'm finished, Will," Susie stated coolly, while gathering her fur from the counter directly behind Chambers.

"Are your nails your own nails, Mrs. O'Donnell?"

She turned to him and asked haughtily, "What?"

"Are your nails natural nails or press-on?"

"They are natural. And for your information, they're not called press-on."

"Do you go to someone to...fix your nails?" Oldman asked.

"Yes, Mr. Oldman. It's called a manicure. I get manicures."

"I'd like you to provide the woman's...or *man's* name and telephone number that does your manicures."

Will nodded as he followed Susie like a whipped puppy.

Susie was at the door when Oldman called, "Mrs.

O'Donnell?"

She turned.

"May I see your nails?"

She whipped around to Will. He sheepishly shrugged. She turned back to Oldman and jutted out her hands. Oldman came over, leaned down and thoroughly inspected her nails.

"Thank you."

She violently pulled her hands away and stormed toward the door.

"We'll need to talk again, Mrs. O'Donnell."

She turned back to Oldman and Cory and spewed with a combative and defiant air, "We'll see."

Susie passed Caroline in a huff as Oldman watched Will follow her down the hall and out the door. He looked down at Caroline and asked, "You ready?"

Caroline placed Neely's suitcase in the back of the gray 4 Runner and shut the hatch. Neely hugged Steven and Jan tightly.

"Try to relax, enjoy the peace and quiet of the mountains and know we're here for you, that we love you," Jan said with an extra squeeze. "I'll call you if anything comes up."

"If Fred gets weird, call me."

"He'll be fine. He's found a new friend in Steven. You may have trouble getting Fred back," she said sweetly.

"You have the number?"

"Neely, we have everything. Don't worry." Jan

reassured.

"I'll call you when we get there," Neely smiled.

Caroline hugged Steven, then Jan, whispering, "I'll take good care of her."

Caroline and Neely climbed into the SUV and waved as they pulled away from the house. Steven placed his arm around Jan as they watched them drive out of sight.

Neely slept for most of the six-hour trip. It was longer than she had slept in the past few nights, in total. When Caroline pulled off the main highway onto the private gravel road to the chalet, Neely woke. She stretched and smiled at Caroline. The road was lined with beautiful, tall pines and the sky was a pale blue.

"Some woman's on the phone, says she wants to talk to the man in charge of Lewter's murder, she wants to get some things from his house."

Cory Chambers held the phone in the air for his partner. Oldman laughed, shaking his head as he ambled over to Cory. He took the phone and hit the hold button. "Agent Oldman."

"Hi," a feminine voice said softly.

He waited. Nothing. "Can I help you?"

"Well...I hope."

"I can barely hear you. Would you speak up?"

"Sorry, I'm a little nervous. Well, you see I was Barrett's...well, his girlfriend, you might say."

"And your name is?"

"Candy. Candy Meade."

"What can I do for you, Candy?"

"Well...I have stuff at Barrett's house I need to get."

"Like what?"

"Our dog, Booger. My hair rollers, makeup, my bowling bag, clothes, stuff like that. And things he bought me, like my doll collection. I have every Marie Osmond doll she ever made. They're worth lots a money, and there's other stuff I can't remember right now."

"His house is a crime scene. Nothing goes in or comes out until it's released. And I don't have the authority to give anything to you anyway. You're going to have to talk to his family about getting your things."

"He doesn't have no family. *I* was his family, and that stuff I told you about is mine...and I can prove it."

"I don't know what to tell you, Ms. Meade. Maybe you could talk with whoever is handling his estate. Maybe his lawyer?"

"His lawyer screwed him. He sure won't help me."

Oldman's curiosity was tweaked. "Who's his lawyer?"

"David O'Donnell."

"Do you know Mr. O'Donnell?"

"Yeah, I know him. I've been knowing him a long time."

"How did he *screw* Mr. Lewter?"

"I don't wanna say."

"Why?"

"I don't want no trouble," Candy said.

"What do you mean, Candy?"

"I gotta go."

"Miss Meade, you know I can bring you in."

"What for? I don't know nothing. Alls I want is Booger. I don't even know if somebody's taking care of him. He could be starvin' right now."

Oldman's mind was racing.

"I don't know why I called you people. I knew nobody was gonna help me."

"Maybe I can find out about the dog. Maybe I can get him for you."

"How?" she asked suspiciously.

"I can try. I'll see what I can do."

"Well, thank you. You know, it's been real hard on me since, you know, what happened to Barrett, real hard. I loved him. A lot of people don't believe he loved me, but he did. He loved me."

"I'm sure it's been hard." Oldman frantically waved at his partner. "How can I get in touch with you, Miss Meade?"

"I have Candy's Catering. That would the best place to get me. You know it?"

"No, I'm sorry, I don't."

"I'm almost across the street from where that woman was killed."

"Really?"

"Yeah, I met her once. She was with Mrs. Glover. She was real nice."

"Were you at your business the day her friend was murdered?"

Oldman's heart was pounding. His partner now sat on the desk across from him. Oldham grinned a shit-eating grin as he nodded to Cory whiled putting Candy on speakerphone.

"Uh huh," Candy answered.

"Did you happen to see anyone enter or leave the building that afternoon?"

Again, there was a pause. "Uh huh."

"Who'd you see?" He took his pen out of his breast

pocket and waved it at Chambers who quickly jumped off the desk and snatched a sheet of paper from the copy machine and raced back to hand it to Oldham.

Candy went on: "Well...Bobby Joe, our UPS man, went to the door around lunch. I saw him leave a note in her mailbox..."

"Neely Glover's mailbox?"

"Uh huh. Then I saw Ms. Lee and a man go up about two. I think it was two. Then the man left about four thirty."

What in the fuck? Does this woman just sit and watch the building?

Could I really be this goddamn lucky? Shit!

"Anyone else?"

"Yeah...a little later."

Holy shit!

Cory silently high fived Oldman!

"Who was that?"

"Daphne Polansky."

"Who?" Oldman asked.

"Daphne Polansky. She works at the Chamber, or maybe it's the Better Business Bureau. I'm not sure. I don't really know her."

Oldham scribbled Polansky's name on the paper. "You know what time that was?"

"I know it was a little past five, because Miss Lula and Shanika had done left."

"Who?"

"They do the cookin' for me...a negra girl and her mama. I can't stop working, you know, just 'cause Barrett's gone. I gotta take care of myself now. I don't have Barrett and I ain't got no family, either."

"Uh huh, but you are pretty sure it was after five?"

"Yeah," she said, suddenly getting suspicious. "I don't let my girls go home 'til then."

"Did you see when she, Ms. Polansky left?" His heart was about to explode.

"Naw, Tony and me started loading the vans for a party right after the girls left. I had to cater a party for the senior center down on Adams. You know it?"

"No."

"Well, it's about two blocks away. It's where they do the Lasagna Dinner every year. You know, where everybody shows their talent?"

Oldham was nodding as his mind raced. "Uh huh."

"I have Tony park the vans in the back 'cause the city gives me a hard time...taking' up space on the square."

"Uh huh."

"I can't see anything from back there."

"Do you know if," He looked down at his pad and all the frantic scribbles. "...Ms. Polansky and Ms. Glover were friends?"

"I don't think so. I never saw her go up there before."

"What about David O'Donnell? Was Ms. Polansky his friend?"

"Oh yeah, they're good friends. She's always with him. She has lunch with him most every day."

Bingo!

"After I get your dog, I may want to get a statement from you."

"When do you think I can get him?"

"Today."

"Really? Oh, Lord, thank you. I mean that. Thank you so much!"

"I'm making it my number one priority, Candy."

Suddenly, Candy's voice softened, sounding flirtatious.

"You're just so nice...is it Mr. Oldson?"

"Oldman." he said sweetly, playing along.

"Oh yeah, Oldman. Well, Mr. Oldman, I promise I'll make this up to you somehow. Maybe I can bring y'all stuff to eat?"

"No, no. You've already been a big help."

"You sure? I don't mind. It'd be no trouble at all."

"I'm sure."

"Welcome to Edelweiss," Caroline smiled, putting the car in park.

Neely looked at the small chalet and smiled, reminded of her early childhood memories when her family skied in Bavaria.

The pine siding was weathered to a soft, metallic gray. Flower boxes overflowing with a mix of red geraniums and purple petunias hung from the front windows, fashioning a welcoming entrance. Atop the high-pitched dark green tin roof, an oxidized copper reindeer weathervane turned in the breeze.

"Ready?" Caroline asked, smiling at Neely.

Neely nodded. The air was chilly. Neely caught the scent of the ancient boxwoods that lined the stone path to the house. They emitted a faint, familiar citrus fragrance she loved.

"Let's get the luggage later," Caroline suggested.

Neely followed Caroline into the house. "It's perfect."

Across the open room, a fire roared.

"Who made the fire?" Neely asked.

"We have a caretaker named Peebo. He's been with us for years. He's in his eighties and as sweet as he can be. I called him when we stopped for gas. He promised he'd put a bottle of champagne in the fridge and start a fire. Let's see if he remembered the champagne."

Caroline put her purse on the navy plaid sofa and headed for the kitchen, which was merely an extension of the living room, divided by a small counter and two barstools. Neely put her purse next to Caroline's and walked up to the big stone fireplace. She held her palms to the heat and closed her eyes.

"Well look here," Caroline's voice called as she opened the bottle with a pop. She came to Neely with two wine glasses and the bottle of champagne. "No flutes, but it's cold." She smiled, handing a glass to Neely.

"Let there be nothing but peace for the next two weeks," Caroline toasted.

"Yes, peace." Neely repeated softly.

Candy was as thrilled to get her little dog Booger back, as Oldman was to give him to her. She thanked him profusely and was eager to give him her statement. Oldman was beyond euphoric. He knew this was the break they'd been hoping for.

As soon as her statement was signed, Oldman and his partner headed for Daphne Polansky's house. When they found no one at home they went looking for her at the Chamber of Commerce. They missed her by about fifteen minutes, and the office staff had no idea where she was going or if she would be back.

"David, Daphne Polansky's on the phone. She says it's urgent."

"See if I can get back to her after lunch or see if she wants to meet me for lunch." He went back to the papers scattered across his desk.

His phone buzzed again.

"What?" he demanded with obvious irritation.

"She says she has to talk to you now, that it's an emergency."

"Shit!" He punched the blinking light. "Daphne, I have just a second."

There was silence.

"Daphne?"

"I'm in trouble, David."

"What's wrong?"

"They've found out."

"Found out what?"

"They know what I did."

"What did you do?"

"They know I killed her."

Moments passed as he tried to make sense of her words.

"David?"

"I'm here."

"You have to help me," she pleaded.

"Who did you kill, Daphne?"

"I killed Wallace."

He couldn't move or speak.

"David, did you hear me?"

"Why would you kill Wallace?"

"I thought it was Neely."

His face contorted into a grotesque manifestation, "Oh my god."

"You have to help me, David."

He couldn't find the words.

"David! I was trying to help you. I did this for *you*, for us."

David drove home emotionally crashing as he tried to entomb the frightening images of what he concluded would be played out. He was thrown, resigned, unbalanced, and afraid that for the first time in his adult life all the lies and deceptions he'd woven to protect his daughter and his private life, would soon be exposed. He was powerless. Thoughts of Neely swallow up his mind and held. She was the only good thing in his life...the only thing he was sure of. He fought a fierce urge to turn the car around and go to her, to hold her, touch her, to smell her, to give up everything for her.

But he couldn't. He pulled into his drive and slowly made his way through his perfectly manicured grounds toward the house. He wondered how his seemingly ordered world so completely masked the absolute monstrous truth of his existence. He parked behind Susie's car and got out. The sound of their bedroom TV could be heard as he opened the kitchen door.

Before going to find his wife, he went to the bar in the

living room and poured himself a glass of scotch. He set the leaded glass tumbler down hard on the bar and walked to their bedroom. He found Susie making the bed. She looked up, surprised to see him.

"What are you doing home?"

David walked to the partially made bed and sat heavily. He hung his head, not knowing how to begin. She walked around the bed and sat next to him.

"What's happened?"

He looked like a shadow of himself as he spoke with almost a stutter, "Daphne Polansky killed Wallace."

"What!"

"She killed Wallace and she wants me to defend her."

"I don't understand."

"She thought Wallace was Neely."

Susie's eyes flamed as her anger exploded. She threw the pillowcase on the floor and stood to face him. "Will this ever end? Will this fucking nightmare ever end?"

"I don't know what to do. I really don't."

"Well, you can't defend her. You see that, don't you! I mean, good god! You have to distance yourself!"

She stared at him, wanting him to relieve her fears but knew he was lost.

She yelled, trying to wake him from the inertia that paralyzed him "What are you going to do!"

"I don't know."

Caroline answered the phone.

"Hi Caroline, this is Jack. How are you?"

"I'm good. Neely and I just got back from a hike. Do you want to talk to her?"

"If you don't mind."

"Hold on, I'll get her. Nice talking with you, Jack."

"You too."

Neely took the phone from Caroline. "Hi, Jack."

"How are you?" he asked.

"Much better. It's beautiful here. It's just what I needed, away from everything. How are you?"

"I'm fine, happy to know you're doing better" He hesitated before continuing. "I'm calling because I wanted to tell you something before you heard it from anyone else. Daphne Polansky has been arrested for Wallace's murder."

Neely had to sit. She asked, "Daphne?"

"Neely?"

"That can't be."

"They arrested her this morning," Jack said.

"Why would she kill Wallace? She didn't know her."

How do I tell her?

"She thought Wallace was you."

Tears rolled down Neely's face.

"I'm so sorry," Jack offered.

Knowing who murdered Wallace left Neely bewildered and angry, and yet, in a queer way, thankful. She now could put a face to the terrifying ghost. But could she really? Trying to fasten Daphne to this horrific figure was impossible. To conjure Daphne attacking Wallace, inflicting the brutal, vicious blows as her friend slept, was beyond reason, and no matter what path she chose as a reasonable frame of reference, all failed.

Caroline opened the back door and entered the screened in porch where Neely sat in a comfy love seat, looking out at the tall pines lining the top of the distant hills. A writing tablet and pen lay on a side table next to her.

Caroline swept her fingertips gently across Neely's shoulders as she passed her. Neely looked up and smiled. Caroline held out a large mug of hot chocolate. "Thought you might like a little cocoa. It's cold out here."

Neely pulled one hand out from under the wool blanket and took the mug. Caroline sat down in the rustic antler chair next to the loveseat. She grabbed a blanket from the stack piled in a big wicker basket on the deck and covered her legs.

"Damn, it's not just cold, it's freezing" Caroline laughed.

"I like it. It makes me feel alive." Neely took a sip, "Mmmm, this is good. Aren't you having any?"

"I'll get some in a minute. What are doing out here?"

"Writing...thinking...trying to make sense of..." Neely's voice trailed off.

"I don't think we'll ever understand. How does one ever get a sense of why a person commits such a terrible act? I don't think we can, Neely. Did you ever think she was *that* kind of crazy?"

Neely shook her head. "Never. I've gone over everything a thousand times. I mean she was crazy but not murderous crazy. It's like one of those bizarre things you see on TV. You find out the guy next door is a serial killer and the only thing his neighbors say after he's caught is, 'He was quiet and stayed to himself.'"

Caroline nodded. There was nothing left to say. There were no words that would ever change the fact her friend was dead. Nothing.

David contacted Weldon Delionback, an old friend from law school and one of Nashville's best criminal trial lawyers. He did his best to persuaded him to take on Daphne's case. His motives were not all selfless. With Weldon as her attorney, he could monitor the potential explosiveness of her testimony without being directly involved. Perhaps people would discount her ravings if he did not defend her or they might just assume the worst. Who knew?

He packed his briefcase with his notes and prepared to head over to the courthouse. His client's child custody hearing would commence in less than an hour and he wanted to go over the testimony since he hadn't even glanced at the depositions.

He left through the back door, not wanting to be accosted by some fool in the waiting room. The day was beautiful, sunny, and unseasonably warm.

Today was going to be better.

"Mr. O'Donnell?"

David turned. Oldman and his partner were no more than a foot behind him.

"We need to have a word with you." Oldman's voice sounded official.

"Love to oblige you, fellows, but I am on my way to court. I have a hearing."

"When would be a good time?" Oldman persisted.

"I'll have to take a look at my appointment book."

"How about I call you this afternoon, so we can set a time? I'd like to do this in the next couple of days."

"Sure. I'll take a look and give you a call." Surprisingly, David managed to sound calm despite suffering waves of sickening panic.

Oldman handed David his card. "I'll wait for your call."

So much for a better fucking day.

He rode his bike to the pay phones outside the Dollar Store. The first call was to Bill. He quickly brought him up to date.

"Don't panic. Keep your head."

"Keep my head? Shit!" David was losing it.

Bill's voice was calm, "There is nothing to tie you to any of this"

"How do you figure?"

"Jack's kept you clean. They'll never get anything they can sink their teeth into."

"Yeah, well how do I explain I didn't know shit about my best buddy's dealings, dealings that got him popped, or my sleazy nephew implicating my ass in everything from the 7-11 holdup to drug running, or my girlfriend's best friend being murdered by my lunatic friend who believed we had an intimate relationship!"

"It's all circumstantial…coincidence. They have nothing they can hang on you."

"Shit."

"When are you supposed to meet with them?"

"I'm suppose call them."

"Talk to Jack first."

"He told me to take a hike. He never wants to see or talk to my sorry ass again. Those were his exact words."

"He'll talk to you. It's business, David. He doesn't want the Company's dealings exposed any more than you do. Call him."

"God almighty."

David hung up and searched for change in the small pocket of his bike shorts. He deposited coins and called Jack.

He sat slumped at his desk looking at the images of his children smiling back at him. A photo of Bud minus a front tooth, dressed in his T Ball uniform, grinned at the camera, while striking a batter's pose. Next to the photo of Bud, Brooke was decked out in a red feather boa, a sequined, lime green bodysuit, and black tap shoes looking years older than her seven. Brooke's familiar, radiant smile could not be masked by the clown-like theatrical makeup. David smiled.

He loved his children, adored them. His eyes moved from his children's photographs to the framed photo of Susie. It was a photo of her taken at the lake. She was a lot thinner, her eyes brighter, and her smile easy. He was overcome with sorrow and sadness for her. He had cheated her. He had never really loved her. He respected her, he appreciated the kindness and love she'd shown his children but he never really loved her. He'd been so unfair to her and …to Neely...his beloved, Neely.

The buzz of the intercom jarred him back.

"David, a Mr. Oldman is on line two. He said you'd know what it's about?"

"I'll take it."

He rubbed his face hard with his hands. He picked up the receiver and forced a smile, "Two great minds, I was just about to give you a call."

"Have you found a time you can come in?"

"Come in?" David faked a chuckle. "Sounds like an interrogation. I thought you might just come to my office."

Oldman remained reserved. "Whatever you prefer."

"How does seven thirty in the morning sound?" David asked.

"We'll be there."

As David hung up the phone, his smile vanished. His brow was wet and his heart was pounding.

The time spent with Caroline high in the mountains had done Neely a world of good. She had time to sort through the pain of Wallace's death, ponder healthy dynamic options she, Eric and their children might establish, as well as time to reflect on the emotional chaos that reared its ugly head with every thought of David. Neely wanted, for the first time in her life, to make herself a priority, to protect herself, to be kind to herself, to choose the right path for whatever was left for her.

She could now, without too much difficulty, engage in meaningful conversation with Jack when he called, she was sleeping through the night more often than not, and she found that the terrifying flashes of violent images struck less often. She spoke with her children and Jan daily. Jack faithfully called twice a week, and yet the one person in the world she wanted to hear from, remained silent.

David arrived at the office a few minutes past six. He made himself a mug of green tea and mulled over every possible question they might throw at him. He felt pretty confident he could field them without too much trouble. He knew he was smarter, plus, he had all the information. He just had to remain cool and collected.

He took a big sip from the mug and pulled out his familiar yellow pad. He flipped through several pages of notes to a clean page. He outlined his own timeline as to his whereabouts, twenty-four hours on both sides of Wallace's estimated time of death. Thank god he was in court almost the entire day and attended an early dinner honoring a local veteran. Having several judges, lawyers, police officers and decorated veterans corroborate your alibi was about as good as it gets. Having lunch with Daphne at Parker's was the only glitch. But who in their right mind would have lunch with a potential partner in crime, the day of the crime? Bill was right. The connections were all circumstantial.

By the time he finished the timeline his tea was cold. He flipped back the pages of the pad and opened the side drawer of his desk. As he lifted some folders to hide the yellow pad he saw a familiar envelope. He pulled it out. It was from Neely. He brought the paper to his face and inhaled as if it were his last breath.

"David?" Janet's voice interrupted.

The envelope dropped awkwardly to his lap as he looked up.

His receptionist couldn't hide her worry, "Can I get you anything?"

"Some more tea," he said.

She walked over to his desk and picked up the mug.

"They'll be here at seven thirty. Bring them right in and under *no* circumstances am I to be interrupted" he said.

"Understood."

It was seven twenty-seven when Janet announced their arrival. David stood.

Janet opened David's office door. Behind her stood the agents. David gestured for them to enter the room, to sit in the two chairs in front of his desk.

"Good morning, gentlemen" he said cheerfully as he made his way around his desk to shake their hands.

"Janet, can we get these gentlemen some coffee? Or tea?"

"Of course. What can…?" Janet began.

Before she could finish, Oldman interrupted. "We're fine. We had our coffee earlier."

David nodded and looked at Janet.

"Anything else?" she asked.

He shook his head. She left, closing the door behind her.

David addressed the men straight on, with a grin. "Well, I'm ready. Fire away."

Cory Chambers opened the briefcase on his lap, removed a folder, and placed it on the desk in front of him.

Oldman looked at David coldly and asked, "How long have you and Daphne Polansky been intimately involved?"

David laughed out loud, as tea spewed across his desk. "You're on the wrong path, boys. I've never been more than a friend to her. Ever." David pulled out a handkerchief from the top drawer of his desk and wiped his mouth and then his desk.

Oldman leaned in toward David, thrusting the folder at him. David picked up the folder and opened it. The ruled white papers inside were covered with what looked like tight, handwritten notes covering almost every inch of the page. David began reading.

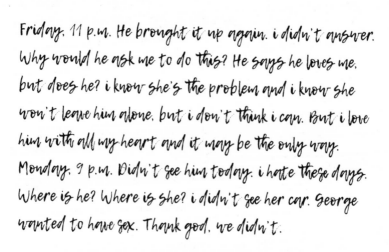

Friday. 11 p.m. He brought it up again. i didn't answer. Why would he ask me to do this? He says he loves me, but does he? i know she's the problem and i know she won't leave him alone, but i don't think i can. But i love him with all my heart and it may be the only way. Monday. 9 p.m. Didn't see him today. i hate these days. Where is he? Where is she? i didn't see her car. George wanted to have sex. Thank god, we didn't.

Cornbread Mafia

Tuesday. 10 p.m. i've told him i couldn't do it. i am not a violent person...he knows that. But i love him and i know he wouldn't ask me to do this if it wasn't the only way. We will meet tonight to talk this out. i love him so much i can't imagine not being with him.

Wednesday. 3 p.m. Our lunch was wonderful. He is so smart and funny. He told me how pretty i looked and how he liked my hair. i wish Bobby hadn't joined us. it spoiled our time. Before he sat down, he told me we would be together as soon as all of this was over with. i'm so upset. i have to, though. i have to. it's the only way we can be together.

Wednesday. 9 p.m. George wants me to go to Nashville tomorrow to pick up a part for his combine. but i promised tomorrow would be the day. Maybe i can go early...be back for lunch with him...i will tell him...going to get the part might actually work for me... yes. Today. NO backing out! Tomorrow's the day!

Thursday. 6:30 a.m. George just left. i feel sick...nervous. Can i do this? Does he really, really love me? She's the problem. She's messed up everything. We want her gone. i have to be strong. i have to do what is right for us. i will do it for him...for us. i love him.

Friday, 12:50 a.m. it's done.

Dumbstruck, David emotionally buckled.

Oldman pressed. "Again, how long have the two of you been involved?"

"I have never been with Daphne. This is ludicrous... insane! It's obvious she's crazy, mentally ill."

"Interestingly, you're the only person we've spoken with who describes her that way. Most say she's smart and, in fact, pretty bland. Her life from what we have deduced includes her work, her husband, her daughter, and their farm. Not one person has described her as insane, crazy or mentally ill. Most describe her as boringly normal."

Without moving a muscle, David said, "I have nothing more to say to you. I want to speak to my attorney."

Oldman was delighted with himself. He had reduced the big fish in the little pond to a minnow.

"We'll expect you in our office, with or without your attorney, first thing in the morning, Mr. O'Donnell, or we will have someone collect you."

"Are you threatening me?" O'Donnell demanded. "Are you saying you're going to arrest me? Are you planning on charging me?"

"You are at this time merely a person of interest, but we will expect you to come to our office in the morning. And, if you will, tell your wife we plan on questioning her again tomorrow afternoon."

He couldn't breathe. His chest heaved in agony.

He looked at the clock on the wall across the room. 8:18 a.m. It had taken less than an hour for his life to end. Everything was, in a flash, so clear. Neely *was* the only important thing in his life.

Janet buzzed him, "Mrs. Michaels, your eight thirty, is here. Can I send her in?"

He sat frozen, "David?"

He picked up the phone. "Give me ten minutes."

"Sure," she answered and clicked off.

He opened his side drawer and brought out her letter. Again, he brought the paper to his face and breathed in her fragrance. He carefully placed the envelope in front of him and picked up his phone. He dialed her cell.

"Hello."

He couldn't speak.

"Hello," she repeated.

"Neely…"

"David?"

"How are you?" he asked.

"Better. How are you?"

He faltered, suddenly unsure what to say.

"Are you okay?" Neely asked.

"No."

"What's happened?"

"Too much, Neely."

"You're scaring me, David."

"I want you to know the truth because it's important you understand…because I love you so much."

David's intercom buzzed. "Susie's here." Janet warned.

"We'll talk soon," he said with sadness.

"David!" she called pleading.

"I promise. I'll call."

The line went dead.

Three days later the chalet land phone rang. Caroline was piling wood on the fire and asked Neely to answer it.

"Hello?"

"Neely?"

"Who is this?"

"It's David."

"I didn't recognize your voice. How did you get this number?"

"Jack, reluctantly gave it to me. I'm calling from a pay phone. I don't want anyone to know I called you. You have enough problems without me making it worse."

He suddenly realized all the things he wanted to say were self-serving. He wished he hadn't made the call.

"David?"

He took a deep breath, "I want you to know the truth about everything, about me. You were right...everybody was right about the drug stuff.   I've been smuggling drugs...for years. Not because I wanted to, but because, when I was just out of law school, I made a terrible mistake that took me...places I never imagined."

"Why are you telling me this?"

"I'm telling you because I don't want you to have to read about it. The only person in the whole world whose opinion matters, is you. I want to tell you the truth, all of it."

She waited.

"I was in the reserves through college and as soon as I finished law school, I went to Vietnam. I'd been married to my first wife less than a year when I left. Shortly after that she had an affair. She got pregnant with my first baby girl, Sandy. I knew about it and I accepted it. Shit, it wasn't like I was faithful to her when I was over there."

Neely said nothing.

Tears streamed down David's face. He roughly wiped them away with his hand and went on. "When I got back we were up to our ass in debt, so when I had the opportunity to represent some mob thug from New Jersey who got caught in Nashville with a trailer load of drugs, I took it. I got the guy acquitted and I paid off our entire debt with a little left to boot. Seven months later, I got a call from the mob asking me to represent one of their bosses in a federal court case. I didn't want to...I knew in my bones it was something I shouldn't do. So I told them I couldn't take the case. Three days later I was paid a visit by one of the mob's lieutenants. He informed me that if I did not take the case, as well as win it, my wife's indiscretions would be exposed. I called the only people in my life I thought could help me...Bill and Jack. The rest is history. I've been working with the DEA since that time. This whole thing with Barrett was part of a sting operation that has been going on for years. It just didn't go as planned, obviously."

"But if you have been working with the government," Neely said, "surely they'll protect you. They know what you've been doing, right? The government knows, don't they?" she asked again.

"Yes, they know."

"Then why are you worried? Why wouldn't they protect you?"

"It's more complicated than it..."

"When will I see you? "She interrupted. She didn't care about the drug stuff; she wanted to see him, to hold him.

357

"I don't know."

She knew it was over and started to cry.

"I have to go, Neely. I just wanted you to know and to tell you I love you, that I will *always* love you. There won't be a day in my life I won't think of you. You are with me...you always will be. Always."

"David, don't hang up! Talk to me. I'm afraid."

"Nothing to be afraid of, sugar. Things will be better for you and you know me, I'm a pretty tough old Marine. I'll land on my feet, like I always have. I'll try to call you back later today. Okay?"

"Promise?"

He answered, *yes*, and the line went dead.

Caroline sat down next to Neely, "You okay?"

Neely recounted the details of her conversation with David.

"You always knew there were missing pieces. You always said something didn't feel right."

Neely nodded. "But why wouldn't the government protect him? Something still doesn't make sense."

Caroline agreed. "Did he tell you who Sandy's father is?"

"No. And there was something strange about that, too."

"What do you mean?"

"I don't know. Maybe I'm off on everything, but when he told me, it was...I don't know...odd...like it was still too awful to tell, yet he easily admitted cheating on her mother." She shook her head in despair. "I need to stop before I go mad."

David didn't call back that afternoon or for that matter, ever again.

Strange how people can go through some of the most horrific circumstances and survive...without any marks or warnings to others, like, "Handle with Care", "Beware/May Be Hazardous to your Health", or "Bridge Out". Perhaps God is truly charitable, allowing us to commit the same crimes, over and over, unencumbered, if that is what we choose to do, or perhaps he is allowing us a clean slate, a second chance, to do better. A choice.

A Year Later

Today marked Neely's one-year anniversary since moving from Summerville to Lake Dunn in Virginia. She bought a stone cottage with a beautiful water view and had dropped out of almost everything, rarely seeing anyone other than the lady at the bait shop down the road to buy milk or bread. She adopted a pair of throwaway dogs, to the chagrin of Fred. She'd weed a good hour a day in both the vegetable garden and butterfly flower garden she'd planted. She spoke daily with her children, Jan, and Caroline. Everything was simple and easy.

And, today, Jack was coming to visit. She hadn't seen him since her move, although he was good to keep in touch with weekly calls and occasionally humorous e-mails and cards.

Jack stayed three days. They went antiquing, grilled out, and had drinks on the porch in the evening. For two full days neither spoke of the bad things, carefully sidestepping any issue that might lead them there.

But the proverbial white elephant in the room merrily danced around them and would not leave. They knew they would eventually have to talk if their friendship was to continue and grow. She decided to broach the subject herself.

"Do you ever see David?"

He looked at Neely, wishing he could erase the pain he knew would come.

He sighed heavily. "Talked with him a couple of weeks ago."

"How is he?"

"I think he's doing all right. Aged a little, but haven't we all?"

She wavered before asking, "Did he ask of me?"

He looked at her with sadness. "Yes."

She smiled with a sigh, "You're the one who got him out of everything, aren't you?"

He looked at Neely and wondered if telling her would help or just give her one more demon to manage.

"I may have helped a little."

"Why *did* you help him? I never thought you liked him much."

He looked down, rubbing his chin. He chose his words with care. "He's not my cup of tea, but he's okay, I suppose."

It was important she understand, so she could put it away, finally. So she pressed.

"Why did you help him, Jack? I found out from Jan that Steven told her if it hadn't been for you, he'd probably be in jail and everyone would know about the drugs and Sandy."

Jack looked startled. Neely took his hand.

He stared at Neely for a long time before saying, "Melissa, David's first wife, was my high school sweetheart. When I left for college, we lost touch." Reliving this period was painful for Jack. He had to force himself to continue.

"Right after David left for Vietnam, she called me. They'd been having problems before he left and she was lonely, thinking about getting a divorce. She asked if I would come talk. I shouldn't have…I knew it wasn't a good idea, but I went. I wanted to see her. I thought at the time, I still loved her. The affair lasted almost no time. There was nothing there and we both knew it. We agreed it was over and that we wouldn't speak of it again. But when she realized she was pregnant, we had to decide what we were going to do. We had two choices: an abortion or tell David. We both nixed her having an abortion...so, ...she had the baby…she had Sandy."

Neely smiled as tears welled in her eyes.

"David was understanding…actually quite generous. He said he didn't want a divorce and that he would raise the child as his own, as long as I never made claim to her and was totally out of the picture. I agreed. It was the least I could do, considering how I betrayed him. They divorced a couple of years later, and when Melissa remarried and started having trouble with Sandy, David offered to take her. She never went back to her mother. The only other person who knows the truth is Susie. David told her before they married."

Jack's eyes too were filled with tears. Neely squeezed his hand tightly.

The last piece of the puzzle…

Christmas

It was Christmas and Neely was in New York. It was wonderfully festive and she was happy. She arrived two days before her children were to join her. With last minute shopping to do, she left The Mark hotel just off Central Park and headed for Neiman Marcus. She walked slowly through the crowded sidewalks, admiring the beautifully innovative store window displays. No one did Christmas like New York.

She felt the hot air and crush of people the second she entered the door. She smiled to herself as she pushed her way through the mass of Christmas shoppers, past the Chanel boutique where she gave the purses a quick look, and on to the makeup counter. Olivia had given her a list of things she wanted and Neely thought she'd get it out of the way before she got down to her serious shopping.

She waited at the counter, three people deep, for about ten minutes before a sales associate offered to help her. She handed the young woman a list of products, and as the woman scurried behind the counter to find them, Neely looked around the store where people were crammed together like sardines. Just a few feet away, at the perfume counter, Susie O'Donnell sprayed perfume samples. Neely quickly turned away, not wanting to catch her eye. But within seconds, she couldn't resist glancing back.

David's wife had gained another twenty or so pounds and looked years older.

A saleswoman called out to Susie above the noisy chatter and asked what she could get her.

"Must by Cartier," Susie shouted back.

Neely smiled.

My perfume.

She realized a fantasy might last forever with the help of something as small and seemingly insignificant as a fragrance.

The End

Cornbread Mafia

Cover Art by Nall

Nall, born in 1948 as Fred Nall Hollis in Troy, Alabama, earned his degree in art, political science, and psychology from The University of Alabama and studied at the prestigious École nationale supérieure des Beaux-Arts in Paris.

His works have been exhibited throughout the United States and internationally. His participation in international porcelain fairs includes the Carrousel du Louvre in Paris; Stuttgart, Germany; the Château de Bagatelle in Neuilly; at Podium Boutique in Moscow, Russia; and in New York's Arts and Crafts Museum and "Murano Memories" group show. His signature dinnerware porcelain has been produced by Haviland and Parlon, Royal Limoges, The Tunisian Porcelain Company, and Monaco Porcelain Company. He has had four postage stamps produced by the Principality of Monaco.

Nall has created commissioned works for the New York's National Arts Club; Cathedral of Saint-Paul de Vence; Prince Albert II of Monaco; The Tuscany Council for Culture; Puccini Festival Foundation; Pisa International Airport, Italy; St. Francis Basilica in Assisi, Italy; and St. Augustine Museum. He was the Monaco Artist in Residence from 2013 to2014. His monumental "Peace Frame" is permanently installed as the doorway to Pietrasanta, Italy and at Monaco's harbor, voted the most photographed site in the city. His latest monumental sculpture "Japanese Magnolia" is permanently installed in Monaco.

Nall has work held in the permanent collections of the Boston Museum of Fine Art and the Bibliothèque Nationale Paris, among others. He is the recipient of Mary Ellen LoPresti ARLIS/Southeast Publishing Award for Best Art Book for "Alabama Art" (Black Belt Press) and works to promote Alabama artists by curating their works into RSA Hotels in Alabama. Nall's work as well as his Alabama Arts Collection is a featured attraction of the Grand Hotel Resort and Spa, Renaissance Riverview Plaza Hotel, Renaissance Montgomery and Conference Center, Montgomery Marriott Prattville Hotel & Conference Center at Grand National Auburn Marriott Opelika Hotel & Conference Center, Renaissance Birmingham Ross Bridge Resort & Spa, Marriot Shoals Hotel & Spa, and The Battle House Hotel.

He received the 1998 Alumnus Art Award from The University of Alabama's Society for the Fine Arts; a Doctorate Honoris Causa from Troy University, Troy, Alabama; and Alabama's Distinguished Artist of the Year award from the Alabama State Council on the Arts. Five hardcover books have been published about his work. For the past 30 years, his passion has been working with young students who have had problems with drugs and alcohol abuse. Nall lives and works in Fairhope, Alabama, USA.

Sheree Le Mon has served on the Nall Art Foundation Board for many years.

Le Mon

Cover Artist: Nall
artistnall@gmail.com

Interior Design: SGR-P Services
www.sgr-pub.com/services

Sheree Le Mon's photography by
David Phillips
davidphillipsphotography.com

Indigo River Publishing
3 West Garden Street Ste. 352
Pensacola, FL 32502
www.indigoriverpublishing.com

Ordering Information:
Quantity sales: Special discounts are available on quantity purchases by corporations, associations, and others. For details, contact the publisher at the address above.

Orders by U.S. trade bookstores and wholesalers: Please contact the publisher at the address above.

Made in the USA
Lexington, KY
19 September 2017